NICO'S GARDEN

CHRIS WOLSEY

Book design by ebooklaunch.com

ISBN 978-0-6481981-5-4

Dedication

To Bill: my Father.
Without him I would have no story, nor the ability to tell it.

THANKS

Dane and the Ebook Launch team created the brilliant cover. Anne Simpson did a helpful edit. Rob Spelta turned formal speech into conversational Italian. Thank you.

ABOUT THIS BOOK

In their sixth adventure Philip, an archaeologist, and Rosalind, an artist, are given a problem to solve: a parcel of scorched pages and broken pottery from wartime Italy. In fact there are three related problems, which involve a mysterious Contessa, a ruthless Mayor, and old families with ambiguous attitudes to ancient tombs. Who were the two giants of Renaissance Florence with an unlikely friendship? The result will change history.

NICO'S GARDEN

CHAPTER 1

Philip and Ros sat on opposite sides of a worn kitchen table. Their feet shared a hot water bottle. The transcript of the latest excavation report of Tintagel headland by Mason O'Flaherty was in front of Philip. His pencilled annotations were as neat as the stack of paper. Ros twirled a length of blond hair between her fingers as she absorbed two paintings from the coffee table book in front of her: the vibrant colours of Sandro Botticelli's 'Primavera' and 'Birth of Venus' glowed in the evening Edinburgh sun. It was that time of the year, mid-summer, despite the bitter wind from the river, when she wished someone would turn off the lights. She jumped as the phone rang, but Philip got to it first.

'Hello Meredith. What can I do for you?' She sounded excited. Philip could hear her sister, Tamarisk, clattering in the background making the tea.

'I have the perfect job for you and Rosalind. You must take it.'

Philip listened to her thinking pause.

'But I can't tell you what it is.'

'Why?'

'Because I don't know.'

'Then why is it so perfect?'

This was going to be a Meredith conversation, or should he think contradiction. In Cornwall her methodical help in their search for King Arthur had been matched by her literal naivety. He looked out of the window. Their flat at the top of Leith Walk had a view north towards Cramond, the Firth of Forth and beyond to the Kingdom of Fife. He tried not to show his annoyance by a long sigh that threatened. There

1

were offers of site supervisor positions on digs in Turkey and Cyprus. Ros was already reading the set texts for the new term back at Art College in Brisbane. But he could not dismiss Meredith's plan out of hand.

Ros looked up and tried to read Philip's face. She waited. What was so perfect?

'Tomorrow then, Meredith.' Philip put the phone down.

After a long afternoon of reading, Ros got up to make the meal. Philip turned over the last page and let his eyes rest on his lovely lady. She was dressed in what she called trakky daks, sloppy joe jumper and Ugg boots. In Oz she'd be barefoot but Scottish weather put paid to that. Her long golden hair was tied back into a pony tail. She looked so relaxed and immersed in the task at hand. He knew there was the most beautiful body hidden beneath those folds, with her socks slipping off, a form just hinted at by little contours in the material. Should he be watching her? Did she mind?

'What?' She felt his eyes.

'You look good.'

'That's not possible. It's me in this.'

She tilted her head towards the pot. Do I add this or not? She tasted it to find out.

'Food's in about ten minutes.'

'Ok beautiful.'

Ros wiggled and blew him a kiss.

§

It was a rare fine and sunny morning as Philip and Ros walked along crowded Princes Street. Mini-skirts outnumbered bell bottom trousers and kaftans in the warm weather. According to newspaper billboards the Vietnam War was ending but the IRA still claimed their victims. The 70s was not a perfect decade. Philip opened the door for Ros as they stepped into the House of Fraser, Jenners' department store. High above Princess Street Meredith sat in a window alcove of the café with her sister. Tamarisk was as slim and petite as Meredith but with more chiselled features, framed by cropped black hair in permed waves. Meredith lifted her hand in a nervous wave as Philip and Ros entered.

She stood up as they approached. 'Lovely as ever, Rosalind,' as she held out her hand. 'Don't you agree, Tamarisk?'

'Yes, she's very pretty: beautiful hair, trim figure, lovely green eyes. You've done well for yourself, haven't you, Philip?'

Ros sat down and studied the menu while she was being judged, like a prize heifer it seemed. But then she relaxed. Weird but they meant well.

Philip nodded and sat down beside her. He had no wish to prolong the embarrassment or the possible inquisition of the love of his life. Then he ordered a black coffee for Ros and tea with no milk for him. When refreshments arrived he spoke to Meredith.

'About the job, Meredith, what CAN you tell us?'

'It's a dig.'

'Good.'

'Peter directs it,' said Tamarisk. 'Our son.' She had their attention. 'Harry and Peter didn't get along. We hadn't seen him for years until he rang Harry, just before his funeral.'

Was Meredith's cryptographic language catching, Ros thought, or did it just run in the family?

'Peter rang again last night. He said he had a problem. But he wouldn't talk about it.'

We're back here again, Philip thought.

'But he asked about you two.'

'How did he know about us, Meredith?'

'I told him how you helped Jeremy.'

Ros and Philip glanced at each other, and Meredith understood.

'I didn't TELL, of course; just how you did things. He thinks you will be perfect to solve his problem.'

'Two problems,' corrected Tamarisk.

'Yes, he is good friends with a local family. They need your help too.'

Philip was getting frustrated. He could see Ros eyeing the door and probably thinking of a polite exit.

'I can hear the thoughts on your faces, you two,' said Meredith. 'Peter digs in Italy.'

'North of Rome, in Tuscany,' said Tamarisk.

'The site is historical and includes a necropolis with frescoes and artwork within the tombs,' Meredith said to Ros. The sisters were working hard to catch their interest. Ros was warming to the idea.

'The other problem, Meredith?'

Meredith looked at Tamarisk. Eyes of sisters for a lifetime met. 'You tell it, Tamarisk.'

Tamarisk sipped her tea, put down the cup and opened her large, black leather handbag. She extricated a much-Sellotaped cardboard box and placed it in the middle of the table.

'Harry was in the war. He was in the Allied push through Italy in 1944. Outside Florence he was badly wounded and invalided home.'

Meredith squeezed Tamarisk's hand on the seat. She knew how hard it had been to live with Harry afterwards; the painkillers and the nightmares. The bomb shrapnel in his back and legs had taken the heart of the man Tamarisk had courted three years before.

'Harry became obsessed with the bits he'd souvenired on the campaign. He couldn't remember much but he never stopped trying to solve things.' Tamarisk's hand shook as she pushed forward the box. 'He wrote letters to people about them. But he wouldn't talk to me.'

That figured, Ros thought. Those who lived through the war rarely did talk. But he'd cut out his wife from something so important to him. There was no point in asking exactly where it came from, or anything else really.

'Would you like Philip and Rosalind to open it now, dear?' Meredith asked quietly.

'No!'

Tamarisk was clear on that. But Ros could see that there was something more.

'In the end the letters were to one person, an Italian woman.'

This was airing dirty laundry, Ros thought. Not easy for a wife of her generation.

'Can you tell us who she was, Tamarisk?'

'I never saw the letters. He burnt them. But I did see an envelope once. The return address was to Contessa di Percussina, Firenze.'

Everyone drank a mouthful in the silence.

'Do you know any more about the Contessa?' Philip's question was to whichever sister answered first.

'Peter knows her,' Tamarisk said. 'Beyond being Italian aristocracy we know nothing more. But when she sees how you deal with Peter's problem she will decide if you are ready for hers.' She paused. 'Peter has described the villas.'

'Plural?' asked Ros.

'Yes. Peter said they are full of astonishing artwork going back to the Renaissance.'

Ros thought back to her book spread on the arm rest in the flat: "Florentine art 1400-1600". Coincidence?

'Is this where I fit in?'

'Peter and the Contessa need you both.' Tamarisk passed over a well-padded envelope from her voluminous handbag. 'Expenses.'

"For Sherlock and his lovely Watson" was written on the front. Ros studied the extravagant copperplate handwriting. The Old World was keeping her here a while longer. The New World would have to wait.

'You won't regret this,' Meredith and Tamarisk said together.

Why are we doing this? Philip and Rosalind's thought was simultaneous, as was the unspoken reply: because we trust Meredith.

Tamarisk handed the box to Ros. 'I don't want it back. But I would like Harry to find peace.'

Meredith's arm was around Tamarisk's shoulders while she zipped up her handbag and draped her coat over her arm. They seemed awfully old as they ambled out.

'That was uncomfortable,' Ros said and wondered why. And how many problems were there: Peter's, Harry's and the Contessa's? That makes three. She went up to the counter and ordered more coffee and tea. 'Ready?' when it arrived.

Philip lifted out a Nazi collar button displaying a black swastika against a white enamel background. Then he laid an ornate brass belt buckle with the double-winged eagle in relief beside it. Below, wrapped in war-time newspaper, were three fragments of ancient pottery. Ros lifted one to the light as Philip did the same.

'Etruscan!' they said together. His archaeology matched her art conservation.

He held a red patterned rim on black background rim with geometric painted decoration. She held a beautifully executed fish tail painted on red clay encircled by shiny black. The dusty pieces of funerary urn gave away the source of these pieces; a cemetery.

One more item remained. It was wrapped in the frayed silk of a war-time map. Philip guessed it once filled the pocket of a German officer or maybe a pilot shot down. He methodically spread it out and then turned over what it protected. How much had Meredith told Tamarisk? Had she quizzed her about what they'd discovered in Cornwall? Of course, but Meredith had promised silence. And Peter? He chose not to doubt.

The page of medieval parchment was badly scorched by the actions of war: a bomb blast, a fire in a villa, they might never know. The vellum leather was familiar territory but the language wasn't.

'Italian,' Ros said triumphantly. 'Some odd words, maybe an old version, but definitely the language.' The limited vocabulary she'd picked up in her art studies would now have to expand exponentially. Etruscan pottery, Renaissance art, as well as a dig that Philip could enjoy; something historical: this might not be too bad. She looked at him poring over the script. There was that familiar zeal. They were hooked. It was only left to Peter and the Contessa to reel them in.

§

As they walked to the end of the close, Leith Walk was the usual wind tunnel, the sky the colour of lead with misty rain. Dreech was the local word. Philip leaned close to kiss but Ros turned and pecked him on the cheek.

'I know, no smooching in public,' he said.

She smiled, puckered her lips and walked down towards the bus stop. He watched her body wrapped up in the trakky dacks and Ugg boots. Then he turned up towards the bus station and the city centre.

'Great Junction Street,' she said to the buxom clippie in white blouse and blue skirt one size too small.

'Five pence, Hen.'

Ros handed over the fare. The conductress set the dial, cranked the handle vigorously and passed over the ticket. Ros watched rivulets of rain meander down the glass as the worn diesel engine whined up through the gears after every stop. Red sandstone tenements scarred by the elements and grime slid past as the leviathan descended towards the river. At the bottom the double decker leaned left into Great Junction. She felt an icy blast hit her back from the rear of the bus. Then she got up and walked on to the open platform. Ros jumped off while the driver slowed for the lights at the bottom of Bonnington Road. It was always fun getting your feet to move at the right speed to avoid face-planting. She dodged puddles up to Junction Place and stepped through the 19th century façade, red sandstone of course, of Leith's Victoria Baths. In the style of the Renaissance seemed appropriate. Another girl clipped her season ticket and Ros walked into the steamy warmth of the "Leith Viccies".

In the female change room she peeled off to a simple, lilac and blue, one piece and pushed her clothes into the locker. A couple of teachers watched her sleek form and swimmer's shoulders as she left the room. They went back to tidying the wooden slat benches of the children's clothes.

Crowded noise reverberated in a space that reminded her of St Pancras Station. Swimming squads from two schools took up most of the Olympic size pool.

'Keep to the left,' she was reminded by the lifeguard as she stood for a moment beside the lapping lane. Three in before her; two older men, regulars that she knew the pace of and one plump wild card who bashed her arms into the rope as Ros watched. The man tumble-turned and she dived in ten metres behind him. The water slid over her like a bath. Hooray for heated pools.

She dropped into the rhythm: arms lifted out of the water to the minimum; mouth turned sidewise for air once every four strokes; her torso twisting gently, her legs with easy power of their own. This was her time. She mulled Italian problems, ancient script and Etruscan pottery; wartime debris that bothered Harry so much. A head in a pink cap rammed her side. Ros swerved around the rest of her without breaking the pattern of strokes. Her Brisbane studies were threatened again. But this was a chance to touch the source of the Renaissance, not just in books. She veered out right to overtake muscular shoulders. What did she feel: that prescient gift that had guided them so well in Cornwall? As she came out of the tumble turn she knew: yes, not easy but good. She was ready.

Philip stepped out of the blustery wind into a different world. The dojan could have been anywhere. As he changed into his Tae Kwon Do uniform he took time to tie the black belt correctly; the two stripes were right. At the door of the hall he waited. The instructor was of an indeterminate middle age with cropped grey hair, lean build and muscular arms. Philip watched him demonstrate their form to a group of blue belts. Every move was crisp and sharp. The material of his suit made a sharp crack as proof. Elsewhere students held boards for one who set up a configuration of breaks in preparation for his black belt grading. Philip worked out the connecting pattern: Eedan Ap Chagi, Jumping Front Kick, followed by Twi-myo Dwi Chagi, Flying Back Kick, turning into Bandai Chagi, Crescent Kick. And for the last he would turn and kneel to break boards with his left and right hands simultaneously. It was similar to his routine not so long ago.

Rab turned towards Philip. Philip stood rigidly upright, legs together, and bowed. Rab did the same before going back to the class. Philip trotted to one side of the room. For the next ten minutes he jogged forwards, backwards, sideways, to warm up his body. Then he dropped into leg stretches. He crouched like a Cossack with his right leg bent and left stretched taut across the wooden floor; then left down and right flattening complaining muscles. Into splits, to forward bends, and later propping a leg over the back of a chair and dropping low. He relaxed with the breath, spread forward so both hands held his foot and moulded his torso over the leg. In a space at the back of the room he stood tightly erect, shut his eyes and slowed his breath. When the moment was right he began Il Jang, the first form. The actions were slow and precise and flowed into Ee Jang, the second, on through to Pal Jang, the eighth form. Everything was clear in his mind as sweat glistened on his chest, arms and dripped off his nose. In the pause before Koryo, the first of the Black Belt forms, thoughts bubbled up. An Italian dig, good. Multiple puzzles and who was this Contessa? He would need to write some letters to postpone other things. But his stomach told him something.

He was about to start Koryo but held back. Rab noticed, as any Master would, but walked over to the board breaking preparation instead. Yes, Philip thought, this was adventure to revel in, to test his abilities, maybe his limits. But now he had to focus. He pulled in air, lifted his hands high and slowly pulled them down his chest. The moves of Koryo began a little rustily but then they flowed, into Keumgang, and finally into Taebek. This had to be perfect to gain his third Dan. Yes, he was ready, Philip thought. Rab agreed.

§

1478 Florence.

One warm Saturday afternoon a week before my ninth birthday Bernardo, my father, and I stepped out of our casa door into the courtyard.

'Good day, Bernardo,' bellowed one cousin from her balcony.

'Good day, Niccolò,' called little Marietta.

'Hello Luigi,' Bernardo said to her father, the patriarch of the Corsinis.

While Bernardo chatted with his old friend about politics and the state of the world I looked at his daughter. Much younger than me she was dark with bright eyes. She stood on their balcony and looked down at me. I did not know what to say. She spent her time with her mother, as all girls seemed to do. I was out most days with Bernardo. What could we say to each other?

There was always family around us in that crowded space. Out in the Via Romana the city buzzed like a hive of bees: some people were going to or from the many wool and silk establishments that were the main industries of this city; others who dressed more opulently were clearly bankers or the clerks that served them; while others like us joined the gay promenade seething towards the Palazzo Della Signoria and the Ponte Vecchio. Bernardo walked at my pace, aside of the main wave of polyglot humanity. This allowed me to look at faces and their owners' movements: the elderly aunts chaperoning teenage girls of marriageable age; the wolf pack of chattering young men who followed them; merchants from Constantinople in turbans and colourful pantaloons; and shopkeepers who barked enticements to lure in customers.

'This way, Niccolò.' Bernardo led me through laneways until we arrived at the printer.

'Welcome Bernardo and young Niccolò,' said a stout man with muscular arms smudged with ink. While he and Bernardo talked about his latest acquisition I looked behind them. Apprentices set the lead type, inked the letters, and turned the handle to clamp the paper, or unscrewed the thread to reveal the printed page. I smelled soot and varnish that layered the floor. Together they bound into ink. Bernardo told me that twenty years ago tens of pages might be coated in a day. Now with these new machines from Germany thousands of pages were made in the same time. For bookworms like Bernardo and me, this was a lucky time.

We stepped into the busy street a short time later. Bernardo had a bundle of loose pages tied with twine: "The Decameron" by Giovanni Boccaccio. It was a year before he could afford to have the work bound. By then he and I had delighted many times in the tales of life over a century ago.

'Bernardo, another acquisition I see,' said a man of uncertain middle age who stepped out of the premises of another seller.

'Bartolomeo, we are on the same errand,' said Bernardo pointing to the book in the man's hand.

'Niccolò, I would like you to meet my friend Bartolomeo Scala, Secretary to the 1st Chancery. Bartolomeo this is my older son Niccolò.'

'I am pleased to meet you, Niccolò.' The men exchanged packages and I studied the pages of Thucydides' "History of the Peloponnesian War" as Bernardo turned them. It had been translated into Latin. Bartolomeo saw me absorbing the text. 'Do you read master Niccolò?'

'Bernardo has taught me to read Italian, sir. Also for nearly two years I have been taught Latin, first by Signor Matteo and now by Signor Battista da Poppi.'

The Secretary nodded approval. 'With a father like Bernardo I am sure your education will progress apace.' As they returned their purchases he spoke to Bernardo. 'You should bring him along to the Confraternity meeting this evening. The discussion might appeal to his lively mind.'

'I will Bartolomeo. Thank you.'

Bernardo and I strolled, me asking questions and he explaining. Of course I spied the dome of Santa Maria del Fiore, our beloved Cathedral at the heart of our city. Who? How did? To my many questions Bernardo gave extensive answers. Filippo Brunelleschi, a goldsmith, had won the competition to build the biggest dome in the world. He invented a special hoist to lift the heavy materials. There was not enough wood in all the forests around Florence to build the usual frame so Brunelleschi designed scaffolding that supported itself.

'The dome is tall because that is what the people of Florence wanted. It is really an octagon.'

'Eight,' I said quickly. My tutor was teaching me mathematics too.

'Yes, an eight sided roof within a frame held together by a special pattern of bricks.'

'When was it finished?'

'The dome was consecrated on March 26th, 1436. I was a boy when Pope Eugenius and a procession of cardinals and bishops came to the Duomo. But the little lantern of marble on top was begun ten years later. Brunelleschi died before it was finished.'

My father led me to the Via de Agnolo because he wanted me to see the sort of men who created such marvels. What I saw was a shop open to the street full of novices at work: some ground pigments in stone bowls to make paint; others sanded wooden panels smooth; and some chipped stone into the rough shapes of saints, ready for the Maestro. Most were young, a few years older than me but their foreman was in his twenties. He supervised three students making charcoal copies of a Madonna and Child. Their master was conversing with two travellers. By their accent they were from Venice and by their clothes they were artists or imaginative people of some variety.

'Do all artists dress like this, Bernardo?' Although grimed by their work each wore a doublet of silk or velvet which was very short. Below was covered in sheer hose, so that every muscle of leg was evident. Men's bums were revealed as though bare.

'Creative minds gravitate towards extremes.'

When they faced in my direction I saw that their pecker was wrapped in an elaborate bag to make it seem as though stiff all of the time.

Bernardo read my puzzlement. 'They believe that they are more attractive dressed like that.'

He did not elaborate. But some of the visitors to the bottega painted colour on their lips and cheeks like women. I turned again towards the foreman. His clothes were of a delicate rose colour and were as revealing as any of the rest. His hair was fair, long and delicately curled. He looked up when he felt my eyes. I could see that he had a beauty that women might choose.

'Why do some of them act like girls, Bernardo?'

'Because they are in their way.'

He saw the confusion on my face. 'Some men like the bodies of other men rather than women.' He let me digest what he had said.

I watched one of the apprentices pretend to kiss another and then laugh. Another only had eyes for the foreman.

'I think I prefer girls.'

'Nico, you are born as a man or a woman. Those are the anatomical bits that you are given. What you do with them is your business. These men choose their way, you yours. No doubt there are a multitude of variations between. But we must respect everyone's private choice.'

'You will marry one day and have children. You can't sire children with men, Niccolò. You will understand the reason when you are a little older.'

That evening Bernardo and I left the courtyard again to walk to the Confraternity of San Girolamo sulla Costa, or La Pietà.

'Why do you come to such a place, Bernardo, when you have no interest in religion?' I had noticed how many evenings my mother, Bartolomea, sang in the choir of Santa Trinità. At home she pored over the right words to fit religious verses she wrote. My father did not.

'You must be careful what you say, Niccolò. The Church can be a powerful enemy if you cross her. She would tell you, "Render to Caesar the things that are Caesar's; and to God the things that are God's". But her representative, Pope Sixtus IV, has more worldly desires. As you will discover Popes covet the things of Caesar and have little to do with God if it suits them. A great many evils are committed in the name of religion, Niccolò .'

Yet one of our favourite books was Dante's "Divine Comedy". Many evenings we would study a canto or two of his journey through Inferno, Purgatory to Paradiso. Bernardo's cherished ancient poet Virgil was his guide for most of the way. At that age I enjoyed the creative punishments for those who had sinned. But my father's explanation was aided by my mother, who showed me the intricacy of Dante's poetry. To him it was a great story of humanity in peril; to her it was a religious text.

Bartolomea fitted poetic technique into everyday tasks.

'What word rhymes with fine? '

'Mine.'

'Yes.'

'Time.'

'No, that's a near rhyme, but still useful.'

'Wine.' She frowned. 'Divine.' She beamed.

'How many syllables in divine?'

'Two.'

'In a sonnet how many syllables are in a line?'

'Ten.' And so I developed the ear for poetic language so that it flowed easily.

During the evening we mixed with businessmen, lawyers and other professionals. Although it was a religious organisation by name it was really a political meeting place where the affairs of the Santo Spirito quarter of the city were decided. I was introduced to Marcello Adriani, a power in the Ist Chancery, Alamanno Salviati, son-in-law to Piero de Medici, and a great many others. Always my father praised my abilities in front of them and I repeated what I had learnt so far in my education. I revelled in the study of so many powerful and interesting minds. Speeches were made in support of charitable causes. Giuliano de Medici, younger brother of the real leader of Florence, Lorenzo, appeared for a short time. Guiliano was as handsome as his brother was not.

'I hope you are well, Signor Giuliano,' said Bernardo when the Medici approached him. 'This is my elder son, Niccolò.'

I bowed and went through the ordeal by praise and the inquisition of my education yet again. My father had no limits when it came to promoting me.

'We would appreciate your literary expertise, Bernardo. Would you call at the Palazzo the day after tomorrow?'

'I would be happy to be of service again to the Medici family. Would it offend you if I brought Niccolò?'

'He is welcome.'

We returned well after darkness. Bartolomea was engrossed in her poetry but she smiled when I recounted our adventure. Yes Bernardo knew everyone of any consequence in Florence.

The next day, a warm Sunday, the 26th April, 1478, our family went to mass in the Duomo. Bernardo had acceded to my mother's request. My sisters Primerana and Margherita, five and two years older than me, sat beside my mother. Bernardo sat between me and my brother Totto, five years younger than me. Soon after we had settled Luigi and his family filed in behind us. We smiled and nodded briefly as we were in a church. Our family was part of a congregation of ten thousand people. Because my mother's piety shone brightly that day we were among the first to arrive, and my place at the end of the row gave me ample chance to watch those who came in. Amongst the ordinary citizens of Florence were the mighty and influential in their finest clothing. Bernardo gave me a whispered commentary. I recognized Giuliano de' Medici easily, and surmised that the dark-haired man with broad torso and short legs was Lorenzo. In the dark skin of his face I could not help staring at his large nose.

'Who are they, Bernardo?' The large group were obviously wealthy and I guessed mighty.

'These are the Salviati family, led by Francesco, archbishop of Pisa. Behind are the Pazzi family, also bankers connected to the Vatican. Both are supporters of Pope Sixtus and therefore enemies of the Medici family.'

'Then why do they sit so close to Lorenzo and Giuliano?' Every pew to the sides and behind the brothers had been taken by the families.

My father shrugged his shoulders. 'That is Girolamo Riario, lord of Imola because his uncle, Pope Sixtus, bought it for him. He walks with his wife, Caterina Sforza, illegitimate daughter of the Duke of Milan who sold him the town.'

'Another enemy of the Medici?'

Bernardo nodded to me, and then to another of his friends in the Signoria. My eyes no longer absorbed the last few people coming in. I watched the backs and the whispering heads of several of the men. There was an agitation to them, and definitely not the quiet observance of my mother.

'Bernardo. Bernardo,' I whispered. I tugged at the sleeve of his tunic. He was trying to catch a glance from another man of importance.

'What Niccolò? Is this necessary?'

'Those men look at them.' Two of the Pazzi were standing up and talking to the archbishop of Pisa. A seat away Girolamo Riario was looking across at another man. He was speaking with his hands. 'They are up to mischief, Bernardo. You can see it, can't you?'

There was quandary in his face. He was not sure. Could I be right? If he got up and spoke to Lorenzo and his brother now, and I was wrong? If only I was a little older?

'What more do you see, Niccolò?'

'Some faces are frightened, others show anger. A few hide their feelings, like...' I thought of one of Bernardo's stories, 'A Hangman by the Window.'

But then the moment was lost. I saw Francesco de' Pazzi and another man move swiftly towards the Medici brothers. Swords and knives were drawn. Giuliano jumped up and Lorenzo was startled with him. I leaned out into the aisle as screams and shouts reverberated around the cathedral. Blades struck the marble floor, and shrieks came from the wounded. Giuliano staggered into the centre. Blood oozed from stab wounds to his chest and arms. Lorenzo stood behind him with a wound to his neck. Then several things happened at once. Giuliano was struck from behind with a sword blow to the head and fell to the floor. One of his attackers thrust and thrust into his chest until there was no movement. Lorenzo saw his brother bleed to death on the Duomo floor. But then he was whisked away into the sacristy by a scholar friend. Bernardo told me later that the attackers could not break in and had run towards the Palazzo Vecchio. While Lorenzo was taken to safety along a secret passageway to the Medici Palazzo the assassins tried to overthrow the Signoria. Through good fortune they failed.

But what of us? People ran out shouting. Others fell in the rush for the door. How could Bernardo keep his family safe in this pandemonium? But he did, by commanding every one of us to stay where we were and crouch low behind the woodwork. In less than a minute there was a break in the panic.

'Bartolomea,' he commanded. Then he pushed me out into the aisle, and led us like a centipede across the marble flagstones and down the steps to the square. Luigi and his loved ones were close behind.

'We must go home straight away. No one is safe.'

Those minutes were like hours. Men with uncovered blades rushed here and there. 'Pazzi conspirators,' someone shouted. 'Salviati must die for this,' came from another. Bernardo kept us close, heads low, our eyes no threat to the madmen around us. We slipped inside the courtyard and Bernardo barred the ground floor door of our casa. There we waited out the day and then the night. Bartolomea spent most of that time praying. Bernardo watched through a chink in the wooden shutters in the kitchen on the top floor. He paced and thought and by morning knew what to do.

After we waited in line behind so many others Lorenzo welcomed us into his presence. He sat in an ornately carved wooden chair. His face looked tired and drawn. The wound on his neck was bandaged and the bleeding had stopped. Standing beside him was his saviour, Angelo Poliziano. He had risked his own life by sucking the blood from the wound in case the knife-edge was poisoned.

'Signor Lorenzo,' Bernardo said with bowed head, 'I come to pledge our family's support in this awful time.' He paused. 'And to express deep sorrow that I could not have done more to save you and Giuliano.'

'What do you mean, Bernardo?'

'My son, Niccolò warned me moments before it happened but I was slow to listen.' He explained as Lorenzo barely took his eyes off me.

'For one so young he has an insightful mind,' said Lorenzo. 'My brother might have been saved. But then without Angelo my life was also forfeit. It is Fortuna.'

'Yes, it is Fortuna,' said Bernardo with the heaviest heart.

As two devout humanists, what else would they say? God did not come into it, whether to save or to destroy.

The city was not safe. When it was discovered that the Pazzi family were involved, mobs rioted and fought in the streets. Conspirators, or their relatives, were summarily executed. Lorenzo's friends acted quickly. Francesco de' Pazzi and Archbishop Salviati were hanged from the windows of the Palazzo Della Signoria. Others were thrown from its windows to be dismembered by the mob. For six months Italy was scoured until more than eighty died for the crime. Bandini dei Baroncelli, who had plunged the knife into Giuliano, had escaped to Constantinople. But the Sultan sent him back in chains and he was hanged from a window of the Palazzo del Capitano del Popolo.

One morning I walked with Bernardo towards the Medici Palazzo near the Ponte Vecchio. Sunlight tried to cut through the edgy gloom that enveloped the city. Florence was attempting to lift itself out of its troubles, most notably the anger of Pope Sixtus IV. He had excommunicated the entire city. I looked up at the Palazzo Della Signoria. The body of the hated archbishop, Salviati, still hung on a rope from a window. Crows had taken its eyes and maggots fell from the desiccated body beneath stained clothing. Bernardo said nothing. He never shielded me from the ugliness of life any more than its beauty. As I looked I noticed another doing the same. It was the tall beautiful man from the bottega. He was sketching the dangling corpse. I watched his rapid, delicate hands move across the paper. What a strange thing to draw compared with the cherubs and saints of his studio. He was engrossed in his work. Tendrils of ink circled the slumped torso as though to give it life. Wisps hinted at the movement of the cadaver in the light wind. Streaks of black dripped from hollow eye sockets and flowed into the crumpled tunic. Exquisitely he captured the dead soul of this grotesque manikin.

§

Ros leant on the ship's rail looking back along the furling wake towards the white cliffs. Her blond mane twirled and whipped against the anorak keeping out the intermittent rain. Beside her stood Philip, immersed in one of his reflective moods. He was looking at those same ramparts of crumbling rock; blacks and greens in patches against the stark white. No doubt he was absorbed in something archaeological, she thought, maybe Dover Castle, just visible, or the Second World War tunnels beneath. They were off again: another dig with a problem, probably plural, and a quest, something neither of them chose to refuse.

'Where are the bluebirds, Philip?' She did not expect a real answer. Seagulls whirled and dived for whatever rose from the disturbed seabed.

'Inside the mental delusion of an American writer who didn't specialise in geography.'

'Too literal Philip, it was a good song.'

Her mood was light, like her inner butterflies. Destination Italy: land of pizzas and amore, history and Renaissance art. It was adventure she could almost touch, like God's finger stretched out to Adam in the Sistine Chapel.

She matched her pace to the roll of the Calais ferry and took a photo of fading England with Philip's lean, tall physique, in polo neck sweater, Levi jeans and desert boots, as the scale. She watched him push away his shoulder-length black hair as it was lashed by the changing wind. Then she linked arms with him as the cut edge of green land submerged beneath the squally grey of sky. Cornwall, and the Roseland Peninsula, that she could only see in her mind, receded and were gone. Their Arthur quest existed merely in memory and a publication or two. A cold wet blast drove them across the angled deck, down the slippery ladder and into the warmth of the saloon. Philip placed the steaming paper cup of black coffee on the table in front of her and held both hands around his unadulterated tea.

As Ros watched the swell rise and fall into the distance Philip looked around the saloon. Two tables away was Frank, a recently retired Yorkshire mechanic. Thick-set, with ruddy complexion and patchy white beard he could have been mistaken for Papa Hemingway. He had emptied the contents of a beaten leather satchel across the blue Formica surface. Methodically he arranged the documents into piles according to time of need. Nearest were those required to get his converted bus through French Customs. Travellers' cheques and petrol vouchers were furthest. Philip could smell his roll-your-own Capstan cigarette smouldering in the ashtray.

Opposite him sat his wife, Margaret. Her short grey hair, spectacled blue eyes and stocky torso contained a keen mind that could compete with Frank's clipped instructions. Her focus was on the map of Europe, as she pencilled in the route through France to Strasburg, into the German industrial heart of Karlsruhe and Stuttgart, before the climb to Innsbruck, and the Brenner Pass into Italy. Between them they had planned each overnight camp according to the leisurely pace of the bus. After a year of Frank scavenging parts, welding and modifying this would be their mobile home for the foreseeable future.

Philip spotted the rest of the group scattered around. Polish-born Sue and her Scottish boyfriend Alan played cards on the other side of the room. Round and maternal she charmed her excessively shy musician with her chatter and canny ways to stretch the cash. Somewhere on deck was Christian, just out of school and escaping the nest. His small, wiry frame was probably sucking in anticipation with every breath of tangy air. Whereas Julian lay inert along a side bench, his feet noticeably over the end to appease the bar staff, his long ginger beard protruding from the leather hat covering his face. Somewhere between Gandalf and Rasputin he epitomized the Hippy era.

It was Margaret who had thought of advertising on the student canteen noticeboard at Edinburgh Uni. "London to Rome in 5 days. Comfortable seating. Friendly company. Share the adventure and costs with Margaret and Frank." Philip applied, automatically thinking of the cheapest way to get to the dig. Even if he had thought of the "expenses" envelope it wouldn't have felt right to use it until the Contessa made her choice.

As the ferry approached Calais docks, the group filed down the stairs to below deck. Inside the bus Ros sat with Philip on a bench seat beside the table. Frank started the old diesel engine and pumped it into life. The car deck behind changed to a hazy blue. Steel chains clanked in rhythm and the ramp boomed and scraped onto the concrete. Files of cars moved out at the deck hand's signal, first row, second, until Frank lumbered into the queue.

'Drive on the Right, Frank,' said Margaret.

'Aye lass.'

He stopped at the guard post as French customs checked papers and walked around the vehicle. Ros couldn't hear the comments but body language suggested they wondered how far the beast would get.

'Merci monsieur.'

Frank waved.

Margaret guided him out of town. Soon she was passing over sandwiches and sweets as Frank cruised at a steady fifty miles an hour. Flickering sunlight through the lines of plane trees either side dappled the road ahead. Christian tucked his legs under him and stared out across the flat farming countryside. Julian stroked his beard and did the same. Sue stretched out and dozed against Alan's chest. Ros and Philip absorbed their books: a paperback on Etruscan archaeology for him and an Italian phrasebook for her. After two hours Frank pulled into a layby and Margaret boiled up a cup of tea on the Bunsen burner. Camp chairs were dragged from the roof and everyone sat around. An hour later they were on the road again.

'This could get tedious,' Ros mumbled.

'Maybe you could suggest that we share the driving, Philip?' after two more tea stops.

Frank revealed his taste in music on the tapes in his cassette player: Yorkshire Brass Bands. Collieries and mills supported their own bands for decades. It was as ingrained as coal. Not all of the oompahs and slightly cracked trumpet work was to her taste but sometimes a song like "Raise Me Up" on a solo cornet touched a memory. Rossini's "William Tell" had a lovely gallop that Frank tapped out on the steering wheel. It made no difference to his speed. By the end of the day they all knew every song on the twelve tapes.

''Ey up lads, gi'us a 'and to set up camp 'fore yer go int' neares' pub,' Frank instructed as he turned off the engine at the designated camp site. They were still in France.

Chores done Philip and Ros walked into the village and found seats on the terrace of the street café.

'Monsieur!' Philip called and raised his arm for the waiter to see.

'I will come,' he replied and shook his head.

'Be patient, Philip,' Ros said gently. 'He knows we are here.'

'See?' Ros patted Philip's arm. 'Five minutes.'

They shared a plate of Coq au vin which steamed like a rich stew. They mopped the sauces with roughly cut crusty bread. The waiter refilled the demi-carafe of Provencal rosé.

Ros enjoyed the calls of crickets in the hedges and the balmy air touching her face. It was nice to be back in somewhere warmer than Edinburgh. Starlight and the occasional car were enough to follow the road back. Sue and Alan were already snoring gently in the other tent. Inside, the bench seats were occupied by Christian and Julian. Margaret's bedside lamp illuminated her book at the other end of the bus.

'Careful,' Ros said as Philip stood on her shins as he came back from the toilet block. With the tent zipped up he slid his legs into the double sleeping bag.

'Warm enough?'

'You'll do,' she said. She steered a wandering hand into hers. 'Goodnight, Philip.'

'Goodnight.'

Margaret's light went out very soon after.

§

'Reisepässe bitte.'

Philip and Ros stood outside the bus with the others as the precise young men checked passports.

'Fahrzeugpapiere bitte.'

Frank produced the required papers for his vehicle. Official eyes were less impressed with his mechanical creation but waved them on.

'It could have been Cheech driving Chong in a Combie van,' said Julian slowly.

'Yes,' said Ros. She looked at him. He'd said barely a word so far. Cheech had made Julian's life easier by skipping breakfast and bringing back that distinctive odour. Frank said nothing.

Ros looked at her watch. Nearly two hours: time to brew up the billy again. Sure enough Frank pulled over from the line of trucks, sorry Philip-lorries. More tea with that soupçon of diesel, she thought? Then back into the grind of gears and views of semitrailers' behinds, with glimpses of the industry of Karlsruhe and Stuttgart.

> '"Wheear 'ast tha bin sin' ah saw thee?
>
> On Ilkley Moor baht 'at
>
> On Ilkley Moor baht 'at
>
> On Ilkley Moor baht 'at."'

Frank led the singing.

'His voice is worse than mine, 'Philip said.

'This is corny,' whispered Ros.

'Yes but it's fun. Look around at the faces. Why not?'

'You don't need a hat on a Yorkshire moor, except to keep out the rain.'

'Too literal, Ros.'

But that did not stop both of them, and the boys belting it out on the autobahns.

'"Oh, Danny boy, the pipes, the pipes are calling,"' was started by Margaret and picked up by the girls. Not quite Yorkshire, Ros thought, but stirring nonetheless.

'"It's you, it's you must go and I must bide."'

It was a song about travelling and leaving people behind, a theme that she could relate to. She was a long way from Oz.

Philip listened and focused on one voice. She's good. I could listen to that all day. Then he read her face and squeezed her hand.

The day ended at a campsite near Ulm. After the usual chores to set up Philip found a quiet spot and practiced his Tae Kwon Do forms. Besides loosening up cramped muscles the repetition of familiar patterns of moves was a form of meditation.

Ros watched for a time.

'If I don't use it I lose it,' he said.

Ros had reasons to thank him for his abilities in the past. Her mind drifted to the positives of their day. Besides their attempts at music she and Philip had read their books, practiced some Italian and daydreamed in comparative comfort. I can think of worse places to spend daylight. Like slides in a projector, images of wet hours excavating at Tintagel headland; of dust and flies at Kara Tepe; of being shot at in Cyprus, dropped through her inner vision.

Margaret rustled up a passable stew, more or less from cans. The site had a circle of rocks for a wood fire. Nobody objected to the crunchy damper Ros, aided by a can of Frank's Heineken Lager, cooked in the coals. After plenty of questions about marsupials, Aboriginals and sharks Ros changed the subject.

'This trip is a pretty big change for you, Margaret. What made you do it?'

'Tha' knows Frank's nobbut middlin' wi' 'is 'eart. An' t' babbis flown nest. So 'twas time to say tarra, ducky, and see a bit 'o world.'

'What about you, Julian?' Philip asked. He was curious what made this quiet soul tick.

'See the world, man, like the lady says: Rome, Athens, the East, wherever the road takes me.'

'What about the money? Can you afford it?' Sue asked.

'I have a bit saved, and you don't need much on the trail through India and Asia.'

'If you're running low you could fly to Australia and earn a bit there. Plenty of my friends do it. Work for three months, live for a year on the road,' Ros suggested.

'We're off to Perugia for a festival. Alan plays the flute really well,' Sue jumped into the conversation again. Her life history followed before Frank asked Alan to play. For the next hour everyone there was "appy as pigs in muck".

'And you, Christian?' He'd been quietly absorbing everyone else's story.

'I've been writing to Giulia for a year. Mum thought it was a good idea if I did a student exchange in Rome with her family. She can stay with us next year.'

His eyes told Ros that he had her photograph. Was this a pen friend or an exotic creature that had already snatched his heart?

Since Alan was in such "fine fettle" the evening ended with pieces by Vivaldi and Mozart, the notes drifting like moths into the night.

§

Frank's fifty miles an hour average was much reduced by the gradient up to the first plateau of Austria but exceeded on the downhill slalom of hairpin bends. Ros saw how he worked the gears to save his brakes from overheating. Then it was down to thirty or twenty on the next ascent as the white peaks moved closer and the air grew colder. Around mid-day, after a brutal climb, they now cruised easily on the short stretch of flat before the next steep descent.

Ros heard what sounded like a rifle shot echo off the high ridges either side of the valley. She saw Frank feel it immediately through the steering wheel. In a second his foot was off the accelerator. He fought the wheel for many more seconds, slowly losing speed with friction and the weight of the vehicle. But whatever he did the bus edged closer to the median strip between the two lanes.

'Sit yer selves down 'n 'ang on,' he shouted through the cabin.

Margaret braced her feet against the dashboard and covered her head with her arms.

Philip jammed his back against the front curve of seat, facing backwards, and tucked Ros deep into his chest, his arms circling her shoulders. He saw Alan do the same with Sue. Julian dragged Christian down the back to Frank and Margaret's bed, where he pushed cushions against the side, and curled them both in tight. For such a slow-moving man his speed was impressive as he took charge of Christian like a big brother.

They felt the sloppy bounce as the tyre rode over the concrete edge. Front left, Philip thought; directly beneath Margaret's seat. Soon the front right joined it on the grass, carving another ugly track deep into the damp earth. On and on, the rear two joined the careering monster ploughing the earth. Frank held on to the bucking wheel as the tyres gouged further. Inexorably the oncoming traffic in the other lane got closer. Everyone in the cabin could hear brakes applied and horns blare. With a last grind, motion stopped.

'Tha' knows to get out!'

Frank helped Margaret out of her seat. Christian sprinted to the door with Julian right behind; Sue, Alan, and then Ros followed by Philip, Margaret with Frank last. The tight huddle of people stopped running two bus-lengths away and waited. But there was no diesel smell. In the meandering tracks Philip could see clear oil but not black. There was heat but no fire.

'Man, I'm vexed,' said Frank.

'It could be worse, Frank. You know how steep the road up here was.

'Reight.'

'And you know what's coming.' Philip pointed to the precipice ahead, sure to be full of multiple bends over sheer drops.

'Ah reckon.'

'Then what were the chances of it happening here, on just four ks of flat road?' said Philip.

'Yer right, lad.'

Philip and Ros walked back to the bus with him and Margaret.

'Sump's scored but not leaking,' said Ros.

'Not much left of the tyre. And there's the oil, from the brake drum.'

Frank just nodded. Ros could see shock in his reactions. But he'd held it together when it was needed. Margaret patted his arm.

'Come on, Philip. How's your German?'

'Not much to write home about.'

She waved down a light delivery truck.

'Sprichst du Englisch?'

'A little.' A young man smiled; all teeth and ears with receding short brown hair.

'Bitte.' Ros led him to the front of the bus.

He looked, shrugged and scratched his chin.

'Mechaniker?' said Ros.

'Me? Nein. Innsbruck! I get mechaniker here.'

'Vielen Dank,' said Ros.

'Velen Dan',' said Frank. He shook the man's hand.

As they turned back Ros saw that Margaret had a brew on the boil. An hour later a large white van with "Altan, Mobiler Mechaniker" arrived.

'He's not German,' Philip and Ros said together.

'This is your call, Philip,' she said.

A muscular, round-faced man of olive complexion strode up to the group. His Ataturk moustache was unmistakeable. Just before he spoke Philip turned to Frank.

'Do you mind if I speak to him?'

'Smashin' idea.'

'Türkçe konu??'

'Tabii ki sorun ne?' Altan's smile spread the moustache across his face. He followed Philip and Frank to the problem.

'Oy, Oy,' were his words when he saw what was left of the shredded tyre and the damaged wheel rim and brakes. Then they followed him back along the tracks to the road. At the point the bus left the tarmac and rode over the concrete Altan picked up something. He turned to face them.

'Allah'a şükürler olsun. Ölme zamanın değildi,' he said. In his open hand was a twisted spiral of metal that had been thrown out by the impact.

Frank and Philip studied the piece of shrapnel.

'We were lucky, Frank.'

'Tha's right, lad. Wha's 'e say?'

'"Allah be praised. It was not your time to die."'

They followed him back to the bus.

'Fren silindiri kırık,' Altan explained. He'd need to order the replacement brake drum from Leyland in the UK.

'How long?' asked Frank.

'Be? gün,' said Altan, holding up five fingers.

'Five days, maybe a bit less,' Philip translated after more discussion. 'That's it, I'm afraid. At least he seems sure he can fix it.'

'What's Turkish for "thank you"?

'Teşekkür ederim,' Philip said quietly.

'Teshkker drim,' Frank said to Altan and shook his hand.

'That's proper champion, tha', lad,' Frank said to Philip.

'It's good that we could help.' Ros was by his side.

Frank shook hands with both of them.

For the evening meal Margaret raided the cache of tins. With Ros' and Sue's help she produced a passable goulash with potato hash. Frank and the lads were on pot duty. In the darkness the steady streams of vehicles came and went between Innsbruck and the Brenner Pass. The small fire of scavenged wood was enough to feel cosy. The coats and jackets did the real job against the mountain chill.

'Margaret 'n me been talkin'. We be reight 'ere until Altan comes by. But tha's best be on your way.'

Philip was tempted to say, 'Are you sure?' but they both knew Frank was right.

Sue and Alan went into a huddle. Ros heard "broken contract" and lots of grumbles but Alan settled her down. Ros was sure Frank would agree to a fair price when it came to settle up in the morning.

'Fifteen quid'll do fur tha' two.'

Philip paid him last thing, ready for an early start. At first light the rucksacks were packed. Ros and Philip finished up their coffee and tea and handed back their rinsed cups.

'Thanks, Margaret. And you Frank.' Ros hugged them both. 'Hope the rest of the trip goes well.'

'Good trip,' said Philip as he shook hands.

They walked fifty metres along the highway, crossed and waited. Several massive pantechnicons drove past without slowing. It would have been hard to pull up in a reasonable time.

'Shake a leg, Ros.'

'As if that is going to work!' She put one leg of her jeans forward and smiled at the van driver. 'Come on. You can do it. Strewth, he's slowing up.'

The driver opened the back and they piled their rucksacks in with the vegetables. Philip climbed the high steps first and Ros followed.

Philip's in protective mode again, she thought. A baddy won't drive off with just him, and he's beside the gearstick.

'Philip,' he said and put out his hand.

'Antonio.'

'Rosalind,' she said before Philip could, and held out her hand.

'Ciao bella Rosalind.' His hand lingered and his eyes ate her.

Maybe I should let Philip play his macho game, she thought. But it is nice to be appreciated, to a point.

Fractured English and even more truncated Italian filled the time while the modern van climbed through twists and turns at speeds Frank would never have attempted. On straight stretches Ros watched the vast snake of trucks behind them in the side mirror. When the railway was close the line of wagons brimming with German coal was equally long. It took fifteen minutes in the queue to pass through the Austrian and Italian checkpoints. The border town of Brenner, on the Italian side, looked prosperous with its station and the trappings of ski tourism. At the supermarket they parted with Antonio.

'Addio bella signora,' and he kissed her hand. Philip was not even in the equation.

Ros didn't have to shake a leg for the next lift. She heard Matteo start the Ferrari Dino Coupe at the petrol station. She looked around and watched the blue envelope, a colour straight from an Assisi fresco, cruise out and pull up beside her.

'Ciao bella,' Matteo purred, just like his car.

The other side of forty, full head of flecked black hair, Armani suit with white shirt, top button undone, easy smile, a touch of class, she thought.

'Philip. Can you put the bags, and yourself, in the back, please?'

He shrugged and did as he was told. It was a lift. Did it matter who made it happen?

Ros waited for Philip to get in. She lay back in the low bucket seat. Unusually the beast had seat belts. While Philip pulled the lap belt tight Matteo reached towards her.

'Scusi.'

He pulled the shoulder belt across her body. She smelled his after shave, musk and something, on the stubble of the night before. There was a click and the sash pulled tight against her chest. He smiled in approval. Matteo took time to snap himself in. Then he leisurely pushed down on the handbrake in the centre, and slid the short gear lever into first.

Philip felt the G-force push him back into the seat. Matteo cut into a tiny gap in traffic. The engine howled with each change of gear. Soon they were on the open highway towards Bolzano. Matteo said surprisingly little. Instead he delighted in showing what this car could do with a beautiful lady by his side. Philip watched the first tight corner approach at lightning speed. Matteo showed no sign of slowing. Almost on top of it he changed down a gear and with the barest touch of the steering wheel flew through the corner.

Ahead was the valley. High green walls of forest towered on either side, the road a narrow cut in Nature. Philip could see better than Ros the series of meandering loops of road ahead, all the way down the valley. He saw Matteo roar forward, almost touching the tail of the car in front, flip out, engine growl, and in again before the oncoming lorry could think of sounding his horn. With the tiniest reduction of speed as he slid down a gear Matteo braked and spun the rear around the hairpin corner. The sounds of a racetrack: squealing rubber, the pain of all the horses inside this thing, all combined into something between thrill and terror.

This was a two seater racing car with a tiny back seat as an afterthought. He sat with his knees jammed into his chest. With the open top blowing a cool wind and the crescendos of noise, he consciously tried to relax. He thought of a positive: if they got to their destination at all it would be fast; very.

Ros lay back in comfort and enjoyed the skill of this driving maestro. The straights were down to a dozen car lengths between corners. The van in front was an approaching catastrophe, and then disappeared as he pulled out, passed, and in again within three car lengths. Touch of the brakes; rear-end spin, a little more rubber on the road, before powering on to the next. His concentration was total so she was free to revel in the experience. She guessed that she was the decoration that improved his sense of being alive. Not that anyone could talk over the noise.

Matteo mostly kept to the speed limit through Bolzano. So the Cathedral, a section of the old Roman Via Claudia, and the Adige River, were more than the previous blur of green. But a business meeting compelled him. The South Tyrolean countryside was rich, emerald and rugged. Trento city was dwarfed by a 13th century fortress: Buonconsiglio Castle. In what seemed a blink another castle, at Rovereto, appeared. Medieval street walls reverberated to the sound of the prancing stallion.

Now they were clearly travelling through the foothill country, still following the icy Adige River above the North Italian plain. Ros might have worried for her safety in the beginning but those first few corners showed his skill. The time had passed in a pleasurable dream of beautiful scenery, speed and the enjoyment of watching someone so skilled in what they did.

Philip climbed out beside a café in the Piazza Bra. Verona's Roman amphitheatre was just across the square. While he unloaded the rucksacks Matteo walked around and opened the passenger door for Ros. She sat forward and extricated herself from the bed-like seat. Matteo steadied her hand.

Ros was not sure what to do next. But then she thought, why not? She leaned forward and brushed her cheek against his, right and then his left.

'Arrivederci, Matteo.'

'Thanks.' Philip shook his hand.

'Buon viaggio Rosalind e Philip.'

As Matteo's steed growled out of sight Philip looked at his watch. It was just before 9; time for breakfast. His espresso and her café nero were accompanied by bread rolls, pats of butter and a small bowl of jam. They people-watched and enjoyed the subtle differences of culture, air and light now that they were in Italy. Both were drawn to the arches of the two-level Roman arena.

Outside one entrance Ros could see wracks of exotic eastern costumes being wheeled in. Through it and another arch, where the great wooden doors were open, she could make out a colossal Sphinx. Ballet was more to her taste but what a setting for an opera, doubly so for Verdi's "Aida".

'A spectacle within a spectacle,' she said. Inside the arena she heard one of the choruses being practiced.

"Gloria all'Egitto e ad Iside

Che il sacro suol protegge;"

The massed voices gave the words grandeur.

'What a wonderful sound. Opera should only be sung in Italian. It wouldn't be the same in English, or German. "Isis" and "Egypt" and "sacred" are about my limit at the moment.'

'Something to add to our repertoire?' he said.

After a comfort stop and what Ros described as a "shush up" they put on their backpacks and trekked out of the centre of the city. The morning began to heat up. This was when she questioned the necessity of every item packed. Philip had the tiny tent but she had the sleeping bag. After half an hour they sat beside a layby and let the sweat cool.

They took turns standing up with a thumb out, looking at the driver's face, willing them to pull over. Tourists sometimes slowed but sped up when they saw the backpacks. Italians in little Fiat Bambinos, or Cinquecentos, 500cc powered bubbles were invariably filled with kids and grandma piled in the back seat. Ros shook a leg and it drew young men to slow up their Alfa Romeos and Lancias. As Philip stood up they roared off again. For an hour nothing worked.

'He's stopping,' Ros said. Eureka, it was on her shift.

The well-worn furniture removal van pulled into the bay and a solidly-built teenager leaned out of the window. 'Ciao bella, dove stai andando?'

Ros heard "dove", "where" and guessed the rest. 'Roma,' she said clearly over the noise of passing traffic.

'Inglese?'

'Australian.'

'Ah, Australiano.'

He climbed out, opened the back and they put the rucksacks in. Ros followed him up the steps into the cab before Philip could get there. He closed the cab door as the boy/man squeezed past the gearstick and closer to his dad.

'Rosalind,' she said and nodded.

'Philip,' he said quickly and did the same.

'Angelo,' said the broad-faced, white bearded father. His eyes pierced like a hawk's.

'Alfio,' said his son. There was no question of his parentage with those eyes, but his skin was swarthier, more like a southern mother.

Maybe there's gypsy there somewhere, thought Philip. But not a thing to say, in case he caused offence.

Angelo pulled out into a big space in the traffic and wound up speed.

'Frank's bus,' said Ros quietly.

'Without the tea stops I hope,' Philip replied.

Angelo's pace on the autostrada was steady and not as slow as they'd imagined. Italian countryside slid by: the undulations, the hill-top towns, the patches of pine forest and the small farms of cropped olive trees, almonds and cherries. Gardens were neat rows of silver sprays of artichokes and climbing grape vines on trellises shading long tables for alfresco family occasions. On their left was the constant presence of the mighty spine of the Apennine Mountains. The range rose steadily in ridges to far snow-capped peaks.

Alfio's leg was squashed against her thigh but whatever went through his brain Angelo's presence limited. Ros dozed for an hour, her head curled into Philip's shoulder. She felt safe with genuine people.

Somewhere in Tuscany they stopped. Ros and Philip had their water and left-over bread rolls and a hunk of cheese from the mountains somewhere near Verona. Angelo opened brown paper bags with hard biscuits, almonds and cherries and some cake. A flask of black coffee finished it off. Each offered to share but was content with what they had.

Ros tried to feel the countryside. This was captured in Florentine art: the paintings of Botticelli, the sculptures of Michelangelo, the sfumato mystery in the backgrounds of Leonardo. She was beginning to sense that awe of being at the Renaissance heart, of where it all began. Maybe it was good to take it in at the pace of Angelo rather than Matteo.

They crawled through Roman traffic in the darkness until Angelo dropped them off in the Via Gramsci. It was out of his way but Philip and Ros could not persuade him to do otherwise.

They were here, she thought, in the ancient soul of Italy. She stopped and looked up at the monumental marble staircase leading to the entrance of colossal Corinthian columns. To one side were carved on a marble panel the words: Accademia Britannica, Via Gramsci 61. This was the prestigious British School at Rome. As they hoisted their bags they felt decidedly underdressed.

'Let's hope Peter told them we were coming,' Philip said as he opened the door.

CHAPTER 2

1480. Florence.

Bernardo was always welcome in Lorenzo's library but after the murder I gained ready access too. My studies with tutors were now supplemented by teachers at the Studio Fiorentino, and all that I could read in this vast collection. Many times I sat with a book open and just listened to the conversations of passing scholars. Angelo Poliziano and his philosopher companions discussed the ideas of Plato, for one of those friends, Marsilio Ficino, had translated Plato's dialogues into Latin. A roughly built man, with the ugliness of Socrates, listened attentively as Ficino discussed ideas from his treatise on Plato called "De amore".

'When we speak of Love, we mean the desire for beauty. The purpose of love is the enjoyment of beauty, but only the meanest form is mortal. For each person is beautiful in some respects but not in others. The greatest love is for one soul to love another, far above the constraints of earthly desires.'

Beatrice, Dante's great love who died too soon, came to my mind: Beatrice who left Heaven to ask Virgil to guide her love out of Hell, to her embrace.

The listener was one of many encouraged and helped by Lorenzo the Magnificent. Clearly the man slept in his crumpled clothes. Others said that he was served the finest food at Lorenzo's table and yet was indifferent to it. After only one year apprenticed to Domenico Ghirlandaio this sculptor and painter now lived amongst the ancient statues of the Medici collection. But Michelangelo was also an accomplished poet, as was Lorenzo. His court dazzled with brilliance.

Another listener that day was a moderately handsome man of average build whose attentiveness caught my attention. Clearly he was a painter in the midst of a work, since his doublet and pantaloons were marked with pigment and resin.

'Artists in each of the arts seek after and care for nothing but love,' Ficino continued. The painter nodded abstractedly. His hand sketched aspects of the folds of the philosopher's tunic.

'The doctors of antiquity have affirmed that love is a passion that resembles a melancholic disease.' The hand paused and his eyes viewed the floor. Clearly this was a man besotted, even to my little experience in such matters. He was a wounded spirit.

'The physician Rasis prescribed, therefore, in order to recover; coitus, fasting, drunkenness and walking.' There was laughter among his listeners but only a muted smile on the artist's face. Who was he?

I went back to absorbing the work of Petrarch as I too had an interest in writing poetry. The structure of his sonnets was eight lines then six, the first presenting a problem to be solved and the second the solution, if there was one. The ten syllables in a line and the precise rhyme scheme made it difficult to master. My limited experience of life made it harder to find a subject. I searched the walls and ceiling for inspiration before looking around the room. There he was poring over a book. With cap balanced on delicate curls and the familiar red doublet and tights: it was the handsome artist.

With the ruse of seeking a manuscript I moved close enough to see what he was reading. It was a copy of Vetruvius' "De architectura" in Latin. He was transcribing sections of text into a notebook. It was clear by his concentration and the gaps in the notebook that he was struggling.

'May I help you, sir?'

He looked up. I watched him process his memory of me. Had he seen me with Bernardo, known as a specialist on the work of the Roman historian Livy? Maybe he remembered me from the visit to the bottega.

'Can you read Latin?' His accent was Florence with a hint of country.

'Yes, quite well.' I looked at the page and realised that Vetruvius was discussing the mathematical shapes of buildings. He let me turn a page and then another one. 'He is describing the best, or correct, proportions of architecture so that they fit the scale, the dimensions, of the human body.'

'What is this word?'

'"Laquearia". It means ceiling.'

He turned to another random page and pointed to the word.

'"Hortus". Garden.'

'And this?'

'"Externus abdominis". That is the body, the torso,' I said pointing to mine.

'Well, you are The Man,' he said and smiled. 'Il Machia.'

'You could be The Scribbler, Il Scribacchino. But I notice your persistence in pursuit of knowledge.'

'Success is difficult. Pesistent rigor is needed to overcome the obstacles.'

'Ostinato Rigore is your motto then.'

'Yes, I suppose it is.'

I looked back to Ficino and his audience. 'If you don't mind, can you tell me who that man is,' I nodded in the artist's direction. 'Another scribbler, I think.'

'A fair comparison, since his work is admirable in many aspects: Alessandro di Mariano di Vanni Filipepi. Sandro created the fine portrait of Lorenzo's murdered brother Giuliano above the Porto della Dogana.'

'Yes, I have looked at it many times.' His eyes enquired and the moment seemed right. So I explained what I knew on that day of the Pazzi plot.

'I saw you drawing the body of Salviati. What a strange subject for your skill.'

'The body in extremis is always interesting.'

I helped him often over the next days and months. We came up with many names for each other: "Piccolo Niccolò" was one I did not like. Eventually he settled on Machia and I chose Ostinato for his dogged determination to achieve.

'Come, we have a visit to make.' Ostinato led me through a part of the labyrinthine palace that I had not seen before. At the end of a corridor we turned left and stepped through the open door of a large room filled with natural light from four windows. It was full of stacked canvases, part-finished cartoons for future frescoes, and piles of drawings. Four apprentices busied themselves as I had seen in the bottega of Ostinato: crushing pigments, framing wood for canvases, working on parts of drapery and landscape that the master had little time for.

'Good morning Sandro. How do you fare today?'

The earnest listener at Ficino's lecture looked up from the sketched out beginnings of a painting of an antique subject. It was Venus, at her birth fully-formed, rising from the ocean in a shell. Her face was beautiful, and I thought her bodily form was too.

'Sandro fares well. How are you, fellow Scribbler?' He watched me study another of his works.

Next to a crate marked "Lorenzo di Medici, Castello" was a painting of a cluster of women and some men in an orange grove. So many flowers so accurately depicted that I recognised dozens I had seen in walks around Mugello. The characters were antique, Venus among them, and Cupid with a bow aimed at three women who must be the Three Graces. All my classical learning was being tested to make sense of this mesmerizing painting. Primavera, goddess of spring, was the cardinal subject, marshalling those around her in their various pursuits. Ovid was there in Sandro's allusions but I would need weeks of research to make sense of the rest. I looked across at the half-formed Venus on the easel and back again at the completed face in the picture. Who was the model, for surely they were the same?

'Do you like the painting, signor Machia?' Sandro asked.

'Yes, and even more if I understood it properly. Is this,' I pointed to his latest work, 'for Lorenzo too?'

'It is.'

'Primavera seems to lead an elaborate pageant that would appeal to his complex mind. May I ask who models for your Venus?'

'Sadly she is no longer with us.' He took a drawing from a pile. Every one was a study of the same person. 'Simonetta Vespucci, former wife of Marco Vespucci: a tragedy on two accounts, her marriage and her early death.'

'You do not approve of marriage?' Ostinato asked. 'Or is this jealousy that she was not married to you?'

'Both. It chains women to unsuitable men, not equal to their beauty or wit. But you are right, if she had been able to choose me that might have changed my viewpoint.'

'At least she still lives inside your mind, signor Sandro,' I said. Ficino had tapped into a man besotted with his unattainable muse.

Over time Ostinato and I developed a pattern of leaving work for each other: he words and phrases that troubled him and me the translations. Sometimes I would visit him at the bottega. I was brave enough to show him some of my drawings and he had the kindness to demonstrate a few tricks to improve them.

One afternoon at the bottega I sat with him as we filled in breaks in his notebook. The page was full of drawings of unrelated things. His brain seemed to be crammed with ideas that just spilled on to the paper.

'Well, boss. Have you found a new friend?' The apprentice was a burly fellow, stronger than Ostinato in muscle. His nose suggested a street fighter. Those beside him waited for whatever came next.

'As foreman I expect more respect. Yes, this is my friend.'

'What does he taste like, old man? Better than the one they nearly hung you for?' He laughed and tapped the bag holding his plonker.

Ostinato stood up. A brawl would help nobody.

'Have you worked for Lorenzo yet?'

The bully scowled.

'I have. A word to our master Andrea and you won't. Without my help you will never have the skill.'

Ostinato walked me outside. 'Loud and aggressive men should never worry you, Machia. Your brain will always win.'

I waved and left. Bernardo explained that two years before the Pazzi Conspiracy Ostinato had faced a charge of raping another man. One of those accused with him was related to the Medici family and the case was dropped. But for months he had faced a death sentence. It was clear that the experience hurt him deeply. By the end of the evening I understood the theory of where babies came from. I remember feeling unsettled that family were created in such a primitive, embarrassing way, like farm yard animals. But then we are not so far away from the beasts, are we?

While Ostinato worked for Lorenzo in the Palazzo I learnt a new skill, rhetoric, at the Studio Fiorentino of which the Medici was patron. I had no interest in business but I had ability with words. With letters and speech I could persuade others to my way of thinking. It was a talent that has served me for a lifetime.

'What is this text, Machia?' Ostinato had surprised me.

'It's"De Rerum Natura", "On the Nature of things", by the Roman philosopher Lucretius.

'Ex causis fit sine motu omnia numina,' he read over my shoulder. '"Sine" is "without", "ex" is "out of" or "from", "omnia" is "everything".'

Ostinato built up the translation by picking out words that he knew. When he was nearly there but slowing I helped. 'All things occur by natural causes without any intervention by the deities.'"

'That is not something our Pope would agree with,' he said. But then he sat down beside me and we immersed ourselves in Epicurean philosophy as interpreted in Rome of the first century B.C. So many phrases stirred our excitement: "What once came from the earth sinks back into earth", "the atoms in the world are used over and over again; thus the death of one thing is needed for the birth of another."

We studied the text for weeks. Whatever Ostinato was supposed to be working on was put aside for this new passion. He revealed that his only education was at the bottega. He had taught himself Latin. The man who had sired him with a peasant girl, Caterina, had denied Ostinato his name or any financial help. Piero had never been a father, whereas I had Bernardo. But we had both known poverty. Together we thirsted for that knowledge to lift us out of it, even to the peak of society.

On the 24th June, at the festival of San Giovanni Battista, the streets of Florence were filled with light and colour. All the confraternities were on parade including ours, La Pietà. Ostinato had been busy with designs for banners and painted ribbons which now hung in the streets, and statues to celebrate Florence's patron saint. Bernardo took me to a play in the Piazza del Duomo. John the Baptist's story was filled with strange animals that lived in the desert and demons sent to tempt him. The spectacle stayed in my mind.

Florence was still at war with the King of Naples who was allied with the Pope. Villages outside the city were pillaged by Sienese troops and in return Florentine mercenaries did the same around Siena. The cities paid the price for the Pope's schemes. Meanwhile the silk and woollen mills traded goods through the port of Pisa. Ships from Genoa and the East brought in and loaded cargo at the docks. Sailors were the first to become sick. In the warm days of summer the first cases appeared in Florence.

'Tumours like small apples appeared between her legs and under her arms,' I heard my mother tell Bernardo. 'When they burst, blood and pus poured out of them.' She had called the priest to her cousin across the courtyard but when he arrived he would only visit if Bartolomea gave him an exorbitant fee.

'Too many friars have died already, along with the doctors. You must pay more,' he had said.

My mother gave what she could ill afford but the man would barely go into the room to look. He pronounced his prayers and left.

'God is punishing our family, Bernardo. You must pray with me at Sante Croce so God knows that you are devout.'

Bernardo saw the desperation in her eyes. 'Tell her family to burn her clothes and wash her body with water and salt. You must do the praying, Bartolomea. I will visit the Franciscan friars at Santa Croce to see what help I can give.'

On his instructions my sisters and brother and I were confined to the house. We watched the first priests in the street outside carrying holy relics. A procession followed it. Flagellants wearing few clothes were everywhere. Whatever the city had done the Lord was showing his anger. Bartolomea's cousin died on the fourth day. There were so many more soon after that the busy courtyard became oddly silent. Around Florence the smell of rotting corpses was the only way the authorities found the dead. No priests gave the last rites. Consecrated ground in the churches was full. Only the rich could afford a Christian burial. The rest were dumped in ditches with a small covering of earth.

'What is being done to stop the Plague, Bernardo?' I asked?

'Nobody knows how. What makes it, Nico? Foul vapours of air? Your mother thinks herbs might help to keep it away, with prayer of course. I know two things: stay away from other people and that the Plague will run its course.'

Bernardo was often with members of the Confraternity or the Franciscan Friars helping wherever he could. When the Plague was at its height he came home.

'Bartolomea, we must take the household to the country; but not to the vineyard at Sant' Andrea. The roads are full of those fleeing south and west. Your family's place is in the north east. We can be safe there.'

'I spoke to cousin Antonia this morning. She is desperate to take her two sons out of Florence,' said Bartolomea.

'Her husband died last week?'

'Yes,' she said tentatively. 'Can we bring them with us?'

'No. All of Florence cries out to escape.'

'But they are family.'

'This is my family.'

'But you must.' Bartolomea pleaded. 'How can you sleep at night?'

'My answer is no. I save our own. I cannot give in to the desperate. And yes, I sleep.'

The following day we packed enough to fill a cart: clothing, food and a few precious books. By early afternoon Bernardo complained of a headache. In an hour he was vomiting. The first boils appeared on his body at midnight. He was clammy and pale when he called me to him.

'Nico, you must take my place and lead the family to Mugello. There you must do everything you can to keep them well.'

'Who will look after you?' My voice was cracking even though I chewed my lip to be strong.

'One of the Friars has promised to help.' Bernardo folded a sheet of paper and put it in my hand. 'If the atoms of my body are destined to join the earth, then you are the head of the family.' There was no mention of God. But I recognised Lucretius.

In the chill of early morning my sisters and I walked towards the Piazza del Duomo. In the cart were my mother and Toto. Brunelleschi's masterpiece and the other great works were insufficient to raise my spirits.

"There is no greater sorrow than to recall a happy time when miserable." Dante's words flowed unbidden.

Tears streamed uncontrollably. My sisters said nothing. I thought of everything good that my father had ever done for me; his wisdom, his teaching, the life he lived through me. What was to become of Bernardo?

Mugello was a more prosperous estate than ours at Sant'Andrea. It was set in upland country of farms and orchards where Bartolomea grew up. The rugged peaks of the Apennine Mountains towered to the east. Bartolomea and the rest of the family settled into a routine of providing for the table and prayer. She aged daily.

'Niccolò, you must help Bartolomea in the kitchen.' I remembered Bernardo's instructions.

'Why, that is girl's work, for my sisters.'

He had frowned. 'You are better than that, Niccolò. You must help her so that you learn to cook.' I was unconvinced. 'Do you know your future?'

'How can anyone, Father?'

'True. That is why you must learn to feed yourself. It is a skill like any other.'

As a child Bartolomea had pushed a stool next to the bench for me to stand on. Alongside my sisters I mixed the flour and water with my hands, broke eggs so that the shell stayed out, cut vegetables for the pot. All the while Bartolomea and Primerana sang songs of the Tuscan countryside. Usually they involved love, hardship and longing for something better. What I remembered was hands working to the beat, and how time flew away. As well as Bartolomea's stress on rhyme and musicality of words.

Now I sourced vegetables when our own land was insufficient. On occasion I would slaughter a young goat and season it with herbs gathered from the hillside; oregano, thyme, rosemary. As the man I gathered firewood when no fearful peasant would come near. From the cellar I would decant enough wine from the urns in the floor. Together we washed ground and cooked whatever we had. At the evening meal Bartolomea would speak gratitude to her God for our survival.

When I was able I spent time roaming the woodland. Ostinato had described his wanderings in the hills around his family home. Now I was doing the same. Etruscan roads cut through stone so that cliffs shaded me from the sun. Remnants of their tombs and scattered stonework of houses were still visible, even though local farmers robbed so much for their buildings. Water was guided in culverts down the hillside to provide ample to drink. Whenever I watched birds I thought of Ostinato. In the evening with a book, thoughts of Bernardo kept me company.

'Bartolomea, why are we poor?'

'We have more than many, Nico. Bernardo works hard to see to that.'

'He has studied law. Why has he no cases to prosecute?'

She pretended to concentrate on mixing lard and flour and steadily kneaded it into pastry. 'It is difficult to talk about, Nico. But since you are now head of the family it is right that you should know.' She scattered flour over the wooden surface. Then she rolled a wooden pin to make the pastry flat before cutting a circle with a knife. Handfuls of turnip, carrot and a little meat, sprinkled with salt went inside. 'In Bernardo's early life, before he met me, he owed money and could not pay it back. According to Florentine law anyone who has been bankrupt cannot practice his legal skills.' A smear of egg went around the edges of pastry and Bartolomea's nimble fingers twisted it into a pie in the shape of a half moon. She started on the next one. There was more she had to say. 'Bernardo's father sired him outside of marriage. He is illegitimate, which also makes it difficult for him to succeed.'

That evening books did not satisfy. What enormous obstacles Bernardo had surmounted to reach the pinnacles of the Medici court. He knew the mighty of Florence. This he had done through hard work and their universal esteem for his learning: his love of books. All this he had shared with me, so that I would have chances he never did.

In the morning light I watched Bartolomea and the girls pulling weeds from between the vegetables. The piles left at the end of each row would go to the milking nanny. Totto helped by shouting and throwing things at the birds. It struck me that her children were her life: feed, clean, teach. While Bernardo and I had been at Confraternity meetings she would sow fabric and compose her verses to God in the firelight. When she was alone my curiosity was too blunt.

'What happened to your first husband, Bartolomea?'

'He died.' She carried on with her work. 'A woman cannot live without a husband.'

Bernardo would have been horrified by my so-called diplomacy.

'Nico, Toto, Primerana, Margherita, come quickly,' she shouted one morning weeks later. Bartolomea stared down the dusty road that wound up to the village. A single horse paced slowly behind a solitary traveller. On its back were two panniers that made the creature sweat even at this time of the day.

'Bernardo,' we each said as he stopped in the courtyard. He was thinner, whiter but still found that familiar mischief to smile.

'We cannot neglect your education,' he said, tapping the satchels of books.

When you have looked at Death and recognised his sneer time takes on new meaning. Bernardo wasted none of it.

True to his word my father found local priests, medical students and retired teachers to teach us.

The teacher of Latin stooped with his hands behind his back as he paced back and forth at the front of the room. 'Amo, Amas, Amat,' he said in a modulated gravel voice. 'Amamus, Amatis, Amant.' I studied his rheumy eyes and sagging jaw. He was like an old dog perusing the last weeks of his life. On some afternoons the sunlight from the window shone through his parchment skin. Yet his eyes sparkled with the joy of sharing his language. 'I love, you love, he or she or it loves, we love, you love, they love.' Amore.

When not in the classroom we wandered in the local woods or explored the ruins of Montebuiano castle. Unlike the local boys and girls we did not have to work as hard in the fields to keep our family alive. Peasant life seemed closer to the earth, too close according to Bartolomea. When I described to Bernardo that I had walked around a corner to see a girl squatting to pee, he just laughed. But my mother failed to find the humour.

'If your father has his way you will talk to commoners and kings. For that you will need manners, in speech and in habit.' Her training intensified. In poetry I was enthralled. To her passing on of the Christian message I listened politely, because it meant so much to her, but in that task she failed.

'They all seem to relieve themselves wherever they are, Bernardo. They squat with their back to you. The girls hitch their skirts and crouch down. The men pee standing up, usually looking far away into the trees or scratching their backsides.'

'It's the way Nature made us, Nico. People believe that we are special compared with all other creatures of the planet. But everything that lives has parasites, diseases, things that live off them and things that want to kill them. Why should people, walking feasts, be any different?'

'But it's ugly, a bit like the other thing.' I described how trysts in the forest were commonplace. At a distance, since I knew that the Plague was still a threat, those coupling were unconcerned by my presence. But they giggled and made all sorts of noises: a piglet squeal, the grunt of a boar. I thought of the Zeus and Europa story from my Classics teacher. My curiosity was pricked, as it were.

'These people do not live long, even when we are free of pestilence. Twenty years, thirty maybe. Few of the babies they produce live to be adults, Nico. You should be more tolerant of their enjoyment.' When I frowned he laughed. 'Your time will come.'

Sometime after my twelfth birthday on one of my rambles I heard laughter. In a patch of sunlight beside a stream lay two people. They were wet and naked. She yelped as her Zeus mounted her. I needed no books to tutor me how it was done. My member grew miraculously. Things happened down there of their own accord, until I wet myself. Or so it seemed at the time. Bernardo had been right, of course.

'Bernardo, you teach me so many ways to be a success when I am a man. Why is virtue so important? We both see quicker ways to the top.'

'That is a valid question, Nico, a good one. Yes I could teach you ways to be a crook. Many men would say that's the best way. It's definitely the shortest route to money, fame, honours of the variety that the Pope hands out. But it's not lasting or satisfying, and not what you would like to review on your deathbed.' I felt the passion rise in his voice. 'Know the bad ways but choose the better. Make your conscience as clean as you can in the game of survival. In the full life I imagine for you it will be tested to destruction, or almost. Choose well.'

On the topics of wine and water Bernardo had strong opinions. 'Our family is lucky enough to have good water from Mugello and Sant' Andrea; clear, without smell or taste. Here at Mugello you may drink from streams that flow from the hills but never from the marshes or stagnant pools. Others less fortunate drink poor water flavoured with wine. In ways that I am not sure of wine cleans the water, even if it does not make it taste any better.'

From the earliest age we all drank some wine, much regulated by Bartolomea. 'Drunkenness is a sin. No child of mine will fall into that, like the most foolish of the peasants. '

When I recalled my bodily discovery to Bernardo he smiled and then sighed. 'It is time to introduce you to another great pleasure, not as immense as books, but definitely as enlightening as fornication.'

At one of the less frequented taverns, of which there were a great many, Bernardo spoke. 'Nico, when the Pazzi tried to kill Lorenzo you proved to be a great student of people. Now look around you.'

I did as I was told. Some of the faces I recognised as those who tilled the fields on our estate. Gap-toothed laughter was all around. One man spoke a great deal but nobody understood. Another leaned and swayed over a smaller man with fists raised. The tavern keeper nodded to a pair of hard-faced men to deal with the problem. In a corner a girl not much older than me had her eyes shut blissfully as a man fondled inside her shirt.

'Wine does this?' I asked.

He nodded. 'It can turn men into sheep.'

I pointed to an old man asleep at a table.

'Or lions.'

I watched the mis-matched men being pushed roughly out into the alley.

'It loosens the mind so that people can escape the drudgery of their daily lives. They can break the chains of convention and do what they really want to.'

I looked at the girl. She was not complaining. It was too noisy to hear any farmyard sounds.

'Yes, it takes away inhibitions to a point of abandonment; what Bartolomea would call drunkenness. Therefore you must be in control of its powers.'

My mother disapproved of our tavern-crawling but what better way to find my limits than in the safety of Bernardo. I looked at the tazza, the shallow terracotta bowl with a low stem, in front of me. With a first drink, diluted from a flask of our water Bernardo carried with him, I felt warm, a little sleepy. With a second my cheeriness increased as did my wish to talk, about anything. But this changed over days and weeks, as the water became less. The first tazza of undiluted wine silenced me, made me look and talk less. 'He is saying more than he should to the crowd around him. She is laughing too loudly, a lioness about to be taken by those men bringing the wine.' A second tazza gave me confidence in my judgements and made me feel like a lion myself. Later in my education Bernardo let me drink a third glass, so that I could hear my speech slurring. My words and thoughts escaped me, and I could see now how vulnerable anyone could be if they drank more than their mind could take. He did not need to offer me a fourth because I could feel the queasiness in my stomach. I did not wish to embarrass Bernardo, not so much a father but an older brother.

'What a wonderful means of enlightenment,' I said to him later the following day, when my head had cleared.

'For you especially: your skills lie in guiding men, the kings and the commoners that Bartolomea spoke of. But Plato in his Symposium served wine carefully to his philosopher companions. It gave them insight. Yet Aristotle's maxim, "Everything in Moderation", applies. Wine is a powerful tool but a terrible enemy.'

In 1482 the plague had passed and we returned to the Via Romana. As soon as I could I walked the short distance to the Medici Palazzo. The library was as rich as ever and academia thrived like Plato's Symposium of ancient times. But there was someone missing. It was Angelo that told me. Lorenzo had become tired of waiting for works to be completed. When a silver lyre in the shape of a horse's head was finished Lorenzo sent it as a gift to Ludovico Sforza, the Duke of Milan. Ostinato had gone with it.

§

Ros awoke to bright sunlight dappled by manicured tall trees in the grounds and the Villa Borghese gardens beyond. After a tent and sleeping bag on hard ground no wonder they'd slept in. In the twin bed pushed against hers Philip was stirring.

'Bags first shower.'

Philip was content to listen to her rendition of Dean Martin's "Amore" while he studied the map of the city. Peter had given them until Saturday to explore. That was three days away. Via Gramsci bordered on the vast park of the Villa Borghese, full of the art that enticed Ros. The British School was minutes' walk from the Piazza del Popolo, where all roads led to somewhere astonishing. West along the Via Cola di Rienzo was the Vatican and nearby Castel San Angelo. South, more or less, was the Via del Corso to the Piazza Venezia and along the Via Dei Fori Imperiali, at the end of which was the Colosseum and the remnants of the heart of ancient Rome. Clearly the difficulty would not be how to fill in three days but how to select only the jewels, according to their tastes. Of course they also had to work on the problem of Harry's text.

'Hogging all the hot water?' as he slid into the shower beside her.

'Not all of it.'

The water slid in soapy rivers down the curves all the way past her toes. He picked up a sponge and started to trace the contours that he particularly liked.

'Ah, ah; before you get frisky. We have things to do. Daylight's wasting.' She took the sponge and squeezed it into his chest as she got out of harm's way.

Along the wide gravel pathways named after Churchill and Washington Philip studied the mature limbless pine trees with their flat shady crowns. An army of gardeners with a good head for heights was needed for such a look. Before the real heat of the day this was the place for walkers, escaping dogs with owners calling in the distance, and fit runners loping like gazelle seemingly without effort. The city was a roar of traffic just out of sight.

Out of the gardens, a short way along the Via del Corso, Philip turned right into a narrow warren of alleys; the realm of pedestrians, tourist shops and cafés. It was disturbed only by Vespa scooters going cross country to avoid the jammed main thoroughfares; and taxis creeping behind oblivious tourists. Soon the view opened into the Piazza di Spagna and the Spanish steps.

'It's bigger than I imagined, even with all the spreading bodies,' she said. They stood beside the Barcaccia fountain and looked up to the Trinità dei Monti church at the top. Ros observed the two storey pink and white house where Keats spent his last days.

'"Here lies one whose name was writ in water",' she said.

He waited for more. Ros always astounded him with what she could quote, and he couldn't.

'One for you, Philip: "The poetry of the earth is never dead."'

'Thank you. Do you want to see inside?' he said.

'Yes, but there's so much to see here in this city, so another time.'

Philip dragged out the map again, folded to cover only the area close by. More back streets and there was the extravagant confectionary of the Trevi Fountain. Down by the water's edge he put three coins into her hand.

'Make a wish.'

'One.' She leaned over and spun the coin. It sliced straight in and spiralled to the bottom.

'Two.' She threw again. 'A two-er.'

'Three.' This time it bounced many times, across to the rocks.

'Anyone else tosses them over their shoulder,' he said.

'Dare to be different! Maybe my wishes will come true.'

At the Colosseum there was an obstacle: five lanes of traffic circled the structure. Pedestrian crossings did not deter the blaring horns and the steady snarl of impatient drivers. Philip studied what the Italians did. One widow in black; small, stooped, and of unknown age, had it mastered. She came to the edge of the sea of vehicles, looked left and stepped out. She then ambled across the lanes at an aged pace, and the tide parted around her. She was a moving island that no one dared to touch.

'Who could ever run over grandma?' Ros said.

'Give me a moment,' he said. He came back from the street stall with a tiny key ring of a Vespa motorcycle. It was contained in a brilliant yellow plastic bag.

'Ready?'

'Are you sure?'

'Come on.' He held her hand and looked left to gauge that the Fiat taxi had stopping time. Then he held out the garish bag and stepped out.

'Don't look at them, just forward.'

He held the bag straight out at shoulder height and kept walking. Ros tucked in close. Time slowed and sounds were magnified: tyres snarled, gears changed and Vespas darted in front of and behind them. The waters parted until they stepped onto the other side intact.

'You're mad,' she said.

'But it worked.'

Ros looked down at the ruined chambers beneath what was once the floor of the Colosseum arena. As she had in Cornwall she could feel the layers of lives and the multiple ways of their demise. It was not a happy place, despite the exhilaration of the crowds. The waves of emotions continued to flood her subconscious as they ambled past the Arch of Constantine, through the remnants of palaces on the Palatine Hill and down to the Arch of Titus. The panel on the south side showed the sack of Jerusalem in 70AD. The seven fluted Menorah candelabrum was carved in the deepest relief at the centre.

Near the Ponte Fabricio onto the island at the heart of the Tiber, they stopped at a café in the Jewish quarter. It was hard to imagine the squalid past of the walled ghetto brutally controlled by the Papacy. The irony did not escape her. Now it was a vibrant quarter of fine food, kosher and otherwise.

'Un café espresso e nero per favore,' Ros ordered, to accompany the Margherita pizza.

'What next, Philip?' she said. The pizza was simple, like the best cooking, she thought. The coffee and a glass of water gave them energy again.

'The Vatican. After we do the sights Peter has organised permits for the Vatican Library. It's time to earn our keep.'

'Sounds good, but why didn't you tell me?'

'I didn't think I needed to.' Philip paused. 'We speak with one voice,' he said playfully.

'Ha. Which one is that?'

'Depends which one is right.'

'Ok. Good answer. Just tell me what you're up to next time.'

'And spoil the surprise? You could just agree with me?'

They entered via the Piazza Pius X11. Ros stood in St Peter's Square and absorbed the Basilica from where the Catholic faithful listened to the Papal address. Photographs in books made it familiar but could not convey its majestic scale. Inside, the many tourists were lost as she gazed up into the dome. The Sydney Opera House, anything short of Ayers Rock, would be swallowed by this cathedral. With Philip in tow she stood in front of Michelangelo's Pietà. Somehow it was smaller and more intimate than she had imagined.

Inside the Vatican Museum one chamber, another corridor all flowed like the tide of tourists. Ornate ceilings, painted opulent landscapes, marble floors that had consumed mountains, all filled her mind until it ached. Looking up at the Last Judgement in Michelangelo's Sistine Chapel she could understand how the congregation were cajoled into doing the right thing on earth rather than face the fiery pit that was so vividly portrayed. It was strange. The sale of Indulgences to the poor to redeem loved ones from Michelangelo's vision was Papal extortion. Yet out of such abuse of faith came great beauty. But if she never saw another reliquary with St Bartholomew's left nostril or big toe she would be very happy.

'You want the Catholic Church to sell everything to feed the world's poor, I suppose,' Philip said.

'Just a couple of rooms of the stuff would do that.' This obscene wealth had nothing to do with Christ and his disciples. It left her feeling angry and sad.

But the Library was a different story. Philip led the way outside and along the east wall of the Vatican towards Ottaviano underground station. Just before the Piazza della Città Leonina he stopped at the gate. Inside the Porta Sant'Anna were three soldiers of the Swiss Guard.

'Ready?'

'Of course.'

'My voice this time?' he said.

She frowned. 'Let's get on with it.'

Philip walked confidently through the gate. The first guard stopped them.

'Excuse me, we are scholars and would like to use the Vatican Library.'

'Go to the police station over there,' was the crisp reply.

Inside the booth Philip repeated but the guard did not speak English.

'Siamo qui per la Biblioteca di Vaticana,' Ros said and smiled.

The guard smiled back. 'Passaporti per favore.'

They pinned on badges with the Vatican crest and continued on through a car park to the Biblioteca Apostolica. Inside the Admissions Office the custodian took their photos and issued ID library cards valid for 30 days.

'Pencils and paper, Philip; that's it,' she said from reading the instruction leaflet. Their small rucksack went into a locker.

After a long flight of stairs they came to the library on the second floor. It was worth it. Ros stood for a moment in the Aula, the main reading room, and stared. The opulence of the decorated ceilings, the apostolic paintings on squared stucco pillars, enormous leather bound books and coloured marble geometric flooring; they all stretched out forever in front of her. This was like no library in the world.

Philip found a wooden desk with numbered panels to reserve books. Ros sat beside him and they read the instructions together.

'Where do we start?' she asked in a hushed voice. It was that sort of room.

'Peter told me to look through catalogues first and then fill in the order slip for what we want. The item will be taken to the Manuscript Room.'

'What do we agree that we want to know?'

'We would like an answer to Harry's problem, which might or might not be the Contessa's problem. At this point we have no idea what Peter's problem is,' he said.

'That sounds very Meredith to me. So we do what we can with what we have. Besides it's a good excuse to fossick in probably the most beautiful library on the planet.'

Philip took out a clear plastic bag with the fragment of manuscript in it. 'If we're lucky we'll get a match for this. We might only get a hint but it will help if we can get a conservator to look at it later.'

For the next two hours they trawled photographs and records of what was in the collection. It was tempting to dally in the early period; in a copy of Virgil's Aeneid or a ninth century copy of Terence's comedies, or maybe the Codex Graecus, a bible from the 13th century. Ros was intrigued by the breadth of the collection; the Codex Borgia for instance that recorded on animal skins the rituals of Mesoamerican culture. They both felt their period was later. She remembered the coffee table book of Renaissance art in the flat in Edinburgh. As sunlight outside grew dimmer they left their order slips with the librarian, ready for a new start in the morning. They swapped their Vatican badges for their passports and walked out past the guards. Their pantaloons and jerkins in the Medici colours of red, yellow and blue, glowed in the late afternoon light. As she walked through the gate they saluted her. Ros felt that she was their entertainment on an otherwise mundane shift of keeping out tourists.

'You didn't get a salute!'

'I'm not pretty.'

'That's good.'

Over the Ponte Margherita they were back at the Piazza del Popolo. Away from the enormous open space, with central obelisk and surrounding ornate apartments, they sat at an open air table in a modest café. For her it was Carciofi alla Romana, artichoke hearts with herbs gently steamed in white wine. Philip annihilated a chicken, pancetta and red wine ragu. A carafe of Vermentino white wine completed the experience.

They walked back in the Italian night: traffic murmur, lights and couples, aromas of food and more. When she put out the light Philip leaned an elbow over the divide. His fingers followed those curves he loved, first outside and then inside her nightshirt. Gently he kneaded the parts that gave her pleasure. Slowly her legs parted. Even more slowly he slid into her.

'One voice?' he said quietly.

'Oh yes.'

'Yours,' they said simultaneously.

§

CHAPTER 3

Dressed and towelling off her hair Ros watched Philip get out of the shower. His physique was lean, long and muscular. She's spent so much time lately looking at artists' portrayal of the male body: Michelangelo's "David" or Leonardo's battle scenes of screeching faces on muscular soldiers. She looked again with curiosity rather than lust. Dimensions of dangly bits were not as important as what he did with them. Not that she was complaining. But it was the closeness, the truth of his feelings that mattered.

'What?' he said, as he felt her eyes.

'Nothing; just looking.'

For a moment he tensed. She saw his reserve, his vulnerability. Yet he was as strong as steel when tested. The worried frown disappeared.

'That's all right then; nothing serious.'

She returned his smile.

'Buongiorno signori,' Ros said to the guards.

'Buon giorno signora,' they replied.

Philip received a polite nod.

Inside the library their approaches to the problem diverged. Ros had not been able to resist requesting to see some of the illustrated medieval manuscripts, mostly Bibles or Books of Hours. A late 15th Century Flemish version, probably from Ghent, had links with Jan Van Eyck and Hugo van der Goes. When would she ever again get so close to such a priceless piece of art? Unfortunately it was in Latin, Philip's domain. He was otherwise engrossed.

His requests stayed within the Italian language. Much of the catalogue contained lists of Cardinals and religious treatises. Papal instructions and correspondence over the centuries were kept nearby in the Secret Archives. Both pored over a copy of Dante's "Divine Comedy", with illustrations by Botticelli. Over two pages the Circles of Hell were mapped in an exquisite parfait-glass drawing. Ros could translate something about an abyss that catches thunder and howling, presumably of lost souls. Botticelli's drawings of naked men bound in chains or tortured souls reaching for the light while watched by malevolent demons were as vividly colourful as when they were drawn. Detailed woodcuts of complicated scenes of tormented humanity reminded Ros of Michelangelo's "Last Judgement".

Philip studied the copperplate handwritten Italian on the other side of the vellum. It was of the style of their fragment but tiny details showed a different hand.

'Dante has given the world so many quotable lines that even I can read them here,' Ros said. "Abbandonate ogni speranza, voi che entrate. All hope abandon, ye who enter here." Or better: "La Natura è l'arte di Dio. Nature is the art of God."

The Cosmography by Claudius Ptolemaeus was another of Ros', since it was translated in 15th century Florence from Greek into Latin. The style and terms of his maps were clearly prototypes of modern atlases. Two thousand years did not seem so long when it was compressed into this place.

By lunch time their minds were full and for the moment they had reached the limit of profitable study.

'I could spend months immersed in these lovely creations,' she said.

'I agree, but we don't know enough to ask the right questions. We'll be back. Rome is not so far from the dig site.'

Outside the Vatican gates they walked along the Via Crescenzio towards the Tiber River. Soon they were at the park which surrounded the Castel Sant'Angelo. Built as a Mausoleum for the Emperor Hadrian and his family, later a fortress for the Popes, it was now a museum. Philip led the way up the dark circular road inside the core of the massive drum. After studying the statue of Archangel Michael high on top they noticed a café tucked into alcoves in the outer wall. Philip stopped and looked at a menu.

'Can we afford this?' Ros said.

'Yes, it seems surprisingly reasonable.'

They sat at a table. Slipped into the ancient brickwork it overlooked the Vatican City and St Peters Basilica. Vistas of the Tiber and the wooded parks of Trastevere stretched into the distance. With her café nero and his espresso they shared the plate of chocolate/pistachio biscotti and sfogliatelle. Ros broke open the thin leaves of this pastry lobster tail. She bathed in the aromas of almond with a hint of citrus. While she pinched herself to appreciate the views Philip studied the map.

'Do you feel like visiting another of Hadrian's marvels?'

'Yes if my brain doesn't explode in the meantime.'

They crossed the Tiber at the Ponte Sant' Angelo. In the middle they stopped to look down at the shallow green river controlled by concrete embankments all along its meandering course. The upturned hull of a small boat wedged against a concrete pier showed the depth. Philip studied the triangular bulwarks pointing upstream on each support of the many bridges.

'The city wouldn't go to that much trouble unless they get serious floods here.'

They followed the Via del Coronari east before turning south into a maze of narrow streets. On the way boisterous groups of young Italians parted ambling tourists.

'Dammi i soldi per favore.' A bedraggled woman stepped in front of Philip and turned her face with pleading eyes into his chest. At the same time she pushed her hands into his.

'Basta, "enough",' Ros managed to say first.

'Turista ricco schifoso,' the woman cursed and rushed over to the next target. Beggars appeared at all the tourist haunts. It was clearly an industry.

Philip turned into the Piazza della Rotonda. In the cobbled square they stood beside the obelisk and fountain and looked at the massive

Corinthian columns of the rectangular entrance to the enormous vault. Inside the Pantheon Philip quoted bits from the guidebook.

'After two thousand years it is still the largest unreinforced concrete dome in the world. It has been a church since the 7th century, which explains why it is so well preserved. This is despite the oculus, an opening to the sky, in the roof.'

Ros had seen pictures of this astonishing building but was surprised that it was hidden away as an aside in the labyrinth of the city.

In the late afternoon they ambled a short distance back to the Piazza Navona. Once the Stadium of the 1st century emperor Domitian where "agones" or "games" were held, now it was a triumph of 17th century Baroque architecture. Bernini's Fontana dei Quattro Fiumi,"Fountain of the Four Rivers", was the centrepiece of the square. Philip checked several menus. After adding the tax for this and another tax for that, which all added up to another third on the total price, he chose a café in one corner with outdoor seating that overlooked another fountain. Two coffees, served with water and a plate of olives and bread savouries, bought them time to watch people.

A crowd of young travellers; long hair, frayed jeans or tie-dyed blouses and long wrap-around skirts, sat around the edge of the Neptune Fountain. They listened to a Swedish girl play Beatles' songs on her clarinet.

'Can you remember the name of the Sophia Loren film where she had a bedroom overlooking the square?' Ros asked.

'No. But I can remember a scene from "Catch 22"beside one of the fountains.'

They sipped their coffees until they were cold. The waiter hovered but left them alone. It was not busy yet. Seated customers usually brought in a few more.

'Are you hungry? We can afford pasta.'

Two plates of steaming spaghetti with dollops of butter arrived with a bowl of Parmesan and some crusty bread. A carafe of house white, something probably sourced from a relative in a local vineyard, was quite palatable.

'One more day?' Ros asked Philip nodded.

Lights came on all around the piazza. The flowing water of the fountains sparkled in colours. The hippies and travellers moved on and the wealthy of Rome filled the tables all around. Many were in suits and spectacular evening dresses. Musical recitals, the opera, and the theatre: Rome was as vibrant at night as it was during the day. She could live in this city for years and never discover all that it had to show her.

§

In the bright sunlit morning they followed Via Gramsci from the steps of the British School, around its curves down to the Viale delle Belle Arti. At the entrance to the Villa Borghese Gardens they had breakfast: pizza al taglio, a slice of pizza from a street vendor. On the grass under a massive denuded plane tree a mother hovered over a baby boy. Like a stork she spread her wings as he tried to escape on precarious legs.

They traversed the Largo Pablo Picasso into the Viale di Giulia. At the fountain surrounded by mighty seahorses they entered the aptly named Viale del Cavalli Marini. Girls in carefully styled short skirts and gladiator sandals walked in long steps south towards offices and hotels in the Via Veneto. Men in tailored shirts and dress shoes, or fitted T shirts and denim jeans, walked briskly in the same direction. One more turn, left into Viale del Museo Borghese, brought them to the 17th century Borghese Palace. On and around the palatial steps were wall to wall people. This was going to be another Vatican museum, Ros thought.

Thanks again Peter, crossed Philip's mind at the same sight. He showed Ros the tour tickets and enjoyed her smile.

'Buongiorno gentili. I am Rinaldo, your guide for the 9 'o'clock tour. Come this way, please.'

He was middle-aged and charming with a grizzled face that begged for a portrait. At the cloak room bags and coats were deposited for the dozen people, mostly British and Americans. Rinaldo gathered up the tickets for the guard and they entered the first of what were once private rooms of Cardinal Scipione and the rest of the Borghese family.

Inside the first room Rinaldo chose a position to one side of the thoroughfare, waited and then began. Philip listened to the history, the stories, the intricacies of the masterpieces of sculpture, painting and ornate ceilings that poured from the guide's mouth. Within a few steps into the chamber Ros was in danger of being overwhelmed. It was crammed with wonderful marble statues that she'd last seen in books. It must be required of Italian curators to fill every surface above and below with art. Walls and floors were covered in multiple colours of marble. Gilt-edged ceilings of Greek and Roman myths sucked her up into their "trompe l'oeil" world of trickery. Self-preservation demanded that she choose her own path through this plethora of richness.

The highly polished marble of Bernini's "Rape of Proserpina" was so real she longed to stroke it. The villain's fingers indented the flesh of the frantically struggling victim. Every woman's nightmare was something exquisite that whispered to her.

'Scusa signora!' Rinaldo politely circled his hand for her to re-join the group.

'Scusa.' Like everything else in Rome she could spend years and not absorb a fraction of its beauty.

Bernini's "David" was full of twisted preparedness for his moment with Goliath. Intensity, determination, a plan were all captured in that anguished face. Yet the reclining nude of Pauline Bonaparte by Antonio Canova was a sumptuous homage to a portrait of the Classical or Etruscan eras. Raphael had taken the standard subject of Christ's body being made ready for the tomb and painted an intensely personal tragedy. "Lady with Unicorn" displayed his distinctive palette of soft colours against a Tuscan background of undulating farmland and distant hills.

'We're being drawn to Renaissance Florence, Philip,' she said as he gently led her upstairs and towards the next room before Rinaldo counted heads.

'With a slight diversion,' she said before her mouth stopped in front of a wall of Caravaggios. That brilliant light was guided by the painter over muscular shoulders and luscious fruit. His young male subjects shouted the worldly arrogance of rough street life. She could see Philip's discomfort faced with Caravaggio's blatant joy of homosexual love.

'Each to their own, Philip.'

'I have no trouble with that.' He read some more about Chiaroscuro, that technique of light and shade that produced such intensity. 'Personally I preferred that Sleeping Hermaphrodite sculpture downstairs.'

Did he mean that? But he spent minutes absorbing skull, book and the aged wisdom of St Jerome. The antique mosaics fashioned from thousands of tiny tesserae, both repulsed and delighted them both.

'Gladiators slaughtering magnificent leopards are not my cup of coffee,' she said.

'But that face of Oceanus is something I could look at forever,' he replied.

After two hours the tour was done and their minds too.

'Time for a coffee?'

'Of course.' He led the way downstairs to the small café and bar.

With espresso and Americano, and a couple of pastries, they flicked through the guidebook to the pieces they had enjoyed most.

'Buongiorno Philip e Rosalind. Come va?'

A muscular, vibrant man of medium height and close-cropped hair stood in front of them. He tucked a photograph into his pocket. His mischievous brown eyes set in stubbly cheeks and tanned forehead studied them.

'Bene, Peter,' she said. A hint of British accent and a wild guess, but it probably meant that her playtime was over.

§

1488. Florence.

With the Plague gone, for the moment, our life in the Via Romana took on a familiar rhythm: education, books, evenings spent at the Confraternity. As before, Bernardo promoted my skills to the rich and powerful; aided by old friends, Bartolomeo Scala, Marcello Adriani, and Alamanno Salviati, son-in-law to Lorenzo's son Piero Medici. But life was quieter inside the casa. Primerana married and Margherita prepared for her wedding later in the year.

Lorenzo Medici ruled Florence in reality but with no title. He was its First Citizen, like the ancient Emperor Augustus. At Lorenzo's court the intellectuals of Europe gathered, and tarried longer in this most beautiful city. Textiles and banking kept Florence wealthy. And Lorenzo's skilful diplomacy maintained the peace. His son Piero, heir to the throne, was anything but peaceful.

'How do you judge Piero, Nico?' asked Bernardo. We had the privacy of our kitchen. Bartolomea was with her choir. There were bread, olives and wine on the table. Our first tazza was half full.

'His mind is not as strong as his father's yet he thinks it is. He chafes against rules.'

'Yet he favours you. Why?'

'I help him, just as I did with Ostinato. Maybe because I am not as old he thinks he can teach me. He and his younger brother Giovanni are not friends so I am the replacement.'

'Giovanni spends much time in Rome. Lorenzo grooms him for the church, where spiritual and temporal powers combine.'

'Do you trust Piero?'

'Not really.' My face showed the dilemma.

'You cannot disfavour him. As heir to Lorenzo his friendship can take you far.' Bernardo looked at me again. 'What else bothers you?'

'He has told me about "meretrice" and where they can be found.'

'Prostitutes. And you are tempted.' Bernardo rested his chin on his folded hands. 'He wishes to debauch you. But out of something bad something good may come. When you deal with commoners and kings there will be many perils such as this. This is a great opportunity.'

In the fading light Piero, two friends and I walked along a quiet street away from churches and the bustle of the Via Romana. It was in the centre of Santo Spirito but you would never know it. Inside the vestibule an ancient crone fawned over Piero, accepted a bag of coin from one of his companions, Ser Seccone, and led us into a room of softly furnished walls and a row of bench seats. They were occupied by smiling meritrice. Each worked her attractions on all of us but said nothing.

'Bring us wine, vecchia Vecchia.' Her eyes registered the insult but she returned with tazza of Spanish wine, the best in the city. Anything less would have brought worse than words.

'What about big bosoms?'

'No, the skinny one with legs forever tempts my preference.'

'Better to go for the round one, with plenty to hang on to,' said Ser Seccone. His eyes showed me too much: cruel subjugation rather than lustful pleasure. I tried to separate my thoughts from the happy couple at Mugello. In front of me were people like me, in different circumstances of birth.

'What about you, Nico? What is your taste?' asked Piero?

'If she is not chosen I would like the one on the end chair.' She was thin, young, with dark hair and inexperienced eyes.

'Take the runt. No one else wants her.'

As I led her away to the furthest room I knew that my attentions would be gentler than theirs.

The place was dark except for one candle. She lay on a straw mattress, spread her legs and shut her eyes. She was frightened. I lay beside her.

'Where are you from?' I asked.

'Scarperia,' she said quietly.

'I know it: a province of Mugello. We stayed there during the Plague.'

Soon we chatted about everything, including what I had seen on my walks. She could have been one of the peasant girls. But then she smiled. 'We are here for business.' She read that my lust for her was nil so she stroked my hair, and then my face. I smelled her skin and other odours, before we removed coverings and caressed all the parts I had seen at Mugello. Yes, I was there. Then I took Bernardo's advice and slipped the lamb's bladder over my rising pony.

'No bastards and no pox, Nico!'

Anyone prying would have heard a range of creatures. We giggled more with each invention.

'Thank you, Luna. Buona Fortuna.'

Eventually I joined the raucous group in the room with the seats. Wine had taken effect. The lions were shouting but their words were slurred. Piero was unsteady enough to be supported by the other two. I helped them back to the Palazzo. My own bed at home was welcome. Bernardo could wait for the debriefing.

'Well, you have survived your trial by ordeal, Nico.' He seemed more pensive as he chose his words. 'There are women for pleasure, and there are those for keeps. Your care for the young one pleases me. But her like will never be mother to your children. ' I waited for his advice.

'You are on the threshold of a brilliant career, if you use that able mind and the skills I have tried to teach you. But you will need a wife. She should be someone like us, and content to provide a loving fruitful home.'

My academic education was interrupted next day. For most of the morning I sat with Luigi's young daughter on a shaded seat in the courtyard of our casa. With a great deal of silence and tentative questioning we judged each other as best we could. Our mothers sat far enough away not to hear. Yes, I understood Bernardo's drift. Marietta Corsini was a sweet, shy girl well suited for her task.

Lorenzo's third son, Giuliano, was a very different friend. He was ten years younger than me and nothing like Piero. Quiet, studious Giuliano was a gentle soul who loved the arts as much as did his father. Although well tutored by the best of Florence I was able to help his skills in Latin. From the simple and direct style of Julius Caesar, as he described his conquest of Gaul, we progressed to the cadence and balance of Cicero's speeches to the Senate. And then there was poetry; Virgil's epic account of the history of Rome, the wisdom of Horace and the loves of Ovid. Those early teenage years always seemed to be striving for things of adulthood without the means. And then there were the complications of love.

'"Carpe diem, quam minimum credula postero,"' Giuliano read the words of Horace. '"Take hold of the day, trust little about tomorrow". And this one, "Pulvis et umbra sumus, We are just dust and shadow".'

'Here are some that your father might favour: "Est modus in rebus, There is a middle ground in things." Or "In medio stat virtus, Virtue stands in the middle."'

'Lorenzo might find this one by Ovid appropriate at the present time. "Fas est ab hoste doceri.

One should learn even from one's enemies."'

Giuliano smiled and looked heavenward. "Dripping water hollows out stone, not through force but through persistence."

I laughed. Giuliano was quoting Ovid back to me.

Lorenzo walked past our seat in the shade of the marble portico. His entourage of Venetian diplomats was in deep discussion but Lorenzo paused to nod in our direction.

'Publius Ovidius, "Be patient and tough; someday this pain will be useful to you." He has much sound advice, even in the arts of love: "Should anyone here not know the art of love, read this, and learn by reading how to love."'

Antonio Ridolfi, his ever vigilant friend smiled.

As he left I felt sadness. His rheumy eyes had struggled to read over our shoulders, and his voice, always harsh, lacked strength since I had last heard it. But his mind was as sharp as ever.

That evening I told Bernardo my observations of Lorenzo. Bartolomea looked up from the latest of her laudi to her very personal God.

'Lorenzo has invited Friar Girolamo to the Palazzo. '

Bernardo was perturbed. 'The Medici thirst for knowledge is legendary but for Lorenzo to consult with a Dominican friar, someone like Savonarola is a bad omen. Why did he ever bring him back to Florence when he is Lorenzo's greatest critic?'

Bernardo took me to the square of San Marco. It was full of expectant faces. The crowd chattered as though a carnival was about to begin. A small, thin man in Dominican habit stepped out to the steps of the monastery. There was silence.

'What doest Thou, O Lord? Dost Thou slumber? Arise and deliver Thy church from the hands of devils.'

I felt the rising passion in this man's speech. The crowd fed off it.

'Chastise and scourge so that the church quickly returns to Thee. Hear me, O my brethren. The only hope is that the sword of God may soon smite the earth.'

'He is very eloquent, Bernardo. When he speaks of the church renewing itself, of cleaning out the corrupt despots who rule it, I feel a lightness of mind. Surely you hear some truth in what he says, Bernardo?'

'You know I have no time for avaricious popes. So there is some truth in what he says.'

'He appears to have a great following among the ordinary people.'

'Were you persuaded by the strength of his argument or his speech?'

'His ideas were simple, and often repeated. So I suppose it was the power of his oratory.'

'If you recall the events of the Peloponnesian war between Athens and Sparta you will remember Cleon.'

'Thucydides described him as an unscrupulous demagogue, one without ideas or morals but very persuasive. Do you see this monk in the same way, Bernardo?'

'Look at their faces, Nico.' He waited for me to perceive their awe and total trust. Among them I recognised Michelangelo and Sandro. Both were impassioned but troubled. Their livelihood depended upon the largesse of the Medici but their souls belonged to God. This orator touched both.

'But he seems honest.'

'That is why he is dangerous.'

'He prophesises that a great danger comes from the north to threaten Florence.'

'Let us trust in the diplomatic skills of the Medici to save us from that.'

During the night of 8th April, 1492, Lorenzo died at his villa at Careggi. He was 43 years old. Girolamo Savonarola ministered the last rites. Lorenzo was buried beside his brother Giuliano in the Church of San Lorenzo. Piero was informed late in the morning that he was now the unofficial leader of the Signoria of Florence.

In a few weeks King Charles VIII of France crossed the Alps and ravaged a path through Italy. Very soon Piero met him at San Stefano outside Florence. There he agreed to every one of the terms demanded. On his return the mob screamed for his blood. That night the Medici family; Piero, Giovanni and Giuliano, escaped into exile. Among the group of five representatives sent to King Charles to negotiate a peaceful settlement was Girolamo Savonarola. They returned with a truce. Soon after that Savonarola was elected Gonfalonier, the Head of State.

'Nothing is lost, Nico. The Medici is exiled but never gone. Work hard to be indispensable to those around you in government.' Bernardo was never daunted by changes of circumstance.

I continued to serve in the office of Alamanno Salviati, Piero's son-in-law. In those times when not required by Salviati I made myself useful to Marcello Adriani in the First Chancery. Both survived the priest's reforms of the constitution.

But Florence was changed. No longer were carnivals the favourite of Florentines. The religious fervour of the people frowned on frivolity and luxury. They were more vocal in their support of Savonarola when the state gave out largesse to help the poor. Urchins of the street were most vigilant in their search for luxuries, such as mirrors and trinkets intended to adorn the ladies of the city. Zeal became theft and thuggery. The city lost its vibrancy and colour.

Florence always had divisions amongst its people. Now there were the Bianchi, the Whites, who were pleased with the changes made to the constitution. The great families now shared power with the merchant classes. The Bigi, the Greys, longed for the return of the Medici, while the Arrabiati, the Rabid ones, hated Savonarola openly. But for the moment the Frateschi, the Monkish ones, held sway. Although another name for the priest's supporters, Piagnoni or the Blubbers, grew in popularity as Savonarola made more enemies, not least Pope Alexander VI in Rome. Savonarola refused to join his Holy League against the French. The Pope politely asked the Friar to visit Rome to explain the nature of his prophecies. Savonarola refused on the grounds that he was needed in Florence and it was not safe to travel. "So it is not God's will that I leave now."

'A wise move,' I said to Bernardo that evening.

'Even a prophet has reason to fear the pleasures of the Inquisition.' Bernardo and I were only half attentive to each other. We watched Bartolomea hunched in concentration over one of her hymns. At every opportunity she had been part of the crowd at San Marco. Her eyes grew in spiritual fervour, which seemed to consume her bodily strength. Now we saw a tired old lady closer to her God than to us.

My mind was also on other things. Next morning I waited in the seclusion of the sunlit garden of Sant' Andrea, our estate south of the city. In the cool shade provided by the outer walls I waited. It was 1495, a year when beautiful things were as dangerous to their owners as beautiful ideas. Lorenzo's humanism, the Platonic ideals of the ancients, had been washed away by religious intolerance. Artists and writers were no longer safe.

'Good morning, Ostinato. Have you travelled well?'

He smiled. 'I did my best to soften the journey.'

Over some wine, fruit and bread, he charted the last two years of looking after his mother, Caterina, until her death. Ostinato cursed Piero his father for not saving him from the scourge of illegitimacy. But the poor, beautiful peasant girl who gave him life he adored.

'Why does man interest you so much, Machia?'

'Yes, why does he? He is selfish, nasty and evil. Insatiable desire matched with limitless ambition. He wants reward and ignores the consequences of his actions. His primary goal is self-preservation. But he also imitates and follows others. Here is the rub. His nature has always been so. That means history has the answers as to how to change him. There are so many examples of virtue, heroism and wisdom in the past. Yet the present is full of corruption and idiocy.'

'The right leader could mould him into something better?'

'Exactly, he imitates for his own benefit. That makes him open to conditioning by superior minds. It is most evident when lives are threatened. Then men can cooperate and even show courage. By virtuous action man can control at least some part of his life and limit the whims of chance.'

'War interests you despite the fact that it repels us both,' he said.

'True, war brings out the utter worst that men are capable of. Yet out of anarchy comes productivity. In desperation humans are at their most creative. They want to survive. Ultimately it leads to peace, until the next time.'

'Gently water builds up, irresistible, unstoppable, until like a dam it bursts. It exhausts itself in the mayhem. It is a cycle of life, ours at least.'

I liked his analogy.

'There is another positive aspect to war. In order to maintain peace your enemy must know that you are ready for war. If he knows you are a pacifist then you are weak enough for him to enslave you.'

'Peace comes from strength.'

'Yes.'

'Your Father had much to do with your love of antiquity.'

'I remember how much labour it took for the Livy. He left three flasks of vermilion wine and a flask of vinegar as a deposit. But he introduced me to modern writers too. Dante we shared over so many evenings. Boccaccio's irreverence rubbed off on us I am sure.'

'I see Petrarch too in your poetry.'

So we discussed into the evening. At daybreak Ostinato was on his travels again.

My life was consumed by labour. Making myself useful, as Bernardo wished, meant doing the work that no one wanted to do. The rich and powerful used me mercilessly. But as he predicted I became indispensable. In the last hours of an evening I would describe the intricacies of life in the Palazzo Vecchio. Was it that Bernardo's grasp of politics was slipping? His mind was always deep in caring for Bartolomea's needs.

In my room in the Palazzo Vecchio I struggled to decipher another missive to the Signoria from the King of France. Beneath the usual obfuscation to ward off any understanding by a prying courier was the perennial demand for money in return for Florence's safety. There was a knock on the door.

'Totto, why are you here?' But I knew really.

Around her bed were Primerana, Margherita and now Totto and myself. Bernardo sat on a stool and held my Mother's hand. Her body was small and wizened. She had neither consumed nor drunk anything for days.

Her eyes flipped open from deep within black eye sockets. 'Repent sinners, delay no longer.' They closed for minutes. 'God will lead you to the Ark.' Light went out of her face but a smile crossed her lips. She sat up with a jerk. 'Am I dying?' she asked in a childish voice. Well into the night she quoted Girolamo's sermons. Sometimes there was panic and sometimes delirious religious zeal. She conversed with the corners of the room, where she perceived her Mother and Father, cousins she had last seen during the Plague.

'What do you see, Mother?' Primerana asked.

'A small boy.' She pointed to him standing near the door.

'What Mother?' said Totto?

'A great fish.' Her eyes swam across the rafters with him. When the room was crowded with absent friends and a menagerie that filled the holds of Noah's great ship Mother closed her eyes. Her body became a shell, a cadaver that bore little resemblance to Bartolomea.

Bernardo looked up at the priest clad in black who closed the door. I read anguish in my Father's eyes. But as the Friar opened the book and began to mumble the words of the Viaticum his gaze softened. It was what Barolomea wanted.

"PER ISTAM SANCTAM UNCTIONEM ET SUAM PIISSSIMAM MISERICORDIAM ADIUVET TE DOMINUS GRATIA SPIRITUS SANCTI, UT A PECCATIS LIBERATUM TE SALVET ATQUE PROPITIUS ALLEVIET."

"Through this holy anointing may the Lord in his love and mercy help you with the grace of the Holy Spirit. May the Lord who frees you from sin save you and raise you up."

Only her breaths were proof of her continued existence. As the street outside became silent in the darkness her long in-breaths and shorter out-breaths moved further apart. Wider and wider silences and then the surprise of her next breath in, the sigh out, and a gurgling rattle in her throat. Each time we waited. Was this her last? But the next one made us jump out of our thoughts.

Totto laughed and we did too. Was Bartolomea playing tricks on us, holding our attention for a little longer? That endlessly stretched sucking of air within. Pause. Then there was the softest of sighs, before a cavernous rattle of corrupted lungs. We waited, and waited; nothing. Her tiny body sunk deeper into the bedding. Bartolomea was gone.

'Oh Madre!' I held her hand and lay my head into her shoulder. In moments her skin cooled as the life force left her. Totto sat on the end of the bed cradling her feet. Bernardo cupped his wife's hand within his. Rivers of tears flowed over what was left of her.

'Come, Father,' said Primerana as she gently touched his shoulder.

'Come, brothers,' said Margherita to Totto and me. We followed the priest out of the room. My sisters began preparing her body for burial.

It was the year of 1496, the third year of Girolamo Savonarola's rule as Gandolfier of Florence. The Medici Palace had been sacked by the mob two years before, when they bayed for Piero's blood. Of that great artistic circle only Sandro remained eking out a precarious living from church commissions. Scavengers roamed the city. Their excuse for breaking into the homes of the wealthy was to remove vainglorious trinkets that would only hinder their owners' entry to heaven. As the poor they could claim their value for themselves.

In May 1497 Savonarola called the Church a whore. In reply Alexander VI excommunicated him and forbade anyone to communicate with him. The Friar answered in his own way.

"Do Penance, for the kingdom of heaven is at hand, Matthew. 4:17.

"Your sins, then, O Florence, your impieties, your fornications, I say, beget these tribulations. This is the cause! If you have found the cause of all this evil, look for the remedy. Remove the sin and you will be healed. O priests, O leaders of the Church of Christ, renounce your pomp and your banquets; renounce your concubines and your boys. Monks give up your extravagant attire, your silver, the fatness of your abbeys. Oh my brothers in Christ let go your luxury, your paintings and vain ornaments. Listen to the words of God or he will punish you. Anything you do not need give to the poor. Give alms to those who have not. Priests, lustful ones, dress in hair-cloth and do penance. All of you who have houses full of vanities and pictures and indecent things and evil books and poetry contrary to the faith, bring them to me to make a bonfire as a sacrifice to God. Mothers who adorn your daughters with vanity, fancy hair ornaments, bring all these things to throw into the fire. So when God's anger comes he will not find them in your house. And thus I command you as your Father."

The crowd, scavengers and the pious combined. Throughout the city people raged through the streets with goods from every corner. Vanities, as Savonarola called them, mirrors, fine furniture, precious manuscripts and paintings, flowed as streams towards the Piazza Della Signoria.

"Renounce!"

Resistance was silenced with curses and blows. How dare anyone defy the instructions of Savonarola, the mouthpiece of God who was trying to save them from eternal damnation?

"All is vanity."

Into the flames poured the wealth of the city. The night sky lost its stars and only the crash and gutter of the fire could be heard above the shouts, chanting and wailing. I was alone. Bernardo remained in the kitchen, fretting over his library hidden behind boards in the walls and floor. There were no familiar faces from the Confraternity or my colleagues at the Signoria. Amnesia seemed to be their answer. Soon it would all go away.

But there was one face I knew. His eyes were impassioned by spiritual torment, but his footsteps resisted every movement. Sandro came towards the fire pulling a cart. In a spot where the heat threatened to ignite not only the contents but him he lifted the cover. Drawings of his precious Venus were first. Each fluttered and rose as a glittering firework in the updraught from the inferno. Then a painted canvas of Athenian philosophers was tossed in; then another of muses and gods of antique times. Tears flowed from the burning pools that were his eyes. Was it tragedy or ecstasy inside his mind? How could he do this?

"Do penance."

I dreaded whatever came next. Would it be the goddess Primavera? Could he possibly remove his Venus from this world? As someone who dabbled in art I knew enough. How could he throw away all that time, hours of his life, the best creations of a most intelligent mind? All that beauty that he could never create again was all given as a sacrifice to his God.

No, I realised. Castello; Lorenzo had adorned the walls of his country palace. They were too far from the hungry hordes or Sandro himself. Fortuna.

Damn you, Friar. Damn you to your Hell for destroying so many magnificent creations of men. Your oratory has passion but what else keeps you alive? The Pope will win, sure as day follows night. But for now you have Fortuna.

I left Sandro at this pit of Hell. Bernardo sat mindless at the family table, alone. I sat down with him and held his hand. What had his world become?

§

CHAPTER 4

Peter shook hands with them both, and ordered another espresso. Ros described their itinerary over the past few days and Philip covered what they had learnt and the little that might relate to a problem, of whatever variety.

'It would be more useful if we knew what her problem was. Meredith and Tamarisk were not too helpful.'

Peter nodded sagely. 'There's a slight change of plan. After you've packed we'll head out to the site. There've been developments that I'll tell you about on the way.'

As they kept up with him through the broad avenues of trees to the height of a double decker bus he explained that more finds had been stolen from the conservation room.

'Only the most valuable, of course, the ones I needed for the sponsors to maintain our funding. The pattern's the same each time: we find it, clean and photograph it; a night or so later it goes missing, with photos or anything else that might prove it ever existed.'

'Could it be a local, maybe someone who digs for you?' Philip asked.

'That's possible. Most of the physical work is done by international volunteers: for the usual bed and board. But we do have some villagers recommended by Antonio, the mayor.'

'What about the Contessa and her problem?' Ros asked. If you don't ask you don't get.

'That's not for me to divulge, I'm afraid.'

'When will we meet her?'

'Whenever she decides.'

'She sounds formidable.'

Peter laughed a deep throaty chuckle. 'Yes, I suppose she is. Someone once described her as a "Rottweiler with lipstick". But that wasn't me, you understand.'

Philip saw Peter's bright red Fiat 500 sports car and instantly knew where he was going to sit. He pushed their luggage down into the back seat floor and perched on the rear bench like an uncomfortable buzzard.

Peter held open the passenger door. Ros smiled.

'Grazie, Peter.'

Images of Matteo were soon confirmed, but without seat belts. She felt the force pushing her into black leather as Peter cut into a space in front of a white BMW. Its horn blared and Peter gave a thank you wave. The engine growled, as though always one gear too low. Before the end of Via Gramschi Peter swerved left into a side street, roared up behind and then around a wandering Vespa and then cut right into a less busy street more clogged with parked cars but fewer drivers. He screeched brakes as a man walked out from behind an airport minibus collecting tourists.

'Lento, stupido!' The suited gentleman crossed his left arm over and slammed an upper cut behind it into the air.

'Occhi, geriatrico!' Peter shouted back, pointing to his eyes.

He swerved round him and changed down a gear to sprint into the next intersection. As traffic crawled to the right he nosed in, inches separating red paintwork from the scraped blue of a Fiat taxi. In the creeping double line Peter chose to cut in front of an immaculate Porsche. A carefully styled head with expensive sunglasses moved forward and her fist blarped the horn repeatedly. Peter smiled.

'God, I love Roman traffic.'

After more snarls, horns and wonderfully articulate gesticulations that left no doubt about meaning, Peter joined the three laned Corso di Francia. He roared across the Tiber through an avenue of massive stone plinths without occupants except for the occasional imperial eagle. In the blur of wind and speed the road veered right to become the Via Flaminia Nuova.

In the warm gale Philip shut his eyes. Occasionally he trusted the protection of his Polaroid sunglasses to mentally record the route. Otherwise he daydreamed through Peter's problem, what the Contessa's might be, and what were his chances of making love to Ros that night.

She watched the jumbled conurbation of factories, high-rise apartments with colourful washing over balconies become sweeping vistas of small farms, olive and poplar trees with a backdrop of gently rising hills softened by the late afternoon sun. The three lane modern highway, still the Via Flaminia, curved over concrete viaducts. Red-tiled houses punctuated the immediate landscape as names flashed by: Castelnuovo di Porto, Rignano Flaminio towards distant Civita Castellana. Inside her head the sounds of the words floated like music. After an hour of acrobatic driving to pass lines of trucks, tourist campervans and overloaded Cinquecentos the red arrow peeled off left towards the hills of Umbria and Southern Etruria.

In minutes they stepped back five hundred years. Single lanes without road markings followed ancient tracks that dissected the fields and scrubby hills. The avenues of trees, quite often poplars, on the high grass verges reminded her of their trip through France. Bitumen gave way to gravel that rose as a dust plume behind them. Peter didn't slow down, he just skidded round corners a bit more. His face was a picture of delight. She speculated that the innate reserve that comes with being British had absorbed the Italian pleasure of living without limits. Carpe diem seemed appropriate in this beautiful landscape.

Peter was forced to slow down a little as the bends became tighter and the potholes more frequent in these less maintained roads. Philip was able to open his eyes without wind or sand blasting into them. It was clear that they had entered a region of upland plateaux, cut by vertical ravines with rivers and streams around a hundred metres below. Fields of wheat, groves of olives and some vegetables hogged any flat bench close to the water supply, the river system of Acqua Gentile. He looked over the side of a 280 degree hairpin bend to the trickling watercourse below. Collapsing dirt, flattened trees, and logs jammed to create shingle beaches: at times these waters must be anything but "gentle".

Peter gave Rosalind a running commentary of what they were driving through. A series of volcanoes just under half a million years ago had laid down a bed of extremely hard rock known locally as Tufa Rosso, or "Red Tuff". Subsequently two other layers had been deposited. One was a much softer tufa formed from the flowing mud or flying ash dated to around 220,000 years ago called Tufa Stratificati, or "Stratified Tuff".

'The uppermost level is the most important in human terms. Around 40,000 years ago Tufa Giallo, or "Yellow Tuff", covered much of this region. It eroded to rich volcanic soil and it produced high pedestals of stone overlooking deep ravines. In short the first inhabitants had fertile soil, plentiful water, good building stone, Tufa Rosso, and easily defended citadels in rugged terrain.'

Peter slowed up for a flock of sheep. Ros looked north towards densely treed hills separated by steep gorges with yellow scars of scree flowing into guessed at rivers.

'What kind of trees make up the forest, Peter?' she asked.

'They're mostly oak. It's known locally as Macchia, or "The Stain".'

Hardly a flattering name, she thought. She studied a patch of it that encroached on the road. At home in Oz she'd call it dense scrub. Being European Oak she guessed it was deciduous. It was a fitting name for a farmer to call impenetrable undergrowth unsuitable for agriculture.

At the head of the flock, fat sheep with one large goat, was a sturdy man with cap and shepherd's staff. His face and bare arms were weathered like walnuts.

'Buon giorno signor Peter.' He touched his cap and his face cracked along fault lines around his blue eyes.

'Buon giorno signor Luigi.' Peter tapped his forehead in a lazy salute.

At Luigi's pace the sheep followed in a flowing tide, kept in check with white Maremma dogs left and right and to the rear. Ros looked at Peter. For one who had driven like the proverbial "bat out of Hell" for over an hour he was surprisingly content. He chewed the fawn moustache on his upper lip and hummed something from Italian opera, Verdi's "La Traviata" probably. After fifteen minutes the last animal had filed through the rough-sawn timber post and two-rail fence.

Just beyond a tiny village, called Posto Alto, or "High Place", Peter stopped and turned off the ignition. At the red stone wall he pointed out the road ahead. It snaked down a kilometre before crossing a radically modern bridge over the Acqua Gentile before climbing two kilometres to the next village, Alta Cresta, or "High Ridge".

'That's where our finds are conserved and stored. And down there, just adjacent to the bridge, is the site, Città Sotto, "The City Beneath".'

Peter pulled up again at the near end of the deserted bridge. It was a massive overstatement for this simple rural environment.

'At home we would call this the result of pork-barrelling, Peter. Did some politician side-track some state money in return for favours?'

'Antonio, the mayor of Alta Cresta, is rather influential. In your endeavours I'd prefer that you didn't cross him. I never do.'

'Peter, why us?' Ros said. 'Your problem needs police detectives not us.'

Peter laughed. 'Inspector Plod is not much help I'm afraid. Besides Aunt Meredith suggested that the pair of you have an uncanny knack of success.'

Philip leaned over the bridge and counted four trenches and multiple previous signs of excavation now being reclaimed by the scrub. Were they all sanctified by government permits, he wondered. Some looked more like rabbit holes tunnelled into the near vertical sides of what looked like a continuous section; a record of habitation from the present to what he guessed was well into the second millennium. On two adjacent benches, tiny fields of pasture set just above the flood level, were tents. This would have to be their abode for the night, as Peter had not offered something more substantial in the village.

Ros absorbed the landscape holding finger and thumb at right angles. Various viewpoints from the elevated bridge would make good compositions. The colours had something of the Renaissance artists but her view was more of a close up. The setting light from the Tyrrhenian Sea just over the horizon was soft and liquid, more Claude Lorrain than Hans Heysen. He had caught the harsh, brilliant beauty of the Flinders Ranges of South Australia in colours anything but soft and liquid.

Peter looked at his watch. '4.30: you have time to sort yourselves out before a brisk walk up to the trattoria for 6. It's aptly named "La Macchia". Ciao.'

At the end of the track down a chorus of 'Hi', 'How are you?' in many accents met them. An exchange of names proved how international the volunteer work force was. Soon the faces disappeared to prepare. Philip and Ros pitched the tent a short distance away from the track and the others. Ros pictured morning sun to warm up and the western sun blocked by the bridge. No shower block, just a swim in the river, toothbrush in hand, and the latrine another tent with a hole in the ground. Just like Kara Tepe, she thought, with the bonus of running water.

They followed the others up the "brisk walk". They looked up to Alta Cresta. It was one of Peter's natural fortresses, sheer on all sides except for the ridge they climbed leading to an entrance wide enough for a bullock cart. It was not hard to imagine a drawbridge. Roughly painted four and five storeyed houses teetered on the brink at disturbing angles. Macchia closed in on all sides.

'Ciao, bella.'

The lean teenager in tight jeans and an Elvis tea shirt slowed and indicated for Ros to slide on the back. She smiled and waved him on. Would she have accepted if Philip was not in tow? After a k and a half she had definitely been tempted.

They caught their breath on the near-level cobbled road into the town. Her impressions were of red curved tiles, much repaired brick and stone walls, open windows with shutters angled to catch the breeze, smells of washing, cooking, and the exhaust of small engines worked too hard.

'Buonasera signora e signore. Siediti.'

Martina led them to a long table made up of three smaller ones pushed together. Plastic checked table clothes gave it continuity. Ros judged her somewhere beyond fifty, slimmed through hard work and her face glazed by too much time in the kitchen. Her manner was warm but efficient. It was good business. Her sharp brown eyes set in a drawn face framed by tied back brown hair judged people in the positive until they disappointed her. At the kitchen hatch her husband watched and waited for the orders.

Ros and Philip sat down on a bench seat with their backs to a white-washed stone wall. Overhead were massive hand-chipped beams supporting the upper storeys. Black and white photographs of Italian soccer players were grouped in clusters around the walls. At the table Ros counted twenty people including themselves. Lots of waves and names circulated but it would take days to get to know them. As soon as it was polite she turned to Philip.

'What are you looking at?'

'The wine arrangements, actually.' He pointed to two barrels set into the wall of the kitchen. In front of each was a small table with well-used lemonade bottles. By the splashes on the wood one supplied rosé and the other white wine.

Martina filled a bottle as they watched. The deep pink sparkled and bubbled almost like an Aussie beer, Ros thought. Maybe it approached a Mateus Rosé

'It has to be young wine to do that,' said Philip.

'Hi, Peter,' said Ros.

He pulled up a chair and sat beside them at the end of the table.

'Hello.' He spotted their focus of interest. 'I cover the food bill but the volunteers pay for their own booze. Martina just totes up the bottles consumed.'

She set a bottle of rosé and three tumbler glasses in front of them.

'My round, you two.' Peter poured generously. 'Here's to problems solved.'

'Problems solved,' they echoed.

'Not bad; and reasonably priced at fifty p a bottle.'

A dozen bottles formed a line down the centre of the table. White bowls, knives, forks and spoons were set in front of everyone. Small dishes of grated parmesan were placed beside salt and pepper grinders. At 6.15 steaming bowls of spaghetti appeared, along with a bolognaise sauce and side plates with cubes of butter. Everyone helped themselves using the wooden utensils. When one receptacle was empty it was quickly replaced.

'An army fights on a full stomach?' Philip said.

'I firmly believe it. These people work hard in dusty hot conditions. So far they haven't grumbled.'

Ros filled a plate with pasta and some sauce with a sprinkle of cheese. Philip added butter to his pile. She ate hers with a fork and spoon. He twirled the tendrils around his fork until it was the size of his mouth and then bent low to the plate and shovelled it in. All around the table Ros could see variations of method. Oddly, three Italian couples at the other end of the restaurant showed as little finesse as Philip. Another myth blasted.

'So what are your plans for tomorrow?' Peter asked.

'I would like to see the conservation room, if that's ok,' said Ros.

'That's no problem. Nico can show you the cameras too, since that's your area of expertise.'

'I would like to start there too: past excavation reports, how the finds are stored, etc. What's the story that you told the team about the reason for us being here?'

'You are visiting academics offering ideas about a different approach to getting the most from the site. A geologist spent months mapping the terrain last year. Early this year an engineer specialising in ceramic manufacture using water machinery spent six weeks studying the medieval pottery industry on the site.'

'It would be useful to work with the volunteers and your local workers too,' said Philip.

'Feel free to do whatever you think necessary.' Peter paused and then decided to say it. 'If you don't solve the problem,' he said in a low voice, 'then there won't be a next season.'

He didn't need to speak quietly. The other end of the table was getting decidedly raucous. An American boy: short, with soft features, curly short black hair and a goatee beard, was telling stories about other digs he'd been on. They all seemed more exotic and productive than this one. The glass of Sambuca arrived and Marina lit the surface to cook the coffee bean that floated on top. Ros could see that Peter absorbed everything but chose to say nothing.

'I've gotten into liking this stuff as the least worst drink at Mom's Thanksgiving. And you wouldn't guess that,' the boy said. With a sweeping sideways gesture his arm clipped the glass and blue flame streaked across the table cloth.

'Whoa,' he said slowly and laughed loudly. To Ros the sound resembled a donkey. He watched the flame's magical course; flickering blue, opaque white and yellow. The river had a life of its own. Bradley was fascinated.

But Marina was not. She dropped the damp tea towel from over her arm onto the liquid fire. Its flow stopped but eruptions squeezed out of side crevices. She swiftly tamped down here, there and there. Her table cloth was scorched but not lost.

'Mi dispiace Marina quanto costa?'

'Niente Peter.' She smiled and waved it all away.

'Bradley.'

Bradley was not listening. His story wasn't finished.

'Bradley. Bradley.'

Philip listened. Peter's accent was slipping from Oxbridge somewhere to Geordie welder. Philip guessed that Peter's building site experience to pay the way into academia was not so different from his own.

'Yeah, Peter.' There was juvenile exasperation in the tone.

'It's time to call it an evening, Bradley.' That was an order that everyone understood.

The walk down from Alta Cresta was pleasant in the warm, Italian night. Layers of cool and humid air alternated. From the enclosing forest bird calls that she didn't recognise pierced the quiet. Ros felt agreeably enervated rather than inebriated. Arm in arm she was not sure which label applied to Philip. He would probably say "pleasantly pishonkered." But his pace was steady and relaxed. Neither of them managed to fall over anything before they zipped up the tent against anything that flew or crawled.

§

'Tutto chiaro?'

'Sì.'

Thud, thud. Soil and roots creaked. The man grunted as the clod gave way. He placed it carefully to one side. Thud, thud, thud. He levered the first side, then the next, and the next until the dirt loosened. The soil and debris were stacked with the turf. The rhythmic sounds of his work merged gently into the heart of night. His toil was masked by the densely tangled macchia.

Thuud, a higher pitch. His blows became delicate, here, there, before a crack and crumbling rock. The steel bar grated on the edges of a neat circle roughly forty centimetres in diameter.

'È tempo Jacopo.'

The boy next to him stood up. The man tied a thin rope around the tiny waist, and then checked it.

'Pronto?

'Sono pronto nonno.'

The man laid a gnarled hand on the boy's head and smiled. Uneven teeth glinted in the starlight.

Jacopo sat on the edge of the hole and dangled his feet. He twisted until he faced the man. Then he found holds for his feet and began the descent. Slowly, carefully he found edges for toes then fingers, until his tiny body disappeared beneath the ground. The rope paying out was the only sign of his existence.

'Sono passato.'

The man stood up and placed his feet either side of the hole. He looped the rope around his waist and took the slack.

'Adesso,' he said quietly.

The rope tightened in his hands. Hand over hand he let it slip until it became loose again.

Inside there was no light, other than a glimmer from above. The air was stale, a bit sweet: a good sign. Jacopo crouched low and felt the ground in the blackness. There were a few stones, some gravel, whatever had fallen down the hole; then in the circular sweeps of his hands he touched the first long, light stick, then it was a pair; he followed upwards to curved rings before, ah, the skull. He moved position, careful not to overbalance or stand where he should not. There, something round, and inside it rattled: a sharp thing. He picked it up gently so it did not cut him, and put it over to his right, all together. He moved his legs, always crouching, and gathered up everything. He felt the edges, and then raised himself to scour the walls for niches that might hold more. His young eyes were open but mostly he felt the outline and size of the room. Soon he could make out the shapes of the pictures on the sides and ceiling. Strange men and women were walking; eating what he knew must be special food. Their faces were different from him and his family. They were the ancestors who had left these gifts for him to find.

'Grazie antenati,' he said inside his head.

Then he unravelled the slim sack from over his shoulder and placed the things inside. He untied his waist and made a firm knot at the top of the bag.

'Nonno.'

Then he steadied it to stop it swinging, and guided it up through the hole. In a few seconds it came down again. After three collections he tied the bag like a bandoleer and the rope around his middle.

'Io adesso.'

He rose to the ceiling. The man above felt his hands touch the edges. The rope slowed, and then moved a little faster. The boy's head rose above the grass and sucked in fresh air. As his arms straddled the cavity the rope went loose. Strong biceps lifted him easily and placed him on the damp earth. He sat and looked at the stars while the wooden cap was covered by the dirt. The man gently pressed the turf into place with his boots.

'Questo è sufficiente. Andiamo.' Then he made the sound of a Tawny owl.

'Ke-wick.'

'Hoo-hoo-oo,' the watcher replied.

Inside the kitchen one light was on. The smells were of hot soup, white-washed walls and stone floor, and the rough cut bread in a bowl at one end of the heavy wooden table. Nonna waited to serve while the men and the boy studied what came from the bag, all laid out on the other end of the table.

A large pottery jar with two handles was circled by red figures against a black background.

'Sfinge,' the boy said pointing. 'Grifone,' he remembered, 'Centauro.' Then he traced the animals hunted and the armour of men fighting on the other two vases.

'Vedi la nonna?'

She looked at the necklace with golden leaves with some Egyptian god on each. When he held the filigreed gold earrings against her cheeks she bent her head close. She held his excited face and smiled. Yes, they were beautiful things. This ancestor was wealthy and generous.

'Ben fatto Jacopo.'

Nonna looked around the room. There were more vases from the ancestors than her cooking pots. Nonno will be generous to his friends, and maybe even sell a few, she thought. But what about the rest; where was she going to put them?

§

'Philip!' Ros whispered loudly. His amore was welcome but not the sound effects. They were in a tent, for goodness sake. He puffed like a train going up a steep hill.

'Shush, Philip. You'll wake the dead.'

§

1497. Florence.

'Bernardo, how are you?' I asked. It was evening, a little earlier than usual. He sat at the table with the Virgil. 'Which part of the journey are you reading now?' I busied myself preparing a meal, since he had forgotten. By the smell of his clothes he had not been as accurate peeing either. I looked around. Nothing had changed since I left early this morning.

'What are you reading, Bernardo?'

'Page 75,' he said slowly. He pointed at the words.

During the meal there was no conversation. He just ate steadily. At times his mouth opened to say something but then it would close again as though he could not catch the thought.

'Where am I?' he said next morning.

When those you love become sick the life flows out of them. Like a piece of stone nothing you say or do seem to change them. It's a mini death, a premonition.

'He is affected by apoplexia,' said the doctor. 'Has he fallen recently?'

'Not that I have seen. But he is unsteady on his feet.' In my mind I saw him lean heavily on the table edge to haul up his body, as he did most mornings.

'Apoplexia often shows itself as a pause in the middle of an action.'

'When we converse at the end of the day he has stopped in mid-sentence. After a few moments he will come back and start a new conversation, as though he has forgotten his place.'

'That, in my opinion, is an apoplectic event, a pause in the blood flow inside his skull.'

'And each one makes him forget?'

'Yes, something is lost on every occasion.'

'There is nothing wrong with me,' said Bernardo when the doctor had gone. 'I have my books. They will fill my mind again.'

In the morning I saw fear in his eyes. 'I will be better next time, you will see.' He puffed and caught more breath. 'I will get better, won't I?' Slowly the fear subsided. I turned away so he did not see my tears.

'Yes, Bernardo, you just need rest.'

That evening he said nothing and I read to him from Virgil. He had forgotten how. Boccaccio's 'Decameron' was more successful. When gullible girls were seduced by fools played by donkeys he laughed uproariously, farting loudly as he did so. His subtle humour was gone.

Bernardo I have my own life to lead, I said in thought. You put me on this earth to do good, possibly great things. That is what I am doing. You would be proud if you were able to understand.

'Tell me your news of the day,' he said. He licked his lips, over and over. There were two pieces of bread on the table. I prepared the rest of the meal.

'It is 1498. Savonarola has been elected again. But his support is slipping. The poor like him but have no power. The rich fear him and hate him. They lost so much in the bonfire.'

Bernardo licked his lips again, before the meal, and after it.

'The Pope schemes against Savonarola. He has a ready ear among the well-to-do families. My work is breathtakingly busy, I suppose because the powerful trust me. I say nothing against Girolamo but I think they know that I do not support him.' Each evening I listened to myself and watched Bernardo's intense concentration to understand. It was always a struggle but he did not know how to give in.

'It is April. I have two momentous events to report, Bernardo. First, you remember that Girolamo prophesised the death of the French King, Charles VIII.'

He gave out a short noise like a laugh.

'Well, he was right. On the 7th April the king cracked his head on a door lintel and died within hours. He was 27 years old.'

Bernardo giggled and waited for more.

'Now the best bit. A Franciscan friar has challenged Girolamo to walk through fire. Before he could find an excuse Fra Domenico offered to risk himself instead. Now the priest is caught. If Domenico dies Girolamo is lost. If he takes the ordeal by fire the people will know that he is a mortal like the rest of us.'

I stoked up our fire for Bernardo. He felt the cold much more. Should I explain the irony? With the repetition, with some shouting to overcome his deafness, was it worth the effort?

I took Bernardo to the show. For weeks I had been reading the mood of those I served in the Palazzo Vecchio. It was a powder keg; waiting for the right moment. A great many people nodded their heads to Bernardo as we walked those familiar streets to the Piazza Della Signoria. Bernardo smiled but clearly recognised none of them. We stood in the noisy crowd and waited.

'Walk through the flames, Friar. We want to see you do it,' one yelled. 'You'll smell like broiled chicken,' shouted another. The pious chanted their prayers and looked to heaven. The hours went by. Girolamo was stalling for time.

'Priest or politician, Bernardo?'

Suddenly black clouds filled the sky above and torrents of rain drenched everyone. Savonarola came out on to the balcony. 'God has spoken. The fire is out.' And more words to that effect. When he cancelled the event and left there were more shouts of anger than religious support. His feet were slipping.

The crowd was not to be put off. So many now marched down to the monastery of San Marco, Savonarola's spiritual home. They attacked the doors, threw rocks at shuttered windows and shouted for his presence. The Friars fought back wildly, anything to preserve their Prior. Pope Alexander excommunicated them. On 21st April the priests wrote a collective letter to the Pope. It was abject surrender. They gave up their "Little Friar".

'It is the 19th May, Bernardo. Two commissioners have arrived from Rome. I heard one say, "We shall have a fine bonfire, for I have the sentence of condemnation with me." It seems the time of reckoning has come for Girolamo.'

'Well Bernardo, even you will be a little surprised at this turn of events. Do you remember my visit to the meretrice with Piero and his friends?' I did not wait for a reply. 'Francesco de Ser Barone, "Ser Ceccone" to Piero and his few friends is to interrogate Savonarola and the two Friars arrested with him. He was a heartless bastard then. Will he spare them because Savonarola gave him sanctuary in San Marco when the Medici fled? I doubt he has changed in his new role.'

Rough hands dragged Girolamo Savonarola, Fra Domenico and Fra Silvestro along the musty stone corridors of the Bargello prison. Dampness from the Arno River above seeped through mossy stone and worn floors. Silvestro was weeping, unable to comprehend that his hiding place in the monastery had been discovered. He had no wish to die for anyone, to die at all. Domenico helped Savonarola when he stumbled inside the cell. He expected nothing less than their martyrdom. Savonarola was pensive, looking for arguments that might even now save him from the cruelty he expected.

'Strap his hands behind his back,' ordered Ceccone. 'Hoist him to the ceiling.' Domenico watched and Silvestro hid his face.

'Tell me Girolamo,' said Ceccone as a friend. 'God did not speak to you, did He?'

'God told me how to cleanse Florence to become the New Jerusalem.' His voice was low and precise.

'Are you a prophet?

'My followers believe so. I have shown some accuracy with the death of the King of France.'

'Did you contact Charles VIII?'

'I wrote a letter, as gonfalonier of the Signoria.'

'Are you a traitor?'

'No.'

The chains holding him up slipped an inch. Ceccone nodded to the minion. Savonarola's body dropped. With a crack of steel it stopped inches short of the slab stone floor. Arms snapped back, shoulders strained to the edge of dislocation, pain burned through every bone and sinew of Savonarola's back.

'Aaaargh,' the cry elongated into a whimper. The Strappado lowered to the flagstones.

'You are known as the Scourge of God. Do you want glory in this world?'

'No,' the chains tightened.

'Did the Friars break the secrecy of the confessional for you?'

'No.' He screamed as muscles stretched while his body lifted off the floor.

'You changed the constitution of Florence so your friends would rule.'

'No.' His breath sucked away as he rose higher.

'You ruled Florence for your own glory, so you could become Pope.'

'No. But if I had succeeded I would have been above any Cardinal or Pope. Florence would be the New Jerusalem.' The chains reached their upper limit. Ceccone's eyes met those of his minion. The Strappado fell for a second time.

Savonarola's body was already weak from self-flagellation, fasting and self-denial. If only the Strappado killed, for mercy's sake. Instead it did not even numb the body, so each fall was as painful as the last.

After the third Savonarola said, 'Take me down and I will write my whole life.'

Domenico wept openly for this broken man.

Next day Savonarola read Ceccone's transcription. 'If you publish this, you will die within six months.'

'Is that the word of a prophet? Sign, unless you need a little more encouragement, a further Strappado perhaps.'

Savonarola signed. It had taken relentless questioning over a week, every day including Good Friday and Easter Sunday. Ceccone had his confession that the Friar had signed. He had not the strength to do anything more.

In the Piazza Della Signoria the protocol was read. Believers were saddened that a New Jerusalem with just laws, righteousness and the rejuvenated Church were just the lies of a priest who thirsted for temporal power. But to the Signoria it was not enough. They ordered a second trial.

'You see, Bernardo, the Signoria was in very dangerous territory. From the start the trial was illegal as a priest could only be judged in a church court. But that was not all of it. 48 hours after Savonarola entered the Bargello Pope Alexander VI praised Florence for the "Timely measures you have taken in order to crush the mad vindictiveness of that son of iniquity". Praise, Bernardo, praise from a Pope. Yes he was happy for the trial to continue in Florence. But once they had finished with Savonarola he was to be tried by an ecclesiastical court in Rome. As a member of the

Dominican order he would face all the elaborate torture devices of the Inquisition. The priest knew too much. Torture would reveal every secret the Florentine government ever had.'

Bernardo nodded, smiled, too many times.

'This second trial was even more barbarous than the first. The Commission of 17, every one of whom had a grudge against Savonarola, had decided that he might have been an hermaphrodite. Do you think that had any relevance? So they inspected his genitals to degrade him a little more. 17 men plus a surgeon forced Savonarola to recant his prophecies, to deny every belief he ever had. This time his confession was written and signed by him.'

'Fra Domenico, why do you follow such an iniquitous villain as Savonarola?'

'Girolamo is a good man who yearns to bring God's kingdom to earth, here to Florence.'

'Has he corrupted the confessional?'

'No.' The Strappado fell. Domenico screamed and then slumped in silence.

'He placed his own supporters in government to gain power.'

'No,' creaking chains stopped, a word and the Strappado fell again.

'Your leader wanted to usurp the Pope.'

'No.' Each time Domenico denied Ceccone the proof that he shouted for. The Strappado fell four times. In his heart Domenico was pleased that he had taken one more than Girolamo.

'It is time for the Stranghetta,' said Ceccone.

Domenico screamed when the iron casings were put around his feet. As they clamped shut the inner spikes bit deep into his flesh.

'Loving God, comfort me in my suffering,' he mumbled barely audibly.

'Give me confidence in the power of Your grace.' The first iron wedge was hammered between the casing and his flesh. His torment left him too hoarse to speak. Fra Silvestro pressed his hands over his ears and shut his eyes. Three more wedges ground sinew and bone into blood and powder.

'Tell me truly that you have never believed that Savonarola is a prophet.'

Very slowly, clearly and just audibly Fra Domenico said, 'I always have and still do believe in the prophecies of Savonarola.'

Ceccone studied this man. His left arm had been dislocated twice, both arms were useless. Ceccone had supervised the wrenching of his limbs, the grating of his bones.

'I have always thought him an altogether upright and extraordinary man,' Domenico said in a frail exhausted voice.

This heroic monk welcomes death. Ceccone turned away. Silvestro was brought in.

Now this is a different measure of a man, Ceccone thought. Silvestro stumbled as he was dragged into position. This was the man who had been pulled from a dark corner of the monastery of San Marco. Savonarola had once been inspired by Silvestro's visions. Now this man lay in the Strappado manacles in abject terror.

'Who came to see Savonarola at San Marco?' The chains pulled tight.

'Adriani. Salviati.' Before the first descent a dozen names of important citizens, their times and dates, and what they had talked about if he had been close enough to listen. The contraption dropped and Silvestro screamed and ranted uncontrollably for minutes on end.

'Who else? When?'. The chains dropped again and Silvestro's body snapped in agony. As soon as the pain subsided, the names flowed again.

It's like milking a cow, Ceccone thought. Was there any need to inflict suffering when the information came without it? It might be that further torment obstructed the flow. By the end of that first day Silvestro had denounced Savonarola, all his claims, and had provided a complete list of all citizens who had regularly visited Savonarola at San Marco.

On May 22nd the two friars and their leader were given the verdict of the Commission: guilty of heresy. In the early morning of the 23rd I held Bernardo's arm in the Piazza Della Signoria. Three platforms with gallows on top and pyres beneath had been constructed on the site of the Bonfire of the Vanities. At daybreak the three priests were led into the square. The first tribunal expelled them from the Church and removed their vestments. The second tribunal, with dispensation from Pope Alexander, forgave their sins. At the third the secular authorities shaved their heads and beards ready for their fate. Clad in white shirts the men were escorted to the gallows.

Silvestro crossed the wooden walkway first. At the scaffold a rope was put around his neck and he was pushed off the ladder. The snare was loose and short so he would strangle slowly and feel the flames creep up from beneath.

"Jesu, Jesu," we heard him mumble over and over.

Domenico did his best to stride along the boards. There was a smile on his face: as before he was glad to meet his maker.

Girolamo Savonarola mumbled incomprehensively as he took that final walk.

'How is your voice today?' asked the executioner as the noose went around his neck.

'No last words, priest?' as he pushed the ladder.

The three bodies writhed and twisted as the flames seared their legs. Their strange involuntary dance amidst the blaze reminded me of carnival clowns. Rocks thrown by the urchins who had once raided houses for vanities reached their marks. Were there images of books and beautiful art in Girolamo's mind in those final moments? A gust of wind passed through the square. A lick of flaring sparks raised his lifeless right arm. He blessed his faithful among the crowd; before their sobbing was silenced by the roar of twisting fire and billowing smoke. Sandro was among them.

As the wind died so the inferno tripled. Stones struck dangling limbs, which severed and dropped into the fire. Guards tightened the cordon. At the order the gallows were pushed into the heart of it. The sentries remained at their post until there were only ashes. Then they shovelled the remains into a cart and drove it to the centre of the Ponte Vecchio. From the highest point the cinders were thrown into the River Arno. There would be no relics here to give the priests martyrdom. Yet Savonarola's sermons were preserved and read many times over by those who revered the three friars from San Marco.

'I did not like the man,' Bernardo said quietly as we walked home. 'But that death was vindictive. The Signoria should have left him some dignity.' Those words were more than he had said in a month.

Next day at the Palazzo Vecchio there was a feeling of excitement and change: the former because the nightmare was over; the latter because new blood was needed.

'Soon,' Scala said to me in a corridor. 'You have a chance this time.'

'The priestly ones will be cleaned out at last. Just bide your time, Machia,' said Salviati. 'This is what your father prepared you for.'

Later I stood in the office of Adriani. He was dressed in the robes of 1st Secretary to the 1st Chancery. 'The Medici will wield power again, Machia, but not overtly like the old days.' He explained clearly as the teacher he had always been.

Four days after the gruesome end of Savonarola and his companions I stepped into the kitchen of our casa. Totto was back from Rome. He got up from helping Bernardo with his food, and served me a plate. It was vegetable stew with a little meat.

'Bernardo, Bernardo, I have some news.' He put the spoon down and looked at me. 'It is what you have trained me for since I was a boy.' His eyes tried to grasp my meaning. 'Today I was voted in as 1st Secretary of the 2nd Chancery.' I waited.

'Congratulations,' said Totto. 'That is a high position with a good salary. You have done extraordinarily well.'

'Yes,' said Bernardo. 'Extraordinarily well.' He repeated it twice more. He understood.

When Secretary for the Ten of War was added to 1st Secretary my workload doubled. I became a roving diplomat who solved the problems of the Florentine Republic. One time I dealt with mercenaries asking for more than the city could afford; on another occasion in Romagna I provided aid to embattled allies of Florence. Too often it was related to Pisa, our commercial access to the sea but our persistent enemy.

I was on my way to the court of Louis XII of France when word came.

"Bernardo died in his sleep," Totto said in his letter. That was probably a good thing since he would not have seen the priest Totto would have called for his final breath. Bartolomea no doubt approved. Apoplexia had exacted its final toll. He had reached his allotted three score and ten years. Totto was left to carry out the proper funeral arrangements. For my elder sister, Primerana had died suddenly months before. She only reached half of her assigned time. On the day of Bernardo's interment I bargained with the king of France for Florence's survival.

§

CHAPTER 5

Ros awoke from a dream that involved running water and exotic birds, in a landscape that was familiar but not quite right. Her ears isolated two purring motors, small and not working very hard: little motorbikes cruising down a long hill. She went back to the birds diving into the crystal water. In her nostrils there was an oh-so-familiar smell: good coffee. Her eyes opened to reveal the back of Philip's neck.

'"There was movement at the station, for the word had passed around.

That the colt from old Regret had got away . . ."'

Now where did that one come from, she thought? Banjo Patterson was a long way from home. Outside the volunteers were stirring. She gave Philip a dig in the ribs. When that didn't work she tickled him until it hurt.

'Ok, ok. I've got it.'

After morning ablutions by the river they walked up to a tent with two Lambrettas parked outside. Inside a gas cooktop roared. The team members lined up for something hot with bread and their choice from an array of jams, marmalades and preserves. They quickly left the queue to breakfast outside or climb up the slope to their trenches. Philip found a patch of grass on which to sip black tea and to carve teeth marks into buttered bread and marmalade. Ros joined him with strong, black coffee and a fresh bread roll plastered with something called Nutella.

'What's that like?' he asked.

'It's sort of nuts with chocolate: unusual but not bad.'

Philip looked around and up. The sun was low over crumbling terraces beside the bridge. There was a sloping plateau above them to the south, and an even higher plug of rock beyond that. Defence just shouted as the reason for this settlement's existence. Greeks, Romans, Etruscans: it all came back to the basics: survival first, water and food second, trade next and the arts a distant fourth.

Ros was letting her mind ramble too. What did she feel? Lots of layers of human existence of course: this was the heart of Italy, a short distance north of imperial Rome. Then there were the burials. Her books were full of the treasures taken from Etruscan tombs. This was a vibrant place, then as now. Like Cornwall this land was full of memories.

They watched a girl approach. Ros saw her short, straight brown hair, scrubbed face hidden by heavy square-rimmed glasses and generous body encased in loose khaki shorts and shirt.

Philip observed manly knees, determined stride and practical boots. He tried not to be judgemental but he'd seen such unlovely specimens of womanhood many times on digs.

Maybe she had a charming personality, they both thought.

'Good morning. I am Melissa Stonehaven, Deputy Director and Site supervisor. You must be Philip Trevasco and Rosalind Bernaud. Welcome to Città Sotto.'

Her handshake was firm. Philip tried to pick the accent: North Country but not Scause or Geordie.

'Manchester?'

'Close; I am from Sheffield.'

'Is that your university too?' Ros asked.

'No. I studied Archaeology and Medieval History at Durham.' There was a moment's pause. 'Peter has requested that I show you around the site. Follow me, please.'

Melissa waited at a grassy knoll quite close to where they'd breakfasted.

'The landscape of Città was formed by three occurrences of volcanic tufa: the earliest being the 50 metre cliffs and the flat platform south of the peak. Next came the addition of 25metres to the north-eastern side, and third was another 25 metres added to the top of the hill. The acropolis,

Città Sopra, or "City Above" is approximately 500 square metres. We are in Città Sotto, "City Beneath". No one has precisely identified its name from the Classical sources so ours serves the purpose. Città's topography makes it a natural refuge with strong defences and quite large areas of flat land for settlement and farming.'

Melissa led them to the first trench perched precariously on the unstable ground above the river. Systematically she covered V, S, K1, 2 and 3, and a number of exploratory excavations of cisterns, man-made water courses and defensive walls. Finds were generally limited but were meticulously recorded. Recent, then medieval overlaid Roman, Iron and Bronze Age material until the natural Pliocene clay was reached.

The earliest level, Phase I, represented a transitory population who left little evidence beyond an inexplicable burning layer. Phase II was more permanent, with numerous post-holes, remnants of a defensive palisade and pollen evidence for farming. Phase III consisted of oval Bronze and Iron Age huts, again on the lower levels. Città Sopra was largely a refuge in desperate times. Evidence for farming wheat and the bones of livestock were accompanied by Proto-Villanovan pottery, with a radio-carbon date pointing to the 11th or 12th century B.C. 200 years later Phases IV and V, with Villanovan pottery, revealed more substantial stone foundations and cobbled floors. Farming was a settled way of life by Phase VI, the 8th century B.C. In Phase VII, the 7th century, pots of copper red ware and painted designs on a cream fabric were created on wheels. But this was the last era of settled life on the site. By about 650 BC debris from above was smothering earlier levels. By Phase VIII Città Sotto fitted its name as it became a cemetery. On Città Sopra the pottery finds dried up. Its inhabitants had moved to a new site nearby.

'Of course there is nothing left on the ground for me to show you. However, Peter has photocopied drawings, photographs and descriptions of each burial excavated.' Melissa passed them a folder. 'Any questions?'

'What about the tented area in Trench V?'

'That's Mike and his team preparing a burial for the grand opening. He won't mind if you watch.'

'Thanks. That's it for the moment, Melissa. What about you, Ros?'

She shook her head.

'You have been very helpful. Thanks again.'

Melissa smiled for a second and walked off towards Trench V. Another group of student volunteers had arrived, from Exeter University, to help on the excavation. Peter relied on this steady stream of labour, willing to work for bed and board, to cut costs. Melissa greeted them and dropped into her guided tour.

'Coffee?' Ros asked hopefully.

After a do-it-yourself in the breakfast tent, they were back on the grass sipping their chosen brew. After looking at the tomb descriptions Philip thought aloud.

'So much of the material has been degraded by erosion and almost certainly by looting. I doubt if you can get excited by the site, as even I struggle to.'

'But the tombs,' said Ros. 'Peter has not found anything to rival the best of Cerveteri and Tarquinia. This necropolis was a country cousin in comparison. But some of the bronze fibulae and pins are exquisite. Look at this leech-shaped bow, with its spring and pin still attached. And this one with the transverse grooves expanding in the centre, matched by the semi-circular catch-plate. Yes I can definitely get enthusiastic over these.'

'This brings us back to Peter's problem: all his best finds get pinched.'

He listened to the wind funnelling through the scrub trees beside the water.

'I'm happy to help but I'm glad we're not here just for the excavation. You'd go mad drawing tiny, badly worn sherds every day.'

'True.'

'But we're hardly qualified as detectives.'

'Time detectives?'

'That sounds like a cartoon show. Have trowel, will travel.'

During the hottest part of the day, between 12 and 2, they alternately read and dozed. That was when they were not woken by machinery working somewhere just down river behind the acropolis of Città Sopra.

'It sounds like a backhoe or a tractor,' Philip said without opening his eyes.

'It seems un-Italian to build things during siesta,' she replied.

'Hello, Mike. I'm Philip and this is Ros. Do you mind if we join you?'

Michael Holland looked up from the wooden board on his lap. On the grid paper was a to-scale drawing of the tufa sarcophagus in front of him. Beside him were several sharp pencils, a good German eraser and clean cloths to put under his arm to avoid smudges.

'Come on in. I won't get up unless you object.'

'That's not a problem. We're not here to stop your work.'

Mike was young and strong in muscle structure from what Ros could see. His blond hair cut short, clean shaven features and faded green slacks and shirt reminded her of Army Reserve. In contrast the petite female with measuring tape was aged somewhere around thirty. Dressed in loose-fitting grey pantaloons and cream blouse she was clearly Italian and chic.

'Buon pomeriggio.'

She looked at Philip and a little longer at her. Just long enough to begin a picture but not long enough to be rude, thought Ros. Her pinpoint black eyes studied the Pentax SLR camera hung off Ros's neck. Then she went back to the tape measure held between manicured fingers and to Mike in readiness for his next instruction.

'Sorry,' Mike said, looking up again. 'Ros, Philip, meet Nicola Corsini. Nicola meet Philip Trevasco and Rosalind Bernaud, friends of Peter.'

'I am pleased to meet you both. But please call me Nico, like everyone else.' She lifted her hand in place of a handshake.

The sarcophagus was of yellow tufa, hand-adzed into an oblong box on four legs with a pitched roof lid. To Ros it seemed short, about a metre and a half, and no more than half a metre wide. The sharp edge of the pitch had been chipped in several places but it was intact. Had it been robbed in antiquity? She would find out tomorrow.

While Nico and Mike finished and then checked the measurements on the drawing, Philip walked around the edge of the trench and then gingerly along the baulk, the thin wall of original soil between it and the next trench. He was trying to make sense of the jumbled stratigraphy of the sections. Everything was tumbled from above, with a morass of tags to show Phases I to VII in a mind-numbing jigsaw.

'Do you mind if I take photographs?' Ros asked.

'That's good. The more the better,' said Mike.

Mike covered the drawing board with a fold-over cloth. Then he packed up his equipment. He didn't leave the trench until the armed policeman arrived. He and his colleagues would stand vigil until the grand event next morning.

Ros helped Nico out of the trench.

'May I look at your camera please, Rosalind?'

'Ros, please. Yes, of course.'

Nico held it carefully. 'Pentax Electro-Spotmatic: 35mm of course.'

'It's an F model,' said Ros.

'What's the difference, Ros?'

'It has an open-aperture meter rather than a stop-down meter.'

'Ah yes. It's still quite heavy, like mine. I have heard that Asahi are working on a K series which will be lighter. Who knows what they will do?'

Nico led Ros back to a large tarpaulin on the ground. On it were a dozen plastic buckets full of dirt and marked with card tags. A range of garden sieves were stacked nearby. Philip followed. Now this was more interesting.

Nico explained how she strained the soil methodically to find the tiny fragments that most digs missed. Peter was adamant that maximum knowledge had to be gleaned from what he knew was limited material. In the final publication it would make his site special.

Philip left Ros with Nico as they worked through the buckets together. They didn't need him. He wanted to know more. Things itched inside his brain. To get rid of them he needed to go high to see the lay of the land. Where better than Città Sopra?

From the site the cliffs were sheer and treacherously soft. He saw no easy path so he climbed the track up to the road and followed it a short way east before cutting along a path into the macchia. When the path forked he went west, up and across the upper plateau. Soon he was in open pasture with sparse trees. The acropolis was like a volcano above his head. He was perspiring but the heat of the day was contracting. Soon he was back in the shade of the macchia. He thought of David Livingstone and impenetrable jungle. But by circling up in a corkscrew spiral he reached the top twenty minutes later. Yes, it was worth it. What rugged country! Umbria merged into Tuscany and the ragged backbone of the Apennine Mountains to the east. Defensive plugs of rock, each with villages and towns on top, dotted the countryside. Defence had been in men's minds for thousands of years here.

By habit he made a survey across the 20 by 30 metre citadel. Within minutes he'd found a range of bucchero, red-ware, coarse kitchen pots, more or less the full range of Città Sotto minus the tombs. But they were sparse. People chose the comparative ease of life down in the valley.

Back on the plateau he headed west. It sloped down to a separate piece of pasture. From the edge of the cliff he could see scars cut into the forest. Had there been a flash flood that had scoured and collapsed sections of overhang along its banks? He was starting to slip on the crumbling rock. No, he couldn't see enough. But he knew how he could. As he headed back east off the plateau Philip identified the spot.

As he approached the site he could see Ros and Nico working the buckets. They were laughing over something. None of his business really, and she was happy. He walked over to trench K1. Bradley and three girls were working in a line trowelling back a clay floor. They were helped by a middle-aged Italian man dressed in worn dress trousers, tan waistcoat and trilby hat. He worked his trowel steadily and it was clear that they were following him. Philip guessed that Peter had assigned a skilled foreman to prevent a Bradley disaster. Behind the line two young men kept up with the buckets of dirt. One in four was tagged and sent to the tarpaulin for Nico and Ros. The rest was dumped on the spoil tip just below the trench. Philip guessed that winter rains would take it away in swollen waters.

Bradley saw him and got up. 'You're the new guy travelled here last night. Philip wasn't it?'

'Yes. I'm Philip and over there is Ros, with Nico. How's it going here?'

'Well, man we're tracing this dirt floor to that bundle of rock, which just might be a wall. You know much?'

'Some. I can have a look if you'd like.'

'That's great. Between you and me I feel I'm drowning but don't tell Peter that.'

I don't need to, Philip thought. 'Ciao. Posso io?' he spoke hesitantly to the foreman.

'Hello, Philip. I am Gabriel. Yes, you are welcome.'

Philip looked up at Bradley, who nodded back. Philip got down and ran his fingers over what they were kneeling on and then over the surface in front of him that needed to be removed. He felt that tingle of excitement when faced by the intricacies of mud flooring. This was like Kara Tepe but closer to home. He crumbled a piece of the hard clay and smelled it. Then he wiped a finger over the new floor and put it to his nose again. That Pliocene clay had multiple uses: pottery, roof tiles, and now ancient floors. He tilted the trowel so the sharp edge was vertical to the clay. He pressed and a piece crumbled; it was seven to eight millimetres thick. He pressed again and another segment split away cleanly. Soon he was in his stride and forgot the girls who tried to keep up with him.

Gabriel gently tapped his trowel in front of the girls. His eyes indicated to step back. Soon Gabriel kept pace with oblivious Philip. The man smiled at Philip's total concentration. The girls became part of the bucket crew. Bradley pretended to inspect some detail of the section but really just observed Philip and Gabriel. It was always good to watch two people who knew what they were doing.

They finished the floor in record time. That tumble of rock was definitely a wall and this floor ran just under it. Peter now had a relative date to work with. In the last half hour Philip chatted to Gabriel, in English since Gabriel's language skill was far superior to his Italian.

'Where have you worked before, Gabriel?'

'Volterra, Chiusi, Sovana, Populonia and a few more.'

'You are an archaeological excavator,' said Philip with a smile. 'How many years?'

'Twenty five years; and my father before me.'

At the end of the day Philip shook Gabriel's hand. 'I enjoyed that. Maybe we can work with each other again?'

'Yes, that would be good. Addio Philip.'

Philip walked over to Ros.

'Posso lavorare ancora con te domani?' she said to Nico.

'Of course, Ros, that will be a pleasure.'

'Come on stinky,' Ros said to Philip, 'time for a swim.'

At the tent she changed into her togs. He reluctantly did the same. Somewhere there had to be a shallow bit. There was a ten metre pond just under the bridge. She looked at the water for a minute and then porpoised in. A dusty brown streak floated away down the river. Leisurely she lifted one arm over the other into an Aussie Crawl.

He slid in from the side. It was cold but refreshing. He paddled out to the depth of his waist and then his shoulders. Not a bad idea, Ros. His nostrils went under as his eyes were just above the surface, like a crocodile he thought. Sunlight flecked through the trees and made patterns in the ripples and eddies. Leisurely he spread his arms and pulled the water, like his version of a breast stroke. He was relaxed because he was not out of his depth. He checked periodically to make sure. Golden sunlight, wind patterns crossing the water like brush strokes, his skin refreshed by the chill of the water: this was pleasure. When he closed his eyes the light was pink. His breathing slowed. Like a meditation he was in the moment. He submerged again to just his eye level. Then he opened them.

There was movement in the reeds on the far side of the pool. It was fast. He looked harder. The something had entered the water. It was swimming, no wriggling in wide loops across the surface, towards him. Half way between was Ros, facing him and with her back to the creature. Adrenalin pushed leisure past his toe nails.

'Ros!'

She continued her lazy strokes and only surfaced every four for a breath.

'Ros!' he shouted.

Something registered. She looked across at him. 'What?'

His eyes were wide and he was pointing.

'What's wrong?'

Philip reached for her hand and began powering his toes through the gravel. Then he made a fair effort at swimming. He was definitely getting out of that water as fast as possible. She turned around to see what the commotion was about.

'Oh, that's it.' She stopped and let go of his hand. A snake swam past her leg: wide head, stripes on a brown/near black body, probably a viper of some kind, maybe poisonous. But it kept going towards the bank. Philip was just ahead of it. The phrase "walking on water" dropped into her mind, just as he got out. The reptile veered away at the last moment and slithered into the shrubbery. She did her best not to fall over or drown as she rolled around in laughter.

'It was a snake!'

'It was only a little one. He wouldn't have eaten very much.'

'You're used to them but I never stayed long enough to become mates with them.' Philip strode off towards their tent.

'Come on, Philip. The creature was on a mission. He was not interested in either of us.'

Oh well, best to leave him to calm down, she thought. Ros went back into the water. Whenever she pictured his face and the rapid exit she tried not to swallow too much.

'Have you recovered your composure yet?' she asked as she hooked her arm in his on the way up to "La Macchia".

'Maybe.'

She went back to enjoying the stroll on a clear evening in Italy. She kept saying that to herself: she was in Italy. To Philip it was close but from

Oz it was half a world away. The sky was turning to red and orange, with a hint of green. The Vespas, each with one, or two, or often three teenagers on them, wiggled around them and laboured up the hill. She must be getting fitter. With a steady stride, not too fast, she was barely breaking sweat.

At the table Melissa was in deep conversation with Peter. She was drawing with her finger on the table cloth. Mike sat on his other side, throwing in comments when the opportunities came. Ros and Philip sat along from him.

'Do you want to fly tomorrow?' Philip asked Ros after his first sip of effervescent rosé.

'Do you need me?'

'I just want to get the lay of the land really.'

'Nico invited me to work with her. I'd prefer that. But I can help you take off and set you up with a camera.'

'It's a deal.'

On the walk back they followed the dancing light of Philip's torch.

'That sounds like the machinery we heard at mid-day.' But as he said it the noise stopped.

'It's still an odd time to work, when everyone is eating their evening meal,' she said.

'Did you check the sleeping bag for reptiles?' she asked innocently as she climbed in beside him.

'I don't think I will bother replying to that. Sleep tight.' His arms encircled her.

'Don't let the bed bugs bite.' She curled into his shoulder.

'I didn't look for those either.'

§

'It's late in the evening, October, 1501, Bernardo. The wind would have chilled you to the bone today.' I looked into the fire, a tazza of new wine in my hand. Totto was far away and on his journey into the priesthood.

'I am 32 and lonely, Bernardo. It is time for that final obligation. Thanks, old friend. '

At dawn the activity began in earnest. Workmen carried in the two Forzieri linen boxes crafted and decorated according to my direction. More men unravelled and hung the Spalliere panels around the walls of the largest room in our casa on the Via Romana. I recognised the hand. All manner of food filled the kitchen. Women from around the courtyard helped with the festivities. There were new faces from the balconies of my childhood. Mid-morning the boxes disappeared.

I stood in the sunlit yard and listened. Beside me were Vespucci and Martelli, my assistants at the Chancery. For three years they had saved my hide from all manner of skulduggery plotted by my rivals while I was away on diplomatic missions. They knew me better than my brother Totto, who now stood in a corner watching the activity.

Music rose above the noise of the street. Soon the first members of the procession entered: Marcello Virgilio Adriani, 1st Secretary to the 1st Chancery, followed by my other old friend Alamanno Salviati, teacher and politician extraordinary. Then it was the Corsini clan, who escorted Marietta, demure and hidden under the veil. Porters carried in the marriage chests, decorated with scenes from Ovid, Petrarch and Boccaccio. 'You approve of my choices, Bernardo?'

'Good journey, Ostinato?' He stood back from the crowd. Yet his style and presence dominated the room. He nodded.

'Bernardo let us admire Ostinato's work.' Around the walls of the main room the Spalliere panels described the traditional expectations of a good wife: virtue, purity, duty, fertility and beauty. But Ostinato had read my love of the antique mind. Ceres, the eternal mother, Diana, the huntress forever chaste, Vesta looking after the home and hearth, and of course Venus, the epitome of beauty.

'Well, Bernardo, our friend loves a pageant as much as we do.' Inevitably, as I stared into the eyes of Venus, I thought of Sandro and his unattainable lady. 'Vespucci, who knows everything about everyone, tells me that on his death Sandro wants to be buried at Simonetta's feet in the Church of Ognissanti. I hope his wish is granted.'

Ostinato stayed for the giving of the ring to Marietta. The dowry had not been easy, since I was not a man of means at this time. After months of discussion with her brother, Lanciolino, it was agreed that I would pay in instalments over a period. Even so I felt the silent approval of Bernardo and his companion, Luigi Corsini. If I succumbed to the many dangers of my travelling life it would keep her and our family from servitude.

'I wish you all that the Spalliere promise, Machia.'

'I wish you safe travels, until we meet again.' He joined his handsome young assistant and the rest of his entourage. With music and colour I was reminded of an extravagant carnival. It was to be a year before each of us were drawn to Emilia Romagna by Duke Valentino.

§

'I trust you are well, Ostinato?'

A man who had seen the prime of life, in rose tunic, spreading blue hat and leather boots looked up from his notebook. Blue eyes set in a well-proportioned face showed no surprise at my presence. No doubt he had watched my approach along the old Via Aemilia. Lines and a mistiness of expression showed his half century of years. His work: haphazard drawings of fortress walls, and bridges. You write with your left hand too since I last saw you. Cryptic notes circled a wonderful sketch of water flowing in pools from the famous fountains of the town, Rimini. Yes, my childhood friend was still a Scribbler.

'I am healthy, Machia, or should I call you Spia?'

His teasing was gentle. As Secretary for the Republic my title was surely Diplomat but we both knew the truth. I was here on behalf of the Signoria of Florence to spy on Duke Valentino. His conquest of so much of Romagna had terrified my masters.

'I am sure the Duke knows perfectly well my role. I am an ambassador, an honest gentleman sent to lie and do whatever is necessary for the good of his state.'

The July heat was softened by sea breezes from across the Adriatic. In late afternoon storm clouds could hold no more. Under cover of a hostelry in Montefeltro we watched the rain sheet across the land towards Urbino.

'So how do you serve the Duke?' I asked.

'With my scribbles, of course. I study his conquests and advise him how to keep them.'

That evening he showed me drawings of strongholds and ramparts which he had improved to resist the new firearms that the French had brought to Italy. As always there were also observations of birds in flight, or distant mountain vistas, water cascading or storms raging.

The following day I sat with him on a commanding ridge in the quiet of an olive grove. Its steep slopes were macchia forest. It could only be for a brief time as the Duke's men were not far behind. My presence threatened his safety. I was surprised when he showed me another notebook, one he kept from the Duke and his spies. A page showed an exquisitely executed drawing of a mosquito injecting its sickness into a man's arm. Around it were vignettes of devices that attached to the creature's abdomen, ponds treated with noxious substances and scientific notes that were unclear to me. But the overall purpose was certain.

'If the Duke had such weapons his expertise with poison would be unrivalled.'

'Precisely so,' Ostinato replied. 'Better that his men see other work.'

He turned over page after page of studies of rock, its composition and his theories about how it came to be. His rambles in the hills surrounding Florence had expanded to Arezzo, Pistoia and Casentino and far beyond since I last saw him. Skeletons of fish that I had never seen in the sea were encased in layers of rock miles from the ocean.

'If they understand this they will call you a heretic. Might I suggest you keep to diagrams of castles and siege machines rather than tempt an audience with the Inquisition, my old friend?'

He turned to another page of the journal. At the centre was an erupting volcano spewing rocks and ash across a lush farming landscape beside a bay. I recognised the Kingdom of Naples and its brooding neighbour, Mount Vesuvius. All around it were cameos of people running, stumbling and hiding. The anguish on their faces was hideous. Others hid in cellars but their end was the same.

'How do you think such things, Ostinato?'

'The ancients described that day. Plumes of gas, rock and ash poured down the mountain.'

On the next sheet were studies of swirling vapour in layers, of jars exploding and men holding their throats.

'They have nowhere to hide, Machia. The heavy mixture follows them into cellars and dungeons. There is no escape.'

'This is also not a weapon for the Duke, for I am sure he would use it. Fear of such a death would win a campaign even before its usage.'

'We agree.'

I travelled the breadth and length of this country. Valentino had given me a pass to look at whatever I wished with no hindrance. My diplomatic role also protected me. Unlike my first mission to France the Signoria, and the Duke, were a little more generous. But I still chose to stay at simple taverns rather than castles. Across Romagna I observed the people as Ostinato studied the natural world. It was a country shattered by war. Conflict does not only destroy buildings and take lives, it makes institutions weak and people lose a confidence that takes years to rebuild. Most evenings I would rub shoulders with peasants who smelled of their beasts: goat shit, chicken shit; cow shit if they were better off. But I preferred their smell to the pomade of the noble elite; French, Neapolitan or Roman. Perfume never hid their filth or the stench in palace corridors.

'The students of Bologna have taken to the streets, my lord,' the spy reported. 'They speak of independence from your dominion.'

'Who supports them?' asked the Duke.

'The former council does, and a number of learned men who speak of setting up a Signoria like that of Florence. '

'I smell the Medici clan in this. What do the rioters do?'

'They do not riot, sir. They talk a lot, shout maybe, but do not destroy property, my lord.'

The Duke took some time to reply. 'Then let them shout. Record who they are, what they say and do but do not intervene. The world will tire of their ranting and move on to other more pressing matters. Then is the time to move. Retribution must be swift and merciless. You might even suggest that the Signoria had their hands in it.'

The Duke's man left with my coin in his pocket. That was a nice touch, to point to Florentine interference in the affairs of Romagna. Was not that my purpose here? I watched the Duke and he watched me. It was a game he played with a smile.

In late August I found Ostinato on another hillside, in the shade of near impenetrable scrub.

'With your interest in the workings of people, this should stir your curiosity,' he said.

I sat beside him. What was he studying? What, ants! Over an afternoon I saw colonies that satisfied the needs of their inhabitants. Some workers built, some foraged for food, and some no doubt protected their queen deep underground at the city's heart. For the parallel with our own was clear to me. Each individual worked for the whole. In return they received sustenance. They had a role to play in the survival of the entirety. I saw farmers of aphids that gave honey. Others were cleaners, so that their habitation would not become hazardous to all inside. But some colonies were of a war-like nature, like the ancient Spartans. A forager met an enemy scavenger, who returned to the nest to tell. Soon armies assembled for war. In the battle groups would tear an individual limb from limb or squirt some burning liquid which dissolved the shell of its foe. Was this to be another of my companion's weapons of destruction? That night I dreamt of cities cooperating so that they became too powerful for any marauder to attack. Not for the first time did I hope for all the states to unite into a country equal to France or Spain; a strong Italy as it had once been under the ancient Romans.

In September he was in Cesenatico planning a canal and port for this lovely seaside town. I joined him again at Imola, where he spent much time on a detailed map of the entire city, as though the view of a bird from the air. The city was contained in a circle with multiple compass points. Every street, church and colonnade was included. The River Santerno was a pale blue line threading through green fields beside pink houses.

When I arrived I saw that Valentino was delighted by this masterful work but was engrossed by another map which covered the entire territory of Romagna. He seemed to cup it in his hands. But no sooner was he able to understand his domain than it was taken away from him. His rebellious captains were frightened by his success.

'Well, Florentines, do you trust them?' This day was overcast and gloomy.

Valentino's smile was easy as we watched the arrival of a small band of dignitaries astride mules, with a few horsemen to the rear. Vitellozzo Vitelli, lord of Montone, Città di Castello, Monterchi and Anghiari, was a condottiero who had fought across Romagna with his lord. With him came Cardinal Pagolo, and the Duke di Gravina, both of the Orsini family. Their pace was slow and measured as they approached the gate of Sinigallia, on this last day of the year 1502.

'Trust is relative to the situation, my Lord.'

Ostinato was distracted by the approaching snow clouds and said nothing.

Valentino's eyes showed surprise before the grin spread wider. The revolt in Bologna had been crushed swiftly: the leaders rounded up in the early hours; their mutilated bodies were found floating in the Arno River. These men before him, jealous of his military prowess and meteoric success, had conspired against him. When he was without arms and friends, hostile armies at his door, I had been sent by the Signoria of Florence to aid him. At Imola he had been desolate. But he rose again. Papal money trained local cavalry; promises to Louis XII produced French infantry and horsemen; guile and diplomacy created reconciliation. Now these captains came to him to show their trust. He smiled at me and then extended his arms in a gesture of peace towards the arrivals.

'Where is Oliverotto?' he said quietly to Don Michelotto, always close to his right hand. The Duke's eyes signalled to fetch him.

Oliverotto da Fermo was with his troops in the square. The others had divested themselves of their men in the castles nearby. Michelotto persuaded Oliverotto to leave his soldiers. When Valentino's four captains were assembled, each between two of his most loyal supporters, the band entered the city.

'Come, it is time to show our mutual regard,' said the Duke. Within a small room deep in the castalan glasses were raised. 'To our future.'

At the signal each of the four were held and bound.

Why were we left to see this? Was it a boast, that his power was so great that witness would spread his fame? Or that he was above such social rules?

He strode out to the courtyard and mounted. As head of his men Oliverotto's fifteen hundred were easily subdued. But the forces of the Orsini and Vitelli realised that something was wrong and fought their way to freedom. As Secretary for the city of Florence I stood back with my friend. This was the Duke's reward for our help and their betrayal.

When his troops moved on from abusing Oliverotto's men to sacking the city, the Duke cornered some and rode them down, so the others restrained their pillage and rapine. Then, with equally decisive action, two of the number, Vitellozzo and Oliverotto were prepared: their wrists and feet were bound, their bodies strapped into seats and the leather cord of the garrotte placed around their necks. Vitellozo readied his soul and asked the Pope for forgiveness for his sins. Oliverotto cried for mercy and shouted that anything he had done against the Duke was due to Vitellozzo.

Oliverotto continued to rave as the strap was knotted and a rod inserted in the loop behind the chair. Vitellozzo closed his eyes and said nothing. But he like us was keenly aware of every movement of his executioner, Don Michelotto. Valentino walked behind them, checked that all was correct and looked at us. How strong were we? I held his gaze.

'No, Machia, no,' Ostinato mumbled over and over. He shook and stared into infinity, mountains, anywhere but there.

The Don and his helper twisted the bars of the garrottes. Shouts became grunts and guttering. The executioners heaved on the rotation until their sweat dripped. The condemned squirmed and twitched. Then their hands and legs shook uncontrollably, before their faces coloured through red to purple. It took an age for them to become still. I clearly heard bones snap as their heads fell forward.

Valentino's coup was not completed until the 18th day of January, 1503. His father, Pope Alexander VI, now had custody of the Florentine clerics,

Cardinal Orsino, Archbishop of Florence, and Messer Jacopo da Santa Croce. The Duke met no opposition in the lofty castle of Pieve, when the Orsinis met the same fate we had witnessed weeks before. No blood flowed in their execution, as the Church required.

What we had observed changed us. My comrade became more of a recluse than before. His mind was disordered so that he pushed away what he did not wish to see. I, on the other hand, felt a strange fascination for this strong ruler who saw men as they were, not what we wanted them to be. Valentino's methods, ruthless and without mercy, created a brief peace in a region that had not known it for generations: but he was feared not loved. His father Rodrigo ruled the Church as his earthly kingdom. The word Trust for such Princes was a tool to be used. Its meaning could never be that of ordinary people.

§

CHAPTER 6

'Spegni la luce qui!'

The flood light rotated past a mechanical excavator, a four-wheeled motorbike loaded with boxes, and a pile of rubble. The beam revealed a shattered hole in a circular building. It was as though an earthquake had collapsed a whole wall. Inside two men worked fully upright. One cut out a section of wall painting. It was of a man and woman seated on a long couch at an ancient feast. The jack hammer reverberated and dust flowed out into the night. His partner lined a wooden crate with straw and fitted the pieces in as they fell off the wall. Both men were white with grime, their faces sweat-lined and ghostly. The machine stopped and the light went out.

'Scemo! Cosa stai facendo?'

'Calmati. Aggiusterò.'

The young man pulled a torch from his pocket. There were the power cables. He followed them over the churned up ground to an alcove around the corner. Muffled with cardboard sheets and hessian sacks was a generator. Good, it still throbbed the way it should. He found the power board and plugged the cables back in.

'Ok?'

'Ok.'

He walked back and stood beside the light. They didn't need to know who tripped over the leads.

Just before dawn he pushed the last bit of equipment back under the army tarpaulin. The boxes had been sealed and removed to a safe place in the village. The other men were back with their wives. He liked this time of day, when the first birds called, the air was cool and the job was done. He whistled gently the tune of a Tony Renis song he remembered from his childhood.

'"Quando, quando, quando",' he crooned as he climbed out of the valley up towards Alta Cresta.

§

'Scusi,' said Mike and coughed loudly.

The poliziotto curled up against the trench wall, with folded arms and nodding head, opened his eyes. He smiled, got up and saluted. Mike swept up any scuff marks, took some more photographs in the early light and then waited. It would be a wasted morning as far as he could see. Local dignitaries were always late. But what choice did Peter have? They had to be kept on side.

By 9 everyone who was anyone had squeezed around the walls of the trench. The volunteers found a space as best they could.

'Buongiorno, signor Sindaco,' said Peter. He held out his hand to the mayor.

'Buongiorno, signor Direttore.'

Antonio Marazzi was a small man, as round as he was tall. His florid complexion was crowned by a bald pate, except for a dozen long strands combed over. Peter shook his hand and escorted him to the best position. Ros and Nico crouched with their cameras on the trench floor. Mike and Gabriel stood beside the sarcophagus with small crowbars. Beside them was a white sheet on which to place the lid.

'Pronto?' Peter gestured to the mayor.

Antonio smiled and a large gold tooth sparkled. He nodded approval.

'Ok, Mike, Gabriel?'

The men slid in the pinch bars at opposite sides and ends.

'Lift,' said Mike.

Ros and Nico took their first photographs.

The small stone lid came up easily. Then, as planned, the two men walked around to rotate it until it formed a cross. The volcanic tufa was as light as a soap stone found in a British bathroom.

The audience gasped and then clapped.

Ros and Nico walked around and snapped from various angles.

'Ready?' Mike said to Gabriel.

'Ready.'

Ros watched them lay the stone on the sheet and turn towards what everyone else could see. The white shroud covered the body of a slim girl, around twelve years of age, her face uncovered and framed by waist length blond hair. Her parchment skin was desiccated and sunken but amazingly intact. Around her neck was a silver torque which sagged where once was full-blooded flesh. The smooth band of metal was finished off by massively horned rams' heads. On her revealed right wrist was more silver jewellery: a bracelet with delicate acorns and horizontal divisions of filigree decoration which framed pastoral scenes. If Ros thought that the bronze fibulae were exquisite how could she describe these? She'd run out of superlatives.

Philip was more interested in the preservation of the corpse. He viewed her from a vantage point on a thin baulk opposite the mayor. On another memorable occasion he and Ros had seen entombed bodies crumble as the air of the present moved into space that had been undisturbed for two millennia. Unlike the Egyptians the bodies were not mummified with natron or other chemicals. In fact many sarcophagi contained cremated remains. Here was a child of some considerable wealth sent into the afterlife properly prepared to continue her status in life. He looked across at Peter. His face reflected his thoughts: at last we have something to keep the American and British sponsors happy. Peter turned to Antonio and smiled. The mayor reciprocated, but then turned back to the open tomb. His eyes glistened like his teeth.

Ros and Nico leaned over the girl and took more photos of specific details; the torque and bracelet, the preservation of her face and hands, and folds of the decaying cloth. Then it was measurements with Mike and Nico.

Now Peter was in a quandary. A body preserved as he could see it would be an archaeological coup. But how could they conserve it with the meagre resources he had; and in the limited time before Nature intervened?

'Quanti anni ha lei?' Antonio shouted to Mike.

He looked up, startled, and dropped his end of the tape. The shell disintegrated like powdered glass. After two and a half thousand years this un-named girl existed as two pieces of jewellery.

'Fortuna,' said Antonio with a shrug. His eyes focused again on the metalwork.

By late afternoon, long after the audience had left, the two items were removed and boxed. Later they would be taken to Peter's conservation and work room in Alta Cresta. There were no funerary urns or domestic items to elaborate. She had kept her anonymity.

But Philip's skills were not required. Mike and Gabriel were more than capable. He left them quietly and walked up the hill, past "La Macchia" and into Peter's domain. It was a large ground floor room of what once had been a factory. A wall of windows gave ample light to work in. It also allowed Philip to observe Peter busy on the annual site report. A profusion of paper sheets encircled him, at the limit of his reach, on a large drafting table. Near his right hand was a glass and nearby two bottles betrayed its contents: Cinzano and Pellegrino mineral water.

Each to their own methods, Philip thought. Maybe a little lubrication was necessary to numb him through the boredom of collating pages of drawings of pottery sherds, spindle whorls and broken pins. Or was it to aid creativity?

'Hello, Peter.'

'Philip. Help yourself.'

'No thanks. I just came to pick up the kite and borrow the Landrover.'

'Be my guest. Would you like a hand loading it?'

'I wouldn't say no. Thanks.'

Philip looked at the page Peter was working on. Yes, it was a nondescript sherd that was not even a rim or a base and had no decoration on it whatsoever. Lunch time Cinzano was probably a good idea.

Peter wandered back as Philip was tying his version of truckers' knots onto the roof rack.

'I'll drop it back late afternoon.'

'That's fine.' Peter waved without turning around.

Ros was waiting at the bridge. 'Here's your camera.'

He looked at a Kodak Instamatic, which was quite small. He knew it was basic, which was a good thing since flying generally required two hands. Ros was the camera buff, not him.

'It takes 110 film which means you have 24 shots, one extra if you're lucky. All you do . . .'

'I know: point and click. I think I can manage that.'

Philip took the rear of the bag and let Ros dictate the rest stops. 30 kilos was a bit wearisome but he knew that she was strong. After twenty minutes they were at the place he'd chosen the day before.

She sat looking down across one of the twin valleys of the Acqua Gentile, which by cutting either side of the knoll made Città Sopra into the fortress that it once was. Directly south were the bridge and the dig; across the valley were the medieval defences of Alta Cresta. She looked back at Philip. He'd unpacked the hang glider, clipped together the frame and attached the blue artificial fabric. As he stood up and felt the wind she walked over and checked his harness. It was a ritual: he had clipped himself in with the climbing carabineer and she made the final inspection. Then she hung the camera around his neck and clipped an extra loop around his shoulder, just in case.

'Good trip.' She kissed him. That was his good luck charm.

'Thanks. See you at 4.' Ros stood within his vision but well to one side. Every few seconds she threw a handful of grass into the air.

Now he was in his own world, preparing his mind for this leap of faith, literally. His eyes locked on to the horizon. He knew the ground in front of him; any obstacles like rocks, and how many steps before he would be airborne. For a second he shut his eyes and felt the wind on his cheeks. He was sensing its pattern. It was an inland site, so the wind direction was changeable. With so many ridges and bluffs it would bounce around. But it was predictable, when his mind was right. His eyes opened; he was ready. The direction of the grass clippings was steady from the south. He waited: one, two, and three; there was the pattern. The gust went through. Philip continued counting. His right leg lifted and pushed, then his left, hard against the resistance of the air and the weight above his head. The third step was always the breakthrough. The fourth was easier. Was he grunting? Ros would tell him later. This was the point. He could feel the breeze picking up. There it was: the breaker. He hit it at his seventh step, and pushed the kite into its power. He was up.

Ros watched him go over the edge like a dart, then the gentle swallow dive down and out, before the climb. After their time in Cornwall, the bad and the good flights, she knew his method: gain height, feel the contours below, discover all he needed to in open space to fly safely before he explored. Her watch showed nearly 1. It was time to get back to work with Nico.

When Ros reached the bridge she followed the climb to Alta Cresta with her eyes. Luckily she didn't have to walk it during the hottest part of the day. Nico appeared above the track down to the site. She pushed the blue Vespa forwards to clip out of the stand. Then she stood astride it and reached down to turn on the fuel line and pull out the choke. From her pocket came the ignition key. Ros noticed the key ring of a heart containing the letters S N. Nico turned the key and kick-started the pedal with her right foot. It caught second time. She nursed the sound for a few moments, closed off the choke and sat the bike upright.

'Hop on, Ros.'

Ros sat on the rear of the seat behind Nico. She thought of holding tight below the seat but as they moved off there was nowhere else than hugging Nico's waist. Nico revved hard and got up to third, where she stayed as the motor whined against the climb. Her short hair spread with the buffeting wind but Ros' streamed behind them.

'Ciao belle ragazze,' came with wolf whistles from the pack of teenage males that weaved around and beside them. Nico dropped a gear and moved ahead. This was a superior motor thought Ros. She looked down and noticed the slim gold band on Nico's finger.

'That was fun. Thanks.' Ros helped her pull back the bike so it sat on the struts.

For the next hour they developed the day's film. Nico bathed the prints in the solution and Ros hung them up on the line to dry. Each batch was clearly marked with date, trench, description and anything else that was relevant. Ros was reminded again that without accurate and detailed recording archaeology was simply digging a hole to see what you could find.

When the last print was pegged up Nico looked at her watch. 'Do you feel like something to eat?'

'I wouldn't say no to a cold drink,' Ros said.

'Buon pomeriggio signore.' The waiter put a bottle of chilled mineral water on the table with two glasses.

'What would you like to eat, Ros?'

'Something light, please.'

'I can choose if you don't mind.'

'Good.'

'Tell me about yourself, Ros.'

'Mm I'm not used to that; Australian of course.

'What about Australia then? I have never been there.'

Ros had time to think before the Arancini risotto balls, grilled asparagus tips, toasted broccoli arrived with a large bowl of salad: tomatoes, cucumbers, feta cheese, olives and red onion rings. Here it comes, she thought, kangaroos clogging traffic in Sydney, koalas causing mayhem in Balmain.

'I ask because Australians like you seem fearless. You are so direct and honest in what you say. What makes your people like that?'

'I do know fear at times but I don't let it control me. Ask Philip about when he first took me up in his hang glider. Yes, it's best to be truthful. Australia can be a hard country, particularly in the bush.' Ros found it easy to talk. Nico was female, of a similar age and showed straightforward interest in what she was asking. Ros talked of her childhood, her experiences out west and her passion for art.

'You and Philip seem so comfortable together. How did you meet?'

Ros was less reticent now. 'We are from different worlds but I think we complement each other. He was a studious, shy academic when I first met him in Iran on a dig. I discovered that he has a great many talents. There is not too much that he would not do to look after me.' She sipped her water and looked at Nico again. This was a seriously intelligent woman. 'But enough about me, what about your handsome fellow, Nico?' She looked directly at her ring finger.

'Stefano,' Nico said and looked into the gold. 'Stefano and I were married six weeks when he took me to Milan for the weekend.' She spoke slowly. 'I can see his brown eyes enjoying the drive along the Autostrada. Stefano was a good Catholic so we lit candles in the Duomo. We walked to the Piazza Fontana to catch a tram to the Museo Poldi Pezzoli. There was a photographic exhibition. I remember looking at the fountain in the centre. The pink granite basins supported by mermaids and dolphins glowed in the sun.'

'You don't have to talk about this, Nico.'

Nico waved her hand. 'The bomb exploded in a bank on the square. I was flat on the road with Stefano beside me. My ears were ringing and my head hurt. Smoke and dust poured out of the windows and doors of the building. I shook Stefano, several times. There were cuts on his head and face. But then he opened his eyes. We got up quickly to get away. He brushed the dust from my clothes as we ran slowly. Around the corner he stopped and looked at me. His fingers looked for damage. I looked at his cuts. "We're ok," he said and laughed. "Come on, we need to celebrate our Fortuna." She paused. The fingers of her right hand twirled the ring around her finger.

'There was a little café. I sat at a table and Stefano got up to collect the two glasses of wine on the bar. He was so happy when he turned towards me. But then his face changed, the glasses fell and he curled into a ball holding his stomach. He looked at me and dropped. The coroner said that he had had a massive aneurism. He was dead before he hit the ground.'

I never do this, Ros thought. But she did it anyway. She got up and gave Nico a big long hug.

'Fortuna,' said Nico.

'Whatever's mapped out,' said Ros.

§

1503. Florence.

'Machia, as your ears within the Signoria, and therefore your friend, I ask you to pay more attention to your wife. For one thing, the Corsinis as you know are well connected, and have a powerful place within the Ten of War. For another you are a father to Primerana, who is now months old. Look after your kids, Machia. They are your inheritance to the planet. All your achievements are a speck in the ocean compared with your children. And, by the way, Marietta is not a cow. Yes you think her life is her offspring; that where they come from is irrelevant. That is not true. Your families decided but she loves you. Look after her.

It is over a year since your marriage and you still owe much of Marietta's dowry. She is not happy, Machia. Pay her the money and come back to Florence. And another thing, your one time friend Salviati is becoming more vocal in his criticism of your lifestyle. By which I mean your whoring and intemperate opinions on every subject, in particular God. Yes our Borgia Pope Alexander and his son the Duke are iniquitous and irreligious in the extreme. But there are many powerful men, like Salviati, who do profess faith. Be careful, my friend. I am your not so humble servant, Biagio.'

'Yes, I had been on the road for too long. I missed the family. But now after a few days of domesticity I am bored, Ostinato.' Rucellai gardens were dappled shade and alternating scents as we sauntered along the pathways that curved around the Florentine hillside.

'What ails you, Machia?' He had noticed that I winced from belly pain in certain poses. I described the stomach wind, the burning regurgitation after some foods. He questioned me: did I eat at regular times?

'That is hardly likely given my constant travelling and the varied food at hostelries.'

'How concerned do you become when negotiating with princes?'

'Very. Sleep eludes me as I grapple with problems and their solutions. Yet it is so simple really. Create a win win situation. Leave your opponent enough space so both win. Then we go back to our Signorias with the good news.'

'Lies are a problem. There has to be some truth in negotiation or that stops trust. Truth and falsehood are absolutes. I deal with the grey area between. I tell them that we are in the same business, and that we all have bosses who have our heads in their hands.'

'So honey for repair,' he mumbled to himself, 'chamomile flowers and a little liquorice for calming, and a modicum of Belladonna.'

'I believe I have a solution to your problem. How is your garden progressing, Machia?'

'My plans are being followed but as always the labour is slower than thought. Images of the ancients appear often and the guidance of water owes much to our Etruscan ancestors.'

'I look forward to seeing its completion on my next visit.'

We sat for a while as I studied his latest thoughts scribed in detailed notebooks. 'I have ideas too but no time to write them. The Signoria demands so much of me.'

'When you retire then, like Xenophon and Arrian, after a great career.'

I return to my study in Sant'Andrea after an evening arguing with local lice over petty things. I miss Ostinato's conversations. But then Agostino's letters from Rome intrigue me. Our dissolute Pope becomes more outrageous by the hour. But his schemes against Florence are dangerous. Thank you for keeping me informed, Agostino.

'Well, Bernardo, the gods are with us. On the 10th August our murdering Pontiff made a mistake. Instead of poisoning his latest enemy he managed to poison himself and his son the Duke. Agostino tells me that it took a week for the father to die and his son is weakened beyond repair. The Borgias are broken.'

'Now who takes their place, Agostino?'

'Marietta has given birth to our son, your namesake, Bernardo. When I look into his eyes I see so much of you there. But Marietta seems happy that he looks like me. '

More letters pile up in my study. The great powers, France and Spain, play with their armies in Italy. If only the great cities would put aside their differences and unite for that great cause, a united Italy strong enough to repel all foreign invaders. In the meantime Florence pays homage to the French, and tries its best to keep Rome and Venice at bay.

'Again, Bernardo, we are at war with Pisa. Our ships blockade the mouth of the Arno against Genoese supplies. But the mercenaries we pay win or lose at the toss of a coin. How can any soldier of fortune win against a determined militia fighting for their very survival? You saw me lobby our Gonfalonier today, Piero Soderini, for Florence to have its own citizen militia. He is open to the idea but the great families of Florence fear any leader with an army at his disposal. They cannot see beyond their own interests. But I have a plan for him that will end this interminable war with Pisa.'

'Will it work, Ostinato?' He was a little older, greyer since our initiation by the Duke, but still vibrant in his passion for an idea. The walls of Pisa were yellow in the afternoon sun. The water sparkled with wind-blown crests of the river at full flow.

'Of course it will, Machia, if your masters fund it properly.' Laid out on desks beside him were maps and proposals, detailed lists of requirements: the number of engineers involved, drawings of two great channels each eight miles long, 2000 labourers per day to make up the 40 thousand man-work days required. Their task: to divert the Arno River away from Pisa and into the sea at Leghorn. No river meant no water and no trade.

'It's a beautiful plan,' Ostinato said. 'Pisa is defeated without Florence losing a man. No bloodshed, Machia.'

'Now to persuade our Gonfalonier that such a feat is not only possible but also fundable.'

I took a deep breath as I walked into Soderini's office and shut the door. Biagio told me once that I had a reputation for getting things done. This was the test. He studied the maps which showed the channels diverting the Arno into the Stagno di Livorno, a great lake before the water reached the sea. An army of labourers not mercenaries was an idea that appealed to both of us. By autumn Pisa would be ours.

Throughout August I pushed every source to provide the huge sum needed to make it work. Every second day I was at the site of the great wooden barrier that now grew across the Arno. Or the wide diversion channels that stretched into the distance. But my enemies were not quiet. Salviati nursed his religion effectively to persuade many like-minded leaders of the Florentine families.

'This goes against God. Once He freed the Israelites by parting the Red Sea. Who are we to dam the flood, to interfere with God's plan?'

'Sorry, Ostinato, the Signoria has decreed that the work can be done more cheaply.'

'More with less rarely works, Machia.' He showed me other plans, this time of a great canal that would link Prato, Pistoia, Pisa and Florence and create a rich corridor of industry. 'If we diverted the course of the Arno from top to bottom we would have treasure in every plot of land.'

But now I saw less of Ostinato. His father, Piero, had died and as the eldest he spent much time over the inheritance of his much younger siblings. The squabbling and rivalry were bitter.

'Are your half-brothers satisfied with their inheritance yet?'

'The lawyers have done well out of their greed. But, yes, I think that it is at an end.'

Ostinato did his best to be fair, with little benefit to himself when the finish came.

In September the winter storms came early. Without enough timber shoring sections of the channel sides collapsed and had to be reworked. Labour on the barrier ground to a halt for lack of men. Bad weather slowed every aspect of the project. The men of Pisa attacked daily and added to the misery.

In October the project was cancelled. Our reputations were sullied. Ostinato travelled to Milan. I was called to our domains outside Florence. Mercenary thugs financed by Venice ravaged the countryside.

Again I dealt with our paid band, which first defeated the marauders and were then no match for the men of Pisa defending their own homes. But Bernardo you told me many times that out of a negative can come a positive. As Secretary to the Ten of War and with the help of Soderini I can at last create a Florentine militia.

It's New Year's Day, 1506. I recruited our first volunteers from villages around Florence. My mind is clear about all aspects of their formation. They will train between ten and sixteen times a year. The armies of France, Spain and Rome fill me with ideas, having studied them for so long. The tactics of Venice are expert and relevant to what can be achieved by Florence. But despite my enthusiasm I am wise enough to realise that I cannot lead or train these men. All the reading of Livy and the ancients has not made me into a soldier. And for that reason I have chosen one fit for the task: Don Michelotto, the Duke's "Strangler".

'Was that a wise choice, Machia?' I could see Ostinato shudder again at the mere mention of his name in a letter.

'Mercy and question are not in a true soldier's vocabulary. We both witnessed his skill and unwavering loyalty to the Duke. If anyone can turn our men into a fighting force, he can. Or so I have convinced Soderini and he in turn has persuaded the Signoria. And so, Ostinato, on the 15th February, a carnival day, 400 of our troops mustered in the Piazza Della Signoria. They were resplendent in their livery of my design: white doublet, red and white stockings and iron breastplate with the Marzocco, the Florentine lion, as their emblem. Surely there was no finer sight. I am sure that Fortuna will favour them in the defence of our great city.'

'August 1507. Ostinato I am again travelling in the entourage of Pope Julius II, our warrior Pontiff. The fear of God is a powerful weapon that Julius uses well. But we know that theocracy is a dangerous form of government. Personal belief based on the simple teaching of Jesus is a powerful guide for many. But once spirituality becomes part of the state the rich and powerful distort it for their purposes. My masters still do not understand the danger Julius presents to Florence. But I hope the militia will be the card that wins the game.'

'Machia, at the risk of sounding like Biagio and the others, your lifestyle is now infamous throughout Italy. Salviati recruits your enemies by the legion, largely with your help. Be more careful, my friend.'

I have no wish to chide Ostinato about the lovers he brings with him. Giacomo Salai, the beautiful peasant boy you bought at market, must be 26 now. Yes it would be good if I could follow his lead. My lifestyle is too conspicuous.

'My life revolves around Pisa yet again. It is now a decade of effort by Florence to take the city. But this year, 1509, is different, because of my militia. I feel that the water of Fortuna flows with me and this enterprise. After raising funds for months we now have a thousand men besieging the city. Our forces clash repeatedly with detachments of Pisan army. The siege has held firm for all this first half of the year. My enemies see that I singlehandedly guide and raise the morale of the men. Salviati himself clearly has not the same respect as I have amongst the men. Ostinato, I wish your bloodless solution to the siege had succeeded. But this is the next best method. By the way, thank you again for your herbal supplies. This dyspepsia I am cursed with is much relieved with their use.'

'June, 1509. It is done, Ostinato. Due to my negotiations on behalf of the Signoria the city fathers of Pisa have surrendered the city to the Republic. There has been no further bloodshed or butchery, as we both have wished. If only all war could end like this? Fortuna overflows.'

'Machia, my friend; watch yourself. When everything goes right then you have a problem. I agree that Fortuna has favoured you of late, and particularly in this venture. The waters have raised themselves from a steady trickle to a good flowing river. But there is also hubris. Do not tempt the gods, those of the ancients, or those of now. Be careful, my friend, and find some humility to hide your success. Remember Fortuna flows both ways.'

§

What was he looking for? As always it was clarity of mind, a de-cluttering of his brain like an aerial meditation. But then it was the unique overview of the land, something impossible to match even from the citadel of Città Sopra. Specifics? Something was happening in the valley that didn't feel right. But "feelings" were Ros' domain.

His eyes again took in the defences of this rugged land. Then the ancient routes through it became clear, north south between Rome and Florence, east west between the sea and across the Apennines. Ros would like this: her beloved Florence and Tuscany so close that he could smell it. But that was only part of his purpose. He practiced his route, started again and held the bar steady at its centre before gingerly lifting the camera to his eye. Squinting through the lens didn't feel good. He would have to judge and do as he had been instructed: one hand to point and click. There were the different trenches of the site. He took twelve pictures in all. That should keep Peter happy. Now came a specific.

Philip turned north and followed the river flow towards where it would eventually join the upper reaches of the Tiber. There, the signs were clear from this vantage point. Great scars were cut into the lowest slopes of Città Sopra. Two photographs; he flew lower, two more of machinery and the destruction they had caused. He saw the diesel smoke and could smell it too. He swooped as low as he dared, quickly clicked some more, let the camera swing and grabbed the bar with both hands again. He gained height and time to think. A reconnoitre came next. He saw people walking through the macchia where it was more open. They were clearly working to a plan, some sort of mapping operation. More photographs. By 3.30 it was time to think of landing. He used up the film, including the extra shot just in case it developed, of the nearest and most scenic of the mountain-top villages.

The air had changed a bit, more of its strength showed, but the direction on the slope was the same. He circled to feel the up drafts and the down drafts. Yes, he was comfortable. Slowly he turned to lose height, down until he felt the influence of the pinnacle and the valley below. Steady, steady, always into the wind, his feet touched in a run, no stumble, he felt the weight return, three steps more and he was dropping the sails to prevent disaster.

'Nice one, Philip.' Ros stood with Gabriel and Mike. They had watched Philip's perambulations through the air and were curious. Ros was not silly enough to refuse a helping hand with getting 30 kg of kite back down the hill. She walked over and unclipped the camera from his neck.

'How did you go?'

'Good. I took the twenty five. But they are definitely point and shoot. I couldn't look through the lens.'

'Oh well. I'll tell you when we develop them.'

"We" presumably meant Nico. Good. She had brains and probably knowledge that they needed. Thinking of which; he looked at Gabriel. He had said nothing but his eyes had taken in the camera, and definitely what Philip could see from the air. Should he simply ask and find out? Gabriel would decide the rest.

'Mike, how many Etruscan cemeteries are in the valley?'

'Seven were recorded on a field survey completed in the 60s.'

'Gabriel, do you know this land well?'

'Of course, my father and grandfather before me; we have all walked this country.'

'Would you walk it with us?' Philip knew that this was the 64 dollar question.

Gabriel was silent. Ros watched him. It was too soon to ask him that.

'Maybe Gabriel needs some time to get to know us?'

Gabriel smiled.

'Yes,' Philip said. 'I was rude, Gabriel. I am sorry to put you in a spot.'

Gabriel nodded and smiled again. But Ros saw more in his eyes.

'How did you ever learn to fly that thing?' Mike asked in between breaths. 'How do you get the lift to take off?' 'How do you turn it?' He was full of questions all the way down. Philip could see that Gabriel took it all in. His English was impressive. It was just a hunch but it might be worth it.

'Gabriel, have you ever flown?'

'Yes, in war time, in a plane.'

Philip, you are pushing your luck again. Slow up, she thought.

'Would you like a flight in this some time? It takes two.'

He waited. Gabriel was a thinker, a careful man.

'Ros has flown with me. She liked it.'

'When I wasn't petrified!'

There was another Gabriel crinkling of eyes and mouth. 'Maybe, some time. Thank you for the offer.'

Mike drove the Landrover back. Gabriel sat in the front seat, with Ros and Philip in the back. At the door of Peter's workroom Gabriel left.

'Arrivederci a tutti.'

Inside the men stood back as Nico laid out the sarcophagus photos like a deck of cards.

'They are excellent, ladies. Well done.' Peter couldn't hide his pleasure.

Ros brought out the torque and bracelet. With gloved hands she placed them on the work table. Peter pored over the details of decoration. "Late Orientalizing period", "550 to 575 possibly" "links to Tarquinia"; Peter chatted away to himself. She turned them over whenever Peter requested.

Peter looked at his watch. 'I need to make some phone calls. Be sure to lock up, please.'

'Do you need me, Ros?' said Nico.

'Thanks, but Philip can help me with these.' She held up the plastic cassette from the Instamatic.

'Time I went too.' Mike walked down the road towards the camp.

For the next hour Ros developed the colour film and Philip hung the wet prints on the clothes line set up in the dark room. The red bulb gave an eery glow to the solution trays.

'Not bad, Philip; Peter should be happy. You could make a Tuscan calendar out of some of these. But what's happening here? It looks like some sort of construction site.'

'Destruction I think; very organised too. There was a name on the excavator but I couldn't get low enough to read it.'

He's pacing again, Ros thought. 'Come on; out with it.'

'I need to check it out on foot, Ros.'

'You mean we, don't you?

'It's probably dangerous.'

'My middle name.'

'Seriously, Peter doesn't need both of us risking our necks.'

'We do this together, Philip, start to finish. Tomorrow?'

'First thing.'

It was still daylight when they closed the safe and locked up. They were late for the meal but Martina looked after them.

'Sei molto gentile, Martina. Grazie.'

That night they cuddled close. It took ages for Ros to slide into sleep. Philip, after his mind buzzed with all the things that could go wrong, eventually joined her.

'It's time, Ros.'

Dawn was half an hour away. Too early for a coffee, she thought. He had his small rucksack with water and the odd stuff he carried. She'd compared it once to a woman's handbag. A brief freshen up and they were on their way upstream. The macchia closed in but there was just enough light to follow faint tracks; probably made by animals that the villagers let loose for acorns or whatever, she thought. When the paths became more definite, Philip climbed out of the water course and tighter into the eroded yellow tufa cliffs. After an hour she was perspiring. It was going to be a hot day. But they'd found what he was looking for.

He held up a finger for quiet. Of course, she thought, I'm not daft as you would say. She took out the Instamatic. That was deliberate. The Pentax was too costly to risk on a venture like this. The photos were sufficient for proof. She snapped at all the things that Philip pointed at, and a few extra of her own. There were the marker pegs in amongst the trees. Lower down were the tracks through the scrub, the machinery half hidden by tarpaulins and cut shrubbery, and the great holes in the hillside. Some still had remnants of the paintwork and smashed pottery. By the second roll of film she was angry.

'What evil so-and-sos could do this?' she whispered to Philip.

She turned her camera towards the excavator. Diesel still pervaded the air. They must have been at work last night, she thought. Yes, I've got it: a name for the thieving cretin.

'Tu chi se?' a solidly built man with a boxer's face shouted at him.

'Cosa stai facendo qui?' an older man yelled at her.

We're separated, Philip thought. The foreman towered over Ros. The worker was the rest of the barrier he'd have to cut through.

Two more came from behind before Philip could turn. They grabbed his arms. Instinctively he dropped low and belted them hard in the groin and gut. Three more rushed in from around a bend in the hill. They stood in front of him, between him and Ros. Hard men, construction workers, he thought. They paused while the other two got up unsteadily.

'Ah.'

The older man twisted her arm up behind her back. She kicked back hard into his shins. He hardly acknowledged the accurate pain.

'Aaah.'

The hold was brutal. It was close to dislocating her shoulder or snapping bone. Philip saw her bend forward in serious pain. Sweat dripped from her face and chin. Thoughts thrashed around inside his head. In open fight he knew he had sufficient. But his weakness was Ros. He couldn't get to her quickly enough to avoid more hurt. And he couldn't let the next bit happen.

'Mi scusi, signori. iamo persi.' Philip held up his hands and smiled weakly. He was not confident. A moment of composure, knuckles cracked, and a deep breath: ready for what came next.

'Perso? Con una macchina fotografica?' The leader laughed.

Lost with a camera? Yes, it was a bit weak, Philip thought. Two punches to the gut, from left and right, doubled him up. A fair swap for what I did, I suppose. But then he forward rolled out of it and crashed upwards with upper cuts to the chins left and right. With the onward momentum he drove his right knee into the belly at the centre. He was through the obstacles, except for one. In the fragment of time before he tackled him

Philip saw the gleam of steel. Whiskery grandad had a hunting knife across her throat. The man tilted his head to one side. Philip shoved the crouched obstacle to one side and faced the leader. A tiny sliver of blood dribbled down the blade. There wasn't the slightest doubt that he would cut her throat like one of his sheep.

'Basta! Basta!' Philip shouted and put his arms loosely by his sides. He looked directly into the man's eyes. The others laid into him. Punches to the head he blocked with his forearms. Kicks and blows to the groin and shins he obstructed with a raised thigh. A few he let through, alternately going loose and turning, or tightening his abdomen so that their knuckles hurt. He did not return the blows. Always his eyes returned to his real opponent. His message was personal: if you kill her then I will kill you.

'Tutti lasciano!'

The men obeyed.

'Porta via il coltello,' Philip said quietly. Fear helped his language ability.

'Ok.' The man sheathed the knife in his belt. The smile grew wider. He twisted Ros' hand just a little, enough for Philip to see more of the pain Ros was trying to hide. Then he let her go. When she made a step towards Philip the man blocked her with his arm. Philip's eyes were relentless.

'Io decido,' the leader said.

Yes, you can have that one, Philip thought, as long as it is the right decision.

As sunlight entered the narrow valley, Ros and Philip sat with their backs to the tufa cliff. Ropes bound their hands and feet. "Il Duce" was still deciding what to do with them. Philip guessed some of his thoughts. No doubt people were murdered in Italy but it was not done lightly and particularly to staff from the foreign dig. But they had seen too much. What he guessed was a lucrative operation was in danger. What would he do in the man's situation? He leant into Ros, gently since it was her sore arm. She felt what he was saying and laid her head on his shoulder. All they could do was wait.

§

'Dear Ostinato, I am at my usual station, at a desk in a tavern, a wench and a tazza of wine close by, a long way from home. Biagio has warned me not to return too quickly. It seems that Salviati and crew have dropped my name into the authorities again. They could not make much of "libertine" or "atheist" in the past, as these are not hanging offences in this liberal Republic. But now they accuse me of being the son of a tax debtor and therefore not fit for office. How naïve! Do they not realise that I paid off Bernardo's debts a long time ago? On his advice since he felt this law all his life and did not wish it to limit my potential.

Pope Julius rages against all those he wishes to conquer, and schemes with those he needs to make it happen. Meanwhile work goes on at the home of St Peter: such wonderful work in the Sistine Chapel and the Papal apartments. You must feel keenly the contradiction in the man, since he favoured others over you. All paid for with indulgences and the widow's mite.'

'October, 1511. Agostino, your Pope has succeeded beyond my greatest fears. His Holy League of Italian states, Maximilian, the Holy Roman Emperor, Spain and even Henry VIII of England is a more powerful force than Italy has seen for a long time. Some would claim God had something to do with it but I am not one of them. My money is on the French forces of Gaston de Foix, an enigmatic leader who has the trust of his men.'

'April , 1512. Biagio, this letter contains good and bad news. The good is that the French have won a surprising victory over the Spanish and Papal forces at Ravenna. That should set back Julius and his cronies for a long time. But the bad concerns me, in my gut. Gaston de Foix was killed. Can they continue their success without him?'

'May, 1512. Ostinato, I feel the river of Fortuna flowing rapidly away. How could circumstances change in just a few weeks? With Swiss help the League has expelled the French from Italian soil. Without them Florence is vulnerable to the schemes of this vengeful Pope. I have good word from his council at Mantua that he has his eyes on our city again. Soderini does not know it yet but soon will; the Medici brothers were close by. I know the schemes of men do not interest you greatly, Ostinato but all this does not bode well.'

'28th August, 1512. Vettori, the 2000 militia we sent to defend Prato against Cordona and the Spanish forces have performed brilliantly well. Against superior numbers they held and have repulsed the enemy. I beg you now to persuade Soderini to use this good fortune to our advantage. Negotiate! Negotiate! Cordona's troops are weak with hunger. He will listen. I will be there within the day to help you.'

'30 August, 1512. Ostinato, such a tragedy brought on by stupidity and pride! Soderini would not hear reason, would not listen at all. There would be no negotiation. For the Spanish there was only one avenue of hope; attack. Starving, outnumbering our militia five to one, they took Prato and slaughtered everyone they could find, 4000 souls by my reckoning. What a pointless waste of life, and the loss of my beautiful militia. I created them and Soderini destroyed them. Innocence lost and stupidity won.'

'But there is more, my friend. Cordona has given us terms: Soderini must step down or he will sack Florence. Vettori and I have written his resignation. Soderini has been spirited out of the city to Siena under armed guard. I must look to my back. '

'Bernardo, you can see that these are difficult times for our family. The Medici rule Florence through their puppet Ridolfi. So much of my work has been dismantled. Why, when I have known the family all of my life? Giuliano and I created poetry together as youngsters. His brother, Cardinal Giovanni, I knew less well but my work is known to him and surely its quality speaks for itself. Piero, thank goodness, left this earth ten years ago. When I write to share my advice I am ignored. In the Palazzo Vecchio I go to my office each day but it seems that I do not exist.'

Diary.

7th November, 1512. I am dismissed. The Medici feel that I betrayed them by working for Soderini.

10th November. I am bound to stay within Florentine territory, with a bond of 1000 gold florins. When have I ever had such a sum of money?

17th November. I am banned from entering the Palazzo Vecchio. They must surely fear my ability to influence others.

24th November. I am accused of embezzling money while I held the role of First Secretary of the Second Chancery. What irony! I am allowed to enter my old place of work to answer questions.

December. Interminable questions. Each day I am grilled by a panel led by that Medici stooge, Niccolò Michelozzi. Each evening I return home to mull over my answers and predict their next line of attack. This is the fourth week.

December. They have found nothing. In fact they paid me a small sum that was owing to me; a victory of sorts.

New Year's Day, 1513. Marietta and the family are with me at Sant' Andrea. As the Medici increase their control there is nothing in Florence for me. Giuliano rules Florence, Giovanni schemes at the highest level in Rome.

January. Biagio visited today. There is another conspiracy against the Medici. Pietro Biscoli, Agostino Capponi, Niccolò Valori and Giovanni Folchi are names that I vaguely recollect. So I asked Biagio why he had risked his neck to tell me. Boscoli mislaid a list of possible supporters if their coup had succeeded. My name was on it.

8th February. All those on the list have been rounded up. This morning I said goodbye to Marietta and the children. It is evening. Welcome to the Bargello. "The path to Paradise begins in Hell." Dante always has an appropriate word or two.

There is no air and it's freezing cold. The damp of the river seeps through the walls. I must remember everything for when I leave here. Yes, Bernardo, I must believe that. Otherwise I am lost. At least I have the rats for company. It's a pity they would not crowd around me to ward off this bitter chill. Pity, yes, I feel self-pity, Bernardo. How are the mighty fallen. My stomach longs for tavern food, a good tazza of wine, a wench rather than an avalanche of rodents to keep away the icy chill.

How can I prepare? My name is on a list but what am I supposed to have done? Fear, anger, ranting against the Medici or my ill fortune: what good does that do? I shut my eyes and join the ancients. They faced such trials with stoicism. I must try to do the same.

But I am in a dark wood stalked by wild beasts. Fear overwhelms me until a familiar mind takes my hand. Virgil, divine face of reason, leads me.

At first light men came, to lead me "into the eternal darkness, into the fire and ice." They tied my arms behind my back and hauled on chains to lift my body to the ceiling. I want to scream but what would that do? Worse it is to know what comes next. No questions yet, so I suppose they choose to loosen up my tongue with pain. The din of iron cranking on iron stops. I swing leisurely looking down from a great height. They wait for their master's word. My torso rotates until he steps out of the shadows. It is Ceccone; greyer, with a stout girth, the reward for his particular line of work. I shut my eyes. I am buried in grotesque images of Savonarola and his two Dominican friars burning in the Piazza Della Signoria. No. My own pain is enough. My own path through it is the way.

These seconds twirling slowly like a carnival marionette are vital. I have no power over Ceccone or his Medici masters or Boscoli and the rest. I am in the lap of the gods. But I have power over myself. Weakness or strength, cowering or dignified, it is my choice how I face the greatest test of my life. I see Bernardo with a quiet confidence in his eyes. Now it is up to me to try to manoeuvre Fortuna.

The chain screeched. I feel weightlessness and then pain, so terrible that I still cannot describe its intensity. Every sinew and nerve in my shoulders, back and neck shout together. My mind hopes for the bliss of unconsciousness but it never comes. I swing gently inches from the stone slabs, all the pain centres still cry in anguish. When will it stop?

'How are you, Machia? Still whoring I hear. Piero would have been proud of you.' His voice holds the confidence of power. The blue milk of his eyes displays dissolution and cruelty in equal measure.

'What would you like to tell me about the Medici, Machia?'

'I have no quarrel with any member of the Medici family. Lorenzo and his sons were good to me in my youth.'

'Then why do you repay them with conspiracy?'

The winch stopped and my body waited in suspension.

'That is not true. '

The chains roar and the pain reaches its crescendo as my body sways just above the floor. I understand why the Signoria chooses such a torture. Each Strappado is the same as the last. Nerves, muscles, sinews feel the exquisite pain. There is no dulling of the senses from first to last.

'You worked for Piero Soderini?'

'Yes.'

'He is the enemy of the Medici.'

My body drops into agony for a third time. At this point Savonarola had said that he would tell his life story if they would only stop.

'I served the Republic. Soderini was my master. There was never any disloyalty to the Medici.'

The metal shouts for a fourth time, louder than my screams. Domenico had taken this many. Whatever his beliefs and misguided loyalty to Savonarola I admire his fortitude.

I drop for a fifth time. I am conscious but not fully of this earth. Questions follow upon question. I hold on to the gentle, proud face of Bernardo. Yes, it is his pride that tells me that I cannot fail.

'Boscoli and the others have revealed everything, Machia. It is pointless to resist.'

'I have done nothing other than serve Florence to the best of my ability.' I can hear the effort in my slow words. But I know now that I have the strength to die.

After the sixth Strappado I see Ceccone standing over me. When I open my eyes he looks into them.

'Tomorrow, Il Machia, we begin again.'

Fitful dreams fill my exhaustion. I roll and turn to find a position that hurts less than the last. This place belongs in Dante's Inferno. Or will I be like Sisyphus pushing the rock up that mountain only to have it roll down again, until Judgement. Rising and falling in pain forever.

Ceccone left me to self pity for days and days. But slowly it distilled into hope and determination. What could I do for my own salvation?

23rd February. Dawn. I woke to chains clanking and laude sung for condemned men. Whispers through the cells told me they were for Boscoli and Capponi. Fools, what pity did they deserve from me, who was only here because of their stupidity? Let them rot in the central well of Hell, waist deep in blood and pus for eternity. Anyway I could do nothing for them, even if I chose. But there was someone who could do something for me, Giuliano di Medici, head of Florence. Would he remember our love of poetry in our youth?

"Giuliano, I have a pair of shackles on my legs

and six drops of the strappado on my back;

my other misfortunes I shall not tell,

since that is the way they treat poets.

These walls are full of lice so big and fat

they seem like butterflies,

and there never was such a stench in Roncesvalles

or in Sardinia amid those groves,

as in this fine dwelling of mine.

With a noise that sounds like Jove

and all Etna were hurling thunderbolts to earth,

one prisoner is chained up and another unbound,

padlocks, keys and bolts rattle together,

and another cries: 'Too high from the ground!'

What worries me most is that, as I slept, near dawn

I began to hear 'We pray for you.'

Now let them go.

I pray if only your mercy may turn towards me

And surpass the fame of your father and your grand-father."

Giuliano made no reply. But Fortuna plays many tricks on mere mortals such as me. Two days before Boscoli and Capponi received their well-deserved fate another died of more consequence; Pope Julius II. After the Cardinals finished their deliberations Pope Leo X was chosen, formerly known as Cardinal Giovanni di Medici, brother to Giuliano. Florence celebrated beyond any occasion before. The Medici ruled Florence and Rome. And in their gratitude prisoners were freed. On the 12th March I walked out of the Bargello a free man.

§

Nico parked her little red Vespa close to the wall. She was early. Peter should have put a guard on the place, maybe even slept there himself overnight. Through the windows everything looked tidy. Peter arrived as she turned the key in the door.

'Buongiorno Peter.'

'Buongiorno Nico.'

Both went straight to the safe. The door was slightly ajar. There was nothing inside. Peter opened drawers under the table to retrieve the photographic evidence. Nico went into the darkroom. The pegs still hung on the clothesline but the prints were gone. They came back to the table empty-handed.

'It's the same pattern as before. They took just the items and the proof of their existence.' With his head in his right hand he shut his eyes and stayed silent.

'Philip and Ros developed film from his flight. The prints are missing.' Nico looked at him. 'Why did the thieves take those photographs?' She broke the quiet. 'Peter, please drive to the site. We need to talk to them.'

The tent was undisturbed. It felt like prying but they did it anyway; Peter going through his bag, Nico hers. Ros's Pentax was still there, clothes and toiletries, and a negative roll inside its metal case. She put it in her pocket. She joined Peter who was with Mike and Gabriel beside the sarcophagus.

'Gabriel says that Philip asked him to walk the land with him. So that's what we should do.' As director he had spoken.

'Peter, this is not for you to do,' said Nico. She looked at Gabriel who nodded.

Peter looked at her.

'If they found something, trouble, then you cannot be connected.'

'But.'

'Antonio, Peter. Think about it.' She spoke rapidly in whispers to Gabriel. 'Please leave it to us, Peter. Report the theft but run the excavation as before.'

Ros was dozing when the man returned.

'He's decided, Ros. Be ready to move.'

Men, who smelled of stale clothes and garlic, blind-folded them and marched them out of the riverbed and up a track. The doors of a van closed behind them. For the next hour they were bounced around the bare metal floor. He felt minor roads, then the motor way, and then slow city crawl until they stopped at the back of what his nose told him was a bakery. The sun was hot but he heard no bustle of people; siesta probably. There was dirt and crumbled rock underfoot. Rough hands pushed his head low and threw him forward onto more powdery dust and rubble. Ros landed on top of him. There was a noise like stone grinding on stone. What little light that came around the blindfold disappeared. They sat up and listened. Soon there was nothing.

'Put your head behind my back, Ros,' he whispered.

She leant into his shoulder and then down and down his side until her hair dragged in the dust. She coughed.

'Thanks. Stay still.'

She felt his fingers touch her nose, then forehead, and then the knot at the back of her head. It had been tightened by men's hands.

'Ow.'

'Sorry. I think I have it.' He held back one strand of the material and pinched and pulled the other, again and again. Slowly it opened up enough to push it up and forward.

'What can you see?'

'Nothing; it's pitch black in here. Turn around. It's your turn.'

By the time she lifted his blindfold her own eyes had adapted. There was a halo of light around what looked like a huge round boulder blocking the entrance. It didn't take a genius to work out that it was guarded on the outside.

When she turned back to back to work on his hand ropes it was easier to concentrate if she closed her eyes. Thank goodness for farm girl's hands. But it still seemed to take an age.

Philip looked around. They were in a cave or a tunnel. Underground at least. Somehow it was appropriate, quite a creative solution to the problem they'd presented. Nosy archaeologists disappear in an underground labyrinth; nothing to connect "Il Duce" to their demise.

'Right; we're free,' he said.

'Sort of; were you speaking metaphorically?'

'Comparatively, really: no bonds and no incapacitating injuries. That's not a bad start.'

'I don't wish to burst your optimistic bubble, Philip, but we are stuck in a cave. The way out is not possible, the way in is a black hole, and we have no light or anything else to help us.'

'All true but we have our wits. So let's use them.'

She knew he was right of course. 'Ok.' What would her Dad say about their chances? "Fair, and if we're lucky middling to good". Negativity was a dangerous luxury here.

'How's your neck?' He had seen her rubbing along what he guessed was the knife imprint.

'Good. I'll live. What about you? Those men were pretty keen to pay you back.'

'A few bruises but I'm ok. So, there's nothing to stop us. Did they leave anything in your pockets?'

'No.'

'Same here. Let's think. What do we know? I think we are in a town or village north of Alta Cresta.'

'Why?'

'We travelled for about an hour: country roads, then motorway, then inner-town alleyways. We'd be in Rome if we went south, which we would have recognised. West is the sea; east are the mountains, therefore north.'

'These fellows rob Etruscan tombs for a living. I'd guess that we are in a necropolis.'

Philip picked up some dirt at his side and rubbed it together. 'It's tufa similar to Alta Cresta. So I would agree.'

They sat for a while, still adjusting their eyes. She pushed away the fear of being entombed, which was presumably the intention. He was thinking of how to get out the way they'd come in. Persuasion presented an awfully slim chance. They had to use the time before thirst or starvation or simply despair ended their story.

'Ros, I am not sure what they can hear,' he whispered. 'I want to play a hunch. Can you talk to me, tell me a story, so I can find my way back?'

'Ok. Once upon a time, there lived a little girl called Goldilocks.'

'Slowly, please.' He leaned forward into all fours and crawled inwards, away from the guards. Every couple of slides he felt for whatever was there.

'Ow.' He cracked his head. The tunnel was narrow, rough-cut, and his body soon blocked all light.

'Damn.' His right knee and elbow struck a rock fall simultaneously.

'Who's been eating my porridge,' Ros said, 'and how about coming back and giving me a go?'

He returned, sat and rubbed sore bits. 'What's your secret?'

'On the farm there wasn't a street light for miles. As a kid if we lost power I got used to getting around with my eyes closed.'

She shut her eyes, partly to avoid poking them with something in the inky blackness, but mostly to finer tune her other senses to what was around. There was more ahead, not just a rock wall. How, she could feel it? Then there was a faint musty, sweet smell that was familiar.

'Who's been sitting in my chair?'

She delicately slid over the rock fall. But the tunnel kept going, and there was a turn or an alcove, she felt something hollow ahead. Her right hand slid over rock and into space. She traced its edges, about the size of the space she was in. There was only tufa wall at her left side. She swung her head into the space, like Dumbo the elephant she thought. Her knees slid into a tumble, not rock but things. She sat on her haunches, just, as her hair brushed the ceiling, and felt through the stash of things.

'Who's been sleeping in my bed?' she said. 'You might want to see this.'

Nobody but me I hope was the thought in his mind. '"See" You're hopeful.'

'Keep coming; slowly.'

He bumped into her side.

'What was your hunch?'

'I thought that the tomb robbers might have left some things?'

Ros flicked the flint. A flame lit up the BIC lighter in her hand, and a kerosene lantern on the floor. She pushed a lever to raise the glass, turned a screw thread to raise the wick and tilted the lighter underneath the glass until the flame caught. Then she turned off the lighter and wound down the wick to give just enough light.

'You've done that before.'

'Yep. Was this what you expected?'

In front of them were small pick-axes, spillones-the crow bars the robbers used to break into the vaults, jute bags for the loot, rope and a lot more.

'A veritable treasure trove, don't you think?' She laughed when he grimaced at the joke.

'Yes, it's more than I hoped for.' He leaned over and kissed her. 'Thanks.'

They loaded up a sack each, tied them on like rucksacks, with extra lanterns hung off the back. They drank their fill from the terracotta amphora of water and filled canteens to the brim. Food would have been nice but neither was complaining. Ros stood up in a crouch and led the way. She could not help thinking that people in the past were a good deal smaller than she was. Stooping in still air, tinged with that sweet smell, she progressed metre by metre into the cavern. Powdered dust retained her footprints. Her movement stirred up a cloud of it which rose above her ankles. She stopped, squatted on her haunches and looked ahead. There were dark spaces either side. Her back and neck were straight for the spell, before she moved forward again. The farther she progressed the hotter it became. Beads of sweat formed on her forehead and dripped off her nose.

Five metres on the first alcove revealed its contents: in a space a metre and a half long and a quarter metre high, precisely the size required, was a wrapped corpse. Wrappings which once had been dyed, expensive material were colourless rags from which long bones and the dome of a skull protruded. Below the space her lantern revealed green algae dribbling down to the floor. With minimal light there was phosphorescence like primeval ooze. Almost toe to head was the next, again with a green glow. The sweet smell of death was powerful. Once the morticians had deposited the carcass, more like jammed it into the space; where else would body fluids go than into the rock. Corpse after corpse lined the tunnel on both sides, often two high, or three smaller cavities presumably for deceased children. The profession of undertaker, cutting these final resting places and then filling them with those recently stricken by some sickness, was not a healthy occupation.

'Nothing has been touched. Our friends must have been disappointed by Christian burials with no trinkets,' said Philip. Ros stopped to stretch and he took over the lead.

When the tunnel turned right and produced another trove of bodies he drew a forward arrow with his boot. Too many people had become lost in catacombs that went for miles and through multiple levels. But what choice did they have other than go on. Soon he added numbers to his markings. Being methodical might dictate their survival.

He still had his watch. They had been shoved into the van mid-afternoon. It was eight 'o'clock in the evening. They had spent more than half an hour among their decaying companions. The access tunnels were cut in parallel lines, like a multi-pronged fork. Minimal effort to store the maximum number of clients, he thought. But ahead there was a space on his left. As he approached it was clear that this was by a different hand. It was definitely cut rather than a natural collapse. Instead of the roughly cylindrical shape they were in this was a rectangle, roughly 80 cms on the short side and 120 cms on the long. It was vertical and had grazed one wall of the catacomb so that it formed a window into this space. He held the lantern through and leant in.

'Whoa, that's impressive!'

'Careful, Philip. What is it?'

'It's a vertical shaft.' Looking up and looking down were the same; the light disappeared into the blackness. But close at hand were small incisions in the long sides of the hole.

'Well, there is good and bad news, Ros. Which would you like first?'

'The bad I suppose.'

'This is a very deep, narrow hypogea, a well cut by the Etruscans in what was probably a fortress city. Our best bet is to climb it.'

'The good news?'

'The builders cut footholds so they could get back up.'

Philip took out the pick axe and widened the hole. Then he reassessed their packs. Claustrophobia was one thing; impeding progress or even getting stuck were real possibilities. One lamp on a rope around his neck, a spare and water in each pack now slung on the chest and he went in first. He stretched for and placed his right foot in a groove, then his left in the opposite. Basically by feel he stepped down two rungs and waited.

'Take your time, Ros. Get your head right before you come through. You're the leader.'

'Why?'

'Just in case.'

'In case of what; me falling and taking us both out?'

'Just in case.'

'Always the gentleman!'

She sucked in what air there was in this mausoleum. Settle your mind, she told herself. This time it was not to face a vast sky but a bottomless pit. At least they were going up. Surely a well had to have a top where a man with a bucket once stood. Ok, let's do it. She leant through the space, saw clearly where the notches were for her feet because of Philip's light and fitted her sandshoes in left and right. That same lantern, since they were saving hers, was enough to illuminate a metre or so above her. To start with she manoeuvred her shadow to see. Soon she felt the pattern and began the automated climb up: left foot then right foot, straighten up. These fellows knew what they were doing. She felt the rhythm and kept it slow. Those ascents to La Macchia were paying off. Steadily up and up, and a rest every ten steps.

Philip was content with the pace. Whenever he looked up there was a gorgeous rump looking down at him in various poses. He wouldn't be a man if he didn't notice. But this was not the time to admire her body as he had in the Edinburgh flat and he pushed away the thought. She was just conserving energy before moving on.

They had been going up for what seemed an age but was probably an hour. Her leg muscles were starting to cramp in the repeated positions. Sweat streamed down her back and dripped on Philip, whose own contributions presumably fell into the cavernous hole below. Her rests were extending. The ten steps up between were more mind than what the body offered.

'Ah.' Her right foot missed. Her shoulder and head slammed into the stone. She steadied herself with her forearm and planted her toe in firmly. 'That was stupid. Sorry Philip.'

'No need to apologize. Are you all right?'

'I'm tough; nothing that a Band-Aid wouldn't cover up.'

'Just rest for a bit; shut your eyes maybe and put yourself somewhere else.'

Yes, she could do that. In fact she was getting to be quite an expert. It was ten minutes before she opened her eyes. She could do this. Her steps were slow and deliberate. She had no wish to test whether Philip could cope with her weight on top of his. Back to ten steps and a pause, like a machine.

'Just stop on the next one, Ros. There's something just above you on your left hand side.'

She saw it. Carefully she rose above the entrance, gripped anything protruding with her hands and slid inside on her belly. It was another horizontal tunnel like the catacombs, but different.

'That was a lucky break. Let me look at you?' He spread her hair away from the temples. There was a stone graze reaching down past her right ear to the top of her cheek. He dabbed with the inside of his cuff and some water. Antiseptic would have been good, particularly after all those putrefying stiffs, but it would have to wait. When she was ready they got up and he went first, marking in the dust as he went.

'This is not for burial or for water, Ros.' At times the tunnel was barely big enough to squeeze through. Then it would expand to something a horse and cart could negotiate. He shone the light on the walls. There was the tufa but then there were traces of something else, glistening like glass with a yellow tinge and much harder.

'Melissa explained the geology of Alta Cresta. What was the name of the hardest rock?'

'Pozzolana.'

'Yes, that was it.'

'It was mixed 2 to I with lime and then water added to make particularly strong Roman cement. The ancient port of Cosa has piers of it under seawater in the harbour. It's still strong after more than two thousand years.' She smiled and waited. His face said; how did you know that?

He nodded. 'You're not just a pretty face are you?' He walked on a bit and took the lamp to more wall. 'Well, this is a mine. Like most ancient miners they just followed the seam.'

To prove the point the walls expanded into an enormous dome supported by massive pillars of tufa rock. At his feet the black hole returned but was much larger. They stood together looking down at a cavern thirty metres across, round and regular in its construction. But they could see the bottom approximately fifteen metres down. It was covered in smashed pottery, rubble and mud. As he walked around part of its edge he could see more of the foot-holds they had climbed earlier.

'The archaeology says that's a later cistern, maybe built by someone in the Middle Ages. Practical men kept these to maintain access.'

'So the Pozzolana miners were later again.'

'Yes.'

'But how did the builders fill the cistern with water?'

'Springs? Or more importantly for us, channels to catch rainwater and divert it in here?'

'What comes in must go out!'

Philip's lantern flickered and then died. He sat down. He found the flint and the next lantern in his sack and lit it. Then they drank the last of the second canteen. He rearranged the last water and lantern into his bag. His watch said 10 in the morning.

'Onwards and upwards,' she said. She led into another passageway and he followed, dragging his toe as a marker at each crossroads. Better than breadcrumbs, she thought; if they had had any. In a short time she found one of his marks, so they chose the other tunnel. This was a maze. One of Philip's words, "higgledy-piggledy" came to her mind. Again and again they came to a familiar crossing of tunnels. Time slipped, hours and hours, and Philip had stopped looking at his watch. But by a process of elimination they were going to find the way out.

'Ros, we should rest for a bit.'

'What time is it?'

'4am.'

'The witching hour. Ok, just a short one.'

He sat with his back to the wall in quite a wide culvert, more like a grotto really, with two side tunnels: the one they came out of and the one they would enter soon.

'Do I smell as bad as you, Philip?'

'I don't think I will answer that one.'

She picked up the lantern. 'Call of nature. Back soon.'

'Don't go far.

'I won't, in case the bogey men get me.'

At least she still had her sense of humour. When she returned he did the same.

'Is this where we tell each other ghost stories?' she said. They were side by side, feet stretched out across rubble and dust.

'I can think of something better.' He told her about Rider Haggard's version of King Solomon's Mines. It seemed appropriate. The second lantern spluttered into the darkness. He finished his story and they dozed. He felt her hand grip harder intermittently as she dreamed. She was scared but wasn't going to tell him that.

Ros woke first. She lit the final lantern and they drank half of the last canteen. It was time to continue their trek. Maybe Philip's special mate, "Murphy", instead of putting obstacles in front of them might just throw them a bone.

A familiar shape, a rectangular space 80cm by 120cm, appeared ahead. The darkness at their feet was matched by the blackness above. Luckily the miners had cut around it. She flattened her back against the side and slid around. Twenty metres further on a shaft cut in from her right. It was regular. Eureka, it had a gentle incline. She felt new energy. Philip was right behind her. Soon her lungs told her something. Not much further on her eyes told her more. She felt like she was in a train coming out of a cutting. Twenty metres on Ros stood on a rock shelf looking out over somewhere Tuscan. She could smell it. It was the macchia, the crumbling tufa stack, and above and below swallows circled. Somehow Tuscany became even more beloved. She and Philip sat on the slightly inclined slab and sucked in fresh air.

He put out the lantern and passed over the canteen. Then he looked around for a way down. Of course this eyrie was high on a sheer cliff. No medieval builder would have provided an easy way for an enemy to enter the city above them. To left and right were grooves cut into the hillside: more catchment for water going into the tunnel and into the cistern. There was no way down or up from there. But below them, probably only twenty metres, was the scree slope, around a 45 degree decline, and macchia scrub. He took out the last item from Ros's bag: a long rope. He measured it out and coiled it again on the rock: definitely twenty eight metres. His mind felt light: he had a task and this was possible. Yes, there were two likely trees, misshapen and distorted by their tortuous choice of home. He looped the rope around one of them, tested it and then tied knots at two metre intervals. Then he paid out its length over the side, down to the nearest patch of green on the tumbled rock. Yes, it slapped into a trunk. He estimated there were two metres to spare.

He read her face. 'Ok Ros. We both know you can do this. When I call take some deep breaths and follow me. Take your time.' He slid over the side and locked his feet on the first knot. Then he gripped with both hands and began the slide down. She was watching as he disappeared from sight.

Breathe, Ros. Get your head in the right place; not here over a hellish drop. Take long breaths in and even longer ones out. Yes, I can do this.

'Ok, Ros, it's your turn. Take it steady.' He sat astride the tree trunk, pulled the rope tight and tied off. Very little wind, he thought. Then he waited. He saw her feet search for the rope and then the knot. Yes, she's got it. Then she concertinad into sight, while her face looked horizontally into the rock. Don't look down, he telepathed. She held there for thirty seconds and then slid down to the next knot. A pause, a little rotation was throwing her. He held off saying anything. She didn't need distractions or instructions.

'Là! Laggiù!'

Just like in the well she was in automatic mode, he thought. Slowly, steadily the space shortened. Say nothing until he had to. When she must be able to feel his presence, even hear him breathing: 'Next step is the tree, Ros.' His voice was calm and almost a whisper. He slid out further and guided her tight into the base protruding from the rock. She gripped both very tightly. Then he untied his end and sent up a flick in the rope. No. He did it again, harder. The line fell out of the sky. He covered her head and his, riding the tree like a bronco. It clipped his right forearm but it was down. Then he looped the same knot and dropped the rope. This time it touched dirt by the second knot.

'Ready?'

'Yes.' She looked down. Not easy but easier she thought. She couldn't fight the elation after the adrenalin burst that had got her there. 'A piece of cake.'

'Come on then, Sherpa Tensing.' He slid his feet down to the rubble and she was right behind him. The rope guided rather than supported. By the time they found the end it was an inert snake that he whip-cracked again and gathered up. After he looped it over his shoulder like a bandoleer he looked up.

'Not Everest, but a pretty good effort, Ros.'

The last fifty metres was a slipping slide from one scrubby tree to another until they entered an orchard of olive trees.

'Hello Ros. Hello Philip.'

Ros looked at the lady who had stepped from the shadows.

'Buon pomeriggio Philip e Rosalind.'

Philip looked at her companion.

'Buon pomeriggio Nico e Gabriel,' Ros said.

'It's good to see you alive.'

Nico was her usual elegant self, in dress and manner, thought Ros. But there's something else besides genuine pleasure to see them. She and Gabriel had gone to some trouble to find them. In fact it was close to a miracle if she thought about it too much.

'If you don't mind I think you will be safer if you come and stay with me.'

'Nico, that's very generous of you,' Philip started to say.

Ros looked at him and then at Nico and Gabriel. 'Philip, this is hospitality, like in Iran.'

'Accettiamo Nico. Grazie,' she said.

The white Fiat 124 saloon was parked in a lane nearby. Gabriel opened the door to the back and Ros and Philip climbed in. Nico started the engine and Gabriel slid into the passenger seat.

Philip leaned forward. 'Gabriel, where are we?'

'Orvieto.'

'Ah,' Philip said. He was ticking boxes that matched inside his head.

'North,' said Ros. She smiled at him.

'What was down there?' Gabriel asked.

'Catacombs, wells, cisterns and pozzolano mining.'

'No photographs?' Nico said to Ros.

'Sorry, that was not quite the priority, Nico.'

On the journey south, down the Autostrada and then into the country lanes, Nico asked questions.

'How did you know that there was another way out?'

'We didn't, but it seemed logical,' he said.

'Why did you not get lost in the dark?'

'Philip guessed that the tomb robbers had left some equipment so we had light,' Ros said. 'Philip left markers on the floor. Whenever we found them again we chose another route.'

'We were lucky,' Philip said.

'You must record your experience,' said Nico.

'Of course,' they said together.

'Someone could also follow our route with Philip's markers,' Ros said.

An hour later Nico knew their story but, other than she and Gabriel had pulled in favours and used an army of children probably with binoculars to wait for their exit, Ros and Philip knew nothing about her. Until they turned up a steep path lined with poplar trees. Ahead were two stone gateposts with wolfhound statues perched on top. The gate was held open by an elderly man. He nodded as she drove through.

Ros said little but observed ornamental, expansive gardens of trees and grass that reminded her of the Villa Borghese. When Nico pulled up on the gravel beside wide steps in front of a portico entrance of Corinthian columns Ros was almost sure she'd come to the Villa Borghese itself.

Nico turned off the engine. 'Gabriel will guide you to your room. Please take your time to freshen up.'

Ros' eyes grew wider as they climbed a circular flight of marble stairs. On the walls were paintings, oh what paintings. She felt like a girl about to giggle with delight. Within inches of her fingertips were Renaissance masters that she could name. And they were not copies, any more than the Gobelin tapestries or the Persian carpets, the silks that Philip so loved.

Inside something like a palace state room their belongings were carefully laid out. By the time they had showered they had both guessed.

Gabriel and Nico waited for them downstairs. His clothes were cleaner but the same as he wore on the dig. His manner was of someone who was a friend rather than a servant. Inside a drawing room, lined with more masters Ros noted, stood Nico in a well cut suit, business but stylish.

'Philip, Rosalind,' Gabriel said in perfect English, 'I would like you to meet Nicolina Eliana Theresa Corsini, Contessa di Percussina.'

'Siamo felici di conoscerti finalmente,' said Ros. She shook Nico's hand but it seemed a strange thing to do with a friend.

'Thank you for helping us,' Philip said as he gently gripped her fingers. He waited with Ros for the Contessa to speak.

'Your dedication to archaeology is impressive; as is how you worked on Peter's problem. What courage when you faced the tombaroli!' She nodded to an unseen servant. 'Please, will you sit down?'

Around an ornate 18th century table the four of them watched tea, coffee and Italian cakes being laid out on Sèvres porcelain with the Percussina coat of arms and monogram "NC". When each had been served she continued.

'Philip and Ros, I would like you to help me solve a problem.'

'Contessa,' Philip began.

'Nico, please; nothing has changed.'

'Nico, we know part of Peter's problem but we have not fixed it.'

'You will. Gabriel and I can help you, for all our sakes.'

That was a bit cryptic, Ros thought.

'Will you help me?' Nico studied the body language between the two. 'Do not worry about the expenses. It is a gift whether you accept or not.'

'Yes.' Ros spoke for both of them.

§

CHAPTER 7

1513. Sant'Andrea.

What a miserable, verminous group of men hobbled out of the Bargello that cold morning. Family greeted some. I squinted in a patch of shade until my eyes adjusted to sunlight.

'Bernardo, we did the impossible. But you would remind me of Fortuna. All it took was the death of a Pope and a Medici replacement.' The others dispersed quickly; a wise move in case someone changed their mind. 'Come, it's time we went home.' I took the first steps across the cobbles towards the Ponte Vecchio. Only the thought of what I had left gave me the strength to endure the pain. Emaciated legs, hunger, and arms and torso that shouted with every step. I looked down at the shallow Arno River through the mist and followed the road south out of the city. Market gardens gave way to olive groves and vineyards. Those who worked them looked briefly and turned away. They knew the cursed place that I had been in and wanted nothing of it for them.

'Was it like this when you walked back to Mugello? You had barely more strength than I have.' But my mind lifted with the sun that broke through the cloud. I was free. Pain drifted away with movement. I had a future.

It was well after mid-day before I entered Sant'Andrea in Percussina. My vitality was not of a young man. Bernardo and I had swapped places. But there was Marietta and the children lined up along the brick wall of our villa. Their faces showed the same thoughts I had thirty years before. I winced when she closed her arms around me and they clung to whatever they could reach.

Marietta bathed my wounds but could not wash away crippled hands and shattered arms. But she did her best with herb pastes of rosemary,

158

lavender and cloves. At meal times I studied my family as if I was a stranger. Marietta was well with child, another son, Piero. Bernardo was nearing manhood at 12, followed by Lodovico, Guido and my daughter Bartolommea, "Baccia". How was I to feed this growing family? Your inheritance, Father, is welcome but hardly enough once Totto has his share. There is no extravagance of a 1st Secretary's salary.

Over days and weeks I walked in the garden, the vineyard and our forest to regain my strength. I was rarely disturbed by visitors. My thoughts drifted to Marietta. What life had I given her? Much of it was my absence, worry and lack of money. Our love was practical, coupling in the dark, cooking and family. Was she content? I guessed that she was fulfilled by the woman's lot: raising her children.

'Vettori, it is good to converse with a fellow diplomat. I pine away here in the sticks. Biagio came to see me after he lost his place when I fell from grace. But most others shun me. Those who serve the Medici cuss at me for serving Soderini during the Republic. Republicans call me traitor because I sought the grace of a Medici to escape the Bargello. I am cursed.'

'Machia, you are alive and have family. Yes, your intellect is not served by those ruffians you spend your hours with in L'Albergaccio, your "Bad Hotel". But you tell me that each evening you enter your study and through your books converse with the ancients. Surely Livy, Catullus, Ovid and the rest have something worthwhile to discuss with you?'

'Vettori, thank you. You are right to stop me wallowing in self-pity. The ancients share their wisdom with me. I add what I have learnt over fifteen years of diplomacy for my masters in the Signoria. There is an embryo of a book, my friend, which I will tell you about when it reaches adulthood. In the meantime keep me enthralled with the antics of Popes and whores, on both of which you are expert.'

'Boschi, how did you cut yourself this time?' I ask.

He sits nursing his tazza in two hands, one with a filthy bandage, as if to keep warm. 'Sharpened me axe, didn't I.'

'And you, Panettiere?' His right arm has burn scabs up to his elbow. He opened his mouth in toothless smile and shrugged.

'Should have been more careful,' says Lamento. He moves his piece four squares on the Tric Trac board.

'Work always cruels ya,' says Meschino. Last week you fell out of a tree.' He looks at the board and scratches his ear. It doesn't make sense so another swig of sour wine will fix it.

'I swung too hard coz me axe was blunt,' says Boschi. He nods at Panettiere and points with his one good eye as Lamento moves another piece. 'They've been going for it like elephants?'

'Who?' says Meschino

'Those two behind the curtain.' The couple in the corner are oblivious, and couldn't care anyway.

'When have you ever seen an elephant?' I ask.

'Don't need to. They're big. My third wine and they're still at it.'

'It's like rowing a boat, really, or sawing a log,' says Panettiere.

'Boschi, are you grumbling again? Always someone else gets the better deal,' I said.

'That's true.'

'Well, let me tell you something. You are alive if you're not dead.' I watched him scratch his head for a moment. 'You are as good as you are until you are not. Simple really, you don't give in until God steps in. You don't believe in him? So? But you don't give in and you definitely don't complain. God is not listening. And the Pope? Which one: the poisoner, the lecher, the warrior, the builder of wonderful things with someone else's money? Which one? He wears a cloak, Boschi, the cloak of religion. It allows him the luxury of pious cruelty, so whatever his actions, however harsh, he is justified. So don't moan. Just have another tazza of this awful wine.'

Everything is based on ignorance. My thoughts drift away from Meschino's shouts of cheat, Lamento's lack of parentage and farthings falling to the floor. Men's knowledge is always limited to one lifetime because they don't listen or read about the past. The crew have no interest in my scribbles on paper from my pocket as ideas start to flow.

Everyone has forgotten history. They're condemned to some Dantean circle of never progressing or learning from the past. If only a few read, the ideas of one man could change the world.

I drift downwards. What does death feel like: slit of a knife, a blow, defenestration from a Palazzo, the body shutting down? I have seen all of them. How does society balance self-interest and the good of everyone? I see Ceccone's stare, no blinks in that reptilian smile versus Meschino's dopey grin. This Bad Hotel stinks. The stench of sweat, seasonal stew as well as bodily fluids and gases permeate the walls. Every day I see the dome, belfry and palazzo towers of my old life from my garden. Every day I am reminded of what I cannot have in this miserable hole of the present. Whatever I have done in the past I can only expect to be judged on what I do now.

But in the evening I leave the tavern of lice and enter my study. There I change rustic clothes for courtly attire. I am welcomed into the courts of ancient men: philosophers, poets, leaders and warriors. We discourse about all manner of things until my weariness disappears. As instructed by Dante I record our conversations so that my conclusions distil slowly into a worthwhile treatise. Yes, Bernardo, I again have something to thank you for. Out of misery comes the beam of light that leads to a better future. It is not the event that destroys you. What matters is how you face it. Can you learn? Can you ride the waves of good and bad Fortuna to grab the opportunity when it comes? Can you turn a negative into a positive?

§

'Nico, can you explain the problem please?' said Ros. She looked at Gabriel. Was it ok to speak in front of him?

'Gabriel's family has worked for the Corsinis for generations. We respect each other's secrets.' Nico got up from the table and walked over to an Italian Baroque cabinet. She returned with a simple oak box, which she placed between Philip and Ros, along with white gloves.

'You first, Ros,' Philip said as he slid them on.

She lifted the clasp, in the shape of a lean black wolfhound, and looked inside. There were two pieces of paper faded into sepia brown. She handed one of thick, porous fibre with text to Philip. The finer one with a fragmentary drawing Ros put in front of herself.

Nico and Gabriel watched silently. Philip pulled out a tiny notebook and pen from his pocket. He recorded the fifteen words of Latin and filled the spaces below with his translation.

Ros was still engrossed in a piece the size of a playing card. On it was a pen and ink rendition of a mountainous landscape. A river snaked in the foreground and low hills led to what she guessed were the Apennines in the background. It felt Tuscan; from paintings she'd seen and a feeling. But the sketch was unfinished, a quick throw down of thoughts which was too free to be sure of the artist. Was it a preparation for a painting that had survived? Could it be from a model book, part of a collection of cheat sheets to be copied when a subject was needed? Aging and the style harked back to the Renaissance masters. Was that too much to hope?

She looked up. Philip walked in from a visit upstairs. He laid out the two sherds.

'Etruscan,' said Gabriel. Nico agreed.

'It is possible they are from the same piece.'

Gabriel nodded.

Then Philip passed over what was in his hand to Nico and Gabriel. Nico took it out of its cloth cover and laid it beside the Latin.

'The same hand wrote both,' said Nico. She pointed out the flourishes on the "Y" and "F".

Philip spent more time but came to the same conclusion.

'What do you think, Ros?'

While Philip told the story of Harry's souveniring, she considered it carefully before reaching the same judgement.

'Not much was spared in the German retreat. When looting was about to happen my grandparents drove out to their country villa and hid paintings and sculptures behind false walls.' Nico looked again at the new text. 'I remember this from a photograph he sent. That's why I am sure they were written by the same person.'

'Where did your two pieces come from Nico?' asked Ros.

'I was told they were from a garden. They were found beside a bomb crater and left here. But the farm worker was killed soon after, before he was able to tell.'

'When was this?' asked Philip.

'July, 1944.'

'So you don't know the place?' said Ros.

'No, just that the garden belonged to us.'

'I assume, Nico, that there were several,' said Philip.

'Twelve.'

'So we could excavate to find something buried or maybe an underground storeroom. But that could take an inordinate amount of time.'

'If we knew more about your ancestors, Nico, we might find out whom, why and ultimately where,' said Ros.

'The Corsini family have detailed records back to 1283. It is a tradition each generation carries on.'

Ros looked around the walls. They were full of portraits. 'Do these provide a full record too?'

'Yes.'

Ros looked at photographs on the marble mantelpiece. Would there be any future portraits, she wondered? Were their severe faces waiting for a mistake? Nico's eyes had followed hers.

'Too many dead people,' Nico said.

Yes too many, but one in particular was not there. Nico had asked questions to make her judgement. Given what she was about to trust us with that was pretty fair. Decidedly those faces were watching, Ros thought. How did poor people remember their loved ones before photographs?

'And yes, you may research everything. There should be no secrets.' Nico looked at Gabriel. He nodded.

'Gabriel would like to show you his home. It is relevant to your research.'

Philip picked up his cup of black tea and then put it down again. 'Excuse me, Contessa, sorry Nico, but we cannot forget Peter in this.'

'We have not forgotten him.'

'We were close. On the flight I took photographs.'

'Yes, we found the negative. You have a record of tombs marked for opening.'

Hence our gear laid out in the bedroom upstairs, Ros thought. 'The men took my Instamatic but we had proof of who funded the robbers. I photographed the machinery.'

'The name was Marazzi, Antonio Marazzi, the Mayor,' said Nico. 'Gabriel and his son followed your tracks when you disappeared. They saw all that you did, as well as you being loaded into the van.'

'That's how you found us,' said Ros.

'So we have not forgotten Peter's problem. Antonio is a powerful man with many connections. We need incontrovertible proof of his guilt. But we also need to keep you safe.'

'How can we get that proof without going back to the dig?' asked Philip. 'Peter's thief is probably one of Antonio's minions.'

'Hang on, Philip. Nico is right. To Antonio we are dead. That's a good thing. You don't have to be on the dig. Gabriel can be your eyes. Nico takes the photographs as before. What would you like us to do, Nico?'

'Do your research. Go with Gabriel and take your camera. We have no secrets.' She cupped her hands on the table in front of her. 'One more thing: Meredith said that you don't TELL.'

Philip and Ros looked at each other. They said in unison, 'Nobody TELLS.'

§

Diary 24th September, 1513.

I am catching birds with nets for our meagre supper. The woodsmen no longer fight as I have pronounced like Solomon and they accept the result. A familiar colourful figure appears at the spring.

'Ostinato. You must be in the wrong place. This is no palace or courtly residence.'

'Machia, intellect hides in many dwellings but rarely in those.' He studied me. 'You look fit and well after time away from the rats.'

That evening, after the family meal, Ostinato shared my sanctuary. Giacomo and the rest were ensconced in L'Albergaccio. Goodness knows what words they had with my ruffians. We dressed in our finest raiment. The ancients listened to our discoveries, mine on the sordid machinations of men and his on their deeper thoughts. Warriors, philosophers and poets looked over our shoulders but thankfully they did not tell.

'People of this time have not been kind to either of us, Machia. But our wits have risen above their pettiness.' We both thought of our days spent in the Medici library. 'Poverty has not defined us but it will always make our security tenuous.'

Over the evening we touched on so many topics.

'It's not that you gain wisdom in old age. It is just that you have seen it all before,' he said.

Ostinato's mind was so full. I know that a writer finds it hard to let go of their work. They always want to improve it. Was that his problem: when to stop, because it is never perfect?

'It must be hard for an intellect like yours to succeed. You spread yourself too thinly, and you know the end before you finish.'

'Yes, when the solution is inside my head then it is done. The execution of it is boring. Time is lost from solving the next problem. Life is too short to waste it appealing to others.'

'Your patrons?'

'They get their share.'

So soon he left to join his entourage on the journey to Rome. This Pope might favour him.

'Trust, Machia. The future might produce the wisdom of the ancients.'

'Yes, if Fortuna favours humankind. I will be ready for when you come again.'

§

Ros heard the knock on the door. She nudged Philip out of his siesta doze.

'I could quite get used to this,' he said shortly after as he stepped out of the shower.

'So could I.' After the meeting Nico had shown them around the Palazzo. What could Ros say? This was the stuff of dreams. It was like rooms at the Vatican without the hordes of people. When Nico excused herself and Philip chose to do as the Italians do and succumb to the heat of the middle of the day she had wandered. There were so many Baroque masterpieces, with some paintings from earlier. She spent ages looking at a Sandro Botticelli roundel of the Virgin surrounded by children. Those colours, the particular pigments of that period either side of 1500, were just luminous.

In the glare outside Gabriel stood beside a 1960s Fiat 124. It was white, nondescript, and by the number of small scrapes and dings well used. Philip remembered the Murat in Turkey. The Lada in the Soviet Union was another clone of this very practical car. Gabriel held the passenger door open for Ros so Philip slid into the back seat. Twenty minutes of accurate, fast driving along country roads and Gabriel turned on to a dirt and gravel road. It slid through open fields, with regular rows of olive trees, and grape trellises stepping up the slopes into the distance. Then he turned into a track lined with Italian pines which had been pruned into a canopy of shade. He pulled up in a yellow gravel courtyard lined with rough stone walls. These were punctuated with windows lined with red brick. Above was the ubiquitous red tiled roof. When he had shut the gate he opened the car doors. Philip could see the ridge of Alta Cresta around five kilometres to the south.

'Benvenuto Rosalind.' The old lady held Ros' shoulders and touched cheeks, right then left.

'Benvenuto Nonna.'

'No, chiamami Elizabetta per favore.'

'Stai bene?'

'Si nonna sto bene. '

'Benvenuto Elizabetta.' Philip held out his hand.

'Benvenuto Philip.'

Her grip was surprisingly gentle for pasta-making hands. She guided them into her kitchen: white-washed stone walls, enormous hand-cut beams supporting lighter ones above, and flag stone floors. In one wall was a red brick curve over a massive fireplace that reminded him of a London railway arch. On the substantial cast iron cooking stove, with oven and cooking rings, ornately decorated with whirling plant tendrils, was an enamel kettle bubbling steam.

'Siediti per favore.'

At the table, steaming coffee in his hand, Philip looked around the room. A window opened wide onto the courtyard. It struck him that the Roman concept still held: Nature and cool, given privacy by four walls. He guessed the farmhouse had been there for a century or more, each generation adding their contribution: an extra room for family additions, shutters to keep out the elements, maybe plumbing was Gabriel's work. Nothing was destroyed only added to according to need. He liked what he saw.

Ros was the first to see what they had been invited for. On a shelf beside one of Elizabetta's enamel cooking pots was a two handled red pottery bowl. She was sure it was a krater, somewhere in the realm of 600s BC, and it depicted Greek soldiers stabbing at a giant as if to blind him. Further along the shelf was a black impasto two-handled bowl, a kotyle, with a bird incised into the side. The more she looked the more she found. It was clear Elizabetta put on show the pieces that she particularly liked. It was probably the bird rather than the rarity that appealed to her. How many more were kept in cupboards out of view? Then she saw Gabriel watching her. His face was a mixture of pride at what he had achieved tinged with anxiety about what would happen next.

'You have an amazing collection, Gabriel. Would you like to tell us about it?'

'Yes I would.' He took a deep breath and explained how his family had taken pottery and beautiful objects from Etruscan tombs for three generations.

'Our work as clandestini is difficult and dangerous. Outsiders, newspapermen, universities do not understand. They call us stealthy, backdoor crooked people. Yet the word means underground too. We are really people who work underground to supply museums and collectors.'

'Why are you helping us, Gabriel?' Philip asked. 'Why do you trust us?'

Gabriel took his time answering. Elizabetta understood enough to know that Gabriel was taking a great risk.

'You and Rosalind came to archaeology from universities. You are intelligent young people. I have watched you. You do not take anything, only knowledge. You are honest. But you could earn a lot of money doing something else. Maybe if you had a family to support it would be different.'

'We will have enough,' said Ros. 'Money doesn't have to equate with dishonesty or crime.'

'To my father and me this life was not a crime. What we found were gifts given by our ancestors. They showed us where to dig. We loved the thrill of finding things. Sometimes we sold things to get a little money when times were hard. But the tombaroli are different. They make a big business of ripping up our heritage and selling it abroad. Italy is losing its culture to these greedy people.'

Philip absorbed the silence at the table as each drank their coffee. Peter's problem was now so much bigger. But the possibilities of change were exciting. He had read about Italian laws that protected antiquities but he had never known about this clash of traditional treasure hunting with systematic plundering by organised crime.

'Thank you for trusting us, Gabriel. I believe archaeology can win here. We can make a good change for the future of Italy.'

Gabriel smiled.

'Will you let Ros take photographs of your collection?' said Philip.

'Yes.'

'And will you let me record what you know about where each piece came from?'

'Yes.'

'Then these pieces will give us archaeological knowledge.'

'Philip, will you come with me on an expedition?'

Ros saw doubt flit across Philip's eyes. He was being asked to break his code.

'Yes.' It was a matter of trust.

Well into the evening Ros took photographs of all the items that Elizabetta resurrected from cupboards. Gabriel told Philip everything he could about the provenance of each. Some went back to his grandfather so the compendium was incomplete. But the hoard was vast.

'Gabriel, you realise that you might have to part with these. Can you do that?'

'I have thought about that for a long time. Yes, I can if they give archaeological knowledge.'

There was a knock on the door.

'Buona sera Tommaso.'

'Buona sera Jacopo.'

'Buona sera, Nonno.'

'Buona sera, Nonna.'

Philip donned the dark clothes, the balaclava over his head like Gabriel, his son and grandson. He carried his fair share of the tools to the Fiat.

'Take care, Philip.' Ros gave him a public hug.

'I will.' She must be worried, he thought.

Gabriel drove slower by only a little. But he avoided loud gear changes, tyre-squealing on corners and rapid pull-offs at crossroads. Philip could work out that their direction was south east. Gabriel explained that each family had their turf. To dig on Antonio's patch would not only be dangerous but against time-honoured rules.

Gabriel slowed, turned left and followed the dirt track to the edge of a field. He turned around to face out, switched the lights off and the group sat in starlight for several minutes.

'Silence now please,' he said to Philip.

Tomasso laid out the tools and sacks on the edge of paper-like stalks. Philip could smell the rows of garlic stretching into the distance. Gabriel covered the car with a tarpaulin. Jacopo looped a sack over his shoulder.

'Andiamo,' Gabriel said, just above a whisper. The quarter moon just beyond the rise ahead cast just enough light. He led them towards the macchia at the edge of the small, flat field. In its gloom he picked a way through an animal track like Philip and Ros had followed to Antonio's diggings. For twenty minutes they meandered up the slope and along the ridge. Gabriel stopped periodically to listen and study the lie of the terrain. Philip could see him retracing steps from wherever he had reconnoitred during daylight. Gabriel stopped again. This time he ran his fingers over branches that leaned over the track like a tunnel. He held one and straightened its broken stem. Tomasso put down the tools and sat down with Jacopo. Philip joined them as they watched Gabriel.

He was scrambling carefully over the scrubby bushes of oak. His feet were light as he used his hands to pull himself up and around the gentle incline. Minute after minute he clambered over the same ground until he held and then straightened a broken twig.

'Spillone per favore.'

Tomasso handed him the thin crowbar. Then he disappeared into the macchia.

Gabriel raised the tool and Philip felt the thud through the earth at his feet. As the dull rhythm of blows began Philip wondered again what he was doing there. He was a trained archaeologist not a treasure hunter. What he was now part of was illegal. A heavy bubble of anxiety sat immovable in the pit of his stomach. Yet, there was something else. In the tunnels he had entertained Ros with Rider Haggard's adventures in exotic places. He had grown up with "King Solomon's Mines" and "Alan Quartermain". They had spurred his thirst for travel and the extraordinary. Archaeology was just a logical extension of his boyhood dreams. Maybe that bubble in his gut was the thrill that Gabriel had described.

'Boom.' The echo through the soil was as different as if Gabriel had struck a bell. Two more blows and the note stretched. He felt the piercing of the ground. Gabriel must have heard the first flow of crumbled stone, like sand through an hour-glass. The work continued until Gabriel had cut a neat, circular incision into the hollow space beneath.

'Vieni Jacopo.'

Jacopo climbed up and stood still while Gabriel tied a rope around his waist.

'Sono pronto nonno,' Jacopo said quietly, like a man. First his feet, then his hands and at last his head disappeared from view.

Gabriel stood astride the hole and let the rope slide through his fingers. In minutes he pulled the first bag to the surface. At the second Philip knew it was time. He stood up and signed to Gabriel that he wanted to come up. Gabriel nodded. Philip tried to mimic Gabriel's style to avoid incriminating damage or prints. He was beside him looking down.

'Per favore.' Philip held out a Kodak Instamatic camera with a flashbulb cube on top. He put his mouth close to Gabriel's ear and explained what Jacopo should do with it. Gabriel stood back and looked steadily at Philip's eyes in the cool light.

'Perché?'

'To record, like archaeology.'

Gabriel still looked at him. Was trust slipping? 'This is the good change, for Italy,' Philip said.

A moment more and Gabriel crouched down. He put his mouth into the hole.

'Jacopo ascolta, per favore.' He repeated Philip's explanation.

'Capire?'

'Sì nonno.'

Gabriel lowered the camera inside the bag. Philip waited. A brief beam of light penetrated upwards to illuminate Gabriel's startled face. He spread his body low and shut his eyes. His clothes glowed three more times.

'Ho finito il nonno.'

Gabriel pulled up the sack and handed the smoking camera to Philip. Then he lowered the rope again and pulled up his grandson.

'Grazie Jacopo,' Philip said.

Jacopo rubbed his eyes and smiled.

'E 'chiaro Tomasso?'

'Sì,' came from somewhere further down the path.

Gabriel capped and covered the hole. Then he packed and checked. 'Andiamo tutti,' before he led them back to the car. Philip was glad to smell the raw garlic that his leg brushed against. He stood beside Jacopo while the men uncovered the car and quietly filled the boot. Gabriel slid into gear and drove by moonlight for a kilometre before he turned the lights on.

'Questi sono fantastici,' Ros said as the jewellery was laid out last. Beside more bucchero and orientalising vases with designs of warriors and fantastic beasts were a necklace and two Egyptian scarabs. The amber in the string of beads must have been traded from the Baltic region, presumably by Phoenicians. Inside the delicate silver scarabs were medallions of turquoise incised with primitive sailing ships that reminded her of Arab dhows.

'The pottery says 6th or 5th century B.C. She must have been very wealthy to have been buried with such things. Ben fatto Jacopo.'

Philip handed the camera to Ros.

'Thank you Gabriel, Tomasso and Jacopo,' he said. 'Thank you for your hospitality, Elizabetta.'

Just after 3am Gabriel drove away from the Palazzo. By 3.30 Ros was asleep on Philip's shoulder. What have we done, he thought? Something good, he replied and joined her.

§

Diary. 1517. Sant'Andrea.

My garden is complete and full of the delights that I have carefully chosen. This morning the Apennine Mountains glow and the belfry and spires of Florence glisten with light. There is nowhere I would prefer to be, except maybe on an errand of importance for the Signoria. But that is not to happen, unless Fortuna looks my way. I hear the squeal of the steel gate opening.

'Ostinato, your travels pause here again. How are you, my friend?'

'Older but I am not sure any wiser, Machia.' His gait along the path to my seat was slower than before. His beauty had declined from youthful vigour but it was replaced by a look of contemplative study of everything around. But clearly slowness was caused by creaking bones. Fingers that once worked miracles now remained half closed like eagles' talons.

'I disagree. You look shrewder than ever.' On closer surreptitious inspection I cursed the cruelty of old age, as I had done with Bernardo.

His eyes grazed antique urns on mounts, and the grotto behind. 'Hades awaits us both I fear,' he said and chuckled. He sat and watched the Florence of our youth glow into magnificence. Neither of us rushed to speak for a time.

'I hear that Machia's life has changed greatly and not for the worse. You found time to write.'

'Yes, from a negative came a positive, as Bernardo would say.' I handed over my manuscript of Discourses on the Ten Books of Livy that I was in the process of final editing. He took it in his left hand, his right being too palsied to grip.

'Writing has saved you. Bernardo would be proud. Even that scurrilous play of yours, Mandragola, is a masterful satire on those who meant us harm for so long. As usual you lampoon ignorance, hypocrisy and of course the Church. No wonder it is dangerous to be your friend. '

'It was well researched in the brothels of a dozen Italian cities. Yes, Bernardo would approve of my full life!'

'And your latest amore is part of that?'

'Of course they all are. You and I are monogamous to a degree, as Marietta well knows.' Giacomo would no doubt agree.

'Back to that familiar topic of ignorance, Ostinato, we're in an era where everyone lives for now. Nobody cares what happened twenty years ago.

Brunelleschi's Dome, they walk past it every day and don't give a damn about what it took to make it or what a marvel it is.

Ignorance is bliss some say. Rubbish, it's a curse. It's not an excuse. How many people feign ignorance? They prefer not to know because then they are not responsible. Ask the Pope, he's a master at the game.'

That evening we two dressed well and my sanctuary became the Medici Library of our youth. The best and deepest of his notebooks and the refinements of my writings we savoured well into the night.

'As usual for these scribblings there are many powerful men who will hang us,' he mused.

'You have avoided that fate better than me.' We looked at each other's damaged hands. I observed the box of pills he had left for me in one corner, as always. Had he devised anew for his ailments?

'There is nothing more for me in Italy now that Giovanni Medici has gone. Surely the king of France will give me more respect.' After a silence, 'What have I left behind, Machia? You have children, an ever patient wife.'

'Your notebooks are your children. Giacomo and Melzi keep you company.'

'I must put my works into some order. My family do not need me. But those books cry to be heard. If only I could have done more with my allotted time.'

Next morning we savoured the Tuscan light from my garden. He looked again at La Bocca dell'Inferno. 'You have caught the Duke's smile! Popes and the Medici can find their own way to Hell.'

I walked with him, he leaning on my better arm, up the path to the gate out to the road. His baggage train, servants, boxes of his works and chattels strapped onto mules, began to move.

'Good journey, old friend.' His arm lingered on mine. Eyes said what the mouths could not.

I was alone in my garden with my thoughts. Ostinato, you are such a secretive, fearful gentleman. You sired no children but you leave the products of such a mind. We are unlikely friends. I am lucky, the future too, that you have trusted me. Our thoughts will find the right minds when the world is a better place.

§

'Buongiorno Nico.'

'Buongiorno Ros.' Nico picked up the Instamatic with the four blown flash bulbs in the cube. 'Have you been teaching Philip some tricks?'

'He's not that bad really. No it was Jacopo. Would you like to see what he found?'

As Ros had expected Nico's dark room was spacious and well equipped. It was almost insulting to develop snapshots in such a deluxe setting.

'They're interesting.' Philip topped up Ros' coffee cup at the drawing room table and offered the pot to Nico. He was quite getting used to espresso. The belt of sugar at the bottom definitely woke him up.

Four photographs were spread on the table. Jacopo had snapped the first, then turned clockwise a quarter and taken the second and so on. There were some long bones and a skull on the floor.

'Quite small,' said Nico. 'Like the sarcophagus maiden.'

Beside her were marks of fingers dragged in the dust.

'Presumably Jacopo collecting the goods,' Philip said. He didn't like to use the word loot. His mind was still reconciling his image of King Solomon's Mines with the reality of tomb theft.

Ros was too engrossed in the scenes to reply. Thank goodness she'd put in colour film. A black and white frieze was punctuated with frolicking dolphins. They were blue, a rare colour that again spelled out wealth. Reclining diners at a feast were entertained by musicians playing lyres and flutes. She followed Nico's finger to a woman surrounded by birds who clearly was waving farewell. Reds, yellows and greens burst with vivid life in this scene of death.

'Gabriel took a bit of persuading but I think he will like the result,' Philip said.

'Yes.' Nico was as enthralled as Ros. 'Imagine if the early excavations had such records.'

'That's the key Nico: records. It's the difference between archaeology and treasure hunting.'

'Philip, slow down. That's offensive,' said Ros.

'Sorry, Nico, and I suppose Gabriel when I see him. I just meant that both methods destroy things. To get to the next level down you know we must destroy the one above. Gabriel could argue that he damages far less than I do. The difference is that archaeologists record as much as they can. That is why we asked him to let us photograph the finds and describe their provenance as well as he could remember.'

Ros saw the excitement in Philip's eyes. His enthusiasm was infectious. Nico's smile suggested that there was nothing to forgive, but something to prove.

'Let me show you some of the results of treasure hunting.' She led them upstairs to the top of the palazzo.

Ros stopped just inside the door of a room that reminded her of Versailles' Hall of Mirrors, it was so enormous. Except instead of silver sheets, her views were through huge windows, built when glass was a vastly expensive luxury. They were of the Tuscan countryside. The Renaissance painters jumped out of the scene, or should she say so many of their backgrounds were of this.

Philip stood still a little further in. Cabinets of wood with glass panels filled the room, row upon row, a little like the reliquaries in the Vatican Musuem. Many were inlaid with scrolled patterns of leaves and vines. Those nearest to him looked ornate like Louis XIV furniture, probably 18th century. A little further on the cases showed more of the heaviness of the Victorian era in Britain. At the far end the cabinets were entirely of glass, with bevelled shelves and modernist gold catches. Inside all of them were Etruscan pottery treasures beyond anything he had ever seen.

'These are records, detailed and until now private, of everything in this room.'

Nico handed him a modern ledger entitled "Beni Culturali, Volume 16". Inside the open cupboard Philip could see the previous fifteen. He opened the first page but didn't need to. The Corsini tradition of recording was as detailed as he had expected.

'What do you know of the Grand Tour, Philip?'

'That the British nobility came to Italy to study the artistic treasures.'

'Many of which they took home as souvenirs.'

Nico is much too polite to also mention the syphilis, or pox, they collected in the brothels of Venice and Naples, thought Ros.

'For a century these dilettanti had free reign. Did you know that the most well-known of the tombaroli was a Frenchman?'

Philip shook his head.

'Lucien Bonaparte, estranged brother of Napoleon Bonaparte, was known as the "Prince of Grave Robbers". It was recorded that in 1828, in a few weeks he dug an area of two hectares to reveal more than two thousand artefacts. Each site was scoured for painting fragments to box up. The pottery,' Nico swept her hand to indicate the cabinets, 'was judged worthless and so was smashed and left. The Corsini family had other ideas. Gabriel's family have worked for us for generations.'

I have just been skewered, Philip thought. To tell her that her family was enlightened in a time of cultural barbarism would just insult her. 'I am sorry, Nico.'

'A bit like the Elgin marbles from the Parthenon, Philip,' said Ros. 'If Lord Elgin had not taken them back to Britain when he did they would not exist. They would probably have been melted down for cement like so much else.'

You're rubbing it in, Ros. It feels like two against one.

'Your books do not tell you these things. But I have read about some of your British archaeologists. For instance Lt General Pitt-Rivers was of some interest to me. At a time when Italian tombs were opened up to entertain British aristocrats on a day's excursion, he believed in method and in recording what he found. Sir Mortimer Wheeler has carried on his work. I think they have done much to create the modern science of archaeology.'

Ros turned away from an exquisite red earthenware jug with a black figure of a high-stepping warrior. 'So you are ready for change, Nico.'

'Yes, the Corsini family has always adapted to the new,' she searched for the word, 'reality.'

§

'I can't tell you exactly where to find Rosalind and Philip, Melissa.'

'Drs Gullet and Fleming from Chicago University were asking for them.'

Yes, I know why too, thought Peter. The sponsors want their trinkets and they have guessed why the two of them are here.

'They had a few sites to visit. I imagine they will turn up with their results when they are ready.'

'You don't know when?'

'I believe soon.'

Peter looked at Gabriel, whose face was as impassive as ever.

Gabriel knew exactly why these men were at Città Sotto. Melissa's ears had been pummelled for most of the morning. It is strange, he thought, how these men believe that they are different from the collezionisti he had supplied. The ancestors are just being generous. But then he thought again. The rules had changed: beni culturali were now owned by the state, and universities and museums were the new collezionisti. For the sake of Jacopo he needed to change too.

In the afternoon he joined Mike and Melissa at the big trench, M1, dug at the start of this season. It was cut on the hill slope beneath the cliffs of Città Sopra. Its purpose was to gain a complete section of the archaeology between the base of the citadel and the river. Melissa was in the upper section trowelling and brushing around several rock markers of burials. She looked up towards the declining sun. Nico would be around soon for photographs. Gabriel found Mike working on a clay-lined cistern. Bradley was close by cleaning back one area of the trench wall. Gabriel joined Mike since he had most to do to be in time for Nico.

Together they cleaned back the lowest of the steps into the water storage. The clay had been beaten into a hard surface. Imprinted in this and the steps above were signs of timber revetments. The wooden structure, long since perished, was there to support but also to contain run off silt from the hill above. Clean water stored in the Pliocene clay would have been used just as today, in the making of tiles. Each summer Gabriel's cousin worked the yellow and red clays into shape with moulds, dried them in the sun, and then fired them in the kiln set into the hillside. Cisterns would catch intermittent storm rain for when water was scarce. In winter he collected the clay in readiness along with macchia timber for the firing. So often the archaeologists were surprised by his intuition but really the methods of making a living had not changed much in three millennia.

Proof of Gabriel's musings was in the refuse dumped in the conical pit in later times: piles of broken tiles along with animal bones and household rubbish. Bradley had barrowed selected quantities of what they trowelled to Nico's sieve site. She and Peter were proud of their record of finding the minutiae that other excavations missed. For a poor site, other than the burials, it was rich in knowledge of how ordinary people lived.

Gabriel watched Bradley on the edge of his vision. He was scraping the section perfunctorily rather than carefully. It was a new face to reveal to the camera the cross section of what they had gone through. But a spirit level, or even a ruler, would show that it was not precisely vertical. Yet the main feature was clear: a cuniculus, a channel for diverting water into the cistern. It resembled a large post hole but viewed from the side rather than above. Many Etruscan cities diverted water into complex systems of tunnels. This one was simple, with occasional natural rock lining its base but mostly cut from the packed soil itself. Bradley's efforts revealed horizontal layers of silt and gravel that had washed in to fill it up when it was neglected in later times.

'Buon pomeriggio Mike e Gabriel.'

'Buon pomeriggio, Nico,' they replied.

'Are we up to your standards, Nico?' asked Mike.

She looked carefully. Mike knew what she expected.

'Si è buono.'

Mike and Gabriel stepped back with their tools. Their shadows did not fall into the photograph. But Bradley's did.

'Excuse me, Bradley. Would you mind moving out of the shot, please?' she said.

'Oh, right lady.' He stepped back and left a footprint in the dust from his scrapings. Nico waited while he brushed the dregs into a bucket.

'Bradley?' She pointed to the print.

'Oh yeah.' He brushed that one out and all those he put in getting there. Gabriel and Mike squirmed but Bradley saw none of it.

'Thanks, Bradley.' Nico took the photographs and went up to Melissa, who stood waiting.

Nico caught the last of the good sun. Bradley was gone. Mike, Melissa and Gabriel put away tools in the tent.

'Buona notte.'

'Buona notte, Gabriel.'

At the road Nico waited beside her car. When he approached she handed him an envelope. She watched his face as he took out four photographs. His smile was more than polite.

'Do you remember such things when you were the age of Jacopo?'

'Yes, of course.' He held them up at different angles. 'He did well.'

'Yes. You must tell him that.' She waited until he was about to hand them back.

'No, Gabriel, these are yours, for your collection; for your records.'

'Philip and Rosalind want me to do more, don't they?'

'Yes. You already have photographs of each item, and your description. Rosalind wants Jacopo to take flash photos inside every tomb you can remember. Philip wants you to write down where each one is. He understands it will not be with a theodolite like surveyors use. But he hopes you can draw a map.'

Gabriel was quiet. He was thinking. Nico wondered if he regretted going this far.

'Today I showed them the Corsini collection and our records. We must work with them. It is the right way, Gabriel.'

§

Ros awoke to that special Tuscan light and Philip's singing.

'O sole mio, o sole mio.'

That's all he knows, she thought. Don't give up your day job, Philip, but that wouldn't surprise him.

'"O sole mio sta nfronte a te!

'O sole, 'o sole mio

Sta nfronte a te, sta nfronte a te!"' she sang.

'Encore. Bellissima,' said Philip.

Downstairs in the drawing room Nico had organised a buffet breakfast that might have satisfied an officer in the British Raj. Ros gathered a plateful of fruit; fresh figs, plums, nectarines and peaches. Philip filled a bowl with yoghurt followed by toast and marmalade. The former could have matched Turkish and the latter beat Robinson's hands down. They both went back for more.

'That's good coffee,' she said.

'Yes,' he said as the sugar and caffeine worked their enervating magic. 'It seems strange not being at the site.'

'You know we can't go back just yet. The tombaroli think they've won. Anyway we have our second task here.'

After the revelations of the Corsini collection Nico had left them to their own devices. Her place was at Città Sotto and later at "La Macchia". They had spent the afternoon rambling inside the Palazzo. For a time they had filled their brains with Etruscan treasures. Then Ros reconnoitred Nico's stupendous art collection while Philip looked at the gardens from every window before venturing outside. At the evening meal Nico's near-invisible servant, Salvatore, said next to nothing but provided for them sumptuously. Afterwards they drank what they judged to be excellent Chianti; that is it tasted divine and it produced clear thinking and mellowness in equal measure.

'Tomorrow we focus on the task in hand,' Philip said as they curled up in bed like spoons. With his arm around her belly he fell asleep almost immediately.

§

'Yes, we have Nico's problem to solve. Peter's is a work in progress.' He sipped the sugary tail of coffee and poured another one.

'We have Harry's souvenirs and Nico's text. The writing goes back to one person, presumably a Renaissance man but not necessarily. Nico has put no limits on our snooping but there must be a problem, something in the way or else the family would have found out before.'

She followed his lead and sat down with another café nero.

'What are you thinking? A black sheep somewhere? Something dangerous to the family name? But Nico did suggest that whatever it was it was bigger than the family itself, a vital piece of history in some way.'

He sipped and thought. 'You seem to get along. Is she telling us everything she knows?'

'Would you?'

'Probably not; family skeletons are usually embarrassing or worse.'

'Maybe she wants to, to solve the problem, but prefers to let us find out. She hopes that the solution is worth the discomfort. Afterwards she relies on our discrete silence.'

'That's an awful lot of trust being put in us, from Nico and Gabriel.'

'Then we'd better get to it, and get it right,' she said. 'I do the portraits and you the records. Gardens are for later I think. Ciao.'

'Ciao Bella.'

Philip asked Salvatore where the family records were kept. He was led to a 19th century room near the kitchen on the ground floor. Philip could see that it had once been a servant's room but the bedspace had been converted. Jammed into shelves on three sides were teetering piles of tomes of dog-eared files.

'Grazie Salvatore.'

He sat on the simple wooden chair at the bare table and thought: what am I looking for? It bought time before he faced the dust and silverfish of neglect. Writing detailed records was commendable; their maintenance less so.

A list was a good start. What do we know? Writings times two, both probably 16th century, by the same hand. One landscape sketch of a similar vintage. That's Ros' domain. Do I go straight for the early files? But then there is the reference to them being hidden in a garden. By whom? Did a more recent Corsini find them and hide them? There was no choice: he had to start at the present and work back. He was looking for discrepancies, for references to a find, or something concerning that had to be hidden. It was all very vague, like following a hunch or relying on a gut feeling. He preferred the more familiar world of a trench. Research was more satisfying when you knew what you were looking for. After three hours he longed to swap shoes with Gabriel.

Ros began by wandering corridors and salons. In her notebook she put down the room and each painting. Portraits were scattered among the Baroque artists, the Berninis and Gentileschis. It was according to personal likes rather than any logical order. One positive aspect appeared early in the search: the female of the species was equally represented with the male. A second was the Corsini eye for detail: dates of acquisition or of the portraiture were added as tags onto the frame. Birth and death dates were nearly universal too. After an hour she needed a coffee.

'Salvatore dove sono i record per i dipinti per favore?'

'Per favore seguimi.'

He led her to a ground floor room near the kitchen. She could hear Philip sneezing loudly in the next room. At a similar chair and table she sat down with her coffee and notebook and began her search. After the first volume her nose exploded a cloud of dust from its cover.

Elimination to find a discrepancy, she thought. Much as she longed to study the art for its creative merits the masters were less likely to give her an insight into a secret than the family portraits. Jump back to the 16th century or start from the present? Method was paramount. She started her list of him and her at the present. Nico's portrait was a stunning likeness, aristocratic in a simple black Armani dress. Her husband was not recorded; too little time for a portrait. I would like to have seen him, Ros thought. Her parents, grandparents, great; they all stepped back into time in a logical order. Giacomo and Elena were in their late twenties when Lucien Bonaparte was pillaging their homeland. Was it the severe Giacomo in dark jacket and black cravat tied loosely around his sun-tanned neck or the pretty young Elena, in red satin with delicate white embroidered edging and cuffs, who decided that Etruscan pottery was worth saving? Throughout the 18th and 17th centuries the family were hardly adventurous. Nothing like a Maja Unclothed by Goya graced the walls. Nakedness was a strictly private affair between a man and his wife. There were suggestions of wealth in clothing and furniture, the symbols of learning like books or a globe, and enough flattery of a man's wife to hide marriages for wealth or elevated status. By the end of the day conservative was the word she wanted to shout but that would have offended.

Ros would call Philip dogged. He needed to be. There were records for everything, whatever was bought and sold, entertainments, chairs repaired, artists paid for portraits. Gabriel's payments, going back to his father and his grandfather, were all there. It crossed his mind that such a cache of truth was dangerous if it ever got into the hands of an enemy. Why would you do it? Most modern businesses kept a second set of sanitized books for tax purposes. He dragged his mind back. Names went like a forest of people growing backwards. At times he read forward again to get perspective of father, disappearing, and son, appearing. Amounts paid showed inflation. Italian lira fluctuated during and after both world wars, and some payments showed up as German Deutsch Marks or American dollars. By lunch time he had reached 1860 when coinage based on the gold florin of the Republic of Florence was the standard currency; except for the Papal States and a few towns nearby like Perugia who paid their bills in escudos. Around 1799 there were even some French francs when Napoleon's troops were involved. He grazed some rather nice cakes Salvatore had laid out in the drawing room. Another espresso gave him the energy to go back to the 17th century. By then the minutiae of a great and wealthy family was passing in front of his eyes without register. It was time to quit.

Salvatore brought out Artichokes alla Romana, sautéed in olive oil, with mint, garlic and oregano, accompanied by simple pasta. The glasses of Vermentino were generous.

'Buonasera Nico.'

'Buona sera Philip e Rosalind.'

'Any news from the dig?' Philip asked.

'Gabriel and Mike are working on a Villanovan round house. Melissa is finding more cremations. I sieved more fragments of bronze that the Romans did not manage to recycle. Peter is getting nowhere with the local police about the theft. They did not even do fingerprint checks around the safe.'

Nico sounded tired. They all were. The weather did not help. It had been hot and sultry for days.

'Have you any leads from the family records?'

Philip noticed how much she enjoyed that word. 'Not yet.'

'I'm not sure. It's early days,' Ros said.

After a shower the bed was like the wine glasses: generous. She curled into his shoulder with only a single sheet covering them. Philip played with her hair and then her navel and all stops between. Their lovemaking was gentle and slow. It was far too hot to be energetic. Sleep was total.

But in the early morning hours Philip was not awake but not entirely asleep. Problems became animated in his dreaming. He dealt with one and the next would appear. Somewhere before daylight he passed the point of efficiency. These venomous reptiles swirled around him like mad broomsticks. He was as helpless as the Sorcerer's Apprentice against their onslaught.

Philip awoke to bird calls, some of which he could guess. Two or three geese were flying close enough for him to hear their cries and the beat of wings. More distant was the screech of some bird of prey, maybe an osprey. The twitter of sparrows was even closer, somewhere in the garden. He got up to look out of one of the windows. A pair of herons was checking out whatever was worth eating in one of the ponds in the parterre, the organised garden of hedges laid out in geometric patterns. Wearing enough to be decent he came back with two coffees, his espresso and her café nero.

'You seemed to be on to something yesterday,' he said.

'I might be but I'd prefer to let you find the person by yourself.'

'No hints then.'

'No.'

'Back to the grind,' Philip said as he walked away from the breakfast table with a second espresso towards the dungeon. He pulled out another decaying folder with possible woodworm and definite silverfish nibbling. It was a visitor list, a who's who at banquets. It seemed that the family always kept close to the rich and powerful. Knowledge was power. More arrivals, children, church ceremonies, guests and extended family filled page after page.

He was in the 16th century. Husbands and wives appeared, unless they had been culled by age. A few dowagers were recorded year after year, to considerable lifespans given the average life expectancy of late forties at the time. Wealth bought time as well as position. One was younger, in her forties, and came with children, five at various stages of growing up and being married off. There was no mention of her husband, ever. Another oddity was that he was sure that the early notations of her visits had been altered. The dates and places were untouched but the paper had been scratched where her name was recorded. Someone had meticulously erased a longer name and carefully scribed a shorter one. It was something to run past Ros at the evening meal.

A quick jog along corridors, another coffee and cake, and he was back to another volume, this one entitled "Giardini". The rest of the day was taken up with details of their creation, with the help of an Italian/English dictionary. As well he carried out extra research in Nico's library on the history of Renaissance gardens, in English. He found them fascinating.

Alberti's 15th century tome, "The Ten Books of Architecture" provided the template for designers in Italy and then across Europe. Drawing on the recently discovered works of Ancient Greece and Rome, mainly Vitruvius and the Plinys, Elder and Younger, Alberti laid down the landscaping rules: a hilltop mansion; symmetrical terraces merging into the wooded hillside; copious water fountains and ponds; and plenty of aromatic features such as citrus trees in pots. Most intriguing were the architectural features such as colonnades, grottoes and secret gardens, drawn directly from the Classical era of Hadrian at Tivoli. With good reason, since the need for shade, cooling water and places for quiet conversation had not changed over two millennia.

As the light mellowed into late afternoon Philip thought of where someone would put something in a garden. He went outside and let the paths guide him without any purpose while he thought. The air was still and limpid. When he leant on the ornate cast iron dog that supported a seat his finger was stabbed by static electricity. The sky wanted to rain but didn't seem to know how. "Hide" was the word. This family recorded everything yet this was a secret.

If Philip keeps drinking espressos like that he'll learn to fly unaided, Ros thought, on her way down to her own level of Dante's Inferno. In another moth-eaten folder of browning thick paper she followed hims and hers back through the 1600s. Then she found the portraits in the corridors and staircases above. Most of the males were a little older and more worldly-wise than their spouses. He was able to look after a younger, pretty wife of limited experience. Sexism was another word that crossed her thoughts; until she came to Marta. Her likeness was forthright. She was older, in her latter forties, and was no longer pretty. Her dress was of dark, silk brocade, with decorated bodice and puffy sleeves. Her eyes looked to her right into the far distance. She exuded an experience of life that was beholden to no one. Two more things intrigued Ros about her. There was no corresponding husband portrait, and there were smaller likenesses of five children along the wall beside her. Was there a purpose beyond the simple record of their existence? Ros had no idea what it was.

She took a break. There was another perambulation around the passage-ways of this private museum: a little Caravaggio perhaps or should it be Guido Reni? Ros felt the same as if she'd walked through a Queensland rainforest alive with birds, the sounds of water and the wind in the leaves. Her mind was relaxed and stimulated at the same moment. Stress and drudge left her body with every step on the complex marble floor. Through the window she saw the beginnings of mirages over the gravel pathways, and faint haloes of steam hovered over the fountains. Even from here she could see the excessive number of cobwebs with an inordinate number of bugs caught in their silk. Had the mosquitoes and flies hatched early she speculated? The spiders were definitely doing well. Yes, she was better off in the cool.

To finish the task she followed the list back to its beginning. She felt that the journey would end by the 15th century but she had to be sure. The pattern of wealthy display, proof that they had arrived, continued. From farming beginnings outside Florence they had joined banking to make their fortune. During turbulent political times, when great families and cities warred constantly, they had survived. Did she admire them? Yes if their success came from hard work and yes for their enlightened attitude to artistic treasures. They could have spent their fortune on the equivalent of the pokies, what Philip called "one arm bandits". On a more practical note none of the portraiture told her anything more.

'Basta,' she said loudly. 'Where are you, Philip?' She heard his footsteps coming in her direction.

'Voila.' He placed a chilled glass of Vernaccia di San Gimignano in her hand and guided her arm towards the garden. The worst of the heat had dissipated and there was a slight breeze. The shade and aroma of the avenue of linden trees worked their sensory magic.

'Marta,' she said.

'Yes. First appears in 1524 and then she seems like a permanent fixture, well for twenty six years to be precise, from 1527. Why?'

'No husband, five kids, she does not fit into the usual newlyweds or dowager empresses. Why?'

'All the early visits are meticulously recorded, as you would expect. But her Christian name has been scraped out of the paper and Marta put in. Why?'

'Is she the black sheep; on the wrong side of the bed sheets? Five is a rather excessive number if that was the case.'

'Gardens,' he said. 'We have to visit lots of them, including places Corsini of course.'

'I won't object to that. And find Marta.'

They touched glasses and ambled back to the Palazzo in time for dinner.

§

CHAPTER 8

'Ciao Nico.'

Ros watched her walk away from the breakfast table. In a khaki safari suit and broad-brimmed white hat she was elegant. Ros heard a distinct high-pitched roar as the Fiat started. There was something about that sound that spoke Italian cars.

'Where to today?'

'A garden, two actually.'

Ros finished her café nero and Philip gulped the last liquid of his espresso. He led the way out into the courtyard. Another sultry day with heat haze obscuring the distant hills.

'Not the Ferrari then?'

'No, this is more my style.'

Ros studied the well-worn Landrover in front of her. It had the short wheel base that Philip liked. Under the dirt, scratches and dings there were solid steel bumpers front and back, and army green paint. The spare wheel was the usual obstacle to front vision. And woe betides that it rain with those silly little windscreen wipers. It reminded her of the dig vehicle at Kara Tepe. She hoped that it was in better nick than that one. At home she would call it a "paddock basher". Philip opened the passenger door for her.

She wound down her window successfully as the diesel engine kicked into life at first go. She reached for and there was a seat belt. Philip slid into first gear without double-declutching or crunching. She felt the pull back into her seat as the powerful engine responded. He slowed at the entrance briefly and pulled onto the right side, which was a bonus. Then he smoothly worked up through the gears until she could only describe his speed as "hooning". She looked at his face as he weaved wildly around scores of pot holes. Yes, he was enjoying himself. She tugged on the seat belt to make sure and then sat back for his version of Italian driving. So far there was nothing on the road. They joined the SS3 and very soon after the E35 near Civita Castellana, which merged into the E45. Fast Italian motorways were not the Landrover's thing. Philip had it in top gear but was overtaken multiple times in the slowest lane. But the smile never left his face.

'What gardens?' she said over the noise outside and in.

'The Gardens really. Arguably they were the templates for all the rest, including the Corsinis'.'

Ok Philip, this is a magical mystery tour, she thought. She sat back and enjoyed Tuscany on a bright sunny morning. The sign said Via Maremmana Inferiore and soon after that they took the exit for Tivoli.

'Hadrian's Villa?'

'And the Villa D'Este. 2nd century Imperial Roman to the 16th century extravaganza of Cardinal Ippolito d'Este.'

Philip joined the traffic of buses, tourists and Italians getting to work. He nosed out in front of an open-top sports car. Its horn sounded and Philip stuck his hand out of the window and waved. At the next crossroads he eyed every vehicle until a tour bus driver made eye contact. Philip hopped into a non-existent space that suddenly appeared when the man took evasive action. Another horn, another wave. At traffic lights he watched until the other lane had a red light and then moved off with the rest of the pack two cars before their own turned green.

'Where did you learn that one, Philip?'

'Tehran, before I met you on the dig. There everyone moved off together, just one block of cars; an absolute misery for any tourist.'

'Hence your liking for this old thing.'

'Well, who's going to risk their paintwork if I get it wrong?'

Philip shoved and merged mercilessly until he saw an elderly Fiat 500 driven by an even more venerable driver waiting for a space. Philip stopped abruptly. Tyres and brakes screeched all around as he waved the gentleman in. His wife, well-dressed and perfectly manicured for an 80 plus vintage, waved a regal thank you.

At one standstill Ros looked across as another older driver squeezed into a tiny parking space that was clearly too small. For the next twenty seconds he took his time to shunt into the car behind, then the one in front, then behind again until he made the space he required. Quite simple, she thought; if you adapt to a new set of rules. Philip was quite civilised in comparison when he rode over the footpath and bounced into a parking spot. There was no crunching of bodywork at all.

Inside the gates Philip handed Ros the guidebook. It was a change from his usual commentary. The square kilometre of pools, baths, fountains and Alexandrian Greek architecture had the faded damaged glory that the 19th century Romantic poets loved. So much had been pillaged during the fall of the Roman Empire. A lot more of the marble and travertine had been burnt down to make cement, a la the Elgin Marbles might have been. Much of what was left of marble and statuary was purloined by Cardinal d'Este for his gardens visible close by. But there were still magical parts, she thought.

They walked around the circular pool of the Maritime Theatre. The fragmentary colonnade of Ionic columns provided some shade as she looked across to the island. There was a replica of a Roman house reputed to be a refuge Hadrian used to get away from the problems of empire. She observed a rectangular pool lined with Caryatid sculptures and columns that mimicked the Egyptian resort of Canopus. The crumbling dome of a temple dedicated to the god Serapis reminded her of the Pantheon in Rome. Logical, of course, since that was a product of the Emperor too. Not for the first time she longed to sit down with easel and paints for the rest of the day; preferably in the shade beside a pool to get away from the oppressive heat.

Philip consulted the guidebook frequently, mostly the map, so that they found the extensive heated baths and holes in the unexcavated section that might have been the start of tunnels. Where would he put something important and secret in such a garden format? Short of the obvious, burying it in some container, he was stuck. After a slice of pizza and a Fanta arancione they joined the queue for the Villa d'Este.

'This man should appeal to you, Ros. Second son therefore he went into the church; archbishop of Milan at the age of ten, at 27 sent to King Francis 1st of France.'

'Francis and the Pope scratching each other's backs?' she interrupted.

'When Ippolito was thirty, with the king's backing, Pope Paul III made him a cardinal.'

Ros heard Philip's sarcasm. 'I suppose he became immensely wealthy and built this estate to show it, on the back of the collection box.'

Their tour of the Cardinal's villa confirmed her thoughts and was brief. Besides, their task was not the study of sumptuous Baroque art but the formulae of an elaborate landscape that leant itself to secreting something valuable.

'You'll be pleased to know that he never reached Pope, and not for the want of trying. However, you might find some saving graces in the man when you look at his garden.'

From the palace terraces they had looked down on the heavily sculpted steep site. Vast quantities of rock and earth had been piled behind retaining walls to form the geometrical terraces, or moulded into miniatures of the Apennine Mountains. Sight and sound was dominated by the sound of water, splashing as fountains, flowing as streams out of gargoyles' mouths or intricately harnessed to produce music.

They stood above the Fountain of the Organ, looking down through spray from the Neptune fountain towards the flat area of the fish ponds. Waves of cool fanned across her. The music from what looked like a thoroughly modern church organ was somewhere between fairground and Elizabethan or maybe Bach to her ear. But it was powered by water so the Cardinal could be forgiven for his musical taste. With the tourists they ambled along the pathway beside the hundred fountains gushing from theatrical masks. She marvelled at the Fountain of the Bicchierone, which the Cardinal had commissioned Bernini to design. Yes it did look like a big glass of water. It bubbled from its receptacle of mosaic stone overlooking a stunning view of poplars, olive groves and misty foothills.

As far as Philip could judge the garden was full of hiding places; the caves and watery grottoes behind the Oval Fountain; the man-made rocky crags above; the Rometta Fountain with its boat containing an obelisk mast, and the statue of Rome Triumphant perched above sultry vine-clad walls; the nooks and crannies within the island supporting the Fountain of the Dragons. If he thought about all the aqueducts and channels guiding water underground the opportunities defied probability. With luck the Corsini versions of this masterpiece would be less complex.

§

Nico walked on site with her camera bag over her right shoulder and her Pentax around her neck. The sun's light cut shafts down into the valley from just above Alta Cresta. Yes, the colours are still intact for an hour or so yet she thought. She walked up to where she was needed: Melissa's Etruscan urn, Gabriel and Bradley a metre away and Mike working on his refuse pit close by.

'Buongiorno a tutti.'

'Buongiorno Nico.'

She chose her position for another shot of the urn. Melissa had prepared: all loose dirt was brushed into a pan and set aside for sieving with the rest. She stood out of the picture and waited. Nico took off the lens cap, adjusted focus and checked her light meter, lined up, held her breath for a moment, click; done.

'Grazie.'

She stayed to watch Melissa go back with her metal spatula. It reminded her of a tongue depressor at the local hospital. Melissa wiped her forehead to avoid drips on to her work. For over a week she had trowelled and bagged the earth to within ten millimetres of the travertine surface. Anything closer was clipped off by pressing the edge of the tool and levering to follow the stone. The lid was of a reclining lady in Hellenistic robes staring sightless into the distance. Around her neck was carved a torque and around her right arm were two twisted bracelets. The decoration was so reminiscent of the young girl in the sarcophagus. With a toothbrush Melissa had revealed intricate folds of the woman's dress. She'd uncovered traces of red and some yellow paint by her careful approach. On the front and left hand side of the lid was inscribed "PANATIA ARATHENAS THRESUS, APACUS PUIA" or "Panatia

Arathenas, wife of Thresu Apucu." The dimensions of the lid, 105cms by 76cms, suggested that this was a cremation.

Nico stood face on to admire the Skylla, a winged sea monster, with the torso of a woman and legs which were coiled fishtails. Was this an ancient mermaid sent to guide Panatia through the stormy seas she would face on her journey to the afterlife? It was a wonderful piece typical of the late 3rd century BC. Nico wiped her brow while she indulged her senses for a minute or two before facing Mike's project. His bandana was dripping with sweat.

With equally painstaking care Mike had followed down the layers of debris inside what was once another water cistern. Each period of use was separated by silt and sand but no household rubbish. It was full of broken tiles, wasted pieces of tegulae, flat tiles, and imbrices, with curved overlaps, many of which had fused together in the firing into distorted plastic shapes. These were not nearly as exciting as a product, thought Nico, but so important in terms of knowledge about the purpose of the site. Roofing tiles had been made continuously here for centuries, and were still the industrial lifeblood of Alta Cresta today. She took her daily record photographs and then looked across at Gabriel and Bradley.

Bradley knelt beside Gabriel. He tried to match Gabriel's technique as the latter traced the floor on which Melissa's urn stood. The millimetres of yellow clay crumbled under the side edge of Gabriel's trowel. Like any craftsman he made the process seem so easy. Nico saw Bradley get it right for a few minutes, and Gabriel would slow down so that they could work together. But then Bradley would lose concentration, probably because he couldn't think straight in the scorching air. But usually it seemed because he was looking around at the urn. Nico could read his mind: why am I scratching a dirt floor when I could be revealing this piece at least as well as Melissa. Gabriel said nothing but in his smile were frayed edges.

After a visit late morning to Peter's work room to develop and hang up the latest prints she drove back to the Palazzo. Salvatore's lunch of aubergine and mozzarella salad with a rosemary bruschetta was delightful. Her eyes had just closed when the telephone rang.

'Nico puoi venire al villaggio. C'è qualcosa che dovresti vedere.'

Her informant waited for her at the medieval gate of Alta Cresta. Together they walked towards the square as he explained.

'Addio Contessa,' he said quietly and left.

'Espresso per favore.' The young man returned with the coffee. 'Grazie.'

'Prego.'

Nico sat at a table in the shaded loggia and waited. Peter's room was across the cobbled sunburnt space. A few youngsters collected nearby on a corner. Their Vespas sat on their raised front pegs in the shade. Smoking Gitanes appeared to be in at the moment. Not people I would rush to employ, she thought. But no doubt they would grow through this aimless stage. She heard another Vespa approach. It stopped in front of the group and a young man stood astride it. She could not hear every word from this distance but the boy was clearly fluent in the Italian of the streets. Then she saw that handshake: a packet in one palm, a folded note in the other. The exchange had been made. Then it happened again: hand in his pocket, the swap and all done in a couple of seconds. Was it just marijuana, she thought, or something more, LSD perhaps? In five minutes it was all over. The newcomer drove around the corner and the aimless ones went back to their conversation.

'I would not have guessed that,' she said to herself. Nico finished her coffee and went back to the remains of her siesta.

§

Diary. 1519.

As usual Fortuna ebbs and flows in my life. Today I learnt of Ostinato's death, far from the home of his boyhood. It grieves me but our bond pleases me. But that same fickle lady took the life of Lorenzo Medici, a disappointment to me and to every true Florentine, and gives us his brother Cardinal Giulio. He is a wise patron of the arts and has much of the political wisdom of the great Lorenzo of my youth.

1520. July. Another of my books is to be published soon, "The Art of War". Better still Giulio wishes me to write a History of Florence. The problem of how to place the Medici family without flattery or insult is a delicate one.

Meanwhile my old boss, Soderini, offers me extraordinary sums to come and serve him in some backwoods republic called Ragusa. But I cannot accept. For all their faults I again serve a Medici.

1521. Bernardo the flow ebbs for me, Florence and for every state in Italy. Once, the powers of Spain, the Holy Roman Empire and France were balanced nicely. But chance has Charles 1 of Spain become Charles V of the Holy Roman Empire too. Leo X, a Medici, dies, and Adrian V1, tutor to the said Charles becomes our new Pontiff.

1522 Plague has returned Bernardo. Florence stands still. Those afflicted are sealed in their homes. You and I watch from afar as Totto is in extremis. We are powerless. Only 47 years, Bernardo.

What an abysmal year. In Rome Soderini's conspiracy against Leo, a Medici, has finally been found out. In Florence my not so erudite friends from the Rucellai gardens now do the same, all in the name of the Republic. Torture and execution everywhere but for some blind reason this time the Medici do not look at me.

1524. Giulio, now Clement V11, has replaced Adrian V1. France and Spain size each other up like pugilists and Clement dares to referee. Why do we have a profession called diplomacy if we decide things with weapons? If diplomacy works there is no need for weapons. It's there to replace war with talk.

Sometimes I write in solitude at Sant'Andrea. At others I party and fornicate with the lovely Barbara. You see, Bernardo I waste not a moment of life. Ah Love and Barbara are such fickle creatures. Her role in my play "Clizia" shows its irony. I wrote it to salve a damaged heart.

1525. Bernardo good and bad is in equal measure. Clement likes my History of Florence. As a Medici I knew he would. And now I am back in harness as his emissary.

The bad news? The French king, Francis 1, is in a prison in Madrid. Charles masses his troops to pounce on Italy.

Clement listens to my advice about militia for every city in the army's path, not least Florence. I put away the pen and sharpen my wits for the duel ahead.

1526. Francis gave Italy to Charles, just to escape gaol, and then reneged on the deal. Francis has Rome, Venice, Milan and Florence on his side. War is inevitable but we are not ready, Bernardo. By the way Clement is an incompetent bungling fool. Where is my Florentine militia when we most need it?

I dash hither and thither Bernardo, since no one else will. We, me and your namesake grandson, inspect and guide the repair of the walls of Florence. At least Clement provides the funds. Would you believe that I have my old room in the Palazzo Vecchio? How the world turns!

Lombardy is next, organising militia of course. But Charles' forces advance inexorably. Towns fall over like ninepins. Francis' League is failing. Milan changes hands again. But, glory be, our forces have taken Cremona. I was there, Bernardo, when we stormed the gate.

September. Why can't people see it? Words drip off their tongues so easily. An apology; yes we will do. Bullshit. Every time they forget and it's me who has to fix things again. It's like batting a ball over a net. Why can't the other fellow hit it back? Has no one read my books? The first rule: beware the enemy within. Treacherous Cardinals have schemed with Hugo de Moncada, a minion of Emperor Charles. A few imperial troops barricade Clement in the Castel Sant'Angelo and he gives away everything we've worked for. What a bambino amongst wolves!

Now Charles pushes south. His goal is Florence itself. No time for the pen. No time for whoring or even Barbara. She is surprisingly constant, even if she shares.

I stood before the walls of Cremona cheering. Now I stand on the walls of Florence and don't cheer. All the theory in the world means nothing compared with the test of reality.

§

'My turn.'

Philip handed Ros the car keys.

'Tell me how much I've got behind me.'

He stood on the pavement and gave hand signals that closed together as she took the last inches. Philip moved to the front and did the same. She reversed hard into the kerb and rode over the edge.

'Get in, Philip.'

She leaned out of the open driver's window and let her blond hair flow in the breeze. 'Grazie,' she said to young male driving a van with "Elettricista" on the side. 'Ciao Bella,' said the two fellows on Vespas who gave her space onto the roundabout. Buckets of smiles and wide eyes came from all ages when the traffic slowed to a halt.

'Perché lo stai guidando?' They pointed to the Landrover and raised their eyes.

'È suo,' she said pointing to Philip.

On the open road quite a few slowed down to look or whistle at the owner of the blond hair. The usual magnet, Philip thought, in this land where the majority were brunettes. Her speed was sedate and yet they reached the country road turn off in the same time. He went back to enjoying the sweeping vista of precise rows of vines on gentle slopes, hazy lines of poplar trees marking distant roads, and elevated villas painted orange by the afternoon light.

Ros pulled up the handbrake and switched off. As their shoes crunched gravel in the courtyard Gabriel opened the door to welcome them in.

'Buona sera Gabriel,' they said together.

'Buona sera Philip e Rosalind.'

Nico rose from the table on the loggia.

'Welcome back.'

In the open stone verandah shade and breeze combined to create a perfect cool. When they were seated Salvatore placed chilled glasses of Pellegrino mineral water in front of them.

'How was your day?' asked Nico.

'Good, thanks. Magnificent gardens,' Ros enthused. She could see that there was something else.

'Yes,' Philip said. 'And so many places to hide something.'

'"Hide", yes, that fits the family legend.'

'Otherwise it would be indoors,' Ros said.

'What do you plan to do tomorrow?' Nico asked.

'To visit your family gardens, now that we have got the general layout,' Philip said.

'Can you fit in something else? Gabriel has a request.'

His eyes studied the table for a few seconds. 'We have been recording our tombs in the way that you asked,' he said, now looking at Philip and then Ros. 'Jacopo enjoys his new talent, and the sunglasses that Nico provided.' His smile was brief. He searched for the right words. 'For your plan to work all the families need to be part of it. Do you agree?'

'Yes, absolutely. Can you arrange that?' said Philip.

'I have spoken to some of them. They feel,' Gabriel paused, 'that they are taking the risk. They need to meet you to know that it is worth it.'

Philip looked at Ros, and then at Nico. His gaze strayed into the garden past the bubbling fountain but really he saw nothing. Peter's problem, still not solved, had led them into something much much bigger. He and Ros still knew very little about the stolen antiquities trade but it had to be large and lucrative. Their kidnap had proved that. If they met the families there was a fair chance Antonio would hear of it. But if he was the head of a clandestini family he would surely want to meet the archaeologists too. But this was Italy, known for its corruption.

Philip was pacing now. I doubt if he would even hear me if I spoke, Ros thought. The look on Nico's face confirmed it. If they agreed to Gabriel's request the risk factor multiplied considerably. Antonio would not be so subtle a second time. But what a prize if the families agreed!

Philip was looking at her now. Yes, she nodded.

'Nico, we will need your help.'

Over an exceptional meal of roast lamb with rosemary and garlic they discussed the next steps. The young Chianti Classico flowed freely to lubricate what Poirot would call the "little grey cells". At the end of the evening it was decided that they would visit the Corsini gardens before the meeting. That would give them freedom to travel for as long as possible.

'Buona notte Gabriel.' Nico and Ros touched cheeks with him, and Philip shook his hand.

'Nico that was a lovely meal; I'm full as a gug,' Ros said.

Nico raised her eyebrows. 'You are welcome.'

'Nico, on another topic, what can you tell us about Marta?' Philip said clearly. A good wine always helped his thoughts.

'Marta is quite a common name. When are we talking about?'

'Either side of 1527.'

'She had five children,' Ros prompted, 'and apparently no husband.'

'There was a recluse about that time. Maybe gardens are a good thing for you to look at tomorrow. I seem to remember being told that she spent most of her time in them.'

'Nico,' he said quietly. 'Is there a second set of books, I mean records? I don't mean to pry beyond our task but most families have secret dealings that they would not like the tax man to know about.'

'Just about Marta, Nico,' Ros spoke into the silent space.

'I will get Salvatore to collect whatever he can about Marta.'

'Thanks, Nico,' they both said.

§

Diary. 1526.

Ever closer. Giovanni de Medici, our best soldier, great grandson to Lorenzo the Magnificent, died in battle near Mantua.

1527. A dreadful year unfolds: war, infamy of leaders, famine and plague. If there is a God, which Bernardo we know there is not, then he has cursed us. I am cold and sick to the belly of fear for those I love most, my family. Marietta nurses baby Totto with the help of Bartolomea. Bernardo and young Guido and Piero study in the city. Lodovico thankfully is in the Levant. I have tried to settle Marietta and Guido's fears with news from the front. Fortuna, where are you?

1527. Spring. We have diverted a force to defend Florence. The walls are repaired as much as I can hope. The Emperor knows it. Hope is all we have left as his army marches under the Bourbon along the Arno. It is 40 miles from Florence. Will he, Bernardo?

A miracle, he goes south! Clement's God help the people of Rome.

4th May. Charles of Bourbon's army is at the gates of Rome.

6th May. Who defended the city? Clement in his inimitable wisdom disbanded his army months ago. All that stood between the Spanish infantry plus Bourbon's fearsome company of lansquenets was a rabble of paupers, old men and boys scoured from the taverns. In a few hours the enemy were through. It cost so little, other than the Bourbon's death. If only Charles V had paid his troops. If only the bullet had missed the Bourbon's leg. If only he had not died outside the walls. History is full of "if onlys". Spaniards and Protestants were thirsty for loot and revenge. It was a sack to match that of the Goths and Visigoths a thousand years ago. Guicciardini and I witnessed rapine and pillage without limit for 8 days. I had survived the Strappado but could I remain sane suspended for hours, or cut with burning irons, my teeth drawn out or forced to eat my own nose, ears and balls? 8 days of Hell on earth that only Dante could describe. Only when Charles himself reached the city and rescued the Pontiff from Castel Sant'Angelo did it end.

11th May. Florence is stunned by the awful news.

17th May. The Medici is again in exile and Florence is once more a Republic. Clement has kindly agreed. What foolishness to give away what you no longer own! For eighteen months I have travelled frenetically from here to there and back again, amidst the filth, disease and carnage that should never be witnessed by any man.

Now I am alone with too many thoughts as I skirt the waters of Lake Trasimeno. The ghosts of ancient Romans, Flaminius and his soldiers slaughtered by Hannibal, come to haunt me. In the late afternoon the sky turns leaden and a cold wind stirs. From the mountains in the east a wall of white rises up. I turn my mules into the cover of forest. There is no inn for miles, and definitely not before this beast attacks. Sleet and ice swirl across the lake. My back is against a tree which shudders with its force. I tether the animals in their panic as eddies of snow pile around my ankles. That night is long and cold and too far from home. I have observed that the hold on life becomes weaker as one ages. If you live long enough you see the patterns. Some give in and want to go but God won't let them in. Others are buried by tragedy and wonder why there is life at all. I feel it now.

In the morning I cross the white wilderness. In the final days of May I reach Tuscany.

Amidst the jubilance around me I should rejoice with my fellow republicans. But they are young men who take power. They have little time for me, one who served the cursed Medici to save their beloved city. It is good to be on my way home to a family that is safe. But I cannot fight the gloom. Everyone hates me from all sides of politics. I take pills for this and that but to no avail. Only the thought of my family around me gives me joy.

10th June. Another takes my place as 1st Secretary of the Second Chancery. I am passed over. My mind cannot face this again. Melancholia grips me like an illness. I take my potions but they seem to make the stomach cramps worse. What a waste there is in death. All that knowledge and experience is lost. That's why I write about history. All that people need is there if they have the wit to grab it.

16th June. The doctor has found blood in my stools.

21st June. Violent spasms wrack my belly. I am spitting blood.

'The Pope doesn't like me,' I tell Lamento.

'Why should he?'

'I didn't get three score and ten,' I tell him.

'Whom the gods love dies young,' he tells me. Where did he learn that?

'Well, that's a relief.'

'Bad bastards live forever,' says Meschino, looking at Lamento.

If this is my time then surrounded by family at Sant'Andrea is not a bad exit.

22nd June. I am Guido. My mother wants me to record my father's words and deeds at this time, in his fifty eighth year.

He is sick in his bed. We all know it is his stomach again. Madonna Marietta, his family and a few old friends are around him. Madonna has called Friar Matteo. My Father agreed, we all know for her sake not his own. He rambles in his mind, talking first to us, instructions for when he is gone. He seems to place most faith in me; although baby Totto, if he had lived, would surely have been his favourite. Then he rants against those leaders who refused to listen to his advice. 'Your task is to protect your subjects from violence and injustice. Instead your ambition and corruption rides rough over law and institution. You show so much stupidity, malice and cruelty.'

'Guido, come and join my friends. They are all here: Biagio, Guiccardini, even Salviati from younger times, and of course Bernardo. There is a story I must tell, a dream actually. In my vision there is a band of ragged, poorly attired men on their way to somewhere. "Who are you and where are you going, I ask?" "We are the saintly and blessed, on our way to Heaven." Then I see a solemnly attired group of noble men of grave appearance. There are Plato, Aristotle and Livy among many others. "We are the damned on our way to Hell," they tell me.'

'Well gentleman, I believe I shall be happy in Hell talking politics and philosophy with the great men of ancient times. In Heaven I would only be bored trying to converse with the saints and those blessed people. '

§

Nico was gone when they arrived at the breakfast table. But in a pile beside it were a dozen files, just as dusty and unattractive as the previous. They ignored them as they selected their dream breakfast: Ros mostly fruit, Philip his yoghurt followed by egg, bacon and what looked like British sausages with baked beans. An obligatory coffee or two and they were ready for anything.

'Gardens first; heads or tails, Ros?' He flipped a fifty lira coin.

'Tails.'

The coin spun on the marble floor. 'Heads; I drive there, you drive home. Ok?'

'Ok. No chance of the Ferrari?'

'I let Matteo have it today; maybe tomorrow.'

She strapped herself in but Philip was more subdued today. Maybe he'd got it out of his system, she thought, all that adrenalin a male needed to get rid of to prove his manhood. Within twenty minutes they turned up a dusty driveway to a Corsini villa. The gate opened as they approached. Nico must have primed the manager of the estate that they were coming. Or else he simply recognised the Landrover.

'Buongiorno. Possiamo guardare il giardino per favore?' she said to the grizzled face at the door.

'Ovviamente. Seguimi.' He unlocked a side gate and left them to it.

'Grazie.'

They walked together but recorded in different ways; Ros with her camera, Philip with maps and drawings in his notebook. The excessive temperature was not helpful but did not deter them from their task.

'Share any of your feelings about the place when you get them, please, Ros.'

'Ok.'

'Grazie.' They smiled at the quizzical face at the gate. His eyes were devouring Ros, Philip thought, but then what was new? They left for the next one. Her Italian was being worked hard as few of the managers spoke more than a smattering of English.

With personal transport it took less than half an hour to get to the second place. Buses would have been a nightmare. Some gardens were quite small, less than two acres, others were four times that. Most had a practical section full of vegetables and fruit. All had the influence of Rome with mythological statues and shady colonnades. Defence was a part, with a commanding hill and high walls. Water was a necessity, for all the features like fountains but also to supply the needs of the house and the working estate of vines and olives. Many had grottoes and caves incorporated in water features like the Villa D'Este. These gardens were lesser versions but more intimate.

'Was the villa damaged in the war?' Philip asked the eighth manager.

'No. The Allies chose a different route.' He left them with a cold drink and returned with a map. An ancestor had pencilled in the paths of the Americans, British, Poles, Australians and the rest. Philip did a rapid copy and Ros photographed it.

'Can you show us where the Corsini estates are, please?'

None of those they had visited so far or the remaining four was in the direct line of fire; although several had narrowly escaped Allied bombers.

As always their work was meticulous and as complete as they could make it. But neither was convinced that they had found it. Ros sat on a shady seat enjoying the damp spray from another Neptune with a trident.

'Any feelings, Ros?'

'Yes but not significant. Lots of layers of people: the important and the insignificant who laboured to keep it all working. There were a couple of cold patches; one in that last secret garden, where I'd guess some unpleasant end caught someone." She thought of Robert Browning's poem "My Last Duchess". "I gave commands; then all smiles stopped together." How many other women were the playthings of powerful men, to be disposed of if they tried to choose their own path?

'My turn.'

She took the keys. Philip strapped himself in and promptly dozed off. He must trust my driving, she thought, as she pulled off. About forty minutes to our villa she calculated. It had a nice ring, "our villa". Most of the trip was cross country, away from the main Autostrada. Her mood was mellow, like Philip's, after so many lovely havens of plants and antiquity. Ahead was a nondescript Fiat parked in a bushy side lane to a field. A man stood by the car as though to wave her down. Something made her look in the rear view mirror. A similar vehicle with a number of men was not far behind.

'Philip. Philip. Wake up.'

'What? Are you ok?'

'Yes but I'm not happy.'

Philip looked ahead and then behind. He cracked his knuckles unconsciously and sucked in air. The man in front stepped out into the road and raised his hand. 'Keep it in gear, Ros.'

'We're thinking the same thoughts.'

'Un problema?' she shouted across as they pulled up.

'Abbiamo uno pneumatico forato,' the man said pointing towards an invisible back tyre. He leaned on their bonnet and smiled.

Philip heard the car behind pull up and the first of what he counted to be six got out. All were strong, young and not out for a picnic. He saw three more come from the field.

'Gun it Ros,' he said just above a whisper.

Ros floored the pedal and the engine screamed. As the car lurched forward the man at the front side stepped out and made a grab for the passenger door. At the same time three of those behind went for side windows and the back door. Philip gave a rapid jab through his window. It connected with a nose and teeth. The man shut his eyes, let go and sprawled so close that the back wheel nearly finished the job. His body tripped the man at that side window and he flattened on top. But the back door opened and the driver's side window fell out. An arm reached through and then a second. He was scrabbling for something to pull on as his feet dragged in the dirt. A hand grazed Ros' hair, before Philip slammed the back of his fist into the face that appeared where the window had been. Now there was one.

The man crouched in the back and reached forward to grab Ros or the steering wheel or both. In his twenties, with black bandana, earring and a two day shadow he reminded Philip of a pirate. His shoulders and biceps were more bodybuilder. As Philip blocked his wandering hands the man grabbed his wrists and reefed him over the seat into the space at the back. Off balance it was all he could do to hold on to stop those forearms pummelling him. Philip twisted to avoid hard knees driven by colossal thighs. Their shoulders slammed into what was left of the window frame.

Ros couldn't see much through the thrashing bulk behind her. Best to concentrate on evading the two cars that were catching up behind.

Where was the speed of a Ferrari when she needed it? With that and having to straighten up whenever the men threw themselves into the side she knew she was in trouble. They knew the roads, she barely. There were not too many advantages with a Landrover. Except she could hit potholes harder and still have a suspension. Thud; that was somebody's head hitting the roof.

Ow, that hurt, thought Philip. I can't move in this tin box. No space to kick or develop any power from the hips to do damage. Another roll and his head was being shoved out of the back door space. One hand held him down and the other was trying to catch the flapping door and crush his head. This fellow is stronger than me. All I'm doing is avoiding being strangled or breaking a bone. I need to rethink this. Where can I get the momentum to multiply my weight and strength?

'Are you all right back there, Philip?'

'Ow, not really.'

'Anything I can do?'

'Aargh. Brake when I tell you.'

'Righto.' I wonder where that came from she thought. That's a Philip word.

Philip twisted and belted, grunted and swore until.

'Brake!'

Ros crushed the pedal until she could feel the metal stress. Thank goodness Nico had maintained it properly. The burning rubber tracks held in a straight line. She just guided the wheel gently and let it have its way. Instinctively she ducked to her side as the two bodies came through.

This was it, Philip thought as he felt the first tug of inertia. His hands were tearing the shirt and skin from the man's shoulders. As the head was pulled forwards Philip threw his weight behind the momentum and shoved with whatever he had. With luck they wouldn't both smash through the window and end up sliding off the bonnet. But no, he managed to push down and lower his head into the man's uplifted chest. He felt the shudder through his body as the back of the man's head connected with the dashboard. Then Philip was tumbled upside down. He expected a blow to the back of his neck at any moment. But it didn't happen. Without kicking Ros too hard he managed to turn himself upright on top of the body. The man was out cold. And the Landrover had ground to a stop.

'Philip,' Ros said as the two cars slowed and pulled up.

'Philip,' she said louder as the men got out and advanced on the car.

'Yes, I've got it.' He found the handle and the passenger door swung open. With desperate strength he shunted the body out of the door.

'Go for it, Ros.' He pushed the trailing legs out as the engine roared, and slammed the door.

'Are you all right?' she asked, pushing in third gear. She could see the others running back to their cars. She didn't have long before she would be outgunned for speed again.

'How are we going to do this, Philip?'

'I'm not sure yet. Which way do you think it is to Nico's?' He clipped his seat belt and pulled it tight.

'Basically west but I really don't know the route. I doubt if we can look at a map or ask anyone either.'

'I agree, west, maybe north west.'

A bumper slammed into the back. Ros fought the wheel to avoid rolling. When the road became wide enough for two cars to pass the second car came up to join the first.

'Bang.'

There was no mistaking that sound, she thought.

'For goodness sake, they're shooting at us. These clowns have been watching too many spaghetti westerns.'

'Bang. Bang.' The glass of the swinging back door shattered. A hole appeared just above the rear view mirror.

'Ok. Well, Philip, this is something we couldn't do with a Ferrari.' She slowed enough to crunch into four wheel-drive. 'Sorry Nico, needs outweigh niceties.' Then she reefed the wheel forty five degrees to the right and shattered a rough cut picket fence. Then she straightened up and drove hard between two rows of olive trees pruned to the height of a bush.

Both cars followed. But there were no shots. She presumed that it was too lumpy to get a clear line of sight.

'Hold on.'

He gripped the Jesus bar above his head as she threw the rover between two trees. Could she see anything? He knew he couldn't.

Ros looked in the rear view. One had made it through but she could see the smoke from the second one. It must have made a direct hit on an ancient tree trunk. But they were running out of olives and there were open fields ahead. Young corn and maize shoots gave a covering of green. That's a filthy sky, she thought; so many colours hinted at beneath that ominous silver cloud line.

She looked at Philip and smiled. 'Having fun?'

'Of course. Always.' He held the bar tighter.

Another crushed fence and they were in a field ploughed and ready to plant. I wonder if it's for artichokes, she thought. I love artichokes. The car grazed paintwork and followed them through.

'Ok, you lot.' Ros turned left and followed the lines between the soft furrows. Her friends did the same. She sped up to gain a bit of space in case someone was trigger happy. When they were well into a second field of soft volcanic loam she turned right, across the furrows. That was west according to her reckoning by the scorching sun. The Landrover bucked and jumped and carved a slewed path through the field. Their followers tried to do the same but ploughed to their axles within seconds. A couple of shots too far away and Ros and Philip were on their own.

'Our tracks are a bit obvious at present. What time is it?'

'The back of 9.'

'That's good. We might chance a road as soon as the sun starts to go.'

Driving without lights was slow but there was no one else on the road. No people that Ros could see anyway. Philip opened the gates into the courtyard and closed them as soon as she was in. The black wolfhounds barked, approached and sniffed. But they settled as soon as they saw the vehicle. Ros parked close to a wall a little way from the front door.

'Buonasera signora e signore,' said Salvatore. He showed no surprise as he closed the door behind them. 'Vorresti mangiare?'

'Sì grazie,' she replied.

'Pizza and Chianti. Not a bad combination' she said.

'Maybe we should talk to Nico about her car at breakfast,' he said.

'A good idea.'

§

'How are you both?' There was concern in Nico's voice.

'Good enough,' said Philip. 'Nothing broken.'

'Sorry about your car, Nico,' said Ros.

'That is not a problem. Salvatore took it to the mechanic earlier this morning.'

The servant smiled and poured more coffee for Ros and Nico. A moment later Philip's espresso curled steam in front of him.

'Now that they have found you it is important that you meet the families as soon as possible. Gabriel will collect you later.' She finished her coffee in her own thoughts. Then she got up and came to their side of the table.

'Stay safe, Ros,' she said and hugged her tight. 'And you Philip,' as she did the same. 'I am sorry that our problems have become so dangerous for you.'

When she left they were quiet for a time. But their eyes gravitated to the pile of papers and record books.

'You pick first, Ros.'

She selected "Giardini" because they'd spent such lovely times in them. He picked up "Finanza", a volume that he did not recognize. Ros sat at the table in the loggia, within the sounds of water and the garden. Her bare feet absorbed the cool of the marble. She curled open a new sheet of her small sketch pad and placed it with pencils beside her. He found an antique writing bureau to lay his notebook and spread open the columns of figures. His Italian dictionary was close. He was oblivious to the lavish surrounds and the portraits looking down on him.

When mid-day struck on the English Grandfather clock Gabriel walked in. 'Hello Philip.'

Philip looked up without comprehending for a moment. 'Oh hello Gabriel, I suppose it's time to go.' He called for Ros and tucked his notebook into his shirt pocket.

'Buongiorno Gabriel.' Her hair was ruffled as though she had been twisting strands. A dozen leaves of paper were folded over in her sketchbook. She put on her shoes.

'Have you got it?' she said as they walked out to the courtyard.

'I think so. Ok if we compare notes later?'

'That's a plan.'

Gabriel's driving was fast and efficient as before. But his eyes constantly checked his rear and side mirrors. The air blew hot through the open windows. Ros enjoyed being driven, and relaxed. Philip was as alert as Gabriel.

His kitchen seemed full of men; sharp eyes from weather-worn faces with stubble watched Philip and Ros come in. No one got up or smiled.

Buon giorno a tutti, 'Philip and Ros said together.

'Buona giornata.' It was mumbled.

Elizabetta brought out coffee and topped up empty cups before disappearing into the back room. Philip sipped his and then spoke.

'I will speak in English. Gabriel would you mind translating, please? Your English is much better than my Italian.' Gabriel nodded. 'We were asked to come here by Peter, to solve a problem of theft from his dig. What we discovered was so much more.'

'Have you found the thief?'

'Not yet but I believe we are close.'

'Where have you worked before?'

'In Iran, Cyprus and in Britain.'

'Have you found precious things?'

'Yes, a great deal of very special things.'

'Why are you not wealthy?' Questions came as rapid fire bullets.

'We are archaeologists. We don't keep anything for ourselves.'

'Why?'

'Because that's not right. We work for knowledge.'

'Why?'

'I suppose it's a code, something we live by.'

'Why did you go on a job with Gabriel?'

'He asked me. Because he trusted me I trusted him.'

'Why?'

'Look there is no trick here. We are what we appear to be. I don't have a particular philosophy; it's just the right thing to do.'

'Are you a hero?'

'No. I just don't react well to bullies. It's a family thing.'

'He does get a bit protective,' Ros said. That probably went over their heads she thought.

'On the other digs the people we worked with trusted us,' said Ros. Whether a woman's voice in the discussion was welcome was not her problem. 'We let them decide what to do with their treasures.'

'We are not stupid. Why should we trust you? You don't risk anything.'

Gabriel cut in above the grumbles. 'They have risked their lives twice.' Into the silence he explained.

'It was you in that bird thing?'

'Yes,' said Philip.

'Photographing Antonio's diggings?'

'Yes.'

The man did a motion with his hand: a circle with his fingers around his head and then blowing across the flat of his hand. The men smiled.

'No I am not mad. We need proof if we are going to stop Antonio destroying priceless tombs.'

'Antonio is too powerful. No one wins against him.'

'We do with proof. And we do if you all work with Gabriel. Together we CAN win.'

'I suppose you want to tell the police everything.'

'We want a solid case for them.'

'Italian cops are in Antonio's pocket.'

'Maybe, so we contact international police.'

'You tell us,' an old voice spoke directly to Ros. 'How did you get out of the Orvieto tunnels?'

Ros started to explain in Italian but their eyes wouldn't let her think quickly enough. In English she told them how they marked the floor to get the right way. Gabriel did the rest.

'And you climbed down the cliff on a rope?'

'Yes.'

'And you drove the car yesterday?'

'Yes.'

'Why didn't you drive?' he said to Philip.

'It was her turn. She's a good driver.'

'What happens to us if Antonio goes down?'

'There will be an amnesty for all the families if you do what Gabriel is doing.'

Philip put his hand up and the noise settled down.

'Change is coming. International police are getting stronger. To be safe you must be part of it. Work with the archaeologists, the museums and universities. You can save Italian culture from being lost overseas.'

Ros decided to chance her arm again. 'Gabriel told us that clandestini open the tombs to get a bit of money in the lean times.' She waited for their interest to come back. 'If you all record everything and work together then there is far more money for all of you. Capofamiglia, this is the future.'

She stopped and waited. Philip met her eyes. Let them work it out. They saw Gabriel answering questions. Jacopo came through and showed the photographs he was so proud of. They were passed around to lots of comment. Ros heard, 'We have things like that' and 'How do you take photographs in there?' Several times she heard Gabriel say, 'Questo è il futuro', 'This is the future'.

Elizabetta came out with plates of freshly made little cakes and more coffee. By late afternoon Philip had explained several times how he flew that thing. Elizabetta got a full account of Ros' driving exploits, so she could tell the other Nonnas when they next met.

Gabriel dropped them off at the Palazzo.

'Thank you Gabriel,' he said.

'Buona fortuna con le famiglie,' she said.

He smiled and nodded.

They walked into the drawing room with new energy. 'We might just be lucky there,' she said.

'You might have to teach me to drive,' he said.

Nico held out two glasses of chilled Chianti, still young and fresh, a bit like Martina's rosé at the trattoria. 'Saluti.'

'Saluti.'

'Well, Philip, have you worked out who Marta is,' Ros said.

'Yes and who she was married to.'

'Let's go out to the garden. It seems appropriate. Nico, after you.'

An intermittent wind of cool and heat blew from changing directions. On a seat under the fragrance of a linden tree Ros asked first.

'Who is Marta?'

'Marietta Corsini, born around 1480, died in 1553.'

'Who was her husband?'

'Niccolò Machiavelli, born 1469, died 1527.'

'The Machiavelli?' Nico was stunned.

'Yes, Florentine diplomat and scholar, author of "The Prince".

He handed a postcard of a 15th century painting to Nico. It was a portrait from the Palazzo Vecchio in Florence by Santi di Tito. It was of a slim, dark-haired young man with sparkling eyes and wry smile.

Yes, Nico saw that. But there was also a fearless observer of men, and maybe a little gentleness towards her sex.

'And the garden? Have you managed to work out that too?'

'You first Ros.'

'No you Philip.' He waited and then she tilted her head in agreement.

'Nico your family bought another estate in 1527. It belonged to Marietta on the death of her husband. The garden is near San Casciano, not far from Florence. The village is Percussina.'

§

CHAPTER 9

Philip opened his eyes to bright sunlight. An espresso was conveniently placed on the bedside table. Ros sat beside the window reading. As he sipped the hot nectar he watched her take in a page then pause to translate facts into thoughts. In between times her eyes scanned the sky as though she was looking for inspiration.

'Thanks for the coffee,' he said.

'No problem. I thought you might need it after twisting and turning half the night.'

'It was hot.'

'Yes. It's a bit too Queensland for Italy.'

'What have you learnt about him so far?'

'He wrote quite a few books besides "The Prince". The Catholic Church didn't like him; he was in league with the Devil as far as they were concerned.'

'Given your thoughts that might endear him to you,' he said.

'The Vatican was a bit hard to take.'

'He's famous for the phrase "The end justifies the means", that is to reach a good goal you can do bad things to get there,' he said.

'That sounds like we're back to the Church again. I'm sure the Borgias would have agreed with him.'

'There is doubt whether he ever said it, as it is not in his writings.'

For the rest of the morning both were engrossed in anything they could find on Machiavelli in Nico's library. At lunch Salvatore laid out dishes of Pasta al Pesto and Spaghetti al Pomodoro on a warming tray, with an Insalata to one side. Ros and Philip's noses dragged them out of the text to the table.

'Well you wouldn't believe what I've discovered,' she said.

'You wouldn't believe what I've discovered.'

'Ok, you first,' she said.

He could see her eagerness had been caught in mid-flight. 'Sorry, you first.' He waited. 'Really, I'm sorry. Come on, love, tell me.'

'Well,' she slowly wound up. 'I looked up Florence and Percussina. Yes he did live there, when he was exiled by the Medici. He travelled a great deal as a diplomat. There was a Borgia Pope and Niccolò met Cesare Borgia.'

Philip listened. Come on Ros, he thought, I did the wrong thing but. Was it an image of his mother that made him put on a smile, show passion in his eyes and keep his mouth shut? But then his interest became real.

'He was instrumental in creating the painting contest of the age, Michelangelo Buonarroti versus Leonardo da Vinci working on opposite walls of the Council Hall of the Palazzo Vecchio in Florence. "The Battle of Cascina" by a young Michelangelo and "The Battle of Anghiari" by an older Leonardo were never finished but through copies they influenced a whole generation of artists. Machiavelli knew Leonardo and gave him work. For a year they worked together on Leonardo's plan to defeat the city of Pisa by diverting the Arno River. Can you imagine Leonardo daring such a technically difficult piece of engineering? Philip, they could even have been friends.'

'Wow that is seriously hard to match. Books, that's the theme I discovered. He lived when books were an expensive rarity in Florence. Rich collectors like the Medicis scoured Europe and the Arab World for ancient texts by Greek and Roman authors to build up their libraries. This was a time of rediscovery of the Ancient World and its reinterpretation by the masters of the Renaissance. Gutenberg invented his printing press just 30 years before Machiavelli was born. His father, Bernardo, worked for a year in exchange for one book, a work by Livy. So Niccolò grew up in a home where books were valued and available. The Medici cut short his diplomatic career. It was no surprise that he turned to writing himself, not just "The Prince" but a series called "The Art of War" and many other works. He went back to what he owed his father, a love of books.'

Whenever Ros got up to get another glass of lime-flavoured water she looked at the sky. It had that silver tinge behind every delicate hue of mist all the way to a distant horizon. Sometimes clouds would appear and move quickly at a great height. Later they were dark and bubbled up into grotesque mountains. Far away she heard thunder and counted. Yes it was a long way off. Just before dark they sat in the loggia. It was too hot to drink wine. Salvatore brought them two chilled glasses of Peroni Nastro Azzurro lager. The heat became stifling humidity, until the first rain drops fell. It began gently but during the meal it became heavier. Nico was elsewhere or just in another section of the Palazzo. The noise of the downpour hid all but them.

Ros lay on her back in bed and listened. Philip did the same. There was a maelstrom of wind and thunder just above their heads. The deluge continued unabated. It was still warm under a single sheet. His fingers walked across and rested on her hand, and then her waist, and then her belly. Ros picked up his palm and put it back where it started.

'Sorry,' he said.

'No, it's not you.'

'As a kid we used to have a house by the river,' she began. 'It was an old wooden Queenslander, with wide verandahs all around. In the garden below were two Poinciana trees that Dad had planted. When they were in bloom it was like a carpet of red flowers. We used to lie down in the fork and read a book, or just look up at the birds flying through the overhead branches.

'What, you were laying in a tree?'

'Yes. What's wrong with that?'

'Nothing. Just that we didn't do things like that where I came from. Well maybe we did but it was a long way up. You make it sound like a chair.'

'Culture gap probably,' said Ros.

'One time it poured for days, then more rain came. This night it didn't stop. I got up and went out to join Mum on the verandah. She was looking down on the river. It roared like a waterfall. We heard cows bellowing as they floated down towards the sea. When it was light we could see whole trees drifting in eddies and whirlpools. Most had snakes or possums and other critters hanging on to them. The water was like thick brown mud. You wouldn't even think of swimming in it, it was suicidal. And then our neighbours' houses started to go under. The peaks of their iron rooves disappeared in the chocolate. Some groaned and twisted and then just floated away, adding to all the wood and debris in that torrent. The flood crept across the lawns of the sandstone university buildings across the river, until each was a little island in a lake. All the books in the libraries, the art work, everything was just gone.' She paused and Philip waited. The river above their heads flowed unabated.

'Philip, this is not good. It feels the same.'

He had learned to trust her feelings. 'What do you want to do?'

'We have to wake Nico.'

'It's better if you do that. I will try downstairs to see if Salvatore lives on site.'

Ros put on her clothes: jeans, shoes, and a jacket that she'd put in, just in case. She started to wander the corridors, putting on lights whenever she found the switches amongst the ancient faces.

'Nico, Nico,' she called gently. 'Wake up, Nico.' She walked and walked in the vast place. Talk about getting lost, she thought, you could hide the five thousand in here. It must be Philip, I'm thinking Biblical. Not that he's particularly that way inclined but more so than me.

'Yes, Ros?' A sleepy voice came from behind a door.

'Can I come in?'

'Yes, do.'

Nico's room was plainer than Ros had imagined: a few more modern pieces of furniture, a couple of Persian rugs that Philip would like, a personal bathroom to one side, and windows to the garden. Nico sat up in bed dressed in a masculine pyjama top and trousers.

'Nico, we have to do something. This amount of rain so quickly is not good.'

Nico rubbed her eyes. 'What do you want to do? Why?'

'The Acqua Gentile is sure to flood. We need to help the dig people in their tents.'

'Oh. You don't think they are high enough up?'

Ros felt the resistance. Nico is not like this. Was she waiting for Fortuna to decide or was she afraid to do anything that Fortuna would turn bad? Maybe she's just swamped by the thought of an emergency. 'Nico, you have to help. Not just the dig people. What about the people in the village and the farmers?'

'You want me to help all of them?'

'As many as you can, yes. It's the right thing to do. Look Nico, I know that you are not mean or hard-hearted but if you help these people now, in what I think is going to be a desperate time, what will come back to you from these people will be immense. You will get far more out than ever you put in. And the families will trust you and Gabriel.'

Nico nodded slowly. 'Yes Ros.'

'One more small request, Nico, if you don't mind?

'Yes?'

'Have you a hat I can borrow? I don't mind being drenched but I'd prefer not to get my head wet.'

Nico smiled and nodded. Australians are strange people, she thought.

Ros closed the door behind her. She heard Nico making phone calls. Downstairs in the courtyard she heard vehicles crunching on the gravel and their engines left running. She saw that Philip had found his beloved Landrover and Nico's Fiat. Beside it was a Volkswagen van, what she would call a Combie. I wonder if Ferrari makes a van, she thought.

Nico walked out in a black leather trench coat, jeans and wellington boots. Before she got into the Fiat she handed Ros a cap: white with a red band around the brim with a yellow shield framing a prancing black stallion.

'Perfect. Does it make this thing go any faster?' she said as she slid on the Ferrari racing cap.

Nico flashed her lights for Philip to go first. Ros followed her in the Combie. When had she last driven one of these, she thought, as they sloshed out on to the road to Città Sotto? As she climbed through the gears, with that familiar over-revving that always seemed to happen with these things, it all came back to her. The rain thrashed in gusts across the windscreen and buffeted the van. Ahead Philip warned of what was coming whenever he crashed through a flash flood. Solid sheets of water ejected from Nico's tyres as she crossed deep puddles. Her lights showed shrapnel from trees and hedges and rivulets of mud.

When they came to the bridge they looked down on the dig trenches and what should have been tent city. There were waterfalls pouring down from Città Sopra into M1, cascades of mud over the baulks and lakes where the sarcophagus and other graves existed. No tent was upright. People frantically tried to save personal belongings like passports. They slithered and fell like amateur skaters. Very, very close the turbulence of Acqua Gentile cut away the ground they all stood on.

All three vehicles pulled up behind Gabriel's Fiat. He groped his way down the path holding on to shrubbery as he went. In seconds they were doing the same.

'Nico, please, can you stay on top and guide them into the vehicles?' Ros shouted through the swirling blast.

Nico nodded.

'Ros, Ros, you have the path,' Philip shouted.

She wondered where he had found a leather Akubra. You're getting more Aussie every day, Philip. She nodded to him just like Nico.

As she stood there she heard the frightened cries of animals. She saw sheep bobbing up and down in the violence of the current. Deep throated barks punctuated the bleating. They were there for a second before they were lost in the darkness beyond the citadel. Their distressed calls became fainter until there was nothing. Her memories of that childhood night returned.

'It's ok, Melissa. Hang on to the branches as you go up. Nico will help you at the top.' Ros watched her slither and slide until she had pulled herself on to the bridge. Students newly arrived from Birmingham and

Durham followed her up. Mike stayed with Philip and Gabriel until there was no one left.

'Where do we take them, Philip?' Ros asked.

'"La Macchia",' said Nico. 'She is ready.'

The convoy slowly climbed the twists and turns of the hill. Extra weight of bodies helped traction, particularly in the Combie. Always light on the back end like a Ute when empty, Ros thought. Her tyres were spinning on the final rises before the near-flat of each turn. But she kept it in third gear, one speed and twisted the wheel against the skids. She thought about getting everyone to bounce but that worked in mud, not so well on drop edges into the macchia scrub.

'Vieni tutti.' Martina led everyone to the fire that her husband had just lit. They dripped volumes over the stone floor as they shivered and rubbed themselves with the towels she had found.

'Grazie Martina,' came from around the room.

'What about the families, Gabriel?' asked Ros. 'Are they safe?'

'I don't know. Some have telephones but many lines are down.'

'Can you guide us?'

'Ros I think we should double up the vehicles,' Philip said. 'What if you and Nico have the van and Gabriel and I the Landrover?'

'Ok by me. Nico, Gabriel?'

They nodded.

'Torneremo a Martina,' Nico said.

A wind gust grew louder and then pummelled the big glass window. It cracked and shattered across the tables and floor. Screams turned into "Are you all right?", "The glass didn't get you?" Mike picked up bigger pieces and put them into the dustpans worked by Martina and her husband. He and Mike taped a sheet over the gaping hole. She stirred and served the minestrone.

'Where to?' Philip and Ros asked. Nico and Gabriel spoke too rapidly for Ros to follow. All she understood was something "In un'ora". Then the pair climbed into the passenger seats.

Ros soon had no idea where she was but luckily Nico did. They did a circuit of her tenant farmers whose houses were low-lying or close to tributaries of the Acqua Gentile. Most had shedded their animals in the afternoon when they saw what was coming. Some had already tied tarpaulins over rooves where a rotten beam had collapsed or tiles had blown off.

'È bello che tu venga, Signorina Nicola,' torch-lit grizzled faces said to Nico.

The men stayed with frightened creatures in their barns but where houses were sodden they were glad of help for their womenfolk and children. Whenever the Combie was packed to the gunnels with chattering bodies Nico guided Ros back to the Palazzo.

'Vieni tutti,' said Salvatore at the door. The Palazzo shone with every light on, like a fairy-tale castle.

'Grazie Contessa.'

'Grazie Contessa.'

Nico looked at her Bulgari watch. 'There is time for another trip.'

We'll make time, Ros thought.

When they arrived back at La Macchia Peter greeted them. 'It's nice to see you both. I have housed most at my place and the storeroom but there are still some lost souls.'

A dozen bodies jammed into the Combie and took a deep breath in to slide the doors closed. They smelled like wet carpet, Ros thought. She pulled off slowly into another heavy shower. The van was unwieldy with the excessive weight crushing the tyres. It was like steering a barge.

Someone with a voice like Frank started to warble, "I'm singing in the rain". Everyone joined in, even Nico who knew most of the words. That was followed by "Here comes the sun".

'Please stay put everyone,' Ros said when the van slewed with too much movement in the back.

As they pulled into the courtyard "You are the sunshine in my life" was sung especially for Nico. Even in the darkness Ros could see her blush. Salvatore welcomed them in with a "the more the merrier" expression on his face.

'We should find Gabriel and Philip now,' Nico said.

At a crossroads five kilometres downstream from Alta Cresta they pulled up behind the Landrover, with all its lights on and the engine running. Inside were the youngest children. Outside Ros counted twenty people huddled against the driving rain.

'Hi Ros. Hello Nico.' Philip gave Ros a hug and Nico a polite touch of cheek on both sides.

Ros felt how cold he was. 'Are you finished?'

'No, there are another couple of farms down by the river, and one more upstream.'

Gabriel guided the youngest, oldest and mothers into the Combie. Another full load, thought Ros.

'Can you drive this thing?' Ros said to Nico.

'I think so but you're better Ros. Let's not change what works.'

'See you in a bit,' Ros said and patted Philip's arm.

Early in the trip Ros agreed with Nico. This weather was not letting up and the puddles just got bigger.

'This is ridiculous,' she said after creating another bow wave like a steamer. 'Goodness knows where the pot-holes are,' as she bounced the Combie suspension yet again.

'Vieni in "gente dell'acqua",' Salvatore said as the latest group arrived. Ros had never heard him say so much.

'Just one more, Ros,' Philip said as the Combie was loaded again. 'Gabriel is concerned about Luigi, the shepherd. We'll see you in a bit.'

'Can every Aussie drive like you?' Nico said to Ros.

'I'm not sure what to say to that. We do get some wild weather in Queensland.'

Ros accompanied Nico as she did a tour of all the rooms of her home where families and the site volunteers were now encamped.

'Grazie Salvatore.'

'Prego Contessa.'

Ros looked at her watch. It was 3am. The weather was as foul as ever.

Philip observed the farm track ahead. It was rutted and the descent was steep. He dropped into low range four-wheel-drive. Did Luigi drive a vehicle on this, Philip wondered? He stayed in first and let the gears act like brakes as he rode the crests above the wheel-deep ruts. The tyres insisted on trying to slide into the craters as he fought the wheel to stop them. The engine whined as he and Gabriel were thrown left and right into the doors and each other. But then the road levelled out on to a sloppy plain of water and mud. Bow waves of the stuff sloshed over the windscreen and left him blind until the wipers caught up. Ahead there was a tumbled stone hut and a lantern.

Philip stopped on a rocky patch where he might not get bogged. Gabriel got out and shone his torch.

'Luigi,' he called. 'Luigi dove sei?'

Philip got out and did the same. Clearly the hut was a shambles after the wind and flood.

'Qui.'

It was faint but they could follow the sound. As they got close the roar of the floodwaters was colossal. There, up to his waist in what was once his barn, Luigi was trying to drag a sheep to dry ground. Its fleece was saturated. Gabriel and Philip both waded in and helped the exhausted old man pull it to safety.

'Are there any more, Gabriel?'

Gabriel asked Luigi. 'No Philip. He's lost everything.'

On cue they all heard a high-pitched scream followed by a sneeze.

'Capri! È Capri!' the old man said and ran towards the noise.

It came from high up. Gabriel and Philip fanned their torches like searchlights over the raging brown sludge. Up in a cleft of a tree stood the billy goat Philip had seen leading the flock. He looked down on them like the god Pan. There was five metres of water to cross to reach him.

'We could link arms and pull him back,' said Gabriel.

'Just wait, Gabriel.' Philip returned with a rope from the back of the Landrover. If it was strong enough to pull the vehicle out of a swamp it would do the job here.

Gabriel said words to Luigi that were lost to Philip in the wind. Luigi tied a knot around himself with an extra length in his hand. Gabriel and Philip did the same, with the last length run out to a boulder that Philip looped around.

'Andiamo Luigi,' Gabriel shouted, and followed Luigi into the water.

Capri rutted and danced to avoid going into the flood. Only Luigi could get close enough to him to tie the rope and not be skewered by the scimitar horns.

'Tirare!' Luigi yelled.

Capri's hooves carved ruts through the bark. With a final screech he leapt towards Luigi and submerged totally. Philip and Gabriel pulled back and Luigi matched them. With the goat still under water they grimaced with the strain as they dragged his weight against the current.

'Vieni, bastardo!'

They slipped and slid into and out of the water until the horns and beard of Capri surfaced. The creature spluttered and shrieked at them until he was out. Then he danced around like a manic banshee until Luigi settled him down with incomprehensible soothing sounds.

Ros saw the lights enter the courtyard. She walked out to the drivers' side and waited for the door to open. Three muddy, sodden men sat in the front seat.

'Buona notte signora,' said Luigi in gearstick position.

'Don't open the back, Ros. Let Luigi do it,' said Philip.

'Ok. Nice to see you in one piece,' Ros said. Dawn was a cloudy grey but the rain had stopped.

Salvatore stood at the door but stepped back when Luigi lifted out a trussed up Capri. He and Gabriel found a solid shed in the garden for him before they accepted Salvatore's welcome.

Philip dallied in the hot shower. He watched a ton of topsoil flow towards the plug hole. Then he lay on his back under the single sheet.

Ros was by his side. Her fingers crept across and curled into his palm. She felt him slip away into exhausted sleep. 'Another time, Philip.' She shut her eyes and joined him.

Around one scorching heat and bright sun poured through the curtains. Philip stretched his legs and arms as far as they would extend. He opened his eyes and sat up. Ros put an espresso in his hand.

'Grazie.'

'Prego.'

'Is Salvatore feeding the five thousand?'

'Yep. Nico has gone out for more food.'

'Does she need us? I'd like to go to the site.'

'I'm sure she'll manage.'

In the dining room Ros and Philip joined the queue. The smorgasbord reminded her of a classy Brisbane hotel, without the Moreton Bay Bugs, Mud crabs and towers of prawns.

'Grazie Philip,' said Luigi through a gap-toothed smile. He was back for seconds.

'Non era niente,' said Philip.

'You're getting better,' said Ros.

The trip to Alta Cresta was slow, even for the Landrover. The flood was still coming down from the mountains onto land that was already saturated. Water-logged fields would take days to drain even with the baking sun. The humidity was like a sauna. In the town debris lay in waves across the cobbles: airborne tiles that had exploded into hundreds of shards; gritty brown sand washed from gardens; and leaves and flowers spread like necklaces. But the original houses with broad eaves and roofed with old Italian tiles received only minor damage. Their ancient shapes, with two thousand years of tradition, had removed the rain efficiently. Hardwood supports would dry out. But the most modern dwellings of pine, with aluminium windows, and clean-cut vertical concrete walls, "toilet blocks" Ros called them, provided most of the wreckage cluttering the streets of this medieval town.

La Macchia was being transformed by Peter's students. A van with Vetraio written on the side was parked outside. Three men were cleaning up after fitting a new window.

'Tutto sembra buono Martina,' Ros said to her.

'Siamo aperti stasera,' Martina said.

'I'm sure the place will be full,' said Philip.

He parked next to the bridge and they looked down on the devastation. There were landslips all around Città Sopra. Antonio's work was visible to everyone. The torrential rain had carved new streams through the macchia. So much of the forest was stacked in tangled piles wherever the current had been weakest. The grass benches of tent city were half their size and decidedly unstable until they dried out.

M1 had survived but a pump was working hard to drain it. So much of the cliffs had slumped across metres of the site, just like their excavations had proved at the start of the season. The baulks, and that section that Bradley had not worked very hard at, looked like sandcastles swept by a giant wave. Peter and Gabriel were down there in the mud supervising the timberwork shoring that might stop their collapse.

'Here's proof for the need to meticulously record,' Philip said.

He watched Mike work a bucket chain to drain the cemetery area. He climbed down and joined it.

Ros looked at Melissa tagging finds that had washed out of the collapse. After a slither and slide clutching at unstable roots she set up her Pentax to complete the record. At the end of the day Ros could not avoid the irony that these were the best pieces, "trinkets" he called them, that Peter had found all season.

'Where are they being stored, Melissa?'

'In Peter's lockup as usual.'

'Is that a good idea?'

'It's up to Peter really.'

La Macchia was full that evening but no one stayed late. Peter and the villagers had found accommodation for all the team inside Alta Cresta.

Their generosity of spirit was tangible. No lives had been lost and livelihoods could be repaired. As Ros said it was people not things that mattered.

Inside the workroom a torch flitted across the floor. The front door was slightly ajar. The silhouette showed no sign of haste as things were replaced as they had been. When the door clicked shut the body language was more than confident, it was arrogant.

'Hello, Bradley,' said Peter. He flicked on his torch and shone it into Bradley's startled eyes. Behind Peter there stood Nico, Gabriel, Ros and Philip.

'Why did you do it, Bradley?' There was sadness in Peter's voice. He really wanted to understand.

'Why? Why not?' Bradley said. 'It's worth a few bucks.'

'It's knowledge, Bradley. That's what it's worth.'

'Whatever. This here is treasure not knowledge. It's all about now. My skull is not in the past like yours.'

'Have you anything else to say before we pass you on to the local constabulary?'

'Nah, don't do that.'

'Why?'

'The cop's with Antonio.'

'You're frightened of him,' said Ros.

'He fits up losers,' said Bradley and looked down at his feet. 'Whaddya want? I can get things.'

'Are you offering us drugs, Bradley?' said Nico.

'You cottoned on to that?' There was something childish in the look on his face, as if he'd been caught out pinching from his classmates.

'What about Antonio,' asked Gabriel? His tone had the warmth of a stone.

Fear raced across Bradley's face again, then desperation, then that arrogance. 'Whaddya want to know? His operation?' He laughed. 'What's your price?'

Peter, Nico, Gabriel and Ros walked a few paces outside and across the square. Bradley could stew for a while. Philip stood beside him and read his mind. 'Thinking of running?' Philip cracked his knuckles. 'I wouldn't if I were you.'

'We want everything you know about Antonio, everything,' said Nico. 'If it is good enough then you get a plane ticket home.'

'Ok. Thanks guys. I'm outta here.'

'Bradley, can we trust you?'

'Sure.'

Nico lifted a miniature Sony tape recorder from her pocket. She pressed the Rewind button. Bradley squirmed until she squeezed the Play button. "What about Antonio? Whaddya want to know? His operation?" he heard himself say, and then his laugh. She stopped the tape.

'Can we trust you, Bradley?'

'Yes.'

It was a week before they could continue the quest. Philip helped Gabriel repair roof after roof so families could return. Nico carried on her refugee soup kitchen and gave cash handouts as each family went home. Interest free loans helped them start up again with seed and stock. At the site the debris was inspected for more "trinkets" and cleared to a new level. Days of hot sun made the ground workable again. Ros spent her time taking site photos and accompanying Nico on her errands.

Philip was right, this is a lousy road. Like him she rode the crests with her tyres and took the steep gradient very slowly in four-wheel-drive low range. Nico laughed nervously as she was thrown around the cabin.

'Ciao Luigi,' Nico said when Ros pulled hard on the hand brake. He was nailing iron sheets onto his hut. The barn was finished.

'Buongiorno Contessa.'

'Buongiorno, Signorina Rosalind.'

'Abbiamo un regalo per te,' Nico continued.

He climbed down a ladder constructed from macchia. His face changed when he heard barks. Nico opened her door and ducked as two young white Maremma sheep dogs dived out. They circled Luigi and then sat either side at his feet. He buried his strong arthritic fingers in their fur.

Ros and Nico stood by the rear door of the Landrover. Luigi opened it and saw four plump young ewes trussed up on the floor. Great tears rolled down his cheeks.

'Grazie. Grazie mille,' he said over and over as he lifted them out and left their legs partially tied so that they did not run into the scrub.

Nico politely refused his hospitality with the excuse that they had more families to help. Ros dropped the clutch and he watched their steady climb out.

'Nico, it's time we went to Percussina,' Ros said at the evening meal. There were just the three of them, and Salvatore, in the Palazzo. She looked around. The portraits seemed to enjoy the return to quiet. Was there also approval?

'I like early starts,' she said to Philip as their feet crunched on the gravel just on dawn. Nico was comfortable at the wheel of her Fiat. Philip opened the passenger door for Ros and got in the back. 'Better than a Ferrari,' he mumbled to himself.

Within fifteen minutes they were on the E35 Autostrada, which was nearly deserted at that time of the day. Nico drove like Nico, not Peter or Philip or Ros, just fast and confident. After an hour they took the turn off for Siena. Its 13th century cathedral rose above the central square, Il Campo. As a passenger Ros could absorb the details. All the clay had been hosed off the cobbles after the Palio horse race days before. Black and white dominated, whether inside the Cathedral, or on the banners of the seventeen Contrada, the districts who fought for the winner's standard. More time, she thought, later when they had completed what they were here for.

Soon they were back on the Florence Autostrada until the sign for San Casciano in Val di Pesa appeared. 'Like Siena this was first Etruscan, then Roman,' Nico said. 'In the 15th century the Florentines fortified it as a military outpost to defend their city.' Nico drove slowly past a seven metre high section of the ancient city wall.

'What happened to this place, Nico?' Ros said. It felt too new and "feelings' bothered her.

'On the 26th July, 1944, the town was destroyed by retreating Germans and Allied bombardment.'

'Italian reconstruction is renowned in the archaeological world,' Philip said. 'It looks like those skills were applied here.'

Nico went south-west before turning right onto the Via Cassia. On this iron-rich sand and clay soil row after row of Sangiovese grapes climbed over hill and vale. After five kilometres in Chianti countryside she followed the Via Scopeti to Sant'Andrea di Percussina.

'The war destroyed so much here too,' Ros said.

'Careful Italian restoration again,' said Philip. How accurate was their work, Philip thought when he saw the thick stone walls of the Villa Machiavelli Ristorante and L'Albergaccio Inn across the road.

They explored the restaurant/museum that was Machiavelli's home during his exile from Florence. Philip held Ros' hand as she tried to articulate what she felt in the Inn where the man spent his hours playing cards. At the end of each day he walked back along the tunnel of thick stone walls to his library.

'It was an unhappy time for him as he recovered after torture,' she said. 'But then there was optimism, out of a negative came a positive. Fortuna smiled on him again. He distilled his diplomatic experience into "The Prince", one of the most read books ever.'

In the covered courtyard of the restaurant they sat with coffees, bread rolls and hard toasted biscuits with jams and preserves.

'It is all so rustic and beautifully renovated,' Philip said.

'But it's not hard to imagine Machiavelli walking there.' She pointed to the vine rows leading down the slope behind his house. 'He worked with the ancestors of those vines.'

'Your family sold all of this, Nico,' Ros said. 'That was one reason why it was so hard to find. It was no longer a working estate. But the Corsinis kept the garden, even when it didn't give them a return. Do you have any memory of it, Nico?'

'I don't know.'

They finished breakfast and walked back into the paved street. Ros shut her eyes for a moment and then looked along the daunting stone façade. Philip and Nico followed her as her hand lightly traced the stonework to a door. Her fingers stopped on a sign that read "Proprietà privata". 'What do you think is over the wall, Philip?'

He raised his eyebrows. How would I know, he thought? 'I'll give you a hog up and you can see for yourself.'

He leant his back to the stone beside the gate, held out his right hand supported by his left. She put her right foot in and Nico steadied her other hand.

'Ready, Philip?'

'Always.'

Ros pushed hard until her shoulders were above the wall. She gripped the top with her forearms and became still. Below was a cobbled path two people wide between more walls. It was straight with occasional long steps as it led down the slope beside the grape vines visible from the restaurant. Immediately below and right was the gate. She saw a large sliding bolt pushed tight into the wall.

'Steady me, Philip.' She bent her knees and pulled herself up until she straddled the wall.

'Is this another one of your talents, Ros?' asked Nico.

'Maybe.'

She swung over and slid down to her finger tips and dropped. Her bent knees took the shock but the uneven cobbles left her on her backside. No need to broadcast that one, she thought as she brushed herself off. She tried the bolt but it was stiff. It hadn't been opened for a long time. No sticks but there were a few bits of rubble. She belted the bolt along its length with a rock.

'Do cat burglars usually make so much noise?' Nico said through the wood.

'I could do with an oil can and a hammer. Not what you carry in your handbag, Nico?'

Ros got enough purchase to turn the bolt sideways but no further. It was stuck tight. 'Philip I think we all need to shin over. This thing won't budge.' She looked up at the wall. There was no way she could jump that high. But she could use that bolt. With lifting her left foot on to it like a step she bounced and went up on three. Her fingers caught the ledge above the door. With muscles she had forgotten she translated arm strength to forearms. Over they went and then a leg scrabble to get her right leg then left to the top.

'Your turn, Nico.'

Philip went back into position. Nico's right foot went into his cupped hands.

'I'll catch you, Nico.' Ros held out her hands as her legs tightly gripped the wall.

Nico took a deep breath and up she went, to her full height. It was not enough, but just enough for Ros to reach down to grip her palms.

'Push her up, Philip.'

He got her up to his chest and turned. 'Aargh,' he cursed to slide her foot to his shoulders. Nico's arms lay over the wall. Ros slid back a bit and pulled first Nico's arm and then her left leg until she sat on the wall with Ros. Nico brushed off cement dust and checked her scratches.

'How about you two move along a bit? I don't want to push you off.'

Philip looked up and down the street. Amazingly there was still no one around. 'Ok.' He went to the other side of the road, took a few deep breaths and focused on the stonework. The strides were few and long. His right foot lifted in the jump to gain leverage on a small projecting ledge. Momentum and the push planted his forearms on the cemented top.

Nico watched taut lines stand out on his forehead and cheeks as he pulled himself up and over the wall.

'Ok you two, Nico first.'

She slid along and then dropped her legs over. Ros was with her as she stretched to the length of her arms. Petite was not always an advantage, Nico thought.

'I've got your arms, Nico.'

'That's them, I have your feet. Just let go and slide down.' Philip lowered his arms from above his head down to chest height. Nico reached out to his hands and he lowered her down.

'Same thing, Ros.' Her fingers gripped the lip like a rock climber but her feet just reached his upstretched palms. Slowly he took her heaviness and lowered her like a set of weights in a gym. He couldn't resist circling her waist as her feet steadied on the ground.

'Well that was fun,' Philip said. 'It's time for you to lead on, Ros.'

'I think Nico should go first. If I'm right she does own it.'

'Thank you both.'

As he took the rear behind Ros and Nico walking together, he studied the stonework either side. It was from a time when labour was cheap: well-built by craftsmen it could be a hundred years old or five times that. The concept of lasting for one lifetime was an alien modern invention, just as it would have been to the Victorians in Britain. After eighty metres the girls stopped at a gate like the last. Ros was busily working out a way over the next wall. As he caught up with them Nico tried the handle. It lowered and the door creaked open. He followed Nico and Ros through.

Ros had seen so many Italian gardens now that she felt almost an expert. She guessed the square of walls contained an acre of land. There were pathways leading across the slope to where they intersected with those going up. It was built into the hillside with views across the farmland interspersed with cypress and oak woods. Misty heat masked an outline of Florence and the distant Apennines in a sfumato haze. She followed Nico's tentative progress along gravel paths that were weeded and raked like a Japanese garden. But instead of hedges there were lines of vegetables. Behind the antique statues of Greeks and Romans were black cabbages, lettuce and tomatoes. She recognised the face of Plato, the ugliness of Socrates, and the aloof grandeur of Pericles. Nico stopped at a grotto cut into an edifice made of tufa rock. Ros recognised the coral-like confectionary of its curved walls, bisected in the ceiling by decorative stone arches which had faces of what were probably actors. The centrepiece was a cameo of ancient Greek masks of Tragedy and Comedy.

Ros turned and saw a man in his forties working in a patch of artichokes. Nico was motionless in front of the grotto. Ros turned back and watched him cut off lower leaves with secateurs and then stake each plant spaced about a metre apart.

'Cosa stai facendo qui?' He stood up and frowned.

'Siamo venuti per vedere il giardino,' Ros said. She smiled and spread her arms in admiration.

'Il giardino appartiene alla Contessa. È privato.'

'Sono la Contessa di Percussina.' Nico was by her side.

He stood silent in shock.

'Come ti chiami?' Nico held out her hand.

'Mi dispiace. Sono Alessandro Pisano.' He took off his hat and shook her hand gently.

Ros listened and was able to translate most of the conversation to Philip. Alessandro had tended this garden since the war. The Corsinis let him use it as his own as long as he maintained it. When fountains broke he could not fix them or afford an expert. So they became ponds of rainwater green with algae. All the hedges were too much work for one man so he replaced them with vegetables for his family. Water piped from springs was enough for his needs.

'What happened here during the war?' Philip asked.

'Molte bombe.' He mimed the shells pouring like rain everywhere. His father came to the garden the next day to see what happened. He did not return. After Mussolini was executed an important lady came to the garden. She called herself Ginevra Corsini, Contessa di Percussina.

'She was my grandmother,' Nico said in English. Then she went back to Italian with Alessandro. Did he remember her coming back much later with a little girl. Nico was remembering things. Yes, he was a young man then. The old lady walked very slowly holding the little girl's hand. She was telling her things. But then Alessandro's sister brought their dog into the garden.

'Io ricordo.' 'Yes, I remember it. It was big and white. Grandma shouted at it but it came anyway. It knocked me over and sat on my chest. His big mouth with teeth dribbled over my face. I remember how frightened I was.'

Young Alessandro had called away the dog and carried the little girl to a seat. Now he pointed to a path lined with statues and two antique urns on marble pedestals.

Nico walked with him to the place. There was no seat but at the top of wide stairs was another grotto. It was a huge concrete gargoyle face, with holes for eyes, and whiskers and hair like a shaggy dog. The open mouth topped with sharp eye teeth was big enough for a man to walk through.

'La Bocca dell'Inferno,' 'The Mouth of Hell. I remember now.'

§

CHAPTER 10

'Harry! Harry! Over here, Harry.'

Harry changed direction and followed the voice. Pickles, with Cec and the Kiwi crew, was ahead of him somewhere, through the dust cloud from the latest shell. He heard another whine of explosive overhead and dropped to the ground. It blasted rock and concrete from what was a building a moment ago. Those Tiger tanks embedded in San Casciano had their mark. After the peppering hail had turned to swirling mist he got up again. There, over there. He dropped into the field drain with the rest of them.

'Was it worth it, Harry?' Pickles slapped some of the dust from Harry's lean shoulders.

'Did you get lost again? You poms have no sense of direction. You start in Sicily and by Rome you've joined the Kiwis.'

He laughed at Harry's big blue eyes staring out of a coating of white and black grime.

Harry undid a couple of buttons of his uniform and produced items like a magician from a top hat: potatoes, a few carrots, onions and a rather scrawny bird that was probably a chicken. While Cec dismantled the bird and threw the vegetables into the pot the dust cleared. German shelling had moved to the western flank held by the Maori battalion. To the east of them the 6th South African Armoured Division was well back. It looked like 5th Brigade, the New Zealanders, would have to take the town by the front door.

'Best to fill our bellies before the fun begins,' said Pickles. It was his turn next. They all said he was a past master at snaffling, hence his nickname.

He watched the British shelling. The Germans were not giving up that hill top; a centre for communications with a commanding position. Soon after RAF bombers produced a spectacular light show. After a second run during the night he wondered if anything existed in that pile of rubble.

Harry watched the sun spread across this warm land of vines, olives and hill-top towns. If he closed his mind to distant shelling and machine gun fire, and maybe ignored the holes like smallpox across the land, there was an ancient tranquillity to this place. But he was tired: of the destruction he'd seen from the Sicily landings, the burnt shells of cathedrals and monasteries: Palermo, Montecassino. The ruins of Naples smouldered while Vesuvius erupted and killed a few more. People said that the Vatican was telling Churchill to protect Italian culture. He'd seen precious little of that happen on his steady slog north. Now, at the Arno Line it was all going to happen again, with Florence in the firing line this time.

'Come on Harry, the show must go on,' said Pickles. Left and right men got out of hollows or from behind rubble and began the advance up to San Casciano. Behind were 22nd Battalion carriers. The infantry carefully picked a route through the results of shells and bombs; and the numerous mines and booby traps. Only sniper fire met them as they entered the town just before 10am. It was the 25th July, nine days before his birthday, Harry thought.

The blast and shouts were simultaneous. A carrier had hit a mine just behind him. There were dead amongst the wounded scattered around the smoking hulk. His name was not on that one, he thought. Over the morning he and his mates picked off the snipers, and the engineers from 6th Field Company cleared enough of the roads to make them passable. Until the enemy poured mortar and shell fire from the east to hamper the proceedings.

On the 26th his crew entered a small village a few kilometres east, with the spires of Florence in the distance. Their digs was a substantial stone building with a tavern opposite. Pickles had been out scouting.

'Harry, come with me.' In the basement was a wine cellar, with a few bottles on the shelves, if they dared to sample what the Germans had left. 'Here.' Pickles opened a door and shone his torch into a stone lined tunnel. It was deep under the road. When they came out they were in the tavern.

'Now that's what I call a worthwhile bit of architecture: your personal access to the pub,' said Pickles.

When they came back to the main living room a rather odd old man was sitting down with an officer. He was sixty if he was a day, thought Harry. His face was red and round, with a huge white moustache that covered his mouth. It took the place of what few follicles grew out of an enormous cranium. He was dressed in a brown suit with a lop-sided polka dot bowtie.

'This is Professor Thomas MacIntosh from the Slade School of Fine Art in London. For the next few days you are to take him wherever he wishes to go. You are to keep him safe.'

'How do you do,' said the Professor through the voluminous curtain of hair on his top lip.

Outside was parked an army jeep with American markings. The officer left after accommodation was provided for the guest.

'I expect you are wondering why an elderly gentleman is here in a war zone,' he said.

'You read my mind,' said Pickles.

'My colleagues and I are here to save and preserve as much Italian culture as possible from the destruction of war.'

Pickles was proud of his knowledge of Italian history. In his eyes he was a bit of a buff.

He looks as though he has walked into this battle accidentally, thought Harry. This fragile academic should not be here. But then he should, because he knows what to save.

'Call me Thomas, gentlemen,' he said as he held up a glass from what Pickles had borrowed from the cellar. None of them were dead yet. Thomas explained the enormity of his task.

'At the start of the war the Italian superintendents of art galleries and museums saw that the cities were targeted by air raids. They decided that the countryside was a safer place for their collections. In Florence alone 3000 crates were filled with art, sculptures, and complete libraries and shipped out to castles, villas and monasteries. Now the combat has come to the country.'

'It's like fighting a war in a museum,' said Pickles.

'Exactly.' Thomas spread out the contents of a satchel. It contained maps and diaries, carefully annotated with his overcrowded notes.

Next morning the jeep started off towards the north east. A carrier followed. Their exploration would cover all surviving villas within the newly liberated zone. Harry drove, with Pickles beside him, and the Professor in the back seat gave directions and a running commentary. He was passionate and talkative. His companions enjoyed the novelty of not being shot at.

'Do you mean that the Nazis plan to blow up every bridge over the Arno?' said Pickles.

'Our intelligence says so: every bridge in Florence, all six including the Ponte Vecchio and the Ponte Santa Trinità. The former was constructed by the Romans, and the latter in the 16th century by Bartolomeo Ammannati, advised by Michelangelo.'

'That's . . .' Pickles blustered.

'Barbarism,' said Harry quietly.

The first villa on the list was a shambles. Paintings, furniture, and glass: everything had been systematically destroyed.

'They even pierced the wine casks,' Pickles said in the flooded cellar.

Harry said nothing as he walked from room to room. The senseless violence against such things of beauty was beyond his mind to comprehend.

The next villa was set down in a hollow. Harry could see it was not in a defensive position like San Casciano. He turned off the ignition and the three climbed out. The sturdy Palazzo looked intact. At the door stood an aged Italian man dressed like a chief waiter. He said nothing as he led them through the dark rooms. Power had long since been cut. Harry felt underdressed in his uniform and army boots. In the centre of the house was a large room. Against every wall were stacked dozens and more dozens of pictures. But one very large one was propped against the table in the centre. He and Pickles just stood with their mouths open. Harry was no art expert like Thomas but he knew Botticelli's "Primavera" when he saw it. This was the most beautiful painting in the world. At least this one, and its mate the "Venus" on the other side, could be saved.

Thomas saw them motionless with silly grins on their faces. He left them while he went off to record what else the Florentine authorities had stored there. By late afternoon they had visited more than a dozen villas and left guards at only three. For the nation that bred Goethe and Wagner Thomas decided that Germany's propensity for villainous destruction was astounding.

After a meal involving bully beef and some local vegetables Harry went outside with a glass of Chianti in his hand.

'Don't get lost, Harry,' called Pickles.

Harry looked down on the rows of vines that probably produced what he was drinking. Instead of a closer inspection he stepped through a hole blasted into a laneway that ran down parallel to the grapes. At the end was a gate. It was unlocked. Inside was a garden that reminded him of his parents' home in Cornwall. Its walls were lined with fruit trees in a similar way. But this was ornate and planned. Gravel paths wound between hedges laid out in geometric patterns. Statues of ancient Greeks and Romans led to fountains. Even without water due to damaged infrastructure he could imagine their sounds and sparkle. Grottoes contained seahorses and dolphins. Rock features had been created out of the local stone. This was a hand-manicured environment meant to be productive and please the eyes and every other sense. Something in his psyche could feel the history of this serene place. He could ramble here forever.

As the light was working down through its colours towards night Harry came back again to the avenue of statues with two Etruscan-style urns on pedestals at one end. They faced a strange grotto with a massive cement head of a creature with long hair, huge hollow eyes, and an enormous mouth with two teeth in its upper jaw. He felt uncomfortable, almost fearful as he stared into that abyss. In all this serenity why put an ugly gargoyle as its centrepiece?

In the distance he heard bombs falling. It was Florence. He could see the plumes of smoke. Yes there were rail yards and maybe some factories but he hoped that something else beautiful had not been taken away as well. He could see the planes, RAF not the Americans. In minutes they were finishing their bombing run. Now they were going back, maybe as far as Malta but probably an aerodrome somewhere closer. He watched them pass overhead, their engine noise receding on their journey south. But one latecomer flew lower. Harry watched as it came in a direct line towards him. No, surely not! Had the pilot leftover bombs he needed to get rid of? No. Not this place. He saw the projectiles leave the hold, a line of explosions, before he dived.

Pickles held him until the stretcher came. Harry groaned as they rolled him on. Some things left his fingers and Pickles picked them up. He saw the wounds in his back and legs. Harry would be lucky to walk again, he thought. He put the bit of papery something and the scraps of pottery into his pocket: something to remember Italy by, he thought, when he tucked it in Harry's pack later.

'Harry. Harry. You're going home, Harry.'

§

Ros linked arms with Nico and led her away from the Mouth of Hell. Philip followed a couple of paces behind.

'There was so much damage from the war, Nico. Your grandmother paid for the restoration. It was painstaking and costly according to the records. I think she wanted to talk to you about what she had done and why.'

'But I was too young. It was just a place that scared me.'

'She died in 1948.'

'I was told it was cancer,' said Nico.

'So she knew that she did not have much time. It was not an opportune moment for the dog to appear.'

'Fortuna.'

Philip continued pacing along the paths after Ros and Nico found a seat. The war damage fitted with Harry's fragment and the sherds, he thought. As he walked his eyes searched as if he were surveying Città Sopra for artefacts. Statues had been repaired, as had one of the urns, the right, in front of the gargoyle. It was expertly done but there were always tell-tale signs: spider-web joins, colour difference or a less-than-perfect contour. If something were hidden underground he could probably ask Nico to fund a metal detector. But then what metal would there be, other than shrapnel from the war? He was stuck for the moment. Maybe Ros could help with one of her feelings? What if Gabriel could see what he couldn't? And then there was always going back to research on the man himself. Surely in his writings there was a clue to his way of thinking.

§

Peter was back in his workroom, the report in front of him, and a glass of Cinzano not too far away. Philip and Ros pulled up two chairs in front of him.

'What did your Dad say about the war, Peter?' Ros asked.

'Not a lot, but it didn't do him any good.'

'If you don't mind, in what way?' she asked.

Peter said nothing.

'We believe that the fragment your father had and Nico's piece are from the same hand, and probably came from the same garden at Percussina. Any bit of knowledge might just help us to solve this,' said Philip.

'Harry was a restless, unsatisfied man. He was domineering and I did not like the way he treated Mum. The war damaged him: not just the pain, or the shellshock, or that he could not remember anything about that day. He just couldn't let go.'

'Was he why you chose archaeology?' Ros said.

'Harry was mad about it and about Italy. He always had his head in a book about Italian history. I was good at English, Geography and History at school. Harry suggested Archaeology at Uni. It seemed like a good idea at the time.'

'But you did not get along,' Ros said. 'Tamarisk told us.'

'That's true. Whatever I did was not good enough. He was always telling me what I should have done. It was easier to stay away, to make a new life for myself somewhere else. Italy was not a bad choice.'

'You see Peter I believe that Harry did not souvenir this piece and the sherds as he had the Nazi mementoes. This one bothered him. He felt it important enough to write letters to lots of people, even though he did not recall where he got it. By chance Nico was one of them and replied to him. My guess is that it was the destruction of so much beauty that made him into the man you knew. He could not stop it happening, and this one piece made him powerless again because he was invalided out and couldn't remember the place.'

§

A familiar horn sounded in the courtyard. 'That's Gabriel to pick me up. When do you think you will get there?'

'Around mid-day,' said Ros. 'Bradley has been quite productive. Nico and I want to follow up some leads first.'

'Take care of yourselves.' He gave Ros a kiss. She didn't mind.

'We don't plan on any heroics with Antonio's people. And you watch out too. Don't let a bomb dig you up.'

'Promise.'

The war-time damage theory fits well, Philip thought as he walked with Gabriel along the paths of the garden. He said nothing as Gabriel made his methodical survey. Harry's fragments were scorched or in the case of the Etruscan sherds just exploded. Nico's paperwork was the same. Ros had spoken about her feelings of the garden later when they were alone. They were jumbled: like the other Corsini gardens but with the shattering impact of war, then the slow reconstruction by patient men. "Too many layers," she'd said, "but quite a few cold spots. I can understand why Nico doesn't like that gargoyle."

'What do you think, Gabriel?' Philip asked when they had returned to a green pond with a redundant Neptune at its centre. The marble edge made a convenient seat.

'The garden has been reassembled from very little. I wonder why the Corsinis did so much but left it for Alessandro to grow kitchen vegetables.'

Both men looked at what was growing: carrots, potatoes, Ros' artichokes, a bit of everything really. Without saying anything more they got up and pulled four inch pointing trowels from their back pockets. "Have trowel, will travel" were Ros' words, Philip thought. A freshly ploughed field, or in this case Alessandro's diggings, was always an opportunity. They diverged left and right to cover the expanse of upturned soil. It was still a gentle light which reflected off overnight dew. Yes there was still a lot of metal in the ground. Philip inspected tiny pieces of shell casing and plenty of slivers of marble that must be adding some limestone to Alessandro's crops. Terracotta fragments were bits of tile and plant container, or the occasional coarse cooking pot. There's nothing of any vintage, Philip thought.

Their survey was a classic grid but there was no need for a bucket to collect finds. Philip saw Gabriel's care not to damage plants or compress the soil too much. He understood a man's need to feed his family. They worked from low to high, towards grottoes cut into the hillside.

'Philip.'

He looked up. Gabriel stood in waist-high artichokes and waited for Philip to join him. He held out a two point five centimetre square of pottery. Gabriel dropped the piece into Philip's palm. It was a sherd of a well-made fabric with traces of black slip. 'Athenian red-figure ware, approximately 5th century,' Philip said. Gabriel nodded. He crouched down and Philip did the same in the next row. Together they gently tumbled the earth as though working back a floor. Gabriel teased up another piece and put it on the path. Soon Philip found another. After half an hour they had covered an area roughly four square metres. The position of each find was marked with a stick. They were isolated to an area two metres long and half a metre wide. The pattern was a comet that emanated from the footpath.

Gabriel and Philip sat down on the pathway and played with the pieces like assembling a jigsaw.

By the time Nico and Ros arrived they had put the bits together. Despite its incompleteness what all four saw was a scene of a body laid out on a cart pulled by two stunted horses or mules. Against the black background dotted with childish clouds a man led the creatures. This was the final journey of the deceased to the underworld.

'They match Harry's fragments,' Ros said.

'Yes. Yes. Yes,' the other three agreed.

Nico led their eyes to the source: the resurrected urn on the right hand side before the steps. She restrained a shiver as the eyes of Hell's Entrance looked back at her. The urn and its pedestal measured just over a metre high. The pedestal was decorated with oval garlands of flowers which framed faces of the ancient world. Nico had avoided any close study of its subjects until now. She recognised Plato, Socrates, and Aristotle. The urn took up over half of that height and its diameter was a little less than half a metre. The motifs inside circular crossed swords were ancient military men. She recognised Caesar, Hannibal and Pericles. The whole piece summarised the statues all around the garden. No flowers filled the basin. Would the restoration work have withstood growing roots, she wondered?

'Have we your permission, Nico?' Philip asked.

'This is a shrine,' Nico said.

'Yes,' said Ros. 'But I feel that it's the answer to your problem.'

Ros watched Nico's face. There was that same reluctance she had seen on the night of the flood. But in the mental process that flickered behind those eyes Ros saw resolve.

'Yes.'

'You know that we will be careful and show respect,' said Philip.

Nico nodded.

Next morning they returned with everything they needed. The Landrover was loaded with three timber uprights on the roof rack; ropes, blocks, wrapping and straps inside. Philip and Gabriel carried everything down the lane, since Alessandro's entrance was even further from the road. Gabriel bolted the timber together to form a tripod. Each beam was four inches by four inches in the imperial measurement, substantial and made of hardwood. Philip belted in the pegs and roped them to the feet to prevent movement. The top block was attached by a chain to the apex of the tripod and a four-rope configuration ran down to the second block. Philip tested it by hauling up Gabriel with ease as he hung on the hook. With blanket padding and straps on the urn they were ready. There was a clear line where the urn rested on the pedestal. The girls walked into the garden during their final preparations.

'Are you ready, Nico?' Philip asked.

'Yes. You and Gabriel clearly know what you are doing.'

I wish you wouldn't say that, Philip thought. Murphy was never far away. He nodded to Gabriel who lifted his hand and looked towards the cocooned urn. Philip began the pull through of rope, a lot of it for a limited and slow lift. Ros and Nico had their cameras ready. Gabriel watched the steady rise from the heavy piece of marble. Nothing shifted under the wrapping. Nothing groaned in the equipment. The urn separated and when it was clear Gabriel's hand signalled down. He held it and swung it clear of the pedestal as Philip paid out the rope. On sacks the urn came to rest. There was nothing inside or under the base.

Philip and Gabriel rapidly detached the wrapping, straps and ropes and readied the pedestal. Gabriel's hand went up and Philip pulled. This was marginally more arduous but hardly a strain with the purchase power of the winch. The bands pulled tight and the cube of stone began to rise. Philip heard the click of camera shutters but could not see from his angle of sight what was appearing. Gabriel wriggled his index finger to keep going up. A pair of bricks appeared, aligned roughly east west, and then a second pair on top at north south. Gabriel's finger kept tapping upwards. The girls gasped and took more photographs. Gabriel's finger stopped and he laid his hand gently against the block of stone to stop any sideways movement. Philip tied off the rope firmly and stepped beside Gabriel. On top of the bricks was a worn leather satchel that a child might take to school.

'Nico, I think this is your task,' said Philip.

She handed her camera to Ros and stepped forward. She looked up at the suspended rock and then at the container. Tentatively she reached and touched it and then quickly lifted it out with both hands. She stood and looked at the object. They could feel her temptation to open it immediately. But then Corsini patience and respect took control. She wrapped it in a spare blanket and placed it in a clear bag of heavy duty plastic. Philip and Gabriel went back to work. By late afternoon they were all back at the Palazzo and the equipment was stowed away.

In the breakfast room Salvatore had laid out a range of antipasti in bowls on a side bench. The 18th century table was covered in a plastic table cloth that Martina would have chosen. On it was laid the satchel and two cameras. All four sat around it with white-gloved hands resting in front of them.

Nico looked around at their faces. Again it was her role. Would there be nothing worthwhile that had survived that blast? She looked down and gently pulled the buckle strap and levered the pin out of the hole. Slowly she slid the leather through the surprisingly uncorroded buckle. The top flap came loose. Nico reached inside and picked out a fragment of paper. She placed it and the following eleven items in a line in the middle of the table. At the bottom of the bag there were a few more bits to fit the jigsaw of the shattered pot. Everyone studied the objects but no one chose to touch them.

Philip saw two more pieces of Latin text that appeared to match Nico's. She tilted her head to try to read the Italian on four scorched bits of fine leather. Ros was mesmerized by the remaining fragments, snippets of paper sketches: a forehead and eyebrows of a female, a nose and lips, another landscape and drawings of raging water. Was it by the same hand? It appeared to be. She stepped out of her reverie when Nico clicked her first photograph. Ros did the same. Then everyone started talking at once.

'The handwriting is the same. Look at the flourish on the "Y" and "F",' said Nico.

'There might just be enough Latin words to match a known text,' said Philip.

'I think these are preparatory sketches for a commissioned piece,' Ros said.

'Lifted up and contained in leather has kept out the moisture,' said Gabriel.

After more photographs and excited chatter it was agreed that each should apply their own expertise: Philip the Latin, Nico and Gabriel the Italian, Ros the sketches. Then the items were carefully put away for further study. The table became a place of eating and discussion over good Chianti; until Gabriel lapsed into a more silent self than usual. Ros was the first to notice.

'A penny for your thoughts, Gabriel?'

He remained quiet while he chose his words.

'Cosa ti infastidisce, vecchio amico?' Nico said gently.

'The job is only half done, Nico,' he said in English.

'Of course,' said Philip. 'Why do I never see the obvious? The Etruscan pot contained all of this, until it was smashed to smithereens.'

'There is one more, isn't there?' Ros said to Gabriel. He nodded.

'The second urn in front of La Bocca dell'Inferno?' said Nico. Gabriel bowed his head again.

Ros watched her contemplations once more. Nico had called this a shrine and she agreed with her. Did Machiavelli, since this had to be his garden, want these things to be found? But Gabriel was right: the task was not finished. She waited with the others.

'Yes, Gabriel, we must do this once more. Grazie, vecchio amico.' Nico smiled and touched the back of his hand.

There was a sense of déjà vu. Ros stood next to Nico watching Philip and Gabriel winching up the urn from the second pedestal, on the left when looking into the great mouth of Hell. Tuscan mid-morning warmth was muted by an updraft over the walls from the valley below. No noise came from the street above. In the seclusion of this Italian garden it was hard to imagine anything but tranquillity. Harry had known different.

Gabriel appeared to be less worried that this intact urn would fracture with the pressure of clamping around the covering and the strain of pulling. He guided it expertly to its waiting bed of blankets. Philip helped Gabriel unwrap the vase. It was empty.

'Surely it contained the equivalent of what was once in the right urn,' said Philip.

'But would the restoration team risk a future breakage,' said Gabriel?

They covered and secured the pedestal. As with the hang glider he checked Gabriel's straps and their safe connection to the winch hook. Ros looked across to her right. No one would ever guess that the other vessel and pedestal had ever been touched. As the second podium shifted slightly Ros took a photo. After Nico's camera dropped around her neck again Ros reached over and held her hand. Nico squeezed her fingers.

The face of Plato seemed to look at Ros as he rose. "The measure of a man is what he does with power" came to her mind. In order to understand Machiavelli she had read a lot of the thoughts of ancient philosophers lately. Nico and her family had qualified rather well, Ros thought. She would like to think that she and Philip were on the right side of the margin too. They would never be wealthy but they had done some good so far. What came next might be what decided that question.

When the stone was half a metre off the ground Philip tied off and Gabriel checked him.

'Buono.' Both steadied any swing.

The eastern sun shone on an Etruscan water jar. Everyone there recognised Heracles battling the many snake heads of the Hydra. It was intact and pristine, except for a wooden cap that Gabriel might have made as a tomb cover. It was sealed with melted bees wax.

What was Machiavelli saying, Ros thought? Surely the man was applying his wit in the choice of topic? Did he empathise with the enormity of the tasks presented for Heracles to solve? He had placed a two thousand year old jar from an Etruscan tomb inside a garden ornament. It was recycled nearly five hundred years ago for whatever purpose he had in mind.

Nico walked forward and lifted the vase away from the "rock" of Damocles hanging above it. She placed it on wrapping. Photographs were taken from every side while Philip and Gabriel returned the two items to their rightful place.

Nico said little on the drive back, which was more sedate than usual. Gabriel and Philip were two car lengths behind. Ros guessed their vigilance for the entire trip. An Antonio accident was not going to happen.

In the breakfast room the table was clear. The jar stood in the middle studied by four pairs of eyes.

'As an Italian archaeologist of twenty five years' experience I think you are most qualified to open the cap,' Philip said to Gabriel.

'Nico should decide that Philip,' Ros said.

'Sorry, you're right. Nico?'

'Yes, you are correct on both counts.'

Gabriel was as painstaking as ever. He levered off the wax from the inside edge of the lid. Every shaving was placed in a bowl. The scalpel in his hand cut around the wood. He put as little pressure on the lip of terracotta as possible. Over and over he scribed and removed residue. Periodically he tried to lever with the grip of his fingers. After a time he was cutting off slivers of wood. Round and around he took an equal measure of timber away so he never threatened the pot. It was nearly an hour before his fingers felt the first movement. But he still did not yank out the cap. His hands continued to work around until he could pry the seal from any angle. He knew it was unattached. Gabriel extricated the cap and put it beside the bowl of wax. Philip handed him a torch.

'There are two books inside,' Gabriel said. With gloved hands he lifted each out and placed it on the table. Both hardly qualified as books. They were each clearly loose sheets of paper placed within a worn leather pouch. One surface had a loop of twisted hide inserted and held from the inside. The other had a length of braided leather to tie up. There was nothing written on the outside. The uneven size of the pages showed that this was not printed on a Gutenberg or later press. These were manuscripts created and kept for Machiavelli's own consumption. On both the connection was loose. After photographs Gabriel opened the lid of each to reveal their first pages.

Philip and Gabriel gravitated to the flowing Italian script that a lawyer might have written. Philip's Italian stretched to "Il Futuro Principe" but was quickly defeated by the antiquated style. Nico and Ros leaned over a page of rapidly executed drawings of mundane things: a river, a bird's wing and sea shells. Between them, with no relation to a page orientated left to right or up to down was a spidery writing. They made no sense of it at all. Gabriel looked at both manuscripts and reserved judgement.

§

Ros woke excessively early. She dressed and made a café nero from the DēLonghi machine on a bench in the drawing room.

'Ciao bello,' she said to Philip.

'Ciao bella,' he said. He was already filling a page of his notebook: Latin on the top line, English translation below. The linen-based paper fragments were laid in a line on acid-free white paper with clear plastic on top. A pencil was stuck behind Philip's ear and another one in his hand suspended in mid-air as he thought.

She looked around the room. Salvatore had brought in two more tables to spread out the finds. On another was the Etruscan water jug, out of direct sunlight against an interior wall. Heracles, or two of them according to the potter, was busily hacking at the serpents' extremities for all eternity. Philip was right: work on the smaller task first. She put her coffee well away. Wouldn't that be a tragedy, priceless antiques destroyed by spilt coffee? She had no wish to explain that one to Nico. Then she laid out the drawings in a line on the same paper and under a transparent cover like Philip. Nico's sketch she placed at the end of the row. She stood back with her cup and contemplated them as she would a new surfing beach. Just like the water there were patterns and she would find them.

Salvatore knocked and walked into the room to see if his services were required. Master Philip was oblivious to all but his translation and the dictionary next to him. Miss Rosalind was rearranging the pieces of ancient paper in front of her. She looked up.

'Altri due café, per favore, Salvatore.'

When he returned with their preferences she had gone. He put them beside a tray of small cakes. Ros returned with her camera. She leaned over each fragment for a close up shot. After an hour in Nico's darkroom she returned with multiple prints. With a pair of sewing scissors that Salvatore had found for her she proceeded to cut them up and build what she would describe as identikit pictures like the police might assemble. By the time Nico walked in she was looking at the first few pages of that strange sketchbook. Her smile confirmed it. Her hunch was right.

'Philip. Rosalind. I am sorry to disturb you but things have moved on with Peter's problem.'

'Philip.' Ros wandered over and tapped him on the shoulder.

'Oh. Ok. I just want to . . .'

'No Philip. Something's come up.' Ros had seen the concern on Nico's face. They sat down together at her table. 'Tell us about it, Nico.'

'I took my photographs as usual. While I was sieving the latest levels from M1 I noticed Bradley talking to Gabriel. Bradley was very animated. Gabriel tried to settle him down but Bradley became frantic. Then he gave Gabriel his trench notebook and started to leave. Gabriel held his arm and said something before Bradley left. He ran.'

'What did Gabriel say?' Philip asked.

'Gabriel didn't tell me but he said to meet him at 12. Then he went after Bradley. You should be there.'

'There's more. Peter was working with Mike on the latest phase of the revetment wall. Antonio arrived with two men. He was very angry with Peter. I did not hear all that was said but he accused Peter of stealing his own finds and sending them back to Britain. He is going to close the site.'

'What did Peter say?' said Philip.

'Peter's Italian is very fluent when he is angry. I heard him say "That is ridiculous" and "Do not threaten me".'

'I think Peter needs to meet Gabriel too,' Ros said.

Nico drove into Gabriel's courtyard. There were four other cars parked. Inside Philip, Ros and Nico were greeted by Gabriel and a number of men. Ros recognised them as heads of families who were there at the meeting. Bradley sat by himself in a corner. Nobody spoke to him but it was clear from the men's eyes that he was not going anywhere.

On the table was a notebook. Peter was engrossed in its contents. 'Bastardi astute.' 'Barbari storti.'

'Has Bradley given us what we need, Peter?' said Nico.

'Oh yes, with bells and whistles.'

She walked over to Bradley. He was sweating with fear. 'Bradley, here is your ticket.'

'Ros and Philip, will you take him to Rome airport, please?' She handed the Fiat keys to Ros.

For an hour and a half Bradley sat silently in the back seat. Two young members of the families sat either side of him. At the airport he constantly looked around at other travellers until his flight to New York was called. The four of them watched security hand back his passport and Bradley walk through.

'What do you reckon on his chances, Philip?'

'Worse than average; Antonio's tentacles appear to go a long way.' Ros looked to where Philip's gaze pointed. She flinched: she could still feel his knife at her throat. 'It's ok, Ros. You are not the target.' Philip and the thug said volumes with their eyes. Then the man smiled and disappeared into the crowd.

Gabriel's courtyard was even more full of vehicles when they returned.

Around Elizabetta's table sat the Capofamiglia. Peter and Gabriel looked up when Philip and Ros walked in. The young men joined their family members.

'We waited for you before I gave the explanation,' Peter said. 'Bradley was very forthcoming.'

'The trade relies on four types of criminal: the thieves who usually work for consignment, the receivers of the stolen goods, the smugglers themselves and the money launderers who are intimately connected. Most of all it relies on the collectors: without them there is no market. Antonio has been funding his building company with stolen artefacts and laundering cash. Beni culturali are smuggled by boat, fast train or in refrigerated lorry into Switzerland, which has particularly lax import laws. The owner of stolen items, who says he bought them in good faith, becomes their legal owner after five years. Then they can be exported to final destinations in Britain or the US.'

Peter picked up the notebook. 'What Bradley has given us is an exhaustive account of how the entire operation works: places, dates, names, everything.'

'What do you plan to do with it?' asked one of the men.

'A copy will go to the Comando Carabinieri Tutela Patrimonio Artistico.'

'Bah.'

'Another will go to a special department in the Guardia di Finanza, another to Interpol, to the British and American police, and to anyone else who can prosecute. And there is one more that I will deliver myself.'

'What happens to us?'

'Exactly as we promised,' said Nico. 'Antonio might try to involve you but he will not succeed. There will be an amnesty for all of us. My lawyers will make sure of that.'

'And the future?'

'The future for every one of you is good,' said Ros. Nico, Philip and Peter nodded in agreement. 'We do not betray trust.'

Antonio Marazzi was in his office in the Council chambers. 'Don't be concerned. This will all blow over. Yes, it can be arranged.' He put the phone down as the door opened. In a second his room was full.

'I have a present for you, Signor Sindaco.' Peter placed a copy of Bradley's report on his desk.

Antonio looked puzzled, then smiled and opened the file. The men grinned as his eyes squinted in disbelief and his face reddened in rage.

'Ti attaccherai per questo!' he shouted at Peter. He lifted an imaginary noose and mimed being strung up.

'Prima tu, piccolo uomo grasso,' said Peter, spreading two fingers to show how small his manhood really was. To emphasise the point he repeated it in English: 'You first, little fat man.'

'He's all sound and fury that signifies nothing,' he said to the others as they left.

§

'Hello Meredith,' said Philip. He could hear her sister drying dishes at the sink.

'Hello Philip. Did you solve Peter's problem?'

'Yes. I suggest you look at tomorrow's edition of The Times. There's an article about Antonio Marazzi.'

'What about Harry and his Contessa?'

Not well put Meredith, he thought. 'Yes we're very close to solving that one too. The Contessa is very happy but I can't tell you about it.'

'Why? Oh I know, nobody TELLS.'

§

Peter was back at work next morning as usual. Melissa and Mike ran the volunteers but Antonio had closed the door on local labour. Mid-morning Nico arrived for her photographic tour.

'Have you any idea where Gabriel is?' Peter asked.

'He is coming soon.' Nico looked at the angle of the sun before taking a shot of Bradley's rejuvenated section. Mike had turned the storm-ravaged earth wall into something Pythagoras would have been proud of. 'Can you spare him for a few days, Peter?'

He looked at her normally inscrutable face. She couldn't hide that glow of excitement. 'Are you closer to solving your problem?'

'Oh yes.'

'I can take the photographs too if you would like.'

'Grazie Peter.'

He looked up. Gabriel and a group of men, older and young, walked down the track. Peter recognised the families and their strong young progeny.

'Buon giorno a tutti.'

'Buona giornata Peter.'

'Where would you like the workers?' asked Gabriel.

'Mike and Melissa can place them.'

Gabriel gave instructions and the young men walked up the slope to MI. 'You know these men,' said Gabriel. Peter nodded and shook their hands. 'They will help you however they can.'

Strange bedfellows, thought Peter: clandestini helping on a legitimate excavation. Is this the future?

§

'How is everything going?' Nico asked as she entered her drawing room. It seemed full of tables occupied with books and bits of paper.

'Good,' said Ros. The composition of her identikit jigsaw now seemed settled. The sketches were on the same table. She sat at another with the Italian pieces, four from the garden and Harry's larger one. Her Italian dictionary was by her right elbow. But she knew that Nico and Gabriel were working on their version. She might just listen first.

'Hello Gabriel.' He nodded, took off his jacket and stood beside Nico. 'I tried to continue your work on the book but I am much slower,' Ros said.

Siesta disappeared. Nico and Gabriel translated: Nico reading and Gabriel scribing. There were two renditions: one into modern Italian and the other into English. Gabriel turned her more literary explanation into fluent spoken English. Some words in Machiavelli's treatise were only resolved with a large Oxford Paravia Italian Dictionary.

'Two out of three is not bad,' Philip said to himself. He wandered over to Ros. On yet another table that Salvatore had found space for were photographs of each page of the sketch book. She was shuffling them like cards. 'They are easier to work with than the originals, safer too.'

'Well, is it time to compare notes?' Philip said to the room, not just Ros.

Nico looked up. 'Yes. We need more time later, of course.'

'Some discussion now might help us see his direction,' said Gabriel.

Salvatore indicated politely that it might be better to retire to the loggia. Ample food and wine were provided.

'Who would like to explain first?' asked Nico. 'What about you, Philip?'

He took another sip of excellent Antico Chianti. 'As I said, two out of three; I am stuck on one. But the other two are sections from "De Rerum Natura: On the Nature of Things" by the first century BC philosopher poet Lucretius. In the book he discusses the nature of the mind and a universe guided by Fortuna, "Chance", rather than any deity.'

'Does that make him an atheist?' Ros asked.

'He did not deny the existence of gods only that they did not create the world or have any influence on it.'

'So what did he think happened in death?' asked Nico.

'He argued that the soul, like everything else, was made up of atoms. At the point of death the atoms drift apart.'

'If that is the case, Philip, you and I should drift together,' she whispered.

'So we are not immortal.' Nico thought for a moment. 'There is no afterlife.'

'We go back into the universe, wherever we came from,' said Ros.

'What lines led you to this, Philip?' asked Gabriel.

'The shorter piece had part of this text: "Nil fieri ex nihilo, in nihilum nil posse reverti: Nothing can be produced from nothing, nothing can be reduced to nothing."'

'We are immortal as atoms,' said Ros. 'What was the other one?'

'This one might appeal to you, Ros. It translates as: "All religions are sublime to the ignorant, useful to the politician, and ridiculous to the philosopher."' I think Machiavelli chose Lucretius because he agreed with his philosophy. These Etruscan jars contained work that was personal, and in this case dangerous. A hundred years later Galileo was brought before the Church Inquisition for a much lesser crime.'

'I like the man. He was brave laughing in the face of Hell. Sorry Nico and Gabriel, if that offends you.'

'You would say, "Each to their own", Ros,' said Nico.

'What is our friend Niccolò saying in your text, Nico and Gabriel?' Ros said to change the subject.

Gabriel looked to Nico to be the mouthpiece. 'We have not finished on the book, "The Future Prince", but so far it sounds like "The Prince": politics, advice but with extra material.'

'We might be better to leave our discussion until we can all read the full translation,' said Gabriel.

'Ok,' Ros and Philip said together.

'What about the Italian fragments,' asked Philip?

'They are all to do with war,' said Gabriel. 'Machiavelli studied and wrote about it for much of his life.'

'Yes, "The Art of War" series,' said Philip.

Nico spoke. 'Let me read out the Italian and its English translation. One: Uomo che lavora machine da una distanza per attaccare una fortezza: man working machines from a distance to attack a fortress. Two: Le macchine sono migliori degli occhi umani, delle orecchie e di altri sensi: The machine is better than human eyes, ears and other senses. Three: Potenza da sole, vento, acqua, calore: Power from sun, wind, water, heat. Four: Rimuovere i crimini di rabbia ed emozione: Remove crimes of anger and emotion. Five, Harry's piece: Dobbiamo ridurre o elimare lo spreco della vita umana in guerra: we must reduce or eliminate the waste of human life in war.'

'This man was so far ahead of his time,' said Philip. 'Machines of war, better than humans, it's the stuff of Jules Verne.'

'With a heart. It's the eternal dream: eliminate loss of human life in war. Let machines pulverise each other, rather than another war to end all wars,' said Ros.

'But what did Niccolò know about machines and power sources,' Philip asked? No one came back with an answer. 'Well Ros, it's your turn.'

'When Meredith asked us to solve Peter and Nico's problems in Italy I never imagined this.' She paused for a moment and smiled. 'The sketches and the book are by one person. What we found in Percussina shows that Niccolò Machiavelli not only knew him but that they were friends. It's the stuff of dreams.' She drifted back into her reverie again.

'Ros,' said Nico. 'Who is it?'

'Leonardo da Vinci.'

After a long pause they all spoke together.

'Machines of war: that is Leonardo,' said Gabriel.

'If it had been mirror-writing we would have guessed its author,' said Nico. 'As it was it was in some personal shorthand and so spidery it was hard to read.' She was standing over the table with his open pages. Was it trust of his friend or deliberate writing for posterity or both, she thought?

'Did you work it out from the sketches or the book?' Philip asked.

'The sketches but the book confirmed it. Should I tell you about it?'

They laughed.

'I felt something about the style first. When I put my identikit cards in the right order I could see that they were studies for the most famous painting in the world: the Mona Lisa, La Gioconda. I need to check but I believe they were done at different periods of his life. We know he worked on it for decades and had it at his death.'

'Are you sure, Ros?' asked Nico.

'Yes, but you should get a second opinion from an expert. I have also done some preliminary research about the subject's background landscape. Some say it was imaginary but I am more convinced that it's of a real place: Montefeltro in the former Duchy of Urbino. It once covered Marche, Emilia-Romagna and Tuscany.'

'Emilia-Romagna was where Cesare Borgia carved out a kingdom,' Philip said. 'Machiavelli and Leonardo were with him during the campaign.'

'So he knew the place,' said Nico.

'With the book I was stuck on the text, not just the scratchy writing. Can you two take on the translation of this one too?'

'It would be a joy for me, Ros.'

Gabriel nodded in agreement.

'You know, Harry was more right than he knew. He put us on to something beautiful and unique,' said Ros.

'People from bottom to top are frightened of change,' said Philip.

Where's he going with this one, Ros thought?

'But from the desperation and destruction of war comes progress and innovation. Niccolò and Leonardo would have approved of what Harry began,' said Philip.

'Decay and growth, like Nature,' said Gabriel.

§

After a week of translation and shared study it was Ros who called it time to share their thoughts.

'Clearly there is enough material here to keep experts busy for years. Which book would you like to discuss first, Nico?'

'The work of Leonardo. Like you I admire him greatly. The thought that one of his treatises should be preserved in a Corsini garden astounds me. Can you start, please?'

Ros looked down at her notes and let out a deep sigh. 'I would be happy to. This book is a collection of eighty pages on forty pieces of paper. Like the Codex Leicester, which was 74 pages written on 18 folded pieces of paper, it deals with geology, the action of water and fossils. But it takes the speculation so much further and includes many studies of human anatomy. In the Codex Leicester he argued against the idea of a Biblical Flood which somehow deposited sea shells on top of mountains. Only movements of the earth's crust and the actions of water, over eons of time, could turn ocean beds into mountains or peaks into sea shores.' She paused to collect her thoughts. Part of her was outside looking in.

'While he worked in the court of Milan Leonardo was known to visit the Alps, where he found fossil bones in caves. It is also recorded that he dissected numerous human bodies. In the Codex Corsini he put these two strands of enquiry together to speculate on the origins of humankind.'

She laid out her playing cards. Drawings of human skulls, so precise that they were proof to the Inquisition of the black art of vivisection, were placed side by side with drawings of monkeys and apes.

'Monkeys were referred to by Aristotle and others in the 4th century BC but Apes were unknown in Europe until the 15th century,' said Philip. 'It was Linnaeus, in the 1750s, who fitted the missing link into the Primate puzzle.'

'Leonardo linked man to the apes,' said Gabriel?

'He went further.' She put more pictures on the table, one that showed simple primates at one end of a row and man at the other. In between there were fossil bones of human femurs and what looked like a

Neanderthal skull. 'And further, his writings pose the question: if man evolved over millennia into what he is now, what made him change? Again he came back to the environment and the geological record. If humans were alive as the earth changed: its seasons, temperature and rainfall, how did people survive? They had to alter. Those who adapted lived to pass on their skills to their children.'

'Survival of the Fittest,' said Nico. 'Charles Darwin published "Origin of Species" in 1859.'

'Evolution not Genesis,' said Gabriel. 'No wonder he hid this book from the Inquisition.'

'He let Niccolò hide his work. That is a friendship based on great trust,' said Nico.

'He also speaks of the soul,' said Philip. 'When I looked at some of the drawings of heads and torsos I began to wonder whether he was looking for the soul through vivisection. When I went through the material again I decided that he was.' He followed Ros' lead with cards of quotes and drawings.

'This skull seems to show the Pineal gland and the Thalamus. He would have known about the concepts of the Psyche from the Greeks and Anima from the Romans. He might have known that Hindus call it the "third eye" or the "doorway to the soul". Descartes called it the "principal seat of the soul", two hundred and fifty years after Leonardo.'

'I am sure there is so much more that we haven't found yet. Nico what do you want to do with the Corsini Codex?'

'Thank you both for naming it. I think it should be available to scholars and the public.'

She picked up their translation of "The Future Prince". 'But I am not so sure about this.'

'It is political. Our country is run by corrupt buffoons. We Italians try to ignore their silliness. Life goes on without them.'

'So you don't want to talk about it Gabriel.

'Nico?'

'Let Philip guide us and we can add our comments.'

'I can understand your reluctance. This is a bleak book but also brilliant in its analysis. It is Realpolitik, a treatise set in the real world rather than the ideal. To him people were essentially evil and selfish but could be moulded by education and good leaders. The ideal state encouraged prosperity, the protection of property and civic pride. It was protected, like an umbrella, by a strong army. In his discussion he touches on the ideas of Hobbes who favoured one individual to rule versus Locke who gave rights to the people to limit his powers. There's Rousseau's liberty and equality of people for the common good. All of this is centuries before they were born. It's as though they plagiarised his ideas.' He rifled through notes to select a few.

'Menial work makes men subhuman, like donkeys in a field. It drains their life force and gives it to the rich and powerful.'

'Sounds like Marx,' Ros interrupted.

'He did not trust the mass of people who are inherently greedy and corrupt. But if people rebel the problem gets worse. In a revolution, one elite replaces another, often inferior if they are uneducated. Niccolò leant towards domination rather than let the masses destroy the civilised things of life such as art and architecture. It is better to let a beast like Cesare Borgia control them from the cradle to the grave.'

'He had seen Savonarola and the Bonfire of the Vanities. So he had plenty of reasons to be hostile towards the Church too,' said Ros.

'Yes, the church kept the elite in power by persuading the multitudes to accept their lot for the promise of heaven.'

'Marx again, that religion was the opiate of the people to keep them subservient to their betters,' Ros said. I almost sound convinced, she thought. Maybe I should stop interrupting.

'He saw the church as a patron of great beauty based on suffering.' He looked at Ros and thought of the Vatican museum. 'At least Cesare would not cover his crimes by acting in the name of God.' He spoke directly to Gabriel. 'In his world you could not ignore him like the Italian government.'

'I saw some good things that Machiavelli wanted to do. He said people were moulded by their environment, so he wanted to change it to improve their lives. His way was to intervene in the capitalist economy so everyone profited not just a few.'

Socialism with a touch of Leninist control, Ros thought. Only in Italy I suppose.

'I prickled when I read about how he would regulate the people: secret police and find every scrap of knowledge about the individual so they could not rebel,' she said. '"An absolute ruler needs to know everything, absolutely". "Without knowledge there is no power". That sounds awfully like George Orwell's "1984". Where's the trust?'

'None of us would like to live in such a society,' said Gabriel.

'To me Machiavelli is trying to find the balance between democracy and authoritarianism, between freedom and control for the common good,' said Ros.

'Autocracy limits the madness of the human condition. Democracy is freedom for untrustworthy and uneducated people to make mistakes. Democracy is messy and lets the stupid hold the reins. It slips into anarchy and barbarism too easily.'

'Democracy is the worst form of government, except for all the others that have been tried,' according to Winston Churchill. Machiavelli was wrong to choose autocracy,' said Ros.

Ros drifted in thought. Well, Niccolò, are you any wiser now, up there? Or are you just part of the atom cloud that just goes round and round. In life the Church was not kind to you. You'd answer, "When was it ever?" But I think history will be kinder. She thought about that. His family home near the Ponte Vecchio; destroyed by Hitler's generals in the retreat over the Arno. Percussina; blown up by the Allies soon after. Maybe it was better to be atoms, Nico.

'I read a lot about him,' said Ros. 'Obviously for me Leonardo was far more interesting. But I wanted to know what made Leonardo become friends with Machiavelli, someone so utterly different in interests and philosophy to him. Let's face it Machiavelli was not a likeable man to a modern audience with his philandering. Why would Marietta put up with him in today's world? But in his time he was a star, political, literary, radical, out there. He rose from the bottom through hard work and talent. Leonardo could respect another able mind whose life was a struggle not so dissimilar to his own.

Machiavelli saved Florence so the barbarians sacked the eternal city instead. Did Marietta appreciate this mercurial spirit who did so much for Florence in his time? I see a much-suffering lady, spending most of her life waiting for him to come home. At the end she looked after his kids and approached your ancestors, Nico. She sold the garden to keep it in safe hands. To my mind there had to have been something good between all three of them.'

'When you put it all together this is a template for social control. He has sacrificed that delicate balance between individual freedom and state authority to create a peaceful society. However unpleasant this is the Holy Grail of political theory.' Philip waited for replies.

'This book frightens me,' said Nico. 'He says he hopes it will survive longer than his masters and accusers. It is left for the Ancients of a more enlightened time in the future. But politicians, Italian or otherwise, are not trustworthy enough to use it well.'

'Prior to finding this I thought Niccolò would have agreed with you,' said Philip. 'His ideal form of government was the Roman Republic before the Caesars destroyed it. How did he become so bitter that he felt totalitarianism was the only way to go?'

'Something else stuck in my craw,' said Ros. 'Even his earlier work spoke of using lies to advantage. But how can anyone trust you if you lie all of the time? There could be no binding treaties or trade agreements, anything.'

'And fear,' she continued. 'Better that people fear you rather than they love you? Fear only goes so far. There are too many examples in history of martyrs for a cause, revolutions against tyranny that is worth the human price.'

'If it was me I would tuck away those I loved and face the bastard,' said Philip.

'Fear doesn't give you happiness, even if compromise fills your stomach,' she said. Thanks Philip, but you know that wouldn't happen, she thought. We would face fear together.

'Surely that is a recipe for a tyrant. If his ideal leader bullied lots of countries, maybe everyone, then there would be a united resentment. You can't intimidate the world and expect to win.'

'And let's not forget the Greek idea of Hubris. Niccolò knew the concept that arrogance, excessive pride towards the gods, leads to your nemesis. Hubris will destroy the best of plans.'

'Something changed him between writing "The Prince" and "The Future Prince",' said Philip. 'Did he finally lose all trust in ordinary humanity? Were they so stupid and greedy that they had to be led with a ring through their collective nose?'

'Was there a change in his thinking or did his thoughts just distil based on his experience,' said Ros. "The Prince" was written just after his time in prison. The Medicis, Lorenzo the Magnificent who commissioned Botticelli's Prima Vera and the Venus. Historians generally see them as the good guys. But in prison their minions dropped Machiavelli from a ceiling. They dropped the poor sod six times, six, to dislocate shoulders, destroy his back, etcetera, etcetera. And he said nothing.' Ros took a moment to still her thoughts. 'The trial showed that he was honest. Successive generations of Medicis continued the betrayal.' She paused again. 'I don't have to like his attitude to women, but I do like the man: a bad boy, but honest.'

'He told what he saw as the truth,' said Philip. 'His private life didn't affect his ability to be good at what he did.'

'But,' said Nico, "The Future Prince" is a dangerous book. I see why he kept it a secret. It is my wish to do the same.'

§

'Welcome back, Ros,' said Nico. She surveyed Ros with a huge smile and then hugged her close.

'Ciao, Filippo. Come stai?'

'Sto bene, Nico. Grazie.' He touched cheeks like a brother.

'You have been practicing, Philip.'

'Poco.' He made a circle with his fingers to show how little, and grinned.

Nico guided them in under the sign that read Museo Alta Cresta. She showed them around the four-storey building on the site of Peter's workroom overlooking the square. It was stonework in keeping with the medieval town.

'Your security system looks rather impressive,' Philip said.

'It was funded by the sale of Antonio's loot, according to the Proceeds of Crime statute in Italian law.'

'How is all that going, Nico?' asked Ros.

'His case will probably proceed through Italian courts very slowly. Then he will be extradited to face charges in several countries.'

'Did he try to implicate you and the families?' asked Philip.

'Oh yes, but my lawyers presented a united front. The old families and the Corsinis are a powerful combination. The police and other authorities chose not to test the partnership.'

They entered a large room on the second floor. Like the Palazzo it was full of Etruscan pottery and relics. Ros noted labels in Italian and English: all items were donated by the Corsinis and other families. Around the walls of this and other rooms were tomb photographs by Jacopo and his friends.

'Hello Gabriel. How are you?' Philip shook his hand.

'I am very well, Philip,' he clasped Philip's hand warmly, 'and Rosalind.' They touched cheeks. She noticed a slightly broader midriff disguised by a new suit. His badge read "Curatore".

Over coffee he explained that the families worked well with the archaeologists. Knowledge had expanded exponentially and the work paid far better than their lives as clandestini.

'Peter is exceptionally happy. The tomb complex beneath Città Sopra is immense, a fitting rival to Cerveteri and Tarquinia. There is enough excavation work to keep him busy for years. He has just bought a house in Alta Cresta.'

Later he walked them past his collection on the way to the third floor. There in the centre, protected by security that rivalled the Louvre, was the notebook of Leonardo da Vinci, on loan from the Corsini family. Gabriel explained that each day he turned over a new leaf for the viewing public. Around the walls were Nico's photographs of the most impressive pages.

'What's this, Gabriel?' Ros was testing her Italian on a tiny leather bound volume of what looked like poetry. She resisted looking at the English translation for the moment.

Gabriel explained. Something bothered him about the garden.

'You had a feeling?'

He nodded. 'Archaeological intuition,' I would call it. 'Nico was happy to let me fossick until I got the result.'

'Now you're showing off with an Aussieism,' said Ros. 'Let me guess. You found it in La Bocca dell'Inferno?'

'Stuffed inside its left nostril,' said Gabriel.

'Of course.' Philip and Ros laughed.

'Machiavelli's humour to the end,' said Philip.

'What is it,' asked Ros?

'"They" is more accurate. Love sonnets in the Petrarchan style to his many mistresses. In the right nostril was his diary.' He handed it to Philip, along with a pair of gloves.

'The poetry might be more challenging,' said Philip. 'Both the technical proficiency, a la Fitzgerald's translation of Omar Khayyam's "Rubaiyat", as well as some of the R rated content I would guess.'

'Translating his poetry might be a good challenge for you, Gabriel. Tap into the romantic side of your soul,' Ros said with mischief. She saw the nearest to a blush she would ever witness in him.

'Does that mean an extension to the museum?' asked Philip.

'I picture a Friendship room, taking highlights from the diary, a few sonnets, photographs around the walls,' said Ros. 'Publication is necessary of course, with access for scholars.'

'Nico will decide.'

At the front desk Philip picked up a copy of the museum catalogue. It was compiled by Peter. According to the blurb he was busy with several books on the significance of the collection, and the tombs in the Alta Cresta region. A poster advertised small group bookings to visit some of them, escorted by local experts. Philip could shut his eyes and see them sitting around Elizabetta's kitchen table.

'Tomorrow afternoon then, Gabriel?' said Philip.

'I will be there. Ciao.'

§

Ros sat on the grassy slope and watched a lot of old men puff up the hill. In between wheezing they were laughing. They were having fun. The weather was, how should she put it, Italian: sun, enough wind, overall a tranquil day.

Philip was ready. She watched him check Gabriel's harness, before Gabriel did the same for him.

'Buona giornata, Signorina Rosalind.'

'Buon giorno a tutti.' She looked at the crowd around her: Elizabetta, her family and most of the womenfolk. On the other side were mainly men and the boys. It was like a village festival..

'Sei sicuro, Gabriel?' Gabriel nodded that he was quite sure thank you.

'Sei pazzo, Gabriel!' The man waved his hand around his head and blew across his palm. There was lots of laughter, except from Elizabetta who frowned. Gabriel bowed to the crowd and blew a kiss to his wife.

Philip stood motionless facing the wind. Everyone stopped talking and waited with him.

'Are you ready?' Philip asked.

'Yes.'

'Now.' He lifted his right leg forward and Gabriel matched him. Their shoulders bowed to push through the inertia. Second step, Ros and Elizabetta saw the strength of their thighs. Third step, the sails of the kite were still fighting. The fourth and fifth seemed like lightning. The sixth, with the strength of two, lifted them up like a child's toy. As they

270

swooped over the valley Philip and Gabriel rearranged their feet into their cocoons. So they resembled two horizontal caterpillars suspended from a giant blue butterfly. When Philip steered the kite back over the slope they both heard loud cheers and clapping.

He worked the thermals to gain the required height. Gabriel was heavier than Ros but the wind was good. Everything just took a bit longer. Gabriel said nothing but Philip noticed his keen interest in the terrain below. When they flew over Antonio's abandoned workings Gabriel smiled. With more height from an updraft over that enormous concrete and tarmac bridge Philip turned north to the farmland beyond Alta Cresta. Over his farmhouse and the hills of his "patch" Gabriel took hold of the Instamatic camera that Ros had provided. He clicked happily "for Jacopo".

'You told me once that you had flown before. Do you mind elaborating?'

'If you wish,' said Gabriel. 'I was a pilot in the Regia Aeronautica Italiana. In 1940 I was assigned to the Corpo Aereo Italiano. We flew many raids over Harwich and Felixstow in the Battle of Britain. On the 11th of November ten bombers took off with a fighter escort which included German Messerschmitts. But bad weather caused us to use too much fuel. The mission was aborted and most of our escort left. Hurricane fighters from 257, 46 and 42 Squadrons intercepted us. Three of our planes were shot down, then two fighters, and many more crashed on landing. Over twenty of my compatriots did not return. When I saw the British I knew the old Breda was too slow for me to escape. Fuel leaked from a crack in the wing. I dived and managed to land. I survived but my plane did not. Your countrymen looked after me in the camp.'

'That explains your excellent English. You were lucky.'

'Yes, Fortuna.'

§

'Benvenuto, Rosalind. Benvenuto, Nico.

'Benvenuto, Elizabetta.' They touched cheeks.

'Buon giorno signore.' Jacopo was inside the kitchen. He was a little taller and more confident. Soon he would be on a Vespa chatting up the girls, Ros thought.

On the table were Etruscan vases, around twenty of them. Each was beautifully authentic in its decoration, and attached to each was a metal tag explaining its provenance: Prodotto in cooperativa Alta Cresta.It was almost as if they knew the original artists, Ros joked to herself. According to Jacopo and his Nonna, business with the tourists was so good that the wives made more money than their husbands.

While Jacopo was showing Nico his work Ros looked around the room. Elizabetta's shelves were stacked with pots and pans. But there was the Duck vase. Ros smiled. A woman can't give up everything pretty.

§

The morning was bright and sunny. Nico stood at the door and watched events in the courtyard. In the middle was her Midnight Blue Ferrari. Philip fiddled with his seat belt and resisted lying back in the passenger seat. Salvatore waited patiently. At last he was able to hand Philip the packed lunch. It contained sandwiches made with Luigi's Peccorino cheese.

Ros started the engine. It snarled sublimely. She put in the cassette tape of Verdi's "Aida" and pressed Play. Perfect. Nico looked at her watch; 9.30. Matinee performance started at 12. Verona in two hours?

'Back in time for tea,' Ros shouted. 'Andiamo, Filippo.'

Nico waved and went inside.

The Ferrari growled along the country roads. It flew on the Autostrada.

'A bit more practice and you might catch Matteo,' Philip shouted.

'You betcha.'

§

Nico sat at an outside table shaded from the strong afternoon sun. The restaurant was at the northern end of the Piazza Navona overlooking the Fontana del Nettuno. She watched two British tourists dangle their hands in the water as they talked. They are a new couple, she thought, from their shy looks and gentle touching. A familiar figure entered the frame: quite tall, blond, shapely in tight jeans and loose-fitting white blouse with an embroidered applique bodice. Long hair touched the black leather satchel hung over her shoulder. She dallied for a moment by Neptune despatching the octopus. The photo was one she would have taken too.

'Buon pomeriggio, Ros. Come stai?'

'Bene grazie, Nico. Tu?'

'Bene.'

'So, what is Philip up to?' Nico said. English felt right today.

'He's enjoying himself in the Vatican Apostolic library. There's a section of the Aeneid in the Virgilius Vaticanus that he thinks Machiavelli might have quoted from on the last one of the fragments.' She looked at her watch. 'I said I'd be back by 4.'

Ros sipped her café nero. 'And how is Davide?'

'He's well. I am meeting him here later.' She was still shy talking about him, even to Ros.

'I have a present for you,' Nico said.

'I have a present for you.' Ros took out what was clearly a book carefully wrapped in yellow paper.

'You first.'

Nico handed Ros a cardboard roll. She slid out and unrolled a blown-up colour photograph of a nearly familiar portrait. It was of a bearded, balding man of later years dressed in a dark coat over a white shirt. Nico's typed description said: "Discovered at the Chateau de Valencay, once home to 19th Century French diplomat Talleyrand. It is reputed to be of Niccolò di Bernardo dei Machiavelli by his friend Leonardo da Vinci. Not authenticated." Ros studied it for a time.

'His eyes have seen too much,' she said. 'My turn.'

Nico opened the parcel. "The Future Prince" by Niccolò Machiavelli rested in her hands. The cover was a watercolour of the Percussina garden. Pathways lined with artichokes and statues led to two urns and La Bocca dell'Inferno. Ros had softened the gargoyle's features so that he was almost friendly. Inside the front cover Ros had written, "Out of something bad good comes."

'Thank you, Ros.' The familiar text was printed in an antique style that suited its author. Nico looked at the paintings that separated each chapter of the translation: the Palazzo, the Museum in Alta Cresta, and views of her gardens. 'I can see that your style has developed since your course at Vinci. They are lovely.' She wrapped it up again and placed it beside her bag at her feet. 'Tell me about your trip to Naples.'

Ros described the flight off Mount Vesuvius.

'How did you get the hang glider up there?'

'There's a road so we loaded it on top of a tourist minibus.'

For four hours they had circled the Bay, with Capri shining in the late sun, and hovered over Pompeii and Herculaneum. Next day they had rattled along in the Circumvesuvio train to the excavations themselves. Philip had surprised her one evening by taking her to a performance of "Giselle" in the Teatro di San Carlo.

'What a sumptuous building with red upholstery against the gold interior. We could see and hear everything from the second floor box.' Ros looked at her watch. 'Can I pay for this one, Nico? I have to go or I will be late for his master.'

Nico stood and they touched cheeks. 'It was lovely seeing you, Ros. And thanks for your beautiful present. We will do this again.'

'Yes, we must.'

Nico watched Ros weave through the crowds coming out of the narrow streets from the Pantheon and the Trevi Fountain.

'Mi scusi, signora, telefono.' The waiter pointed towards the bar. Is something wrong with Davide, she thought? Nico quickly picked up her handbag and went inside.

'Ok Davide. A presto.' She hurried off towards Barberini-Fontana di Trevi metro station.

The waiter cleared the table and picked up the parcel. The lady was gone. He shrugged his shoulders and put it on the bar, in case she came back.

§

"Study the past, if you would define the future." Confucius.

"Fortune favours the diligent and times are changing fast."

"We are embarked on a journey to fully build a modern socialist China."

"We launched the first Chinese-built aircraft carrier."

"(We must) remember history and pray for peace."

New Year Speech to the Chinese people. 2018. Beijing. President Xi Jinping, the new Prince.

§

'Which way is Fortuna flowing for him, Ostinato up or down?'

'Bernardo, what do you think?

'Hubris, Machia,' they replied, as they studied their feet.

§

BIBLIOGRAPHY

Atkinson, James B. and Sices,David eds. Machiavelli and His Friends: Their Personal Correspondence. Dekalb, IL: Northern Illinois University, 1996.

Bondanella, Peter and Mark Musa, ed. The Portable Machiavelli. New York: Penguin Books, 1979.

Borchia, Rosetta and Nesci, Olivia. Codice P: atlante illustrato del reale paesaggio della Gioconda. Amazon. 2012. (Landscape is Montefeltro seen from heights of Valmarecchia).

Cavendish, Richard. History Today, execution of Girolamo Savonarola. Volume 48, Issue, 5 May 1998.

De Grazia, Sebastian. Machiavelli in Hell. New York: Vintage Books, 1989.

Hale, J. R. ed. The Literary Works of Machiavelli. London: Oxford University Press,1961.

Kay, Robin. The Official History of New Zealand in the Second World War 1939-1945.) Italy Volume 11: From Cassino to Trieste. 11 The Pesa Valley. Historical Publications Board. Wellington. 1967

Mansfield, Harvey C. Machiavelli's Virtue. Chicago: The University of Chicago Press,1966.

Marriott, W.K. Translator. Web edition. University of Adelaide Library. South Australia 5005. Sinigalia incident with Cesare Borgia. 2014.

Najemy, John M. Between Friends. Princeton, NJ: Princeton University Press, 1993

Potter, T.W. A Faliscan Town in South Etruria.
Excavations at Narce 1966-71. British School of Rome. London. 1976.

Rose-Greenland, Fiona. Looters, collectors, and a passion for
antiquities at the margins of Italian society. Working paper.
University of Michigan. March 2014.

Singer, P.W. Military Robots and the Laws of War,
The New Atlantis, Number 23, Winter 2009, pp. 25-45.

Singer, P.W. Wired for War: The Robotics Revolution and Conflict in
the Twenty-First Century. Penguin. 2009.

White, Michael. Machiavelli A Man Misunderstood. London:
Abacus. Little, Brown Group,2004.

White, Michael. Leonardo da Vinci. The First Scientist. London.
Abacus. Little, Brown Group. 2000.

SOURCES

As in previous adventures I have included a great deal of researched fact, supported by personal recollection. The Etruscan site of Narce in Umbria, a short distance north of Rome, was my first foreign dig. Like so many I fell in love with Tuscany. The clandestini intrigued me at the time. In this book I speculated how they could be part of a solution to the scourge of antiquity theft.

The two "giants" definitely knew each other and worked together on two projects: Cesare Borgia's subjugation of Emilia Romagna and the Arno diversion project. Michael White and others have suggested a friendship between the two.

Marietta Corsini, daughter of Luigi Corsini, probably came from a less-than-affluent background similar to her husband's family. There is no apparent link between her family and the ancient Corsini family with connections to the Medicis and Popes, or their descendants today. I speculated that Marietta might have reverted to her maiden name to avoid any retribution on her family from the church or others. My story is a work of historical fiction. Any resemblance to actual persons living or dead is purely coincidental.

ABOUT THE AUTHOR

Chris has written much of this book from personal experience. Born in Stafford, England, he studied Archaeology and Fine Art at Edinburgh University. During the 1970s Chris worked on sites in Italy, Cyprus, Turkey and Iran. His last dig was at old Kandahar in Afghanistan, just before the Russian invasion. It is this excavation life that he has reworked into historical fiction.

Memories of his first foreign dig, an Etruscan site in Umbria, and his love of Renaissance history fuel this Italian adventure. After raising two sons he and his wife now live in the hills north of Brisbane, Australia.

www.ingramcontent.com/pod-product-compliance
Lightning Source LLC
Chambersburg PA
CBHW070118120726
47909CB00002B/644